WHAT'S DONE
IN DARKNESS

Also by
Kayla Perrin

We'll Never Tell

Winter Break

Spring Break

The Delta Sisters

The Sisters of Theta Phi Kappa

Anthologies

An All Night Man

The Best Man

WHAT'S DONE IN DARKNESS

Kayla Perrin

ST. MARTIN'S GRIFFIN
NEW YORK

Published in the United States by St. Martin's Griffin, an imprint of St. Martin's Publishing Group

WHAT'S DONE IN DARKNESS. Copyright © 2015 by Kayla Perrin. All rights reserved. Printed in the United States of America. For information, address St. Martin's Publishing Group, 120 Broadway, New York, NY 10271.

www.stmartins.com

ISBN 978-1-250-85752-1 (trade paperback)

Our books may be purchased in bulk for promotional, educational, or business use. Please contact your local bookseller or the Macmillan Corporate and Premium Sales Department at 1-800-221-7945, extension 5442, or by email at MacmillanSpecialMarkets@macmillan.com.

First St. Martin's Griffin Edition: 2022

10 9 8 7 6 5 4 3 2

For Jennifer Enderlin.
Your infinite patience, coupled with your
belief in me, mean the world.
You rock. Seriously.

ACKNOWLEDGMENTS

The fact that you are reading this is a small miracle. I never set out to write a sequel to *We'll Never Tell*, and once all of my readers convinced me to do so, this book still almost never happened.

Writing isn't always easy. Sometimes, it's downright excruciating. I wish I could be the kind of writer who can put her personal life on a shelf, pull her sleeves up, and get to work, but it turns out I'm not. Sometimes, life gets in the way and knocks you down.

Shortly after I started writing this book, my father's health took a turn for the worst and he died of cancer. It was a devastating time in my life, and admittedly, it shook my world to the core. He was too young to be gone, my mother was now alone and heartbroken, and I simply wasn't in the mood to put pen to paper. I couldn't complete this book—for a very long time.

Despite the circumstances of my extreme writer's block, another publisher might not have been so compassionate and understanding. Another publisher might not have given me the time I needed to complete this book. But Jennifer Enderlin, who acquired the book, never pressured me. And when I turned in the book extremely late, she never made me feel bad about it. Jennifer and the entire team at St. Martin's Press have been completely supportive and nothing short of amazing. So I gratefully thank everyone at St. Martin's Press for allowing me to complete this book and making its publication a reality.

No acknowledgment would be complete without thanking my literary agent, Helen Breitwieser, who has been by my side for over a decade. Like with any relationship, there have been bumps in the road during our time together, but Helen has always been there when I needed her. She's seen me at my worst, and also at my best—and she's been there with me through it all. So with utmost gratitude, I thank Helen Breitwieser for her incredible patience and support of me and my career.

Last but not least, I have to thank you—my readers. You asked me for a follow-up book to *We'll Never Tell*. And yeah, some of you actually pestered me—ha! But if not for you, I would never have written this book. I'd never planned to write it. In fact, because my readers asked for this book so adamantly, I was able to convince my editor to agree to a sequel so many years after the fact. And I have to say, it was an absolute pleasure to delve into the world of Katrina and play around in a crazy mind.

So to my readers, thank you. Thank you for supporting my career and for your feedback. I hope you enjoy this story!

*For nothing is hidden except to be revealed,
and nothing concealed except to be brought to light.*

Mark 4:22,
New English Translation

PROLOGUE

University at Buffalo campus
Five years ago . . .

The night air held a biting chill, and the sky was darker than usual, filled with thick black clouds that looked almost ominous. The dark masses crept toward the moon, finally covering it completely—and providing the much-craved darkness on the street thousands of miles below.

With a final look around to be certain no one was in the vicinity, Katrina Hughes said, "Let's do this."

Going down onto her behind, Katrina lay flat on her back, then quickly slipped beneath the front of the car.

Rowena James blew hot air onto her gloved hands, trying to keep them warm as she glanced from left to right, keeping a lookout. At least there was no snow on the ground, but damn, it was cold.

The light from the flashlight came on, illuminating the ground beneath the car. Rowena suddenly felt queasy. Was this truly necessary?

"Are you sure you want to do this, Kat?" she asked. "I mean, it's not too late to change your mind."

"Are you kidding?" came Katrina's reply. "Even the parking-lot light is out—a stroke of luck I couldn't have planned. It's fate. I *have* to do it."

Rowena said nothing, but she wasn't entirely sure that she agreed with Katrina's reasoning. This whole tampering with Shemar's brakes . . . the way Rowena saw it, this was too risky.

"And of course, Shemar had his car checked out earlier today. Got the all clear for his trip." Katrina chuckled. "The jerk won't suspect a thing."

Rowena tried to imagine the moment when Shemar realized his brakes were shot. Maybe it would happen long before he was on the interstate. Maybe the crash wouldn't be fatal. . . .

"Pass me the knife," Katrina instructed her.

Rowena bent low and placed the handle of the knife in Katrina's extended hand. "Are you even sure this will work?"

"Of course it will. I worked on plenty of cars with my dad. I know exactly what to do."

"But how do you know the brakes won't fail while he's driving out of this parking lot?"

"Because it's about putting a tiny hole in the brake line. That way, the fluid will escape gradually—most likely when he's going full speed on the interstate—before he realizes there's a problem."

Rowena stood slowly, glancing anxiously around the parking lot. Earlier that evening, Katrina had gotten Shemar to park in this exact location, under the guise that it was a great area to make out without prying eyes. Not that they didn't have rooms where they could get it on, but she had appealed to his sense of adventure and exhibitionism. And of course, Rowena could imagine that once Katrina had started to give Shemar a blow job in the car he stopped thinking.

Katrina's plan had already been in motion. She'd scoped out this spot and knew that it was a blind spot that the university's security cameras couldn't see.

In the distance, Rowena thought she heard a car, and tingles of fear spread through her. She bent low, saying, "Look, I was thinking . . . maybe we shouldn't. I mean, I don't think he'll ever—"

"That's right. He never will." Katrina peeked her head out from under the car. "And you know why? Because he's going to be fucking dead."

Rowena bit her inner cheek, trying not to let any emotion show on her face. But she wasn't comfortable with this. Not at all. Shemar . . . he hadn't been part of the plan. The others, yes, she could understand why. But Shemar . . .

"But what if it doesn't kill him?" Rowena asked. "He could be injured, sure. Maybe even paralyzed. But he might not die." And the last thing they needed was for Shemar to survive—and point the finger at them. Nothing about what they were doing could be construed as heat of the moment. Any charges would be of the first-degree, premeditated variety.

"Shit, will you stop worrying? I know exactly how to do this. He'll crash on the interstate. He won't have a chance."

Rowena stood tall and shifted from foot to foot, trying to keep warm. But the chill she felt was internal, and she knew it had nothing to do with the sub-zero Buffalo temperature on this brutally cold January night.

"I need you to get down here and hold the flashlight," Katrina said.

A quick look around the parking lot confirmed for Rowena that no one was coming. Then she did as Katrina had asked, carefully lying on her stomach. Katrina passed her the flashlight, and Rowena shone it under the car.

"Angle that light a little, will you?"

She turned the flashlight in a few different directions until Katrina said, "Good. Hold it right there."

The seconds seemed to tick by like hours. This was taking too long.

"How much longer?" Rowena asked.

"Just a moment. I want to make sure I hit the right spot. And it can't be obvious; otherwise the police will be able to see that the brake line was tampered with."

As Rowena's eyes went back to scanning the area, she suddenly said, "Oh shit."

"What?"

She quickly shut off the flashlight. "I think it's security or something. A car's coming!"

And in that moment, she found herself hoping that Katrina hadn't had enough time to do the deed. That the brake line remained intact and that Shemar wouldn't die.

"Maybe we should do this another time," Rowena said, unable to hide her anxiety.

"Are you in this with me or not?" Katrina snapped. "Because if Shemar brings me down, you go down, too. Is that what you want?"

Rowena swallowed. "No. Of course not."

"It has to be now. Shemar's leaving for Albany in the morning."

The car sounded like it was getting closer and slowing down. Was it entering the parking lot?

"That car is in the parking lot!" Rowena said in a panicked whisper. "We've got to go!"

Katrina emerged from the car but stayed low, glancing around. Still crouched, she made her way around to the rear of the vehicle. "Okay, then let's go."

Rowena followed her, her heart pounding. Damn it, they couldn't be spotted!

Katrina took the lead, creeping low behind the row of cars at the back of the parking lot to avoid being seen.

After about thirty seconds—when they heard a car door slam shut in the distance—Katrina slowly stood to her full height. "Someone just got out of the car," she said. "Walking away from us."

Standing upright, Rowena followed Katrina's line of sight. About fifty feet away, a male was walking briskly toward the nearest residence building.

"We're cool," Katrina whispered. "He's not even looking this way."

Rowena started to jog toward the main path.

"Slow down," Katrina told her. "Walk calmly. No need to draw attention."

"I know. I just want to get out of here."

"We're two friends out for a stroll. Nothing suspicious."

Except for the fact that it was four in the morning and it was too cold for anyone in their right mind to be out on the campus grounds taking a stroll.

How did Katrina remain so calm while Rowena's heart was spazzing out?

"Did you do it?" Rowena asked after several seconds.

Facing her, Katrina's eyes lit up with malicious pleasure. "It's done. This loose end has been tied up. Shemar's as good as dead."

CHAPTER ONE

Present day

SHAWDE

Shawde Williams knelt onto the grass beside the tombstone, the tears already blurring her eyes. Five and a half years had passed. Five and a half years and her grief was still strong.

"Hey," she said softly, placing the bouquet of flowers in front of the tombstone. Five and a half years later and the fact that her brother was in a coffin six feet below this spot was still surreal.

Her eyes landed on the etching of her brother. Every time she came here, she was amazed at just how well his essence had been captured on the headstone. His handsome face lit up in a smile, those eyes twinkling, his dimples as charming as they had been live. She fingered the etching, the only way she could touch her brother now.

Then she fell onto her bottom, crying softly. She'd lost more than her brother on that horrible day in January.

She'd lost her mother, who had become a shell of herself as the despair had ripped her apart.

And most recently, Shawde had lost her fiancé because of this tragedy. Maurice had told her that he couldn't take it anymore. Either she let go of her obsession, as he'd called it, or they were done.

Shawde had called the wedding planner the next morning to tell her to cancel all the plans. Then Shawde had met with Maurice to give him back the ring. As long as she lived, she would never forget the look on his face as she'd placed the stunning diamond into his palm. The look of despair had damn near brought her to her knees. But he'd stood his ground, and so had she. If she wasn't over her obsession, then they were over. And she could never be over Shemar's murder—not until the killer was brought to justice.

Maurice didn't understand, and maybe Shawde couldn't expect him to. He hadn't had his family ripped apart because of a murder.

"What proof do you have that it was murder?" Maurice had asked before they'd finally called it quits, exasperated when she'd failed yet again to get the police to reopen the case.

"Shemar knew cars inside out. There's no way he would have missed an issue with his brakes. He would have given his car a complete inspection before a long road trip. I'm one hundred percent certain of that. And it's not that the cops didn't believe the brake line had been faulty. They just can't prove that it was deliberately tampered with. According to them, Shemar could have hit debris in the road."

"Exactly."

"But he didn't. That's not what happened."

"How can you know that?"

"Call it intuition."

"Intuition?" Maurice had thrown his hands into the air. "Do you even hear yourself?"

His patience had been wearing thin, and Shawde couldn't entirely blame him. Perhaps if their situations had been reversed, Shawde would feel the same sense of exasperation. But this was her brother, and she could not go on until she got justice for him.

"Why would his girlfriend want him dead?" Maurice demanded.

"Some people are evil at their core. They get off on hurting others. People like you and me can never understand them."

"I don't understand you," Maurice had mumbled.

Shawde figured he hadn't thought she'd heard him, but she had. Loud and clear.

She'd slept alone that night, and a week later Maurice was telling her that she had to either let go of the past or forget about their future together.

"Maurice and I are over," Shawde said now to the tombstone. "He wants me to give up trying to solve your murder. Of course, he doesn't think it *was* murder. Dad's convinced, but thinks it's eating me up. And Mom . . . well, she can hardly talk about it. She's not the same, Shemar. She's . . . cries all the time. She retired, because she's too depressed to work." Shawde wiped at her tears. "Which is one of the reasons I *have* to keep going. Once Katrina pays for what she did, we can all heal. Finally put this past us."

As Shawde so often did, she stayed quiet, listening to see if she could hear the voice of her brother on a whisper of wind. Every fiber of her being believed that he was looking down on her, that he could hear her. That he was with her at this very moment.

It was one of the reasons she couldn't give up her fight.

Shemar had been her little brother. She'd protected him in grade school. When that bully in his second-grade class had been beating him up, Shawde had given the little bugger a beatdown. He'd never bothered Shemar again.

A smile touched her lips as she recalled the memory. But it quickly faded.

The time it had mattered most, she hadn't been there to protect him. From that bitch Katrina. The moment she'd met Katrina when she'd visited the university in the fall, Shawde hadn't liked her. There had been no warmth in the smile she'd plastered on her face. In fact, it felt as though all the positive energy had been sucked out of the room when she'd entered, replaced by something cold and unsettling.

Shawde had told her brother that she didn't like Katrina, that something about his girlfriend didn't sit well with her. But Shemar hadn't dumped Katrina. Not that Shawde had expected him to.

Nor had she expected Katrina to kill him.

The last thing Shawde's brother had said to her was that he thought she was right. He'd learned something about Katrina, something upsetting. He hadn't shared with Shawde what that thing was but said he'd update her when he'd gotten to the bottom of it. He was planning to fill her in on all the details in person when he got back home to Albany.

Then his car had lost control on the interstate. For some inexplicable reason, Shemar's car had crossed the center line and collided with a truck. That had sealed his fate.

A fate that Shawde was certain Katrina had maliciously planned for him.

At first, the cops had speculated it was suicide, as the witnesses all said that Shemar hadn't applied the brakes. Further investigation of the burned car had shown that the brakes had failed because the brake line had been ruptured, but there had been no conclusive evidence that the car had been tampered with.

"I know you want me to keep going," Shawde said to Shemar. "And I know you'd do the same for me."

Shawde fell silent again. It was weird how five years could pass and yet a part of you still couldn't quite believe what had happened.

Looking at her brother's name, it was never quite easy to believe.

SHEMAR LEWIS WILLIAMS

Then she read the inscription below the dates of his birth and death, even though she knew it by memory.

CALLED TO BE AN ANGEL AT THE AGE OF 21.
YOU LEFT A HOLE IN OUR HEARTS,
WHERE THERE HADN'T BEEN ONE.
OUR LOSS IS HEAVEN'S GAIN.
WE TRY TO REMEMBER THAT THROUGH OUR PAIN.
OH, HOW WE MISS YOU!
AND WISH WE NEVER HAD TO PART.
GONE TOO SOON,
BUT ALWAYS IN OUR HEARTS.

Every time Shawde looked at that inscription, she wanted to scream. She had wanted an inscription that reflected the truth. *You weren't supposed to die* or *Taken before your time* or even *Murdered by a devious bitch* would have indicated the reality of his death.

Shawde's anger was brewing, and she drew in a deliberate breath in an effort to calm herself. She had long ago stopped wearing an elastic band on her wrist, which she was supposed to snap against her skin when her thoughts began to overwhelm her. Such a stupid idea. It simply didn't work.

"One day," she said, smoothing her hand over her

brother's face. "One day, Katrina will have to pay for what she's done. She's already killed again. I told you that. Her parents. I didn't realize it was so easy for people to get away with murder." Shawde snorted. "Hell, maybe I should just take her out."

She heaved a weary sigh. "Of course, with my luck, I'd get arrested. No, I'll just wait for her to slip up. Because I'm sure she will. The friggin' psychopath has killed and gotten away with it, so she's even more confident now. She'll kill again, but her luck will run out. And when it does, I'll finally get justice for you. I promise you that."

CHAPTER TWO

I stared from a distance, the sickening sensation in my gut intensifying with every second. I watched the graduating class gathered on the lawn. *My* graduating class. It was a day of celebration on the University at Buffalo campus.

The action in front of me played out like a scene from some corny made-for-TV movie. Graduates smiling from ear to ear, giggling and chattering, prancing around on the pristine lawn, posing for photos with their smartphones.

I swallowed as I stared at Wesley Morrison, who was standing with his group of friends near the stone front steps. He looked especially handsome today, dressed in his graduation gown. I could imagine a photographer from the university paper, *The Spectrum,* wanting to use Wesley on the cover of the next issue. He looked that good.

He resembled a younger Boris Kodjoe, with that golden-brown skin from his biracial heritage, tall, lean frame, and goatee that looked so damn sexy. Unlike Boris, Wesley wasn't bald. He wore his hair closely cropped. Like Boris, Wesley had actually done some modeling as a kid.

I felt a pang of nostalgia as I stared at him now, re-membering the first time I'd laid eyes on him in my creative-writing class. I hadn't been the only woman to be smitten by his good looks.

But I'd been the one to ultimately claim his heart.

Which made it all the harder to see him now. If he missed me, he was doing a good job of not showing it. Not with that huge-ass grin on his face.

I'm not going to your graduation.

It's not my fault you missed a semester. And no one cares that you're not graduating with the class. It's not the end of the world.

We need to talk about Seattle. About what I suggested.

And I told you already that won't work. Damn it, you make it seem like we're going to die if we don't see each other for a few months.

It's like you just don't care. How can I support your "big day" tomorrow if this is how you're talking to me?

Fine. Stay in your room and sulk, then. Seems that's what you do best these days anyway.

I had left him feeling that he didn't care. And indeed, he certainly didn't appear to right now.

I was standing behind the trunk of an old maple tree in the distance, unseen. Everyone was too absorbed with their own happiness to notice that I was even there, completely miserable.

I should be by Wesley's side. But after our argument yesterday, I didn't want to give him the satisfaction of knowing that I had come after all. That I had watched his proud moment from a distance.

Maybe I was being stupid. Maybe his reasoning about Seattle made perfect sense. He had to concentrate on work, and I had to concentrate on school.

My pride began to dissipate. If I didn't support him now, how could I ever expect things to work out between us?

I began to step out from behind the tree—until I saw Michelle appear out of nowhere and scurry over to him.

Michelle, who until two days ago had been the friend who I'd believed would always have my back. The text message I'd found from her on Wesley's phone had changed all of that.

Halting, I stayed where I was, watching as my suspicion grew.

Wesley's grin widened, and I saw his eyes take her in from head to toe. Did he like her new look? She'd cut her hair into a short, cute bob with longer layers at the front, and I had to admit the new style had done wonders for her. But was Wesley seeing her as sexy and desirable? As someone he would date?

He opened his arms and wrapped Michelle in a hug that was too long to simply be friendly. Then, instead of releasing her, he pulled her close to his side. She was five foot five while he was six foot one, so her head rested against his shoulder. Extending his left arm to hold up his iPhone, Wesley lowered his face to press it against Michelle's. Both of them beamed as they posed for a picture.

My gut twisted. Would that be his new Facebook profile photo? Did his status already reflect *IT'S COMPLI-CATED?* Or, worse, *SINGLE?*

The picture was taken, but Michelle's hand was still looped through my boyfriend's arm. How often had she listened while I'd complained about Wesley, telling me he was a jerk or insensitive and encouraging me to move on?

Well, now I knew why. She wanted him for herself.

I moved out from behind the tree. My pulse thundered in my ears, sounding like a herd of angry elephants charging. The rage swallowed me whole, and I embraced it.

And here's the thing: You know how people always claim that they lose control at a critical moment, that their anger takes over and they couldn't stop themselves if they tried?

Well, I knew that what I was about to do—in front of

Wesley's family and friends—was wildly inappropriate. In fact, as I marched across the lawn a big part of my brain tried to warn me against doing it. And yet my fury outweighed my reason.

I was pissed. Pissed that Wesley could treat me with so little regard after dating me for two years. And I was equally as pissed off with Michelle, the bitch I had once considered a friend.

I stalked toward them, no one noticing me until I was a few feet away. Michelle was the one to look in my direction first, and her smile instantly went flat. Wesley noticed me next, and shock came over his face. Shock that was quickly followed by panic flashing in his eyes.

"So, Wesley is an insensitive ass and I'm better off without him?" I said, facing Michelle. "Was this your grand plan—to move in on my man?"

Michelle stepped toward me, both hands up in a sign of surrender. "It's not what you think."

I slapped her across the face, sending her flying backward on the lawn. I heard Wesley's parents gasp—two people who had said that they loved me like a daughter. If only for their sakes, I should have tried to keep my cool.

But what was done was done, and I felt great.

Instantly Wesley went to Michelle, who was crying. He helped her up from the grass before turning his attention to me. "Have you lost your mind?"

"Have you?" I countered. "You're screwing my best friend!"

"Oh dear God," Wesley's mother uttered. I could see her look of disdain from my peripheral vision, hear the embarrassment in her voice. She was a churchgoing woman who had grown up in Barbados, and she'd always hated public displays of emotion—amorous or otherwise.

Wesley helped Michelle to her feet, then stepped toward

me and placed a hand on my shoulder. "You need to calm down."

"Don't touch me!" I yelled. I violently wriggled from his touch. "Last night, you told me you needed space, that you didn't want to be in a relationship with anyone right now. And now here you are, with Michelle?"

Michelle was sobbing and clutching her cheek, perhaps hamming it up for effect. And her act was having the desired result. Because Wesley turned from me abruptly and took Michelle into his arms, offering her comfort.

"That's right, bitch. Cry your crocodile tears. That's the only way you can get a man."

"For God's sake, Jade," Wesley's father said. He was tall, blond, and, at fifty, still lean. Wesley had definitely gotten his height from his dad.

I whimpered, feeling a pang of regret as I looked at him.

"This is graduation day," Mr. Morrison went on. He gestured to the crowd at large. "You're embarrassing yourself."

"Do you know what your son has done to me?" I challenged. "What he's had me do for him?"

"That's enough," Wesley said, his tone a warning.

"You think he's perfect," I said, addressing both of his parents now. "He's not. He's far from it."

Wesley glared at me. "Jade, *stop*."

"Why? You don't want your parents to know the truth about your life?"

"She's off her fucking pills," someone in the gathering crowd said, and I whipped my gaze in that direction. I saw people snickering, their eyes wide with amusement.

The laughter, the comment . . . suddenly I could see myself from a different vantage point. As if I were a spectator in the crowd.

I was becoming unhinged.

I didn't like it.

Wesley's mother took tentative steps toward me, as if she feared I would slap her, too. "Oh, sweetheart. We know this year hasn't been easy for you. Which is why we told you that you could call us at any time. Any time at all."

"That's not what this is about," I said, but my voice faltered. "This is about Wesley sleeping with my best friend!"

The buzzing among the crowd was louder now, people openly giggling as though I were a circus act.

"Jade, do you hear yourself?" Wesley asked, angry. "And you don't see why I need a break from you?"

"You owe me," I said, wanting to say more but knowing that I couldn't. Oh, I wanted to. But if I told his parents and the world what he'd had me do for him, he would never forgive me. I would never get him back.

A tear spilled onto my cheek. Didn't he see how I was hurting? And yet it was Michelle he was cradling.

I couldn't stomach it anymore. I moved toward them, grabbing at his arms, clawing at them with one hand while I tried to wrench Michelle free from his grasp with the other hand.

Michelle wailed, and Wesley's father got into the mix. He grabbed ahold of my arms from behind, allowing Wesley the time to whisk Michelle away.

"How could you do this?" Mrs. Morrison was asking, tears brimming in her eyes. "Embarrass us like this, yourself? How could you?"

The Morrisons hated me. People were laughing at me. I spun around and took off, running with shaky legs across the grass. The lawn sloped toward the street, and I almost tumbled in my haste to get to my car.

I was angry. I was sad.

I was lost.

My tears blurred my vision, but as I got to my car I threw a look over my shoulder in Wesley's direction once more. Michelle was still in his arms, Wesley's parents and friends fussing over both of them while some looked in my direction.

I brushed at the tears stinging my eyes, then got into my car and slammed the door. The moment I turned on the accelerator, I hit the gas, pulling into traffic carelessly, forcing myself into the lane in front of a car that was far too close to me.

The driver blared the horn. I stuck my hand out the window and gave the driver the middle finger. Sure, I was at fault, but I didn't care. I was in crisis mode.

I drove at a faster clip than allowed for the speed zone, zipping in and out of traffic until I got to the entrance for the 33 expressway. I had no clue where I was going, and it wasn't exactly like I cared. Part of me wanted to head to the I-90 and drive west to Erie, Pennsylvania, and home and never look back at the University at Buffalo. At that moment, I didn't particularly care about the fact that I still had a dorm room filled with my belongings.

I drove, the tears coming harder, as I reflected on the mess that was my life. Why were kids always fed a ton of bull when it came to college? *Best years of your life. Study hard, and the world and your dreams await you. Experience true love.*

There was one important thing that had been left off of the bullshit brochure. No one told you how your life was going to be ripped apart when you watched your boyfriend graduate without you. Because that boyfriend suddenly realized that since he was going to head clear across the country to begin his career, he didn't want to hold you back. He was selflessly breaking up with you for *you.*

"Asshole!" I yelled, and hit the gas. I had been prepared to wait for him, to plan my own career in Seattle once I graduated next year. Or I could even transfer colleges now.

But no, Wesley didn't want to hold me back. He figured

the test of the strength of our relationship would come from a year apart. Which was really his way of breaking up with me because he wanted to see other people.

People like Michelle. I wasn't stupid.

My eyes were swimming with tears when I switched lanes. And again I got a blaring horn.

"Screw off!" I yelled, craning my neck to look at who had hit the horn so I could flash them a dirty look. I wasn't in the mood.

When I turned back to the road in front of me, I had no time to react. I was straddling two lanes. The barrier between the exit for Oak Street and the lane that continued on the expressway loomed before me, moving toward me at a rapid pace.

"Shit!" I uttered, and jerked the car to the left to correct my position.

But I jerked the car too hard. Because it swerved and spun. And then it crashed.

The air bag exploded in my face.

And then everything went black.

CHAPTER THREE

My eyelids fluttered as I slowly came awake. A strange sensation of disorientation hit me like a ton of bricks. As I tried to fully open my eyes, pain pierced my head. I raised my hand to bring it to my forehead, only to find it constricted.

My eyes popped open, and the disorientation intensified. That's when I saw my sister, Marie, sitting beside me. A look of concern mixed with disapproval marred her pretty features.

"Mar—" My voice croaked, and I stopped.

"You crashed your car," she said, her words sounding like an accusation.

"I—I did?"

"You don't remember?"

I shook my head, narrowing my eyes as I stared at Marie. She was wearing her nurse scrubs, which led me to believe she'd been by my side. Her hair was pulled back in a tight bun, the way she wore it at work. She had flawless skin the color of hot chocolate, and with her hair pulled back and no makeup she normally looked like a teenager.

But not today. She looked like she had aged two de-
cades.

I could hear the constant beep of a machine beside my
bed. I was in a hospital. The curtain drawn around my bed
told me that, as surely as the IV I noticed in my hand.

"Are we in Erie?" That was where my sister lived and
worked. Where I lived when I wasn't at school.

"Erie?" She scoffed. "No, you made sure to crash your
car on the 33 expressway in Buffalo. Heading west. Were
you planning to head home—or were you just being reck-
less?"

I closed my eyes tightly, trying to recall what had happened. The 33 expressway. Yes. It was coming back to me.
Driving. Being angry. Losing control.

Wesley.

I was hurt. I was in the hospital. So why did my sister
seem pissed off instead of relieved?

"Why are you angry?" I asked, my voice weak. "If I
was in an accident, I could be dead right now."

"Accident, right." Marie snorted. "I heard the witness
accounts from the police. Jade, you're out of control. Losing it."

"Huh?"

"Witnesses said you were all over the place. Driving
like an enraged maniac. What were you doing—*trying* to
kill yourself?" She held my eyes, giving me a pointed look.

"No," I said. "Of course not. How could you ask me
that?"

My sister simply tightened her lips and shook her head.

I angled my head away from her toward the window
where sunlight spilled into the room, pain slicing through
my head as I did so. I knew what she was thinking. Why
she had asked the question—one that hadn't been rhetori-
cal. I also knew why she didn't seem to believe my answer.
Just over a year ago, when our stepfather died of cancer, I

had unraveled. With him being our only caregiver after our mother died fifteen years earlier, I hadn't known how to cope with my grief. And in that state of devastation, I'd done something incredibly stupid. I'd taken a handful of sleeping pills.

But it wasn't like I'd *wanted* to die. Because after I took all those pills, I was smart enough to call my boyfriend and tell him what I'd done. I'd been rushed to the hospital, my stomach pumped, and in the end I'd been fine.

Physically anyway. But I hadn't been able to function, so I had taken a semester off of school to try to emotionally recover. Which was why I didn't graduate with the rest of my class.

"You know I love you," Marie said, and sighed wearily. "I'm just . . . afraid for you. This thing with Wesley—"

"It's not a *thing*. It's a relationship."

"And life goes on. He said he wanted to take a break. In a year if you still love each other, then you'll know you have the real deal. Trying to kill yourself—"

"I did *not* try to kill myself."

"No?" my sister challenged me. "Wesley told me he saw you getting into your car, that you tore off like a madwoman."

"Wesley . . ." His name escaped my lips on a ragged breath. "You—you talked to him?"

"Yes."

"Where is he?"

Marie didn't answer, and the expression on her face said that she didn't want to tell me.

"Where?" I demanded.

"Look how you're already getting yourself worked up. This isn't good for you. Isn't healthy."

He had watched me get into my car. Such a small, insignificant thing—but it made me feel better. He hadn't been as wrapped up in Michelle as I'd believed.

"So he knows I'm here?"

Marie nodded. "He said for me to call him once you woke up."

I felt a flutter of hope in my heart. Which was crazy, I knew. But maybe knowing I'd been in an accident had given Wesley a different perspective. Maybe he'd changed his mind about us.

It was hope, and I was going to hang on to it.

Later that day, when Wesley stepped into my hospital room, my heart perked up immensely. Forgotten were his words about wanting to take a break, and the racy text from Michelle. All I could think when I saw him was that we were going to pick up where we'd left off. That everything between us would be fine again.

"Hey," he said.

"Hi," I replied softly, my physical pain all but gone.

Wesley fingered the bandage on my forehead, then the one on my cheek. "Damn it, Jade. What happened?"

I'd suffered one hell of a night, but now that Wesley was here it was all better. "Lost control in the car," I told him, trying to force a smile to lighten the seriousness of the situation. All things considered, I was very lucky to be alive and have escaped with only some lacerations and a mild concussion. "Idiot, I know. I looked away for a second, and next thing I know, I'm plowing into that big orange barrier they put near the exits. Thank God for the air bag. I hear it saved my life."

Wesley shook his head in dismay. Then he took my hand in his.

And I swear, I almost cried from happiness. The accident had almost been worth it, just for this moment.

He continued to hold my hand as he folded his six-foot-one, muscular frame into the chair beside my bed. There were worry lines etched on his handsome face, but all I could think about was how gorgeous he was. He was just so sexy. . . .

"Seeing you here like this . . ." His voice trailed off.

"You were worried about me?" I asked him.

"Of course I was worried. When I saw you tear off like you did—" Wesley abruptly stopped, his expression changing. In his eyes, I could see that he was thinking.

"Wait a second," he said. "You didn't . . . you didn't *do this on purpose*?"

"No," I replied quickly. And I was disappointed that he'd even asked.

He narrowed his eyes, and I could see the doubt. Like my sister, he didn't believe me.

"You know I didn't, baby," I went on. "I wouldn't. I was angry about you and Michelle, yes, but—"

He pulled his hand from mine, dragged it over his face. "You always get so emotional, Jade. Too emotional."

"I lost my dad. You think that's easy to deal with?"

"Yeah, but it's like you want to hang on to your pain, let the world know you're suffering."

I said nothing, because I didn't know what to say. Wesley had both of his parents. He couldn't understand what I was going through.

"Damn it," he uttered, and I knew what he was referring to. The thought that I had deliberately hurt myself.

"I didn't do this on purpose," I stressed, my voice holding a pleading tone. How could he not believe me?

"No?" he challenged. "I mean, you did it before. And I saw that you were unraveling again. . . ."

"That was different. That was . . ." My voice trailed off.

"You can't hurt yourself just because things aren't working out for us."

"I didn't do this on purpose," I stressed, needing him to believe that. The one thing I hated more than anything was the way people seemed to believe that one bad decision on my part meant I would be a fragile flower for the rest of my life. "You know that the other time, it was about me losing my dad. My whole world had fallen apart. Honestly, I don't even think I was forming coherent thoughts. All I knew was that I wanted to be able to get some rest and forget."

Wesley gave me a doubtful look.

"I made a stupid decision," I admitted. "But I wasn't in my rational mind."

"Just like yesterday."

"No. Yesterday, I was angry." I opened my palm, wishing he would take my hand again. "We can work things out," I ventured, hoping that he'd had a change of heart since last night. Even if it was just that seeing me in this hospital bed was what made him realize he cared too much for me to let me go. "Obviously, you care. You heard about the accident, and you came."

"Of course I came."

I was emboldened by his response. "We can see each other every other weekend."

Wesley's lips twisted. "I'm going to Seattle. It's not around the corner or just a couple of hours away."

"That's why God invented airplanes," I said, offering him a smile. "We can do this, baby."

He blew out a harried breath. "It's like you didn't hear a word I said the other night."

I swallowed. "I don't want to take a break. I don't want to test our relationship. It just seems stupid. Honestly, this won't even be an issue if I just apply for a transfer to a college in Seattle."

"No." He was shaking his head. "You spent all these years at UB. You should graduate at UB."

"Fundamentally, I agree with you." But for me, not graduating at UB wasn't the end of the world. My relationship with Wesley was more important than where I finished school. "That's why I'm willing to travel to see you."

"It's just . . . so much work."

Not if you love me. . . .

"When you're done school," he went on, "it will be so much easier. And we'll know for sure how we feel about each other."

I started to tear up. "I already know how I feel about you."

"I don't want to rehash this conversation. Long-distance relationships are hard. I think we'll both be happier knowing there's no pressure to stay committed."

My jaw tensed. "That way, you can screw whoever you want."

"Jade—"

"Did you already fuck Michelle?"

Wesley shook his head, but it was more in reaction to my question rather than a denial of what I'd asked him.

"This isn't about Michelle. I love you . . . you know I do." He paused, took a breath as if he was measuring his words carefully, and then continued. "But how many people actually end up with their college sweethearts for the rest of their lives?"

And as I stared at Wesley, at the boyfriend I'd started dating my sophomore year, it felt like I didn't know him at all. Who was this person at my bedside, and why was he saying these things?

"Lots of people," I told him. "Because they love each other, and they make an effort to work things out."

"Maybe in a romance novel," Wesley said. "But this is real life."

The tears threatened to spill from my eyes, but I willed them to stay put. "I can't believe you."

"You know that next year on campus some cute dude is gonna step to you and you're gonna be flattered. Do you really want to be attracted to him but have to worry about staying faithful to me?" He paused. "If we're meant to be, we'll be. Let's take the year to figure things out—without any strings. If, after that time, we're missing each other like crazy, then we'll know."

A year . . . it seemed like a lifetime. One I couldn't bear to spend apart from him. How could he bear to be away from me?

As I stared at Wesley, my chest filling with pain, I began to hate him. Because how was it that we'd dated for two years, had been a tight couple at UB, and now he was letting distance force us apart?

"Get out," I said, an angry whisper.

His eyes narrowed in response to my statement, but he stayed put.

"I said *get out.*"

"Jade—"

"You want to take a break from me, you may as well start now. I don't need you coming here out of pity."

"This wasn't pity. I still care what happens to you."

"Really?" I snapped. I wanted to punch him. "Get out already." I glared at him. "*Get out!* Get out! Get out! Get out!"

Wesley sprang to his feet, his eyes volleying between the room's door and me. He was panicked, as though he feared someone would come in and think he'd done something to harm me.

Which he had.

The man I had loved for two years had broken my heart.

CHAPTER FOUR

Over the next couple of weeks, the proverbial dust settled, but I didn't feel much better.

I was getting used to my new reality, one where Wesley wasn't in my life. Oh, he still claimed it wasn't an official split, and he called and texted every few days from Seattle, but clearly things weren't the same between us. In fact, the more I heard from him, the more it hurt. Because inevitably I would ask if he'd changed his mind, only to learn that he hadn't.

I was in a funk. But trying to move forward.

I'd moved out of my dorm room and was back home with my sister, where I felt like I was walking on eggshells all the time. Because every time I got even a little emotional, she treated me like a baby. Fussing over me and telling me to talk about my feelings so that she would know I was okay.

"I'm not suicidal," I'd told her one day when her concern was too much for me to bear. "I messed up; I know I did. But that's all."

I know she didn't believe me, and I supposed I couldn't blame her. Looking at the situation objectively, I did appear unpredictable. I'd lost control when our dad died. Then I'd lost control again at the graduation. But I was seeing things more clearly now, and I was trying to move on with my life and deal with the reality of having a long-distance relationship.

A couple of days later, I was in my room lying on the bed with a book when there was a knock on my door. I looked up to see Marie entering, wearing her nurse scrubs, and was surprised that she was home at this hour.

"Hey," she said.

"Why are you home at noon? Aren't you in the middle of your shift?"

Marie walked into the room. "I can't take another day of coming home to see you sulking, so I decided to do something about it."

I narrowed my eyes. "Sulking?"

"You know you're depressed."

I did my best not to roll my eyes. "Something like what?"

"I spoke to a friend of mine—we both pledged the Alpha Sigma Pi sorority at UB. She's from Atlanta, but she's now living in Florida where she recently started her own business. It's a small coffee shop, catering to tourists. As we got to talking, she was saying that she could really use some help. And I ended up telling her that my sister could really use a job. She was excited. She said my call to her must have been intuition, because two of her staff quit a few days ago and she's been running ragged."

"You suggested to a friend in Florida that I'd work for her?" I asked.

"I'm sure it's not what you want to do for the summer," Marie said. "But it's a job. And more important, it will get you away from here."

I made a face as I looked at Marie. "You're worried that if I stick around here I'm going to what? Jump off a bridge?

How many times do I have to tell you that I'm not going to hurt myself before you believe me?"

"I didn't say that. But . . . I'd be lying if I didn't say I wasn't worried about your mental health. A change of scenery is always a great thing after a breakup."

We didn't break up, I almost said, but didn't bother to explain that fact again. Maybe it would seem like I was clinging to Wesley in an unhealthy way, but I had decided to take him at his word. And the last thing he'd told me, even though I'd sent him running from the hospital room, was that this wasn't a permanent break. If he said he wanted to test the strength of our relationship, then that's how I needed to see our time apart. Because when I didn't believe that, that's when I started to feel despair.

It wasn't just the loss of Wesley that I was feeling but also the loss of my best friend. I hadn't heard from Michelle since the incident at graduation. Of course, she had unfriended me on Facebook. Nonetheless, I'd tried to reach out to her, but she hadn't responded to my texts or my social media messages.

"I know you don't always agree with me," Marie began, "but I think this will be good for you. Even Lucy said that you should do something for yourself. And Florida? Palm trees, sand . . . what's not to like?"

Lucy was my therapist. The one I'd seen after the pill incident and the one my sister had dragged me to see after I got out of the hospital.

Though in part I resented my sister arranging to have me go to Florida, I was nonetheless intrigued by the idea. Putting my book down, I sat cross-legged on the bed. "Florida's a beautiful state. But damn, it's got to be hot now."

"But it's got beautiful beaches you can enjoy. Let's face it—the scenery will be a lot better than here." When I didn't say anything, Marie sat down on the bed beside me.

"I know you've been frustrated with me, thinking that I'm treating you with kid gloves."

"You have. I'm not a basket case, even if I've made mistakes."

"I think that Florida will be good for both of us. I know things have been stressful these last couple of weeks because we haven't had our own space. Trust me, if I didn't have my job here, I'd jump at the opportunity to go to Key West."

Yes, things had been stressful—but not in the typical way. Ever since I'd come home from the hospital, Marie hadn't been her usual abrasive self. We may have been sisters, but we didn't always get along. We could fight like cats and dogs. Something that hadn't happened since I'd come out of the hospital. Even when Marie and I had a disagreement, Marie didn't raise her voice. Instead, she tried to mollify me.

Which only annoyed me more. Because it told me that she believed I was lying. Lying about being okay mentally.

"You're not saying anything. You think it's a bad idea?" Marie asked cautiously.

"I didn't say it was a bad idea." Perhaps it was a good idea for me to go away, branch out on my own, and do something different. Show my sister—and Wesley—that I wasn't this fragile flower they all thought I was.

"It's just a lot to process," I went on. "I wasn't expecting it." I gave her a pointed look. "And I don't expect you to call in favors from friends on my behalf."

Marie offered me a sheepish smile. "Okay. You got me. But bottom line, you have a job if you want it. She knows it's only for the summer, because I told her you're going back to school in the fall."

My sister, older than me by six years, spoke as I imagined my mother would. Making sure to guide my decisions. I didn't remember much of my mother, because I'd been so young when she had died.

"Katrina said that she'll be grateful for the help," Marie went on, "for as long as she can have it."

"Florida," I said softly, more to myself.

"And Key West, Florida," Marie stressed. "We're not talking Orlando here, with hordes of children and no ocean breeze. You've always liked writing. Ernest Hemingway lived in Key West for a long time. Maybe you'll get some inspiration and actually write that novel you've been talking about."

The idea was growing on me. Maybe Marie was right. Sunshine, blue skies, the ocean. I could do a lot worse for the summer.

And I just might find that inspiration I needed to do some serious writing. I knew I loved stories and that I wanted to write a novel, yet I could never find the time to write a word. Not with school papers and Wesley and friends and other distractions. As well, Lucy said it would be a good idea for me to start journaling. She said that putting all of my emotions down on paper would be healing.

Perhaps there was no better place to heal than Key West.

"I'll go," I said.

Marie beamed, as though I'd just agreed to go into rehab. "Great. I'll let Katrina know."

"I'm going to miss you," Marie said a couple of days later, hugging me hard as I stood outside of the Chevy Malibu that had once belonged to our dad. It was mine to borrow for the trip to Florida, which I supposed spoke volumes. My sister trusted me to get behind a steering wheel again.

I'd been to see Lucy, and she was supportive of this trip. She reminded that I could call at any time if I needed her and that she could also refer me to someone in Florida if required. I was grateful for her. And for my sister. It had hit me in the last couple of days that Marie was the only real family I had left. The extended family who hadn't been around after our mother died weren't around now. So while I knew that Marie, perhaps along with Lucy, had cooked up this plan to "save" me, I couldn't be mad at her. In fact, it finally dawned on me that she was looking out for me because she loved me.

So here I was, about to venture off to a place that offered endless sunshine, and I knew that the hope on Marie's and Lucy's parts was that I would have time and space to forget about Wesley and reclaim my life.

When Marie released me, she said, "I wish I could take the drive with you, but I can't miss any more work."

"I'll drive carefully," I assured her. Normally, I might give her a smart-ass remark. Because on so many levels I'd always shunned her filling the motherly role. But my sister had put up with my mood swings over the past two weeks in an effort to get along better with me, and I appreciated her for it.

She pulled me into her arms one last time. "I love you. Never forget that."

"I know. I love you, too."

A few days later, I was finally in South Florida, my end goal in sight. Only three more hours and I would be in Key West. I had done the drive over three days, taking my time because there was no need to rush. And I found that the long drive listening to music and audiobooks had done a lot for my mental well-being.

I was okay with the time and space Wesley had suggested, and looking back on my behavior, I knew I was lucky he even said he still loved me at all. I was still afraid that in a year's time he would have moved on or that we wouldn't really be able to pick up where we left things off. But as Marie had said, people broke up all the time and life went on.

The clarity I'd achieved after three days of driving almost made the hours I'd spent in therapy after my stepfather's death seem like money wasted. Perhaps all I'd needed to do was drive across the country for a number of days to get in touch with my thoughts and my pain. There's something about being in a car by yourself that allows you to think on a deeper level. And in the three days I'd been driving and thinking, I'd had a profound understanding regarding my relationship with Wesley and why I'd reacted so badly to his rejection. I'd figured out why it had hurt me so much and why I'd been so desperate to cling to him. Because his rejection made me think of my biological father's rejection.

When I was just five years old, my father left us. And it wasn't like he left but still remained in my life and Marie's. He was simply gone, as if he'd never existed.

As long as I lived, I would remember the day he'd sat us all down, explained that he couldn't "do this" anymore, that he needed a break. I remember crying, begging, pleading. But his decision had been made, and no amount of tears from his daughters had made any difference.

I'd been devastated. I had loved my daddy so much. Marie had been angry. Eleven at the time, she'd known that what my father was about to do was unforgivable. Me—I'd simply wanted him back.

Before he moved out, Marie had tried to comfort me by saying that since our parents fought too much, maybe it was best that Daddy leave. But when the day came and he hugged us good-bye, all I could see was that I was being rejected by the man who was supposed to love me the most.

Wesley walking away from me felt like the same kind of inexplicable abandonment. Where a man would tell you,

Hey, I love you. It's just that we can't be together. It didn't make sense to me when my father had said it, and it didn't make sense when Wesley had said it.

When I finally connected the dots, I'd felt a sense of relief. And with it came the attitude of what would be would be. My mother had moved on, found my stepdad, and he'd been a great father. I didn't have to be devastated forever if things with Wesley didn't work out.

In fact, the love my mom had found with my stepdad had been the real deal, the kind of love that made her laugh and smile all the time. She'd truly been happy with him. The tragedy was that she hadn't been able to enjoy that happiness for more than a couple of years before cancer claimed her.

"No sad thoughts," I told myself, and looked out at the stunning stretch of the Atlantic. In the distance I saw pelicans flying low above the water, and a smile touched my lips. My mother had loved birds of all kinds, and whenever I saw a flock of birds while having a bad thought I figured it was my mother sending me a positive sign. True or silly, I didn't know, but it did help me to feel better.

I didn't want to be sad. The road stretched before me—a road of possibilities. Who knew what adventure awaited me? Perhaps it was time I be like my friends and find another man to hook up with when I got to Key West. That's what they did to get over a breakup. Found another guy.

Maybe I'd been far too young to be involved in a relationship so serious anyway.

And wasn't Florida filled with attractive men who liked to walk around without their shirts on? Surely I could find someone to pass the time with, to help me forget about Wesley.

As I saw the mile marker indicating that Key West was only thirty miles away, I felt a sense of excitement.

Whatever awaited me, I was ready.

CHAPTER FIVE

An hour later, I was pulling up in front of A Book and a Cup, the coffee shop where I was to meet Katrina Hughes. People populated the large patio, and a woman wearing a black shirt, black skirt, and white apron was wiping down a table as two women stood waiting behind her. I'd seen Katrina's photo on Facebook, so I knew that this tall, athletic redhead was not her. I was looking for an African-American female who was about five foot nine, light skinned, and on the thin side.

I exited my car and damn near yelped as a tsunami of heat enveloped me. Wow. It was seriously hot here.

I pulled at my shorts, which were clinging to my legs after sitting in the car for so long. Then I made my way through the wrought-iron fence that bordered the patio. I approached the waitress as she turned around, and she actually jerked backward. Finding a person standing in her path had clearly startled her.

"Sorry," I said.

"You want a table outside, it's gonna be a little while."

"Actually, I'm wondering where I can find Katrina?"

"She's inside."

The redhead opened the door and held it for me, and I entered the café, noting that by contrast it wasn't busy at all. Only a few tables were occupied, and all of them by people with laptops. Clearly, people were opting to sit outside in the beautiful sunshine.

I saw a man behind the counter, but no females. Then, a moment later, a door in the back swung open and out walked a woman who had to be Katrina. When she saw me, a smile popped out on her face. She walked toward me, slinging the dish towel she was holding over her shoulder. "Jade?"

"And you must be Katrina."

She extended her hand, and I took it. She shook my hand lightly, not much of a shake at all.

"So nice to finally meet you," Katrina said, a hint of a southern drawl to her voice.

I nodded. "Likewise."

"How was the drive down?"

"Uneventful. Easy. Peaceful."

"Good. Excellent." She went over to a man behind the counter, a five-foot-nothing Hispanic male. "Tony, hold down the fort for me, will you?"

"Sure thing," he told her.

Turning back to me, Katrina said, "Follow me."

Katrina seemed to glide, her body elegantly poised as she moved. Perhaps she had spent years as a child walking with a pile of books on her head to ensure a perfect posture. She had an air of sophistication about her, and I could imagine her being a southern belle. Her hair was flat-ironed straight and had a middle part and hung past her shoulders. Her complexion was smooth, her application of makeup so flawless that it looked like she was wearing no makeup at all. And either she had those eyelash extensions or she was naturally blessed in that department.

She was stunning.

I followed her through a door at the back of the store. From there, a staircase led up to a second level. Once we reached the top, Katrina used a key to unlock the door there and stepped inside.

I went in behind her, my eyes scanning the large apartment. It had a brick wall interior that had been painted white and dark hardwood floors. The place was open concept, with a kitchen near the door and the large living-room space near the window. A small breakfast bar with two bar stools was the only thing separating the kitchen and living room. It provided additional counter space for the small kitchen, while also giving people a place to dine.

"It's two bedrooms," Katrina explained, starting to walk to the right. She showed me an average-sized room with a queen bed that was unmade. I assumed that room was hers.

"This is my room," she said, confirming my thought. "Your room will be over there." Katrina gestured to the door across the expanse of living room, then walked over there. She pushed the door open wide.

I looked inside. The room wasn't very large, but neither was it too small. It had a twin bed, a small desk, a chest of drawers, and a ceiling fan. It would do. I didn't plan on spending much time inside anyway. Not when the beach and palm trees beckoned in this hot weather. "There is a second bathroom," Katrina said. "Thank God. It barely holds a sink, toilet, and shower, but it's super convenient." She showed it to me, and I was amazed that a bathroom so small had been constructed. "I figure it was a closet that was converted into a second bathroom." Katrina shrugged. "Now, so you know, a friend of mine is staying here. Actually, my boyfriend. He's from England, and we've been dating for a while. He's out right now, but in case you came in while I wasn't here, I didn't want you to freak out."

Katrina's smile was genuine, warm. It made me feel a lot better about sharing space with a stranger. I was struck with the sense that I'd made the right decision by coming here, and I was hopeful that this stay would be a wonderful one.

"Now, what do you want me to do in the shop?" I asked.

"Have you been a coffee barista before?"

I shook my head. "No. Never."

"Don't worry; we'll find something for you to do. Most likely, if you're comfortable serving customers, you can do that. It'll be great also because you get to earn tips, better tips than the girls get at the front counter."

"Ahh, yes, that would be nice." I hadn't considered the aspect of making tips. I could use all the money I could earn to help with my final semester of school. And, possibly, for a trip or two to Seattle. Wesley had been right to scoff at the idea of twice-monthly trips. What had I been thinking when I'd suggested that? We couldn't afford to do that.

"This is a nice place," I said. "You own it all by yourself?"

"I suppose you're wondering how I can afford to run this place," Katrina said, summing up exactly what I had been wondering. "Prime real estate in a great location? My parents died a year and a half ago."

"Oh, I'm so sorry."

Katrina waved a dismissive hand. "It was a tragic carbon-monoxide accident in their home. I wanted to do something meaningful with the money I got from the life insurance policy. My parents had always dreamed of retiring in Florida, but they just never got the chance. I came down here to scatter their ashes in the ocean, fell in love with the place, and here I am. A year and a half later, with a business I know they would be proud of."

"Wow. That's amazing." Katrina had lost both parents in one tragic accident, yet she seemed so positive. Upbeat. Stronger than I was. "I know what it's like to lose your parents. Mine were years apart. Losing them both at the same time . . . that's got to be tough."

"It was. But I take comfort in knowing they went together. I don't think either of them would have wanted to live without the other one."

Maybe she was right about that. My stepfather had never remarried after my mother had died, and it had been easy for even a child to see that he'd desperately missed her. On his deathbed, he'd tried to comfort me, telling me that he was finally going to be with my mother again.

I whimpered slightly as the memory hit me.

"I heard about your father dying," Katrina said. "I'm sorry for your loss."

"Thanks," I said, putting on a brave face. Maybe I needed to start thinking about my father and mother being together in the afterlife. Maybe that would help me get a sense of real closure. "I love what you said about opening this coffee shop to do something meaningful with the money from the life insurance."

"I'm not making a fortune or anything," Katrina said, "but I'm doing okay. Making enough to get by, and for living in paradise—who can complain? I was so glad to get out of Atlanta—which is a lot hotter in the summer than Key West, if you can imagine. Here we have the ocean breeze. It makes a huge difference."

"My sister says you went to the University at Buffalo," I said. "What did you originally plan to do? Sorry, I'm not trying to say that running a coffee shop isn't what you planned for."

"Don't apologize. Actually, I always figured I'd go to medical school. But four years of pre-med stressed me out, and I knew I could never be a doctor. Besides, that was always my father's dream for me. I'm twenty-eight now, but I'm one of those people who really didn't know what they wanted to be when they grew up. I loved college life, being a sorority president . . . but beyond that? I guess I thought that the college years would go on forever," she finished with a chuckle.

"I hear that. One minute, I was a freshman. The next thing, everyone I started school with was graduating." Realizing what I'd said, I quickly explained, "I missed a semester after my dad died. I just . . . needed time."

"I get it." Katrina smiled warmly. "I was considering finally going to grad school when my parents died. Then I came down here, found this place, and decided to try my hand at a coffee shop. It took four years of college, and some years working at jobs I didn't like, but I think I found my calling."

I admired Katrina. She wasn't making any excuses about how life had gotten in the way of her plans. She was admitting what most students didn't want to—that they didn't have their ten-year plan all mapped out. It was hard when you were eighteen and going into college to know what you really wanted to do for the rest of your life.

"What about you?" Katrina asked.

"I like to write," I found myself saying, something I rarely told people. "But that's not what I went to school for. I majored in economics, though, in all honesty, I hate it. I don't really know if I can make it as a writer, but I'd like to give it a try."

"Awesome. What do you write?"

"Short stories, mostly. But I hope that I can end up writing a novel."

"Well, this is where Hemingway got so much of his inspiration."

"Yeah, my sister said the same thing." I paused. "Other than that, I figured I was going to go to teachers college. Teach economics in high school or something. But then my dad died, and I missed a semester of school, and I'm not sure anymore . . ."

My voice trailed off as it suddenly occurred to me that I didn't know if my sister had told Katrina everything. I looked at her searchingly, but if she knew anything about what I'd recently been through her eyes gave nothing away. Katrina simply nodded, making me believe that no, she didn't know about my emotional breakdown and how I had ended up overdosing on pills and having to miss a semester.

And for that I was glad. It wasn't the kind of story I wanted people to know, so I was grateful that my sister hadn't told Katrina this. At least it didn't appear that Marie had.

Katrina clapped her hands together. "Okay, I've got to head back downstairs. Work calls. Why don't you get your stuff, settle in. Maybe take a walk around the town, get acquainted with the area. You've had a long drive. You don't have to start work today."

"I appreciate that, thanks."

Katrina's smile was easy, welcoming. "Don't thank me yet. Tomorrow, I'm putting you to work. And you'll be busy."

"Busy is okay," I told her. "In fact, busy is great."

I awoke with a start, frightened. For a moment my strange surroundings had me confused about where I was.

And then I remembered. Florida. The coffee shop. Katrina.

My heart was beating hard, a sense of terror spreading through me. Had I just heard a crash?

I lay in my bed, perfectly still. For several moments, I heard nothing.

And then, another loud bang. Like something had been slammed against the wall. And a scream.

I bolted upright now. Was Katrina okay?

As I sat, terrified, I thought I heard the sound of whimpering. Katrina *wasn't* okay.

I was in the process of throwing the covers off, ready to head out of my room to check on Katrina, when I heard: "You fucking asshole!"

That was Katrina's voice.

"You're the one acting like a bitch."

That was Christian, Katrina's British boyfriend, whom I'd met late in the evening. I'd barely said hello to him and shaken his hand before I retired to my room to get some sleep. Alone in my room, I had sat on the bed, stunned that Katrina was dating someone like him. With his lanky body, less-than-average good looks, and pale white skin, they were an odd couple if ever there was one.

Both of them were now screaming at each other. I glanced at my bedside clock. Three fourteen in the morning. Why were they even up, much less fighting?

"I didn't come all the way from England to be treated like this!"

"Then why don't you just fucking leave?"

I put my hands over my ears, trying to block the sound of their yelling. But then I damn near jumped off the bed when I heard the sound of something shattering against a wall.

Holy, what was going on?

I didn't know if I should get up and go check on them. I didn't want to interfere in a private matter. But I also didn't want things to get so out of control that someone got hurt. . . .

The screaming match continued, with more banging sounds that truly alarmed me. Should I call 911?

I didn't know what to do. This was my first night here. I didn't want to call anyone unless I knew that someone was being murdered. If Katrina and Christian were simply having a spat, albeit one that was scaring the crap out of me, did I really want to involve the police in this matter?

". . . I fucking swear, Katrina . . ."

Hearing those words from Christian, I threw off the covers and got out of bed. What if those words had been a threat? A threat to do harm?

Better I intrude on them than stay silent in my room while someone got hurt.

Quietly opening my bedroom room, I walked across the living-room space to Katrina's room. I put my ear against the door, listening.

"Come on, babe," Christian was saying.

"Don't touch me," Katrina replied.

Their voices were lower now, and I hoped that meant that the argument had ended.

"No, Christian." But Katrina no longer sounded so insistent, and I actually thought I heard a giggle.

I stood, waiting, afraid of being caught at the door but also afraid to go back to my room without any clear sense of direction. I'm not sure how many minutes passed—maybe just a couple?—but I began to hear what sounded like groans of passion.

"Oh yes, baby. Right there . . ."

"You like that?" came Christian's response.

"You know I do. Yes, yes!"

I jerked backward at Katrina's loud, passionate cry. Had all of this commotion simply been a game of kinky sex?

If they had been arguing earlier, they most definitely were not now. Which was a relief. But I stayed at the door, listening a little longer, feeling like a pervert as I heard their passionate groans intensifying.

Indeed, the lovemaking was just as vigorous and intense as the fighting had been.

Satisfied that World War Three had been averted, I made my way back to my room. And suddenly I was missing Wesley. I missed having him put his arms around me when we slept in bed. Missed the makeup sex after we'd fought.

In my room, I retrieved my phone. The next thing I knew, I was texting Wesley, asking him how he was doing and telling him that I missed him.

After all, it was only after midnight in Seattle. He might still be up.

And then I waited, and waited. Twenty minutes later, there was no reply and I felt one hundred times worse.

"Idiot," I muttered to myself. Then I turned off my phone, curled into a ball on my bed, and prayed that sleep would come quickly.

CHAPTER SIX

SHAWDE

The ringing phone jarred Shawde awake. As her head bopped up and she opened her eyes, she realized that she was at her desk. She'd fallen asleep there, her binder of research open beside her.

Shawde quickly reached for her cell phone and looked at the screen, hoping to see Gordon's name flashing on it. Instead, she saw Cathy Campbell's name and picture.

As the phone rang a third time, Shawde debated not answering. But she knew Cathy would be concerned if she didn't hear from her, so she swiped the icon on her smartphone to accept the call.

"Hey, Cathy," Shawde greeted her, injecting a light tone into her voice.

"Shawde, hi. How are you?"

"Good. I've been busy. But good."

"Yeah?" Cathy sounded skeptical. "You sure?"

"Uh-huh. Yeah."

"I've been worried. You broke up with Maurice, and I haven't really heard from you."

Shawde swallowed at the mention of Maurice's name. "I needed a bit of time, but I've been okay."

"That's good to hear, Shawde. Really good. Do you have plans for Friday night?"

"No."

"Great. Because a few of us are planning to go out on Friday night to celebrate Alyesha's birthday. Me, Vanessa, Caitlin. We're going to head to a restaurant, then out on the town for some dancing. We'd love for you to join us."

"Oh." Shawde paused. Then she said, "I'll try."

"Oh no, you don't. Don't blow me off. If you don't say yes now, you won't show up. We all haven't been out in so long. Please say yes."

Shawde opened her mouth to speak, but she didn't know what to say. If Maurice didn't understand, how could her friends? She wasn't in the mood to go out and celebrate when all that mattered was seeing her brother's killer brought to justice.

"Shawde?"

Her phone beeped, indicating that she had another call coming through. Easing the phone away from her face, she saw Gordon's name on her screen.

"Cathy, I've got another call coming through. I've got to go."

"Will you join us Friday night?"

"I'll call you back," Shawde said, then quickly answered Gordon's call. She'd been hoping to hear from him tonight. "Hi, Gordon. How are things going?"

"It's been quiet, but one interesting thing happened."

Shawde sat up straight. "Oh?"

"I told you about Christian, Katrina's boyfriend who showed up last week. Well, another person arrived who's staying with them as well."

"Who?"

"Her name is Jade. I don't have a last name yet. We only

exchanged a few words when she brought me coffee. She mentioned she's down from Buffalo."

Shawde bit down on her bottom lip as she thought. "Buffalo? You think she went to school with Katrina?"

"She's younger than Katrina, that's for sure. Maybe she just came down for work. But she's living upstairs with Katrina and Christian. That much I was able to ascertain."

"If she's living with them, there must be a connection," Shawde said. "I know you'll find out what it is." She sighed softly, then went on. "Thanks, Gordon. I appreciate you being down there for me, keeping an eye out."

"No problem. Shemar was like a brother to me. I'm glad I can help out."

Shawde appreciated his words. Yes, she was paying him, but he was charging her less than his normal investigator rate because he'd gone to school with Shemar from grade school through high school. And at least Gordon didn't think she was crazy. He'd listened to her arguments about Katrina and believed that she was behind Shemar's death.

"Let me know if anything changes," Shawde said. "And try to find out Christian's last name. I want to know why he's here from England, how he and Katrina met."

"Of course," Gordon said. "I'm trying to keep a low profile. For now, I'm just a regular customer who comes in every day and works on his laptop. I'll find a way to strike up a conversation with Christian and get back to you."

"Thanks," Shawde said.

As she ended the call, her eyes went to her binder of articles and notes about Katrina. Shawde had had it open to the page with one of the articles about the carbon-monoxide accident that had claimed the lives of Katrina's parents.

Accident. Yeah, right. That's how the incident had been

termed, but Shawde knew better. And she'd tried to en-
lighten the police with an anonymous phone call.

"You need to look into Katrina Hughes, their daughter,"
Shawde had said when she had called the Georgia state
police from a blocked number.

"Who is this?" had been the officer's reply.

"It doesn't matter who I am. You just need to trust me.
The Hugheses didn't die accidentally. Look into Katrina.
She's behind this."

"I'm going to need your name and number," the officer
had said. At which point, Shawde had hung up.

She hadn't wanted to leave her name. She was fast getting an idea of how the police worked, and she wasn't impressed. If she'd left her name, they would find out that
she was Shemar's sister and that she'd alleged Katrina was
behind his accident. Considering the police in upstate New
York had never taken her seriously, she knew the Georgia
police would determine she was a nutcase who couldn't
accept the truth.

Which, she had to acknowledge, was how a lot of people
saw her. Even her friends, like Cathy. If Shawde were to
tell Cathy that she had an investigator in Key West trailing Katrina, Cathy would tell her to get some counseling.

Shawde didn't need counseling. What she needed was
Katrina behind bars.

As Shawde reread the article, hoping for some clue she
hadn't picked up on before, she yawned. When she got up,
she thought about Katrina. When Shawde went to work,
she wondered what she could be doing differently to help
prove her case. And when she came home, she looked
through her binder again, studying the various articles and
going over the notes she'd taken from the conversations
she'd had with some of Katrina's former schoolmates and
sorority sisters.

Shawde flipped to the section of the binder labeled

"INTERVIEWS." Everything was catalogued in alphabetical order and also according to the interviewee's college year at the time that Shemar had been murdered.

Jennifer Adelaide was the very first name in the file. A sophomore. She had dropped out of the Alpha Sigma Pi sorority after only a few months.

Shawde had recorded every interview she'd had on the phone with witnesses and then had transcribed them and put them in this file. It was easier to reread the interviews, slowly study every word to see if there was something she had missed.

" 'Was there anything strange you recall about Katrina?' " Shawde said softly, reading aloud the first question she had asked Jennifer.

Strange? Um, well, Katrina wasn't very nice, that's for sure. She was a major hard-ass. She loved to make us pledges do a ton of shitty things. Like seriously, was there really a need for us to scrub every toilet with a toothbrush? She got off on making us suffer. I call that strange.

Shawde had wanted to keep Jennifer on track, so she'd asked, *How did you interact with her on a day-to-day basis? Outside of whatever she made you do as a pledge?*

Shawde remembered Jennifer laughing at the question. *Interact with her? We were beneath her. If you were a pledge, she didn't see you as an equal. She saw you as a nobody. Some girls kissed her ass to try to get her approval, but I wasn't about to do that. My mom was a legacy in that sorority—three generations of my mom's family were Alpha Sigma Pis—and Katrina acted as though that didn't matter. In fact, I think she gave me a harder time because of it. I had to drop out of the sorority because Katrina made my experience there unbearable.*

Shawde underlined the word "unbearable." Should she have asked Jennifer to elaborate? Should she call her back and ask for more details?

Frowning, Shawde decided against doing that—the same conclusion she had come to before. The sense she'd gotten from Jennifer was that she was bitter about a negative sorority experience. Yes, Katrina had been a bitch, but she hadn't hurt Jennifer. She had left the sorority because she couldn't stand Katrina, not because she was afraid.

Unlike Angelina Wright.

Shawde knew that Angelina had left the sorority house under a cloud of suspicion. Apparently, she'd been attacked—just a couple of months before Shemar's murder—and she'd left the University at Buffalo. But while people knew that Angelina had been attacked, no one had been able to tell Shawde whether or not her attacker had been caught.

Some suspected the Bike Path Rapist, a rapist and killer who had terrorized students at UB for years and remained uncaptured until just about five years ago. However, Shawde hadn't found any information connecting an attack on Angelina to the Bike Path Rapist.

One way or another, Shawde had to track Angelina down. In Shawde's heart she believed that Angelina had answers.

Answers that would help Shawde prove Katrina was guilty of murder.

CHAPTER SEVEN

The next morning when I got out of bed, I found Katrina and Christian in the kitchen. Their backs were to me, Christian standing behind Katrina, his hands on her hips as she filled the coffee carafe with water. They certainly looked like a loving couple. Not one that had been ready to kill each other the night before.

Christian nuzzled his nose in her neck and lowered his hands to the hem of the oversized T-shirt Katrina had no doubt worn to bed. "Babe," Katrina said, feigning protest, "you're not helping me get ready."

"You're the boss." Christian's hand smoothed over the skin of her bare thigh. "Who says we can't sneak in a quickie before you open up shop?"

Katrina lowered the carafe and splayed her hands on Christian's legs. He was wearing only white boxers, and I was seeing far more of his skinny legs than I cared to. They were covered with too much dark hair to be considered attractive. But Katrina clearly didn't seem to mind, because she stroked them lovingly with her fingers.

When her hand went higher, heading for his groin, I loudly cleared my throat. Katrina quickly threw her head over her shoulder. Seeing me, she gave me a sheepish look. Then she straightened and said, "Oh. Hey."

"Good morning," I said.

Stepping away from Katrina, but staying behind the breakfast counter, Christian turned to look at me. "Morning."

Again I was struck by just how much of a mismatch they seemed to be as a couple. All that pale white skin looked even paler because of Christian's mass of curly black hair. Glasses capped off what I would describe as a nerdy look. And while I hadn't asked how old he was, if the gray at his temples was any indication he was nearing forty—which made him about a decade older than Katrina. Too old for her, in my opinion. Katrina was young, and even without any makeup on she was stunning. What was it about Christian that she'd fallen for him?

I thought of Wesley and his good looks and how that made him attractive to practically every woman out there. Wasn't I smart enough to know that looks weren't everything?

Maybe Katrina wanted a guy she could trust to be faithful. One who was more mature and ready to settle down. Maybe Christian was that guy.

"Did you sleep well?" Christian asked.

Was that his way of asking if I'd heard them? I nodded. "Yeah. Pretty good." Then, facing Katrina, I said, "I smell hazelnut-flavored java."

She held up the open container of coffee grinds. "Oh yeah. I always make coffee upstairs. I know I could just as easily have some in the shop, but I need that first cup to get me going."

Especially if she'd spent most of the night fighting . . . and then making up. I felt the dull ache from a fatigue headache, so I knew Katrina had to be tired. "Makes sense."

"I'm gonna shower," Christian announced, then gave Katrina a peck on her forehead. He quickly exited the kitchen area on the far side—away from me—and I guessed that he was trying to hide a hard-on.

"Make it a cold one!" Katrina called after him.

I grinned as I stepped into the kitchen. Whatever had brought these two together, they seemed to have a healthy sexual appetite for each other. Had their ugly fight last night simply been a one-off?

A look of understanding flashed in Katrina's eyes as she met my gaze. Clearly reading my mind, she said in a lowered voice, "You probably heard us last night."

"Yeah," I told her, my voice barely above a whisper. I was glad she was willing to address what had happened. "Is everything okay?"

"We just had a fight," she explained. "It got a bit heated, yes, but we'd both been drinking. Everything's fine between us now. I'm sorry if you were worried."

My shoulders drooped with relief. "I *was* worried, yes. But I didn't know if I should bring up the subject, so I'm glad you did."

"I can only imagine what you thought. And your first night here."

"I was definitely startled."

She made a face, as though embarrassed. "Gosh, I really am sorry."

"It's okay." It sounded like it was one night of crazy behavior, and for that I was glad. I was worried that I'd moved into a home with two people who were emotionally unpredictable.

But my relief came to a screeching halt when Katrina began to fill the coffeemaker with water and I noticed a bruise on the back of her arm. Just how rough had things gotten between them last night?

"Hey," I said, deciding not to pretend I hadn't seen her arm. "Your arm."

Turning, Katrina looked at me. Then, seeing where I

was looking, she craned her neck over her shoulder to look down at the back of her arm.

"Shit. Didn't notice that."

"Are you sure you're okay?" I asked.

Katrina turned the coffee machine on. "Yeah. I told you, it was a stupid spat. That's all."

I eyed the bruise, making out what appeared to be the shape of fingers. I wasn't convinced.

"Did Christian come from England to be with you here?" I asked. "Or did you meet him here?"

"Actually, I met him here."

"You did?" I was surprised. I figured for sure they'd met via online dating.

"He was down here in January to run the Key West half marathon."

"You're a runner?"

"Me? God no. I met Christian when he came in here and we got to talking." Katrina's lips curled in a smile. "He was really sweet, and he'd recently lost his brother to suicide. I could relate, because I'd lost my parents. He went back home, we stayed in touch, and things bloomed."

I nodded. "And how long has he been here?"

"A few weeks."

Katrina certainly seemed happy, and at least she and Christian had actually met in person. I could see why they'd connected, but for him to be living with her already? It was one thing to get to know someone on the phone and online, but living with a person in the real world wasn't always the same.

"How well do you know him?" I asked. "I mean, look at your arm."

"That was . . ." Katrina smiled sheepishly. "That was from . . . after the argument. Sometimes we like it a bit rough."

My face flamed. Now I felt stupid. "Oh. Um . . ."

Katrina chuckled. "Sorry. I'm sure you heard more than our argument. I think we'd better lay off the tequila from now on."

I said nothing. I was too embarrassed.

"What about you?" Katrina asked. "Do you have a boyfriend?"

"Me? Um . . . I guess so, yeah."

Katrina narrowed her eyes. "You don't sound too confident."

"We're sort of taking a break," I told her. Then I explained how Wesley had moved to Seattle and that he'd suggested we take a break for a year.

"You love him," Katrina said, and I almost detected pity in her voice.

I shrugged, my chest tightening. "Yeah."

"It's good you're here," she told me, then opened a kitchen cupboard that housed mugs and plates. "There are a lot of guys down here. If you need a distraction, I'm sure you'll easily find one."

"I . . ." My voice trailed off. I didn't know what to say. I got the sense that if I told her I wanted to wait for Wesley she would tell me I was naïve.

The carafe now filled with hot coffee, Katrina poured herself a cup. "Want some?"

"Yes, definitely," I told her. Some days, I was amazed that there had been a time when I'd hated coffee. Four years of college and I had come to depend on my daily dose of it.

"Milk and cream's in the fridge," Katrina said as she took down two more mugs. "Sugar's on the counter. By the way, I know we haven't discussed this yet, but you need to provide your own food. I've cleared out some space in the fridge for you. I'm not big on cooking. I usually grab something from the café."

"Of course," I said.

"Coffee, however, you can have as much as you like."

"That's a major bonus."

She smiled. "A woman after my own heart. The last girl who worked here hated coffee. Imagine that? It wasn't a good fit."

I opened the fridge and took out the creamer. "I used to. Before college. Hard to believe, I can't start the day without it now."

"Well, I've got all sorts of flavors. Light roast to espresso. Whatever your heart desires."

I found a spoon from a drawer and began to stir my coffee. "That sounds like heaven."

Katrina started out of the kitchen. "I'm gonna grab a quick shower. I open at eight."

I glanced at the wall clock. That was in thirty-two minutes. "Oh, yikes. That doesn't give me too much time to get ready."

"Take as much time as you need. Christian and I will get things started downstairs."

As if on cue, the bathroom door opened. Christian appeared, a towel wrapped around his waist. His legs looked like twigs beneath the towel. Physically, he and Katrina were a definite odd pair.

Good grief, I told myself. *Stop being so judgmental.* What did looks matter when you connected with someone on an emotional level?

I took my coffee mug and went to my bedroom, where I rummaged through my suitcase for clean underwear and something to change into. It struck me that I hadn't asked Katrina if there was a specific dress code, but I noticed that the staff yesterday had each been wearing dark pants and a T-shirt, so I opted for a similar look. My clothes in hand, I headed to the bathroom.

A couple of minutes later, I was in the shower. As the warm water sluiced over my body, Wesley popped into my mind. When I'd gotten up, I'd checked my cell phone and seen that he hadn't responded to me. Which only made me feel stupid for having texted him. He wanted space, and it was becoming clearer to me that if I wanted things to work out between us I needed to give him that.

Then I thought of Michelle, her betrayal of our friendship, and the whole ugly incident at grad. My stomach tightened as I began to feel angry. Why couldn't I just turn off my feelings for Wesley and forget him once and for all?

If only I could wash him from my heart the way I was washing the grime from my body. But I knew that was wishful thinking.

I took my time in the shower, washing my hair and generally luxuriating beneath the warm stream of water. So when I exited, I figured that I had to be alone in the apartment.

Until I thought I heard the sound of a voice.

I eased closer to the bathroom door. "No, no. It has to be sooner than that."

That was Christian. Were he and Katrina still in the apartment?

"Are you kidding me? Why would it possibly take that long?"

I didn't hear anyone else speaking and assumed that Christian was on the phone.

"Unacceptable," he said after a moment. "I've already told you, this needs to be taken care of. Now." Pause. "You don't need to be concerned. You just need to do it."

Silence ensued, and I kept my ear to the door, listening for more of Christian's conversation. Instead, about a minute later, I heard the distinct sound of a door closing.

I waited a beat, then opened the bathroom door and peeked my head out. I looked around, saw no one. Christian was gone.

I slipped out of the bathroom and headed to my room, wondering whom Christian had been talking to.

And I also wondered why I had the feeling that I couldn't trust him.

* * *

Downstairs, I was pretty much thrown into work with minimal instruction. Katrina told me that I should take orders and she would help me put them into the computer. This wasn't the kind of coffee shop where people went to the counter to place their orders and pay there. It was more of a sit-down café and restaurant, because she also had a liquor license. Patrons sitting inside could go up to the counter and pay if they wished, but not those sitting outside.

I was surprised at how many people were already here at nine in the morning. Most were sitting out on the patio, friends and family members soaking up the morning sun. Those with laptops were inside, headphones on and lost in their own world as they did their work and got their java fix. I imagined some were working on the next Great American Novel.

Mostly, I cleaned tables and took orders only if I was beckoned. By the end of the morning, I was figuring out how to use the computer system. Alexis, the woman I'd first met yesterday, was working the busy patio. She also helped Katrina make the various coffee drinks and smoothies.

There was a small kitchen, where extra pastries and desserts were kept and the sandwiches and French fries made. Christian was the one who prepared the sandwiches and fries, while the desserts and pastries came from a bakery a block away.

Lunch was hectic, with noon marking the start of when alcohol was served. Many people from local businesses stopped in for coffee and a sandwich to go, and I helped take the orders while Katrina filled them. Alexis was busy on the patio, with more people wanting to sit outside and enjoy a beer or a coffee beverage.

"The place is busier than I thought," I said to Katrina when I brought her an order for two BLT sandwiches and fries, plus two fruit smoothies.

"Lunch is always busy," she said. "And the weekends."

When one thirty rolled around and the crowd had thinned out, I was relieved. I'd been worried that I was going to screw something up, but all had gone well.

"You survived your first hectic lunch hour," Katrina said, coming to stand beside me at the far end of the counter, where I was taking a moment to drink some lemonade.

"Thanks."

"You're a natural. Really great with everyone, from what I saw."

I smiled. Then noticed an older lady, who'd been sitting by herself and sipping a tea for about half an hour, beckon me over.

"That's Mrs. Sturgess," Katrina explained. "She comes in every day. Lost her husband four months ago, poor thing."

I made my way over to the table. "All finished with your tea?" I asked.

"Yes, and I'd like another. I'll also have one of those chocolate chip cookies."

"Sure thing."

"Can you warm it in the microwave? Katrina knows how I like it."

"Absolutely."

I went to the counter to ring in the order. "She said she'd like a chocolate chip cookie, warmed. She said you know how she likes it?"

"It's the same for everybody. Fifteen seconds in the microwave."

I found the largest cookie from the pastry display and brought it to the microwave on the counter while Katrina got the peppermint tea bag and a small kettle with boiling water. Once everything was ready, I carefully carried the items over to Mrs. Sturgess's table.

"There you go," I said.

"Thank you, dear. And whenever you're ready, you can bring me my bill."

"Of course."

Suddenly Mrs. Sturgess tsked, and I looked at her with concern. "Such a shame, isn't it?"

"Excuse me?"

With a flick of her head, she gestured to the television perched high on the wall behind the counter. It was set to an all-news channel and had no volume. "That couple in Mexico. Murdered just outside of their hotel."

"Oh?" I'd been too busy trying to learn the ropes to really pay attention to the television.

Mrs. Sturgess shook her head. "That place has become far too dangerous."

I looked over my shoulder, saw the photo of a smiling young man and woman in a corner of the screen while a male newscaster was speaking. The closed captioning was on, and I quickly read the summary:

Honeymooning couple murdered in Cancun.

"Gosh, that is awful," I said, and frowned slightly. "And on their honeymoon."

"Their poor families. I lost my George four months ago, but at least it was a heart attack. The good Lord took him. It's been hard, but I can't even imagine how those parents must feel. Losing your children to murder."

"Oh God. I know. It's so sad."

"Jade?" Katrina called.

"Excuse me," I said to the woman, and made my way back to the counter.

"Figured you could use some saving," Katrina explained in a hushed tone when I got there. "Mrs. Sturgess is very sweet, but she can go on and on."

"It's hard, losing your spouse. My dad was never quite the same after my mother died."

"Let's not start on about your dad again," Katrina said.

Her blunt tone caught me off guard. *Start on about my dad again? Is that what she thinks? That I went on and on about my loss?*

"I just mean," she quickly went on, "that now is not the time to get all weepy and depressed. We've got a full house, and we have to remain upbeat."

"I'm sorry if you think I'm going on and on about my dad," I said, hurt and stunned by the comment. I didn't get why she would say that, especially since she'd talked about losing her parents. Certainly she understood the pain.

"That's not what I meant," she said. "Look, I know it hurts, but when we lose people, we just have to move on. We still have to live." She started to bend down. "I know; I'll change the music."

She reached under the counter, and several seconds later the music changed from mellow to funky. As she stood tall, she began to shake her head to the beat. "Ahh, that's more like it. Nothing better than a bit of shoulder bopping to get you through the rest of the day."

"Right," I said, my voice tight.

"Jeez, Jade. Lighten up. Are you always this sensitive?"

Was I being sensitive?

"Guys don't like it when women whine and get depressed." She gave me a pointed look. "Just saying."

My lips parted, and I gaped at her. So now she was saying that my attitude had sent Wesley running? She knew nothing about my relationship with Wesley!

"Excuse me," I said, and started for the back of the shop. Tears were already burning my eyes, and I felt my ire rising.

How dare Katrina make me out to be some sort of emotional cripple? I barely knew her. What gave her the right to make those kinds of judgments about me?

I went into the bathroom, locked the door, then reached into my apron pocket and withdrew my cell phone. I was ready to call Marie, tell her I was returning home. I wasn't about to spend the summer working for someone so insensitive.

My fingers hovered over the phone, about to write the text. And then I remembered Wesley's words at the hospital.

It's like you want to hang on to your pain, let the world know you're suffering.

Was that really how I came across to people?

"Shit," I muttered. Then I blew out a frazzled breath. Maybe *I* was the problem and I was too blind to see it.

No sooner than the thought came into my head, there was a knock at the door. "Jade?" came Katrina's voice.

"I'll be out in a minute," I said.

"Look, I didn't mean to be harsh. I just . . . I don't want to see you sink into depression. You're in Florida. Endless sunshine, great weather. A chance for a new start."

I opened the door and forced a smile onto my face. "I know," I said. "And I get it. I'm going to do my best to keep the past in my rearview mirror and focus on the future."

Katrina grinned from ear to ear. "That a girl."

"By the way," I said. "We didn't talk about it, but do you want me working till nine?" That was when the shop had closed yesterday.

"If it's not too much, yes."

"It's fine," I told her. "The more hours I work, the more money I make."

"As I expand, I hope to eventually hire staff to work a morning and an evening shift. I'm even thinking of keeping the shop open until ten or eleven a few days of the week. I'll see as time goes by. For now, I'm still feeling my way around the business."

"Like I said, I'm happy to work."

And work was good. It would keep me too busy to sit around worrying about my life.

CHAPTER EIGHT

A week later, I was getting into a flow at the café. I knew how to use the computer, and I was starting to learn to make some of the specialty drinks. I was enjoying being a waitress and definitely loving the tips.

But I was still learning all of the ropes, so I was surprised when Katrina asked me to oversee the coffee shop on Thursday afternoon, saying that she and Christian had to run out and do something.

"Oh," I said. "You're sure?"

"It's always slower in the afternoons," she said, taking off her apron. "And between you, Tony, and Alexis I'm sure you can handle it."

"And if we can't?" I asked, feeling a spurt of panic.

"You'll be fine."

"Where are you going?" I asked.

She just gave me a little smile, then headed toward the front of the café, where Christian was waiting. When she met up with him, they immediately linked hands and walked through the door.

They were an enigma. One minute so romantic, as

if they couldn't bear to be apart. The next, fighting intensely.

I guessed some couples got off on that kind of drama.

Katrina and Christian returned to the shop around five, but a quick glance to see that all was running smoothly was all that Katrina gave it before she and Christian went upstairs. After six, they both came back down, wearing different clothes. As Katrina walked by me, I could smell the whiff of freshness. She'd showered.

She and Christian went into the kitchen, and Alexis sidled up to me behind the front counter. When I looked at her, I saw that her lips were twisted in a lopsided grin. "I swear, those two screw like bunnies."

And they fight like cats and dogs, was the thought that popped into my mind, but I didn't say it. In the shop at least, Katrina and Christian seemed to be harmonious.

"I still don't get it," I said. "The two of them together. And it's not just that they seem mismatched physically. Christian started asking me to play chess with him because Katrina never will. I barely understand the game, but I felt sorry for him so tried playing with him a couple of times because Katrina dismisses him completely. I never see them sit down and watch a show together. In fact, Katrina seems annoyed when Christian watches *SpongeBob* and *South Park*. She's only interested in *Law and Order* and reality crime shows."

"Not to mention that the only time she runs is when she's heading into a store to go shopping," Alexis said. "Every morning, like clockwork, I see Christian jogging by my house. I find it so hard to believe they connected during a marathon."

I shrugged. "Sounds like they connected because of loss. He lost his brother; she lost her parents."

"Perhaps. I also know that the day after he arrived, she went on a shopping spree."

"What?"

"She bought some expensive shoes and clothes, a new laptop, and that big TV in the corner of the café, as well as those two armchairs in that corner nook." Alexis angled her head and gave me a curious look.

"You think she's using him for his money?" I asked.

"Hey, who am I to judge? Obviously, Christian's getting something out of the relationship or he wouldn't be here."

He sure was. A ton of sex. But I wondered if Alexis would have a different opinion if she knew how much they fought.

"But if she *is* using him, I wouldn't be surprised," Alexis said. "Christian Alexander Begley," she went on, feigning a British accent. "He's loaded."

"How do you know that?" I asked.

"I Googled him."

I took my phone out of my apron pocket. "Christian Alexander Begley?" I asked. "*L-e-y* or *l-y*?"

"*L-e-y*," Alexis said.

I typed his name into Google. As results were popping up, I heard Alexis say, "Oh, sorry. Did you want to order something?"

I looked up and saw Gordon, a guy who had been a regular since I'd started working at the café, was standing on the other side of the counter. "I did, yes," he said.

I slipped the phone back into my pocket. "Sorry, Gordon. Did you want another cup of coffee?"

"At the risk of giving myself a heart attack, yes." He smiled warmly. "And I was looking at these treats."

"Did you want another Colombian coffee?" I asked. "Or perhaps a lighter brew?"

When I reached for a new mug, Gordon said, "Actually, let me just get my mug from the table."

I grabbed a menu and walked around from behind the counter, then went over to his table. I'd been chatting, slacking off when I should have been working.

Gordon snagged the mug, then turned. His eyes widened in surprise when he saw that I was at the table.

"I'll get you what you need," I told him. "You sit."

"Oh, okay."

When he sat, I passed him the menu. "We've got sandwiches, treats. French fries."

Gordon nodded as he regarded the small laminated menu. I figured he was familiar with the menu, however, considering he came in every day. A creature of habit, he occupied this table near the front window every day. He arrived early and stayed for hours.

"I think I'll just have a toasted bagel with cream cheese," he said. "And what would you recommend instead of Colombian coffee? Something gentler on my stomach?"

"Do you like Irish Cream? Or French Vanilla? Or we have a light roast. It's really good."

"I'll have the light roast. Black."

"Sure thing."

"So how are you liking Florida so far?" Gordon asked before I could turn to head toward the kitchen.

"Oh. I'm loving it. It's beautiful. I've got no complaints, since I love the hot weather."

"It's a lot hotter than Buffalo."

"For sure," I agreed. During one of our brief chats before, I'd told Gordon that I was a student at UB. "Although Buffalo can get pretty hot and uncomfortable in the summer. At least here, there's the ocean." Glancing outside the window at the patio with happy people, I nodded. "I love Florida."

"Yeah, what's not to love?" he agreed.

He was grinning at me, and I wondered if he had a crush on me or something. He was average looking and on the heavier side of lean. He looked to be of mixed heritage, African-American and something else. If not for his kinky beard that needed a trim and his unkempt Afro, he could pass for Hispanic or even Middle Eastern.

"You come in every day with your laptop," I commented. "Are you a student or something, studying over the summer instead of taking a break?"

Gordon threw his head back and laughed. "No. But thank you for the compliment. I've been out of college for seven years now."

"Oh. Then what do you do here every day?"

He gave me a sly look. "Maybe I'll tell you once you get me my bagel and coffee."

"Coming right up." Then, grinning a little, I turned on my heel. I didn't know if he was flirting with me and he wasn't my type, but the banter was nice.

I went into the kitchen and got a bagel from the fridge, then popped it into the toaster. As I waited for it to toast, I went into the fridge and got the packets of cream cheese. I noticed then that the back door was slightly ajar, so I wandered over there to close it. And that's when I heard Katrina's voice.

"Just stop for a moment and think about what you're saying, okay?" she said, sounding angry. "You threaten me, you threaten yourself. I know you're smart enough to figure that out."

Was she fighting with Christian? So soon after they'd come downstairs from making love?

"I already told you that you'll get your money!" She exhaled a frustrated groan. "Look, it's just going to take a little longer."

Money? What? Was Alexis right about Christian having

helped Katrina out with money and now he was giving her a hard time?

"If something happens to me, the police will be coming after you. You'd better believe that."

Someone was threatening Katrina. Christian? I pushed the door open to go to her aid, expecting to find both of them. Katrina jerked in my direction when she heard the door. I had a moment to notice the cell phone at her ear before she lowered it and yelled, "What the fuck are you doing? *Spying* on me?"

"Spy—? No." I was caught off guard, finding her alone. "Of course not. I—I heard you, and I was worried that you were fighting with Christian, so I came out here—"

"Bullshit!" Katrina snapped. She shoved her phone into her apron pocket and glared at me as she breezed past me. I had to flatten myself against the door so that she didn't knock me over.

"Katrina," I said.

She gave me the finger without looking back.

I stared at her back as she exited the kitchen, the air oozing out of my lungs. What the hell had just happened?

Catching my breath, I remembered Gordon. His order. I quickly went to the toaster. The bagel had already popped up and was no doubt cooling, but I didn't want to toast another one and keep him waiting. So I put the slices on a plate and added packets of cream cheese on the side. Then I drew in a deep breath and went into the café, where I saw Katrina behind the counter emptying coffee grinds.

Shit, I would have to walk past her in order to get Gordon's coffee.

I hesitated. Then I squared my shoulders and went to get Gordon a fresh mug of the light roast. What was I going to do—avoid Katrina forever? I couldn't very well do that while still working for her. I wasn't impressed with how

she'd torn into me, but I'd surprised her during a private—
and heated—conversation.

As I poured the coffee for Gordon, I saw Christian enter the café from the kitchen. Maybe he'd been upstairs.

I took Gordon's order over to him and forced a smile
as I placed the items on the table in front of him. "There
you go."

"Thank you." His eyes narrowed, and he regarded me
with concern. "Everything okay?"

I waved off his concern. "I'm fine."

Either he was exceptionally intuitive or the stress between me and Katrina was palpable, because his gaze flitted toward her before he looked at me again. "Are you
sure?"

"It's nothing," I said.

"I thought I heard some yelling."

Damn. "Katrina was having a private conversation. She
thought I was eavesdropping. We'll sort it out."

Gordon nodded. "How'd you end up working here, by
the way? Did you know Katrina from before, or did you
just pull up and apply for a job?"

"My sister went to school with her," I explained. "I
needed a summer job, Katrina needed the help . . . so here
I am."

"Ahh."

"Anything else I can get you?" My heart was beating
fast, and I knew I sounded harried.

"Didn't you want to know what I'm working on?" he
asked.

"Yes, that's right." My temples were beginning to throb
because of the tension with Katrina, and I was no longer
in the mood for small talk. But nonetheless, I said, "What
are you working on?"

"A novel."

His words made me perk up. "Really?"

"You think I'm crazy, right?"

"No," I said. "Not at all." I felt an instant affinity with him, knowing that he shared my passion for creating stories. "Actually, that's one of the reasons I'm in Key West," I told him. Not exactly a lie. I hadn't come here for that reason, but now that I was here I was going to try to get the inspiration to work on my own book. "I'm hoping the setting will inspire me to write a novel."

His eyes lit up. "No way. You're a writer, too?"

"More like I'm *trying* to be," I corrected him. "But honestly, I just can't find the time to write."

"No one's going to hand you a block of time on a silver platter. You have to make the time. Even if you write every day for only half an hour, you'll soon see the pages adding up."

"You're right," I said. "I didn't think of that."

"What do you write?" Gordon asked.

"A bit of this, a bit of that." Nice and vague. It was easier than admitting that I had a lot of great ideas . . . but never got beyond writing a few pages of any of them.

"I'm working on a historical mystery," Gordon told me. "A bit of a spin on the Lizzie Borden story. Deranged young woman who kills her family and anyone else who gets in her way."

"Sounds gory."

"It is. But I always say that true crime stories are a lot worse than anything anyone could ever come up with."

"Which is why I avoid them. It creeps me out to hear just how deranged people can be."

Or how freaking unpredictable. What the hell was Katrina's problem anyway?

My heart was still beating fast from my interaction with her. And when I looked to my right and saw her walking toward me, my stomach filled with dread.

"Jade," she said sternly.

"If you need anything else, let me know," I quickly said to Gordon.

"I'm not paying you to stand around chatting," Katrina said.

I wanted give her a snarky comeback. I wanted to tell her that it wasn't my fault she owed someone money and not to take her problems out on me. Instead, I held in my anger.

And when I had a moment, I sent my sister a text, asking her what the heck was up with Katrina and what she'd gotten me into.

CHAPTER NINE

SHAWDE

Shawde answered the phone the moment she saw Gordon's picture flashing on her screen. "Gordon, hi."

"I've got something," he said without preamble.

Shawde lowered her fork onto the package of the microwaved meal she had heated for dinner. "What is it? What happened?"

"Nothing yet," Gordon said. "But I found out more about the guy who's living with Katrina. His name is Christian Alexander Begley. I Googled him. He's filthy rich. His parents started a pastry company twenty years ago and the business grew over the years to a multi-million-dollar enterprise."

"Really? And he's working at a café in Key West?"

"Tragedy struck the family seven months ago. Bradford, Christian's older brother, committed suicide. It was horrendous, actually. He threw himself in front of a train."

"What?"

"People on the scene thought it was an accident—said it looked like he'd fainted and fallen backward—but it turns out he left a suicide note."

Shawde shook her head, digesting what Gordon had told her. Had it been an accident . . . or had Bradford been pushed? "Was Katrina in England during that time, perhaps?"

"I don't know about that. But there was no foul play. Witnesses saw him fall onto the track when no one was around him. Christian went to Florida in January to run in the Key West marathon. That's when he met Katrina."

"And Katrina learned that his family is loaded, and she sank her teeth into him," Shawde said, more to herself than to Gordon. She got up from the table and went over to her binder.

"That's the way it looks."

Shawde scrawled Christian's name on a blank page at the back of her binder. "Katrina just happens to be dating a rich guy from England. She's up to something. You need to warn him."

"I found out that he runs every morning—alone. I'm going to start doing that, too. Try to start talking to him."

"You need to tell him that his life is in danger," Shawde insisted.

"I've got to tread lightly," Gordon said. "If there's a moment when I know something for sure, I'll definitely speak up. But I can't just go tell him that he's in danger. That'll risk my anonymity when I go into the café every day."

Shawde bit down on her cheek, pouting. Then she sighed. She knew that Gordon was right. Without knowing exactly what Katrina was going to do, how could Gordon warn Christian? And yet Shawde knew Christian was in danger. Just as her brother had been.

"Also, I got to talk a bit more with that new girl. The one from Buffalo."

"Yes," Shawde said. "What's the deal with her?"

"Her sister used to go to school with Katrina. That's the connection."

Shawde frowned. "Why's she down there?"

"She said she's a writer. That she came here for a break and some inspiration for her writing. I told her I'm a writer, too. I could tell she wanted to form a connection. There'll be more chances to talk with her. I may even ask her out."

"Find out who her sister is," Shawde said. "I want to know if I've already spoken to her."

"I will."

"Thanks, Gordon. I appreciate your hard work."

"I'm gonna need you to wire me some more money for the hotel. Another couple of weeks would be good."

Shawde cringed. This investigation was costing her, and her savings were dwindling. She hoped Gordon would be able to find incriminating evidence on Katrina soon, before Shawde had to think about selling her car or getting a home equity loan.

"Of course," she said to Gordon. "I'll send you an e-transfer this evening."

"Thanks."

"No, thank *you*. I appreciate what you're doing."

He might not be a licensed investigator, but he was able to be eyes and ears where Shawde couldn't be. She hoped he'd be able to learn something incriminating about Katrina soon so that she could finally pay for the crimes she'd committed.

Unfortunately, Katrina was cunning. She was good at what she did, and likely the only chance she had of being caught was if she committed another crime.

And when she committed crimes, people died.

Christian? Was he her target? Or did she actually love the guy?

Her meal forgotten, Shawde opened up her laptop to Google Christian Alexander Begley.

Son of millionaires. Nothing like Mummy's Pastries.

Bradford Begley, son of Charles and Henrietta Begley, founders of Nothing like Mummy's Pastries, dead in apparent suicide.

Bradford Begley is survived by his parents, a brother, Christian, and a sister, Melody.

Shawde quickly picked up her phone and sent Gordon a text, an idea popping into her mind that terrified her:

When you talk to Christian, tell him to take things slowly with Katrina. I wouldn't be surprised if she suggests they get married. That's a guaranteed way to get at his fortune. Make sure he doesn't do that!

Because if Katrina was going to benefit from her relationship with Christian, the best way to do that was by marrying him.

CHAPTER TEN

Hours later, I was lying in bed, trying to sleep off my stress headache, when I heard my phone trill. Easing up, I reached for my phone on my night table. As I brought the screen to life, I saw a text from my sister:

What's up? Something happen with Katrina?

I wanted to call Marie, but I didn't know if Katrina was out in the living room and I didn't want her to hear anything I was saying. So I sent a text back:

Had a bit of a tiff with her earlier. She seemed to overreact. Just wondering if she has a temper?

Marie's response was quick:

She's probably just having a bad day. We all know what that's like. Stay positive. I'm sure things will be fine.

We all know what that's like. I lay back on my bed, knowing what Marie was getting at. I'd certainly had my own issues keeping my temper under control.

I blew out a frazzled breath. Maybe Marie was right.

Still, the tiff and the fact that I was holed up in my room now avoiding Katrina reminded me just how alone I was here in Key West. She was basically my only friend here— which wasn't saying much, considering I barely knew her. I didn't have Wesley to call, nor one of my girlfriends from UB. In the past, when I fought with my roommate I could always go to another friend's dorm room and hang out there until I felt better. Or, of course, Wesley's room.

Wesley . . . I'd told myself that I would put him out of my mind, but it was hard to simply turn off your emotions for someone. I'd been good, though, not checking up on him for a week now. But as I lay in bed, bored, I opened up my Facebook account.

It opened to my wall, where I saw the same messages from after graduation: *Sorry about grad. Hang in there!* And the one that annoyed me the most, a poem about how challenges in life made you stronger.

No new private messages, either. But I'd already known that, because I had Facebook synced to my phone and got alerts when I received new messages or postings on my wall.

A feeling of sadness gripped me as the reality that I no longer had friends I could count on hit me.

I drew in a deep breath. Then, though every part of me told me not to, I ventured over to Wesley's page. The first thing I noticed was that his relationship status had changed from *IT'S COMPLICATED* to *SINGLE*.

My stomach fluttering, I then went to Michelle's page. She had unfriended me but so far hadn't blocked me, so I could still see her wall. Her new profile picture was one of her and Wesley on graduation day. But it was her current status that made my stomach drop:

I got the job with Amazon! I'm moving to Seattle!

As I stared at her status update, my head began to swim. She was moving to Seattle?

I blinked, feeling the tears stinging my eyes. Obviously, this wasn't a coincidence. Since when had she even been applying for jobs at Amazon? Wesley was in Seattle and now she was moving there, too?

Suddenly I could see it all. The wheels that had been in motion from months earlier. Michelle had clearly wanted Wesley, and she had probably been lying to me about wanting to head to New York City after graduation. She must have applied to Amazon a while back, knowing that a job there would put her in the same city where Wesley would be living.

Their relationship hadn't been a spontaneous thing. This had been her plan all along.

"Bitch!" I yelled.

I pressed the COMMENT button to reply to her latest status update. Anger flowed through my body, right to my fingertips. *Don't do it,* a part of me cautioned. *Just forget it.*

I went back to Wesley's page and typed on his wall: *MICHELLE IS A WHORE!* Before I could change my mind, I hit the ENTER key. Then I tossed my phone onto my bed and sat up.

As my heart beat harder from the anger pulsing through my veins, I got off of the bed and started going through the clothes I'd hung up in the small closet. I wanted something tight. Revealing. It was time I hit the town and got over Wesley once and for all.

I settled on a mini tube dress. Black. It hugged my large breasts and my butt. Then I did my makeup in a dramatic style. Lots of mascara, bright red lips. I capped off the outfit with hot red pumps. I took a look in the mirror and I knew what men would see when they looked at me. I looked like I wanted to get lucky.

And I did. Anything to make me forget Wesley.

I opened my door, hoping that Katrina was in her room. But I gasped in shock when I saw her standing outside my door.

"My God," I said. "You scared me."

She offered me a smile, one that looked genuine. "Sorry." She paused. "And sorry about earlier. I just talked to Marie—"

"What?" My eyes bulged. "Marie called you?"

"Actually, I called her. I sort of figured you would call her about our tiff, and I wanted to talk to her . . . make sure she knew not to worry."

Katrina had called my sister before coming to speak to me? Damage control?

"You caught me at a really bad time," Katrina began, "and I blew up with you." She exhaled harshly. "I know you weren't spying on me. It's just . . . I was talking to my ex, and . . . I owe him some money. He's pretty insistent that he get it quickly."

I folded my arms over my chest. "I see."

"I was upset with him. Not with you. I know I was rude and hurtful, and I'm sorry for that."

Rude and hurtful . . . She'd been more than that. She'd been downright scary.

"What?" she asked, guffawing. "You're not accepting my apology?"

"I . . ." I swallowed. Her tone was rubbing me the wrong way.

"You've never overreacted in your life?"

"Of course I have." I nodded. "I accept your apology. And I didn't intentionally eavesdrop on you."

"I know." Smiling, she extended her hand to me. "Truce?"

"Truce." I shook her hand. Then I asked, "You owe your ex money? A lot?"

"It's significant."

"Why don't you ask Christian for the money?" I found myself saying.

Katrina's smile fell. "Why would you suggest that?"

"Um . . . it's just . . ." Shit, I didn't want to let her know that Alexis had told me he had money. And maybe the truth was that his family had money, not him. "Just wondering if he can help you out, that's all."

"I'm not into using people," Katrina said. "I'll sort this out myself."

"Of course."

She turned on her heel, and my stomach sank. So much for the truce we'd just made. . . .

But Katrina suddenly faced me again. "Where are you going?"

"Honestly—I don't know." I shrugged. "I just figure it's time I meet some people. Maybe some guys."

A knowing look in her eye, she nodded. "Good. Head to Duval Street. Turn right; walk three blocks. There are a lot of bars and clubs there. If you're feeling a bit more adventurous, you can head to Garden of Eden, a clothing-optional garden roof bar."

My eyes bulged. "Have you been there?"

"Hell, no."

I chuckled, relieved.

"Well, not yet," Katrina amended.

My laughter dying, my eyes widened again. Was she serious? But then it occurred to me that maybe I needed to change my entire outlook on life and love. What I'd been doing so far wasn't working for me. "Actually, sounds like a hot spot."

"This is Key West. I think the possibilities are endless . . . if you keep your options open."

I gestured to my outfit. "That's kind of my thinking right now."

"You have your cell?" Katrina asked.

"Yep."

"Christian's out getting some groceries right now, but maybe we'll meet you for a drink later."

I smiled. "Sounds like a plan."

CHAPTER ELEVEN

Dusk was slowly being swallowed by night as I made my way down the street, following Katrina's directions. Even if she hadn't told me where to go, I would have known when I was nearing Duval, because I could hear the buzz of excitement in the air.

Duval Street was most definitely the center of the nightlife here in Key West. Everywhere I looked, I saw restaurants and bars. Neon lights lit up the sky, proclaiming the names of the various establishments. And the street was populated with people.

Four young women wearing tight skirts and high heels strolled into the intersection, their arms linked. They were chatting and laughing, and the sight of them made me think of my own friends. Of Saturday nights in Buffalo and going out with my girlfriends for a night on the town, just like these women were doing now.

It was a glaring reminder of the fact that I was alone here. Sucking in a deep breath, I straightened my spine. *No—don't you go feeling sorry for yourself. As Katrina said, Key West has a whole host of new opportunities for you.*

And it was time to explore those opportunities. That was exactly why I was bravely venturing out on my own tonight. It was time to make new friends, find a new groove.

I looked left and right on Duval Street, feeling the energy of the place lift my soul. This was what I'd been missing since I'd gotten here. I hadn't gone far from the shop for the first week, not with the hours I'd been working. On Sunday, the only day I'd had off, I had finally headed to the beach, where I'd dipped my feet in the gorgeous water but not gone for a swim. My true reason for going to the beach had been to sit with my laptop and try to get some inspiration to write my novel.

In the near future, I wanted to go to the Ernest Hemingway Home and Museum. Be in an actual place where a literary genius had spent his time. But tonight was about partying.

The girls I'd seen walking together now crossed the street and trotted toward Margaritaville. I glanced around, trying to decide where I should go. Close by was a place named Irish Kevin's. It had a lineup, but the folk music I heard was not my style. Sloppy Joe's Bar seemed to be a popular spot, with a lot of people sitting on the patio and also lined up to get in. Too busy. I looked down the road and saw another apparent hot spot. But the people hanging outside and lining up to get into the Bourbon Street Pub were all men. Nope, definitely no women in the crowd. The place had to be a gay bar.

A car drove past me, and a guy stuck his head out of the passenger window and whistled. He was probably drunk, but I smiled nonetheless. The attention was nice.

Then, suddenly, my body jerked forward as someone slammed into me. In the next instant I realized that my clutch purse was no longer under my arm. Had I dropped it?

As I looked down, I caught the guy in a denim jacket running in my peripheral vision. And then it clicked. He'd bumped into me on purpose and snatched my purse!

"Hey!" I screamed, turning to give chase as he ran around the corner. "Stop!"

I ran as fast as I could, silently cursing the fact that I was wearing four-inch heels. Rounding the corner where the guy had disappeared, I stumbled to a stop as I saw a man tackle the guy who'd taken my purse. They fell onto the sidewalk, arms and legs flailing.

My adrenaline pumping, I hurried over to them. The guy who'd done the tackling jumped to his feet, producing the purse. "I believe this belongs to you."

"I—thank you," I said, then watched as the man who'd robbed me got to his feet and took off. "Shit, he just took off!"

As the man ran down the street, the stranger watched him, then faced me. "Are *you* okay?"

"Yes, thank you."

He began to brush grit off of his thighs, which was when I started to *see* him. Dressed in a T-shirt that hugged an incredible torso and jeans that were slung low on his hips, this brother was the definition of fine. Golden-brown skin. Bald. He had muscular thighs, and my God, those biceps. His arms were ripped, his shoulders wide.

He stood tall and regarded me, and I felt a jolt of heat.

Good Lord, he was gorgeous. Though he was bald, he had a goatee . . . a seriously sexy look on him. This man looked absolutely scrumptious.

Where had he come from?

"What?" he asked, the edges of his lips curling as his eyes narrowed. "Why are you looking at me like that?"

"Um, I . . . it's j-j-just . . . ," I stammered. "It's just, suddenly you were there." I knew I hadn't properly voiced the question that I wanted to, but for a moment I could barely think straight. It's like my tongue wouldn't work.

"Ahh. Where did I come from?" he said, summing up my question. "I was on the other side of the road when I saw that guy swipe your bag. So, I went after him."

He was grinning at me, his eyes crinkling. Honestly, I wasn't sure I'd ever seen a more beautiful man. It was distracting.

"I'm glad you were there," I said, finally finding my voice. "My phone, my money, my ID . . . it's all in my purse."

"I'm glad I was here, too," he said, and his eyes held a little glint, and I couldn't help wondering . . . or hoping that he was flirting with me.

"Where were you heading?" he went on. "Margaritaville?"

"I was planning on it."

"Then let me walk you over there."

He placed a gentle hand on my shoulder blade and guided me across the street. But as we approached Margaritaville, I was no longer sure I wanted to go there. The line was long, and I was sure that the place was packed inside.

My eyes ventured to the establishment right beside it, named Pippa's. It was smaller, and as we neared it I could hear the sounds of lively jazz coming from the open windows. As with many of the establishments here, there was a patio filled with people.

"Actually, I think I'll go to Pippa's," I announced.

The sexy stranger glanced at me as we stepped onto the sidewalk. "What—you're not meeting someone?"

I shook my head. "I'm exploring Key West on my own."

He gave me a questioning look. "Really?"

"It's not a crime, is it?" I asked, my voice light.

"Of course not. I'm doing the same thing. Maybe we can explore Key West together. . . ."

My stomach flinched from nerves. "You, um, you're here alone?"

"Not anymore," he answered.

He *was* flirting with me! A part of me wanted to tell him that he was wasting his time, that I had a boyfriend. But I quickly mentally chastised myself. What was wrong with me? I'd just seen on Facebook that Michelle was heading to Seattle to shack up with my man.

"What do you think of Pippa's?" I asked.

"I like the vibe. Let's go there."

I turned to walk toward the front door but felt the man's hand on my shoulder, so I faced him. "By the way, I'm Brian," he said. "If we're going to hang out, we should know each other's names."

"Of course," I said, blushing. "I'm Jade."

"Nice to meet you, Jade." He extended his hand, and I shook it. And again he grinned at me. It was a breathtaking smile that lit up his face. Good Lord, what a smile. It reminded me of a Shemar Moore or Taye Diggs kind of smile that made Brian even more attractive. I could only imagine it had had many women dropping their panties.

Together, we started toward the entrance to Pippa's. I was surprised that there wasn't a bouncer at the door, but once we got inside I understood why there hadn't been. Two of the tables I could see had adults with their children. Perhaps this was still the dinner crowd before the night action took over.

This was a far cry from the hip-hop clubs I'd frequented with Wesley and my friends in Buffalo. Ones crammed with sweaty bodies.

This place was more mature. It had a casual yet refined aura. There was a large palm tree near a stage area, which was lit up with a string of lights threaded around the base.

A few people were setting up a microphone, keyboard and guitar onstage, which confirmed my feeling. Family dinner time was finishing up, and the party would soon begin.

A hostess hurried over to us. "Good evening," she said brightly. "It's going to be about a ten-minute wait for a table. But if you want to go to the bar—"

"We'll head to the bar," Brian said quickly.

And then he put his hand on the small of my back, and I had to suck in a breath. His hand felt good on my body. Really good.

There were a few open bar stools, and Brian stood until I was seated before settling on the stool to my right.

The bartender, an attractive and tanned blond, made eye contact with me as I sat. Then he smiled, which transformed him from attractive to gorgeous.

Damn, there were some seriously fine men in Key West.

The smile still gracing his lips, he came over to us. "How're you-all doing this evening?"

"Good," Brian and I said at the same time.

"What'll you have?" the bartender asked.

"A beer," I responded. "Whatever's on tap."

"I'll have the same," Brian said.

"You have some ID, beautiful?"

I should have been expecting that. I was only twenty-two, and I knew that I could pass for a lot younger. "Of course."

I retrieved my driver's license from my purse. The bartender nodded, satisfied, then began to pour the first beer. As he did, I shifted my body on the bar stool so that I was facing Brian and the stage. A woman in a long white dress and wedge heels was standing in front of the microphone. She was beautiful, with dark hair that flowed down her back. I assumed she would be singing.

"Test one-two," the woman said.

As I continued to check out the place, a man and woman who had been sitting near the door rose from the table. The woman lifted a toddler into her arms, while the older child, a boy around eight years old, picked up his coloring sheet and crayons. They started for the door.

"You want to head to that table?" Brian asked.

"I'm okay here. If you are."

"Right here's good for me," Brian said.

"Two draft beers," the bartender said. "You guys want to open a tab?"

"Naw," Brian said, placing a twenty on the bar. Then he turned to me. "You hungry?"

"I could eat something, sure," I said.

"You have a menu?" Brian asked.

The bartender glided to the far end of the bar, and I shamelessly checked out his beautiful body. But it was more so to avoid looking at the man beside me, who I was certain would be expecting me to go home with him at the end of the night.

I lifted my beer and took a sip. And I must have winced or made some kind of face, because Brian said, "You don't like beer?"

"It's not really my favorite drink, but I got used to it in college. It's cheap."

"Why not get something else?" Brian suggested. "I'm buying."

"I don't want to waste this."

"I'll drink it. Just get what you like."

I nodded. "Okay."

So I summoned the bartender over. "Actually, I'd like something other than beer. Maybe something popular in Key West. What do you suggest?"

"How about a key lime martini?"

"Ooh, that sounds good. I'll have one."

As the bartender began to prepare the drink, I perused the menu.

"I've seen you before," Brian suddenly said.

I met his eyes. "What?"

"You work at that coffee shop, A Book and a Cup."

"You've been in there?" I asked. If he had, how could I have forgotten someone like him?

"No. I was walking by earlier today. I saw you on the patio serving drinks."

"And you remembered me?" I was flattered.

"A woman like you . . . you're easy to remember."

My face flamed. He was most definitely flirting with me.

"One key lime martini," the bartender announced, and placed the drink in front of me.

"Thank you." I was grateful for the reprieve from Brian's intense gaze. He was attractive, absolutely. And I had butterflies in my stomach, something I hadn't felt since meeting Wesley. But I wasn't sure I was ready to jump into bed with Brian.

I sipped the drink. "Oooh, this is good."

"That's better." Brian's lips spread in a seriously sexy grin. "You should enjoy what you're consuming, not just suffer through it."

The band onstage was beginning its set, and I turned my attention to them. The guitarist and the keyboardist began playing a lively song, and the singer stood in front of the microphone, tapping her hand on her thigh in beat to the music.

I listened to her start to sing and was impressed with the unexpected soulful sound that came from her lips.

"So, Jade," Brian began. "What brings you to Key West?"

"I wanted to spend a summer somewhere other than

upstate New York. I ended my year at UB—University at Buffalo—and wanted a change of scenery."

"Buffalo."

"Have you been there?" I asked.

"Rochester, yes. Buffalo, no. How did you end up working at a coffee shop in Key West?"

As the singer's voice filled the bar, I held up a finger to let Brian know I'd answer in a moment.

We listened to the woman sing, and when her song was finished I spoke again. "Why am I in Key West? My sister went to school with the woman who owns the café. They were in the same sorority, actually. She needed help, I needed a break . . . that's why I'm here."

Brian's eyes narrowed. "What's the name of this guy you need a break from?"

My pulse picked up speed. "What makes you think it's a guy?"

"Just a sense I get."

As I sipped my martini, the woman onstage began to sing again. So I leaned forward and spoke loudly, saying, "His name is Wesley. And I'd rather not talk about him."

"His loss is my gain," Brian said into my ear.

A shiver of desire trailed down my spine. Glancing down, I blushed. Then I looked up and asked, "What about you? Why are you in Key West?"

"A friend of mine is getting married," he answered. "He's having dinner with his fiancée's family tonight, so I headed out on my own."

"And you like it here?" I asked.

He eased back and looked at me, his eyes holding mine. "What's not to like?"

I giggled, then reached for my drink. Oh, he was good. Saying all the right things.

Just how far did I want things to go with Brian? Lord, he was sexy. Just sitting beside him, my body was in a state of constant sexual awareness. What would it be like having those muscular arms wrapped around me, his lips on mine?

I brought my glass to my lips and finished it off. Perhaps a little liquid courage would help me seal the deal with Brian.

"Want another one?" Brian gestured to my empty glass.

"Sure," I told him. Saying yes meant spending more time with him, and I was fine with that. "And how about an order of nachos? We can split it."

"Sure thing."

Brian summoned the bartender and ordered another drink for me, plus an order of nachos.

"Where are you from?" I asked.

"Ohio. Akron."

"And what do you do in Akron?"

"I'm a fitness trainer," he answered.

"Ahh," I said. With that muscular physique, it made sense. And with his easy charm . . . "I'll bet most of your clients are women."

"Mostly men, actually. Yes," he added, seeing my look of skepticism. "I'm serious."

The bartender slid my drink onto the bar, and Brian passed him some money. "I'll pay for the nachos now as well."

I lifted the martini and took a liberal sip. Then I asked, "Are you single?"

"I wouldn't be hitting on you if I weren't."

I guffawed. "Yeah, sure."

"Why the cynicism? Did Wesley cheat on you?"

I swallowed at the mention of Wesley's name. "We had our issues," I said, not wanting to get into it.

"And you're still in love with him." A statement, not a question.

I didn't speak right away. "I'm here. Seeing where life's going to take me."

Brian nodded, then sipped his beer. "You said your sister was in a sorority. You too?"

"Me?" I laughed. "No. Sorority life wasn't for me."

"No conforming to house rules and being exactly like everyone else?"

"Definitely not."

"Sounds like you like to buck the status quo."

"Maybe a little."

"And maybe even authority," he surmised.

His eyes held mine, as though he were reading my secret in their depths. The secret of just how far I had gone to please my boyfriend.

I glanced away.

"By the way," Brian began, "you said you ended your college year. Did you graduate? Or do you have another year or two to go?"

Another sore topic. But maybe he was simply trying to gauge how old I was. "I have one more semester to go," I told him. And I left it at that. I didn't want to go into why. Remembering how Katrina had accused me of going on about losing my father, I figured Brian didn't need to hear my sob story.

"But enough about me." I looked him in the eye. "Tell me more about you."

"What do you want to know?"

I was enjoying our conversation. And I was especially pleased that we were actually talking, not just flirting. "Any crazy stories as a fitness trainer?"

"Crazy stories. Wow. Def—"

Whatever Brian had been about to say, he stopped abruptly as his gaze ventured beyond me, in the direction of the front door. His eyes widened slightly, something else obviously having just gotten his attention.

Another woman?

"Brian?"

He said nothing, apparently not hearing me. I all but smirked and reached for my drink. I was certain that another woman had entered the place and caught his fancy.

My ego imploded. God, were all men so completely unable to keep their eyes off of another attractive woman when in your company?

I sipped my martini, but it now tasted sour to me.

"Excuse me for a second," Brian said.

I shrugged, not meeting his eyes. And when he walked off, I wasn't surprised. But I was surprised that he didn't head in the direction of where he'd been looking. Instead, he turned and went toward the back of the restaurant, where the restrooms were.

Maybe his girlfriend had entered the place and he was worried about being seen with me. Sure, he said he didn't have a girlfriend. But someone as hot as him . . . was I supposed to believe that?

Or maybe he just needed to use the bathroom. Maybe I was being overly cynical without a real cause.

"And one order of nachos."

I glanced at the bartender and smiled as he pushed the plate of nachos toward me. "Thank you."

I set about trying to relax as I watched the show. Of course Brian would return. Not only had he not finished his beer, but we also had the order of nachos to eat.

But a few minutes passed and still no Brian. I knew women often took an extra long time in the bathroom, but men were typically faster than this.

More time passed. I got my phone out of my purse, about to check the time, when I felt two hands grip my shoulders. I jerked upright, startled. And as I looked over my shoulder, Katrina began to laugh.

"What?" she said. "You look like you've seen a ghost."

"You scared the crap out of me."

My eyes ventured to Christian. He was dressed in jeans,

sandals, and a blue T-shirt. Katrina was wearing a form-fitting white dress and glittery gold flip-flops.

"I told you we'd come and join you," Katrina said.

"Yeah, but you said you'd call." My heartbeat was slowly returning to its normal pace.

"I did. You didn't answer the phone."

I looked at my cell phone. Indeed, there were two missed calls. "Oh. I can't believe I didn't hear the phone."

"No worries, we decided to just come find you," Katrina said. "We went to a couple of other places first, then came here. We didn't even see you at first, and almost left. The place is pretty crowded."

"Yeah," I agreed. The bar had filled up since I'd arrived. "I like it."

Katrina's eyes wandered toward the partially consumed beer. "Are you with someone?" Her eyebrows rose, and she gave me a curious look.

I shook my head. "No. I mean, someone was here. We were chatting. He went to the bathroom and said he'd be back, but he hasn't returned yet."

Katrina pouted. "You think he took off?"

"Who knows?"

"Ah, don't worry about it," Katrina said, and patted my arm. "There are other guys."

"I wasn't interested anyway," I lied. "I was just passing the time talking to him."

"Are these your nachos?" Katrina asked.

"Uh-huh. Dig in."

Katrina scooped up a large tortilla chip, smothered with cheese and sour cream, then popped it into her mouth.

Christian, who had slipped between my seat and Brian's to get close to the bar, turned and asked Katrina what she wanted to drink. Katrina hurriedly munched on her mouthful of food, then answered, "I'll have a margarita."

"What about you?" Christian asked me.

"I'm good," I told him. "I haven't finished my martini yet." And now that it was looking less likely that I was going to get laid, I no longer needed more booze for liquid courage.

And then, through my peripheral vision, I caught sight of Brian on the far side of the restaurant. He was winding his way through the crowd en route to the front door.

Which only confirmed what I'd just thought. Nope. I didn't need any liquid courage tonight.

"Jackass," I muttered.

"What?" Katrina asked.

"The guy I was talking to, he just sneaked past me to the front door!" I shook my head. "I'll bet his girlfriend came in here and he had to make a quick getaway because he was talking to me."

"I thought you weren't interested," Katrina said.

"I'm not. But does he think I'm blind? Going out the bathroom window would have been a better move."

"Maybe he just went for a smoke," Katrina offered.

"Yeah, whatever." I shrugged. "Who cares?"

CHAPTER TWELVE

Katrina, Christian, and I made the rounds at the popular Key West bars. We went from one establishment to the other, and at each bar Christian drank more and more.

I found it disconcerting, but Christian was a happy drunk tonight. He and Katrina seemed completely lovey-dovey, all giddy and expressive with their affection for each other. Sometimes they made out right in front of my face, which made me feel like an oversized third wheel. But hey, I wasn't their chaperone and I wasn't about to tell them to tone it down.

We went home after one in the morning, Christian stumbling much of the way there. Upstairs, Katrina led him to their bedroom, accomplishing that task on her own.

"Good night," I told them before they disappeared into the room.

"Good night," Katrina replied. Christian only grumbled.

And then, exhausted, tipsy, and still disappointed about Brian bailing on me, I retired to bed.

* * *

A loud sound jarred me awake. Frantic, my eyes flew open. As my brain became conscious, I registered the now familiar disturbance.

The loud voices. And the sound of objects hitting the walls.

"For goodness' sake," I whined, grabbing the second pillow on the bed and throwing it over my head. How much of this aggressive lovemaking did I have to deal with? And did these two *never* sleep? It was one thing when they'd been living here without me, but couldn't they exercise some discretion? Couldn't they see that they ought to tone it down a bit?

Unexpectedly, things got quiet. Thank God, Katrina and Christian had come to their senses and remembered that I was in the apartment. Relieved, I made myself comfortable on my pillow once more and hoped that I would fall asleep again soon.

Then, *bam!* The sound of a crash had me bolting upright. Surely that wasn't simply lovemaking.

"Get out!" Katrina yelled at the top of her lungs, making it clear that they were fighting.

My body tensed as there was more yelling, but I couldn't make out distinct words.

"I swear to God, Christian!"

The voice was louder now. Katrina had moved from the bedroom to the living room.

"Stop it! Get the fuck away from me!"

Was Katrina in trouble?

I lay in the bed, paralyzed with fear. Every fiber of my being told me that this was a bad situation.

The voices got louder. "Then why did you tell me that you loved me?" Christian demanded. "What was today about?"

"Let go of me!"

My stomach tightened. The situation was escalating. Was Christian going to hurt Katrina?

"Why have you been messing with me?"

"You're drunk!" Katrina yelled.

And then I heard something, a slap perhaps? I jumped out of the bed, unable to take any more. I threw open my door and found Christian and Katrina standing in the living room, staring each other down. Christian's hand was on his left cheek, as though nursing it after being smacked.

"What are you doing?" I asked. Both of their eyes flew toward me.

Katrina's face crumbled, telling me that she was relieved I had come to intervene. I rushed forward, instinctively standing between her and Christian.

"Keep out of this," Christian told me.

"Keep out of it?" I looked at him as if he were crazy. "How can I, when the two of you are fighting like raging bulls?"

Katrina whimpered, and I faced her. She wrapped her arms around me as she started to cry.

"Stop the bullshit, Katrina. You're the one who slapped me."

I looked over my shoulder at him, saw him rolling his eyes.

"He gets like this every time he drinks," Katrina said, her voice soft, shaky.

"Jesus, Kat. What are you on about?"

I released Katrina so that I could face Christian. He smelled like a brewery. "I think you should go back to the bedroom."

"So she can fill your head with lies?" His eyes moved from mine to Katrina's. "Why'd you have me come here from England?"

"Because I didn't know you were a raving drunk!" Katrina shot back.

"Stop it." I extended my arms between both of them to keep them apart. Not that that would truly stop either of them from lunging at the other.

"What about today?" Christian asked. "You're supposed to be my wife."

Wife?

Katrina's eyes bulged. She shot me a quick look before meeting Christian's gaze again. "*Wife?* Do you hear yourself? Shit, you don't even know what you're saying when you're drunk." Then she faced me, her face contorting with pain. "You were right the other day. My arm." She extended it and pointed to the now faint bruise. "It didn't happen while making love." She sniffled. "It was Christian, out of control."

"*What?*" Outrage filled Christian's eyes, mixed with what looked like a tinge of confusion.

"When you're drunk, you don't know what you're doing," Katrina told him. "Every day, I keep thinking you'll be better the next day. But you keep disappointing me."

Fleetingly I wondered why Katrina hadn't told Christian to stop drinking while we were out. Instead, she'd imbibed with him, and she'd never once pulled a beer from his hands.

"You drank as much as I did!" Christian yelled, echoing my own thought.

Then he took a step toward her, and Katrina flinched. I jumped in front of her again. "Don't touch her."

Christian glared at me. "Fuck you. And fuck you, too, Katrina."

Pointing a finger, he moved toward me. I sucked in a breath and braced my shoulders, preparing for the worst.

But then Christian turned and stalked off into the bedroom.

"Stumbled" was more like it.

My shoulders drooped with relief.

When the door slammed shut, Katrina whimpered and pulled me into another embrace. She began to cry even harder, her body trembling. I let her get it out for about a minute before saying, "God, Katrina. What have you gotten yourself into?"

"It's his drinking. He just gets so out of control."

I eased back to look her in the eye. "Why did you keep drinking with him? You know how he gets. It doesn't make sense."

Looking down, pain streaked across Katrina's face. But she said nothing.

She looked so vulnerable, not at all like the strong woman I'd come to know her as. And then my stomach tensed as I remembered what Christian had said about her being his wife. Had he conned her into doing something incredibly stupid?

"What was Christian talking about when he said that you're *supposed* to be his wife?" I asked. Angling my head, I eyed her with worry. "Please tell me you didn't do something crazy."

"He . . ." Pausing, Katrina sucked in a deep breath, and my concern intensified. "He proposed today," Katrina explained. "He set up this whole romantic scene at the beach. . . ."

"What?" I quickly looked at her left hand. "He gave you a ring?"

"He offered. I told him I couldn't accept it. Not yet. We've been fighting a lot . . . you've heard us. I think it's just too soon."

I gripped her by the shoulders and looked dead into her eyes. "You may have known him since January, but he's been here in Florida with you less than a month. That's way too soon to be proposing marriage."

"I know. . . ."

"Maybe this whole arrangement . . . you ought to re-think it. He may have seemed nice when you met him, but you've really got no clue who he is. He could be a serial killer for all you know. I'd tell him to leave."

Katrina began to shake her head. "It's only when he's drunk that he's a problem. I'll talk to him, make sure he stays sober. Things will be fine."

"Are you really that into him?" I asked, knowing that my words sounded harsh. But from everything I'd seen, they had nothing in common—except their insatiable sexual chemistry.

"He's a nice guy, and he's got a big heart. He wants to start a foundation in his brother's honor, a resource to help people fighting mental illness. His brother suffered depression all his life, then committed suicide last November. We're both passionate about making this foundation a reality."

Learning that about Christian surprised me, and for a moment I didn't know what to say. Suddenly I was asking, "You're concerned about mental illness?"

Was that a flash of irritation I saw in her eyes? But her tone reflected sadness when she began to speak. "My college boyfriend . . . he suffered from depression, too. One day, he was driving home. He drove right into the path of a truck. All witnesses said he didn't hit the brakes." Katrina's voice cracked. "I couldn't help thinking about our last conversation, how he said he felt like a failure and didn't think life was worth living. I . . . I thought that going home to his family would boost his mood. But I was wrong."

"Oh my God," I said, and placed a hand on her arm to comfort her. "I'm sorry."

"I always thought I'd marry Shemar," Katrina went on. "And since he died, Christian is the first guy I've met who really gets me. And he really loves me. A part of my heart is still with Shemar, but Christian loves me completely."

I didn't know what to say.

"Maybe I'm in denial," Katrina said softly. "Maybe I was just tired of being lonely."

Finally she was getting it. "I think you need to kick him out," I said gently. "At least until he gets his act together."

"I don't want to hurt him."

"So it's okay if he hurts you?"

Katrina's lips turned down in a frown. It was obvious that the idea of hurting Christian was causing her grief.

"Maybe I will," Katrina finally said after a moment. Then she offered me a small smile. "Sorry for waking you up."

"That's not even an issue," I told her. "I'm concerned about you."

"I'll be fine."

"How?" I asked. "Christian is in your bedroom. He's still drunk. At any moment he could become irrational again."

"I know," Katrina said. She bit her bottom lip, and that told me that she was afraid, even if she didn't want to admit it.

And then, not even knowing what I was doing, I walked to her bedroom door and opened it. "Christian, you need to leave."

No response.

"Christian," I said, louder.

And then I heard his snoring. He was on the bed, already passed out. Sensing Katrina, I looked over my shoulder. She was standing behind me, looking into the room as well.

"He's sleeping it off," Katrina said. "Yes, he's an ass when he's drunk, but he'll be fine in the morning."

Short of calling the police, we couldn't get him out of here anyway. He was out cold.

I decided to trust that Katrina knew what she was talking about. That once sober, Christian would be fine.

At least I wanted to trust that. So I let the matter go, but it didn't sit well with me.

Not at all.

CHAPTER THIRTEEN

The next day, Christian acted as though nothing had happened the night before. In fact, he and Katrina seemed to be back to their lovey-dovey selves while working side by side in the café.

I, however, was on edge. I couldn't stop thinking about what I'd said to Katrina. Christian had come here from another country. He had no ties to the U.S. He could do something insane, then get on a plane and take off and never be heard from again. Never apprehended. God only knew who he really was or what he was capable of.

His anger frightened me, so I was certain that it had to frighten Katrina. But I suspected that she didn't want to admit that. Either because admitting that she was scared would mean admitting that she'd been foolish to have a man she didn't know cross continents to come and live with her or because she was one of those women who were willing to excuse away bad behavior. She could blame Christian's anger on his drinking all she wanted, but the bottom line was that the guy was irrational and she needed to be wary of just how far over the edge he could go.

I couldn't help wondering how her decision to keep

Christian around would affect *me*. I didn't want to get caught in the middle of a relationship war.

I was cleaning a table when I saw Christian walking toward me. I tensed, then tried to force myself to relax. I hoped that he hadn't caught my unease. I didn't want to appear afraid around him.

"Jade," he said softly. "I just wanted to apologize for last night."

I didn't face him, just kept wiping down the table, although it was already clean.

"I don't even remember what happened," he continued, "but Katrina told me I was a little shit. I was drunk, and I'm sorry. I promise to keep my drinking under control."

I glanced at him then, saw that he was making the sign of a cross over his heart. "Sure, whatever," I said. Then I lifted the tray with dirty plates and mugs and started toward the kitchen.

Christian fell into step beside me. "Listen, I know you don't know me well, but I want to assure you that I'm not the kind of guy who would hurt anybody. I don't even know what to think about what Katrina said. I don't remember putting a bruise on her arm."

"Which is exactly the problem," I muttered.

"What was that?" Christian asked.

Now in the kitchen, I placed the tray on the large metal counter meant for dirty dishes. "You say you're going to stop drinking, great. Which tells me that you know you have a problem."

"I never said I was perfect. But I do love Katrina."

"Good. Then you'll do what's necessary."

Then I exited the kitchen, hoping that the conversation was over and done with.

I went back to work, feeling a little better as the day went on. All a stranger watching Christian and Katrina together would see was two people in love. Maybe last night had been the wake-up call that Christian needed to change his behavior for the better.

Their situation had been like a weight on my shoulders, keeping me on edge. But being in the café, working, and chitchatting with the customers made me feel better.

As I was heading back in from the patio, Gordon waved me over. Smiling, I approached his table.

"How's the book coming along?" I asked.

"Good," he said. "I hit a bit of a block, but I'll work through it."

"You want more coffee?" I asked. "Something to eat?"

"Can I get a plate of fries and another coffee?" he asked.

"Sure thing."

Several minutes later, I was bringing Gordon his order. "Thank you," he said. Then, "Hey, I've been wanting to check out Hemingway Home. And since you're into writing, too, maybe we could go together? It might help inspire you to do some writing."

"That's a great idea. And probably exactly what I need. I'd love to go. When?"

"How's tomorrow?"

"It'll have to be in the evening, because I'm working in the day. Do you know how late it's open?"

"I'll find out."

"If it closes early, I'll work something out with Katrina. I'm sure I can sneak away for a couple of hours."

"We can figure it out tomorrow. Go whenever's convenient for you."

"Sounds great."

I smiled. Gordon's suggestion was an unexpected and welcome surprise.

The unexpected took on a new meaning when, as Katrina and I were cleaning the restaurant at the end of the night, she said to me, "Let's go to Mexico."

I stared at her, confused. "Pardon me?"

"Christian and I were talking about it, and we think it would be fun."

"Are you—" My protest stopped mid-sentence as Christian entered the restaurant from the kitchen. Had this been Katrina's idea—or his? "You're not actually serious," I said in a hushed tone.

"I'm totally serious."

"Why would you go to Mexico?" I asked.

"Why not?" she countered, loud enough for Christian to hear, making it clear she wasn't keeping the conversation from him. "I've always wanted to go to Mexico."

Christian slipped his arm around her waist and pressed his lips against her temple.

My eyes flitted between both of their faces. Was Christian coercing Katrina into going away? Suddenly I was leery of that whole story about him losing his brother to suicide. Maybe Christian was some nutcase who had wormed his way into Katrina's life.

"First of all," I began, "you've got your shop. Second of all, it's June. It's beautiful and hot right here in Key West."

"And that's why it's the perfect time to go. Because there are some insane deals right now. Christian saw a few on a travel Web site. Do you know how cheap it is to get an all-inclusive in Cancun right now? Air included? It's practically free."

"What about your business? You shut down to go to Mexico, you're going to lose money." I'd witnessed that explosive phone call between Katrina and the ex whom she owed money. Why was she even considering going away?

Katrina's eyes met Christian's before she looked at me again. "Money's not the only thing that matters in the world."

So this *was* Christian's idea. I didn't like this. What was he planning to do? Get her out of the country where he could hurt her . . . or worse? "You basically have Mexico right here at your doorstep," I pointed out. "Constant sunshine, palm trees. And the beach, which is stunning."

"It's about doing something different, seeing some place different," Katrina explained. "I could use a break. Christian and I need some time to just be a couple. And you came down here and jumped right into working long hours for me . . . why not come with us to Mexico so we can all have a good time?"

I stared at each of them in turn. Christian hadn't said anything, something I found suspicious. Suddenly I was thinking about the various crime shows I'd watched on television. People vacationing together in the tropics. One person in a relationship secretly wanting to get rid of the other.

"Mexico isn't exactly the safest place right now," I pointed out.

"Hogwash." This from Christian. "The media always sensationalizes things. Sure, that couple got killed recently, but sometimes people are stupid when they go on vacation. They go out and try to get drugs and they don't know who they're dealing with. We won't be doing any of that."

I held Christian's gaze, hoping that he didn't see my suspicion. Because I was suddenly very aware of the fact that *I* needed to be careful, not just Katrina. I had no clue who he really was, and I was living in a city where I had no family.

Katrina looked up at Christian. "Babe, can I talk to Jade alone for a minute?"

"Sure." He softly kissed her lips. "I'll be upstairs."

When he was out of earshot, Katrina stepped toward me. "I can tell you're concerned. Obviously, things with Christian and I have been . . . well, rocky. That's why we could both use some time away. I've been stressed with starting this business, and Christian came from England to be with me and I've thrown him right into working, so I'm sure he's stressed about that, too."

"Have you forgotten last night?" I asked. "And what he did to your arm last week?"

"No. That's what I'm trying to explain. We didn't get to start our relationship off right. Everyone else gets to date and have that honeymoon phase. We've had this coffee shop keeping us busy, and I know that's caused stress and tension in our relationship. We need time to bond as a couple."

How much more bonding time did they need? Even Alexis had commented on their open affection and how the two seemed to spend as much time making out as they did working.

"Look, if you guys want to go, that's fine," I said. "But I think that I would be a third wheel in any kind of scenario where you guys go to Mexico." It was already bad enough having to listen to their lovemaking in the apartment. "It just doesn't make sense for me to join you."

"Oh come on," Katrina said. "What are you gonna do—stay here and keep hoping that Wesley will call and tell you he wants you back?"

"This isn't about h—"

"It's time for you to have sex with someone else. Discover that there are other guys out there."

"I'm not pining over Wesley," I said. And to prove it, I added, "In fact, I'm getting together with Gordon tomorrow night." It wasn't a date, but Katrina didn't need to know that. I just didn't want her thinking that I was still crying over Wesley.

"Gordon?" Katrina looked stunned.

"One of the customers who comes in every day. Works on his lapt—"

"I know who he is," Katrina said. "I just didn't realize you guys had a thing."

"We don't have a *thing*," I said. "But we're going to go

out tomorrow. He seems really nice, and he's easy to talk to . . . who knows?"

"You and Gordon?" Katrina asked, as though the idea of us as a couple were inconceivable.

"We started talking because I see him here every day. And conversations about where I'm from, my school experience at UB, and my writing led to him asking me out. It's nothing major. We're just gonna hang out, get to know each other better."

Katrina gave me a curious look. "That's odd, him wanting to know about your school experience?"

"Why? Obviously he's interested in me as a person. He's not one of those guys who just want to get into a woman's pants." I hoped that I'd said enough to convince Katrina that I wasn't hung up on Wesley. Not that I had to prove anything to her.

Katrina narrowed her eyes. She wasn't buying my act. "What?" I asked.

"Or maybe he's trying to pretend he's someone that he's not. Passing himself off as a nice guy when he's really got ulterior motives."

I wanted to tell her that she was describing Christian. Instead, I asked, "Why would you think that?"

"You may as well know the truth. Before you arrived here, he asked me out. He seemed curious about my UB experience, too." She glanced away, as though contemplating something. "Said something about researching sororities."

"He *is* a writer."

"Yeah, but I've seen him talking to lots of girls. I think he's a player, Jade."

What was this, Katrina trying to compete with me?

"My gut says not to trust him," she went on.

Why was she making such a big deal about this? "It's just a date, not a commitment."

"Forget the guys here, Jade." Katrina's eyes lit up. "Go to Mexico. Find a real man who will rock your world."

"Katrina, I'm not going to Mexico."

"Come on." She pouted. "I want you there. You know the saying. The more the merrier."

"There's also another saying. 'Three's a crowd.' I'm not going, Katrina."

"Fine," she said, sounding irritated. "I guess it's a stupid idea. I just thought it might be fun. But obviously you want to have fun in Gordon's bed."

"That's not what I said."

"Then what's keeping you here? If someone invited me to Mexico, I'd jump at the opportunity."

The thought crossed my mind then—did Katrina want me along on the trip so she didn't have to totally be alone with Christian? Did she not trust her boyfriend as much she claimed to trust him? And if that was the case, why bother to go at all?

I didn't like this. Not one bit.

As much as I felt bad for Katrina, even given the look of disappointment on her face, I didn't change my answer. Some things in life people thank you for later. If my not going stopped her from going, well, I was fine with that. The way I saw it, I was possibly saving her life.

I thought that was the end of the conversation until she said, "I'm sorry if you don't like Christian, but you shouldn't judge him harshly." She held my gaze a beat. "After all, you're not perfect, are you?"

My eyes narrowed as I looked at her. What was she getting at? "Excuse me?"

"I know about Buffalo. What you did at your boyfriend's graduation when you saw him with your friend." She paused. "And what happened afterward."

Fuck! Marie had told her?

And suddenly that knowing look she'd given me after

we'd had our own spat days ago made sense. She'd known about Buffalo then but hadn't said anything. Instead, she'd hinted at it.

"I've taken a chance and let you come here and work for me, regardless," Katrina said. "I don't think you're a raging psychopath."

The words were like a kick to my solar plexus. Instead of seeing stars, I saw the various negative comments on my Facebook wall float before my eyes.

Crazy.

Insane.

Few screws loose.

Can you say psycho?

"My point," Katrina went on, bringing my attention back to her, "is that people make mistakes. You should understand that."

I felt my ire rising. I couldn't believe what I was hearing. "I'm done with this conversation."

"Looks like you're getting hot under the collar," she pressed, as though hoping to get a rise out of me to prove a point.

I drew in a sharp breath, trying to calm down. "Do whatever you want to do, Katrina."

Her face softened. "Marie told me that in confidence, and I probably shouldn't have told you that I knew. It's just . . . you know all about losing your temper. But does that make you—"

"Can we *not*?"

Katrina raised both hands, a sign of surrender. "Okay. Sorry. I'm just saying, we don't always do the right things all the time. I figured you of all people would understand that."

I walked a few steps to the right, trying to distance myself from Katrina and this conversation. I checked out the state of the café, which looked ready for business tomorrow morning. "Everything's good in here?"

"Sure. We're done."

"Good."

I all but ran up the stairs and went straight to my room. I was miffed. I wanted to call Marie and scream at her, but I didn't. How dare she tell Katrina my personal business? I was embarrassed enough because people I knew had witnessed me making a fool of myself. Now I had to live here with the knowledge that Katrina knew what I'd done?

I stayed in my room and watched a movie on my laptop and tried to chill out. And I waited for the other shoe to drop.

That shoe being Christian's temper.

I guess I *wanted* to hear him lose it, so I could assure myself that I was nothing like him. But the hours passed and I heard nothing. Nothing but laughter and easygoing chatter in the living room.

And the next thing I knew it was the morning and I was waking up and I hadn't heard any type of disturbance during the night.

"What kind of coffee do you want, babe?"

That was Christian. The two of them were up and going about getting ready. A normal couple starting the day.

I remembered Katrina's words from the night before. How I of all people should understand that people make mistakes.

I hadn't been impressed with the comment at the time, mostly because I'd been angry that my sister had betrayed my confidence. But maybe Katrina was right. Maybe I was judging Christian too harshly.

I *had* lost it at grad. Totally become unhinged. In my anger, I'd become a different person. Someone I didn't want to be again. Surely I could allow for a mistake on Christian's part. And who knew—Katrina could be on point with her assessment that stress was playing a big part in why they were fighting.

It suddenly struck me why Wesley didn't trust me. Because of how crazy I'd gotten. Hearing Katrina talk about it last night was giving me new perspective. Maybe I needed to apologize again, let him know that what I'd done had been completely my fault. Not Michelle's or his. Mine. A temporary reaction because of the stress of not graduating and the fear of losing him.

I also had to let him know that I was fine with a long-distance relationship . . . as long as he didn't close the door on us altogether.

So I sent him that text, with the goal of convincing him that I was a changed person.

And I prayed that he would be willing to give me another chance. I didn't want to be single. I wanted to work on saving the relationship I already had.

CHAPTER FOURTEEN

The next morning, I entered the café and noticed Gordon outside the front door. His laptop bag was slung over his shoulder. But what struck me as odd was that Katrina was outside the door talking to him.

I watched, curious. I had planned to ask Gordon about what Katrina had said, see for myself where his head was at. But I watched in disbelief as, instead of coming into the café and assuming his regular table, Gordon turned and walked away.

Katrina watched him go, then came into the café. I went over to her immediately. "Where's Gordon going?" I asked. "Why is he leaving?"

"Because I talked to him. Told him I didn't appreciate him leading you on."

"That's what you said?" I asked, feeling alarmed. And embarrassed. Shit, I didn't need Gordon getting the wrong impression.

Katrina shrugged nonchalantly. "The fact that he left shows his true intentions."

I frowned. Why would Gordon leave if Katrina had talked to him about leading me on? Wouldn't he have told her that she was mistaken? Perhaps even laughed off the idea as crazy?

I looked at Katrina—and knew she was lying. But why?

"I need to talk to him," I said.

I started for the door, but Katrina grabbed hold of my arm, stopping me. "Let him go, Jade. He's no good."

"But this doesn't make sense."

"What—that he's a liar?"

Pulling my arm free of Katrina's grip, I blew out a frustrated breath. I wanted to talk to Gordon. Find out why he'd really left.

But he was gone now. I'd have to ask him later—if he came back to the café.

"You've got customers waiting, Jade," Katrina said.

I didn't respond, just went back to work. And every time I heard the door chimes, I looked in that direction, hoping to see Gordon returning.

Every fiber of my being told me that Katrina had lied to me, and I wanted to know why.

Later I was delivering drinks on the patio when I got the overpowering sense that someone was watching me.

I quickly looked over my shoulder, expecting to see Gordon.

Instead, I saw someone else. And my heart stopped in my chest.

Brian!

He was about twenty feet away, resting against a light pole. Definitely staring at me. He smiled.

I blinked, making sure that my eyes weren't playing tricks on me. Because the way Brian had abandoned me at that bar, the last thing I expected was for him to be here now—and smiling at me.

But my eyes weren't betraying me. Brian was actually here.

As I turned away, my breath caught in my throat. Then I glanced in his direction again, confused. His smile brightened, and he actually waved.

I stood, dumbfounded, unable to react. My God, Brian was here. And even with the distance between us, I felt the heat that I had when I'd first met him.

He beckoned me over. That's when I felt a wave of irritation and finally reacted. Guffawing, I turned on my heel and started toward the café's front door.

"Jade!" I heard him call.

My hand paused on the door's handle. Something inside of me melted. The sound of his voice . . . God, what was it about him that drew me to him like a moth to a flame?

"Jade," he repeated, his voice softer. He was closer. I could hear a plea in the way he'd said my name.

I wanted to run. Lord, how my brain told me to run. But instead, I drew in a breath and turned. He was a few feet away, on the outside of the patio railing.

"I'm working," I said. No niceties.

"You can't spare a few minutes?"

"Oh, that's priceless." The question annoyed me. More reason to simply walk away from him. But as I glanced through the glass into the café, I decided that Katrina would survive without me for a couple of minutes.

Then, swallowing, I made my way out of the enclosed patio area and to Brian.

"Hey," he said softly, his smile charming.

The hypocrisy of that smile angered me—as if he hadn't left me in that bar waiting for him to return!

"I find it ironic that you want me to spare you a few minutes now when you couldn't spare me a few minutes to tell me you were leaving me at the bar. So why the hell do you want to talk to me now?"

"Can we go over there and talk for a minute—without

an audience?" He gestured to the alley at the side of the café.

"Are you going to answer my question?"

He placed his hand on my elbow. "Come talk to me."

My breathing was erratic, as was my heartbeat. A part of me was pissed that he had the nerve to show up here and expect me to give him the time of day. But another part was all giddy and elated that he wanted to see me.

Once we were around the side of the building and beyond earshot of patrons on the patio, I said, "Why don't you come into the café and have a seat? Order a drink—and perhaps some nachos." I gave him a pointed look.

"I'm sorry I left you that night," he said.

I hadn't expected the apology, and for a moment it made me lower my guard. I looked into his eyes . . . such beautiful, striking eyes . . . and I wanted him.

I hated myself for it.

Looking away was the only way to save myself from whatever power he had over me. "You're sorry?" I snorted in derision. "If you came here to apologize, then you've wasted—"

"Something came up," Brian interjected. "I know it sounds flaky, but it's true. I'd have to be crazy to walk away from you without a good reason."

"Oh, I'm sure you had a great reason." I faced him again, needing to see the truth in his eyes. "What's her name? Your girlfriend. Or are you actually married?"

Brian shook his head. "There's no one else."

Damn it, I believed him. In his eyes, I saw only honesty. And desire. "Then why'd you take off?"

"It was work related," Brian explained. "I went to the bathroom to take a call, and then I had to leave. I saw that you had company, and . . ." He shrugged. "And now I'm here."

"And you expect me to jump for joy?" I asked. Though

that's exactly what I wanted to do. Being close to Brian like this, I felt a thrill. Alive. "And what do you mean you got a call?" I asked when my brain registered his paltry excuse. "Your phone didn't ring. You looked around, saw someone, and quickly got up. Do you really think I'm stupid?"

"If I thought you were stupid, I wouldn't have come here to see you today."

Again his words stopped any protest in my throat. I'd believe him even if he was trying to pass off swampland as a prime real estate location.

"Brian, I've got to get back to work. Katrina is going to be wondering where I am." I paused. "If you want to . . . if you want to talk, why not come in and get a table?" What? Why the *hell* had I said *that?* He'd had his chance with me and blown it and I was welcoming him back into my life with open arms?

"I can't," he said.

Two words, but they deflated my bubble of hope and left me feeling stupid. Scoffing, I lowered my head. I knew I should have walked away.

"But how about I call you?" Brian asked.

Stunned, I raised my eyes to his, the hope returning.

"Or you call me," Brian continued. "You have a pen?"

I withdrew one from my apron pocket. "Here."

I thought Brian was going to ask me for a piece of paper, but instead he took my hand in his. Heat tingled along my skin where our hands connected. He opened my palm and began to write.

"I'll leave the ball in your court," he said as he wrote. "This is my number. Call, or text. If you're not too upset with me."

I glanced at my palm, then met his eyes again. Our gazes held. And as one beat turned to two and then to three, I waited. Waited for him to kiss me.

"Sometimes," he began softly, "timing makes all the difference."

I frowned. "What does that mean?"

"The ball's in your court," he said.

Then he walked away, leaving me standing breathless in the alley.

Only after he'd gone and I looked at the number on my hand did something strike me as odd. Brian had said that he was from Akron, Ohio. So why had he given me a number with a Key West area code?

CHAPTER FIFTEEN

I was dreaming. I was in a library or an office—somewhere someone was typing on a computer.

I tried to open my eyes, but my eyelids were heavy. I snuggled into my pillow and settled back into my weird dream.

"Hey. Jade. Wake up."

At first when I heard the voice it didn't totally register. I thought it was part of my dream.

"Jade."

The combination of my name coupled with the feel of a hand on my leg jarred me awake. Goose bumps popped out on my skin as fear seized me.

"Jade."

My heart was pounding a mile a minute, but I quickly made sense of what was going on. Katrina was in my room.

I rolled over, squinting as I faced her. The light in my room was blinding. "Kat?" I said, my voice groggy. And in the next instant I felt a spasm of panic. "Is everything okay?"

"You need to go to Mexico."

I blinked, not sure I'd heard her correctly. "What?"

"You need to go to Mexico," she repeated.

Maybe I *was* dreaming, because this made no sense. But I didn't feel as though I were sleeping.

My brain in a fog, I craned my neck to look beyond her at the bedside clock. It was 3:04 a.m., and she most definitely had woken me up. *To tell me that I needed to go to Mexico?*

Anger swept over me like a massive wave.

"It's three oh four in the morning," I spat out. "What the fuck?"

"I had an epiphany," Katrina said, completely unfazed by my ire. "Mexico's what you need to move on, finally put Wesley in your rearview mirror."

"Kat, why are you in my room? It's the middle of the night."

"I was just online checking prices for Mexico, and there's a ridiculous deal right now."

Through narrowed eyelids, I looked toward my desk. She'd been on my computer? "I don't understand what you're doing. You wake me up when I'm trying to friggin' slee—"

"Because the price I found will probably be gone by morning. I can book yours; you can pay me back."

"Are you insane?"

"For helping you out?" Her expression said she thought I was the insane one. "Besides, I have a friend there," she continued. "He's been working at a resort in Cancun, and he said he's interested in meeting you." She patted my leg. "I just *know* the two of you will hit it off. You don't want to miss out on meeting the love of your life, do you?"

I was slowly becoming more conscious, and I wasn't impressed. Huffing, I rolled onto my side.

"Come on," Katrina urged.

I wanted to tell her to get the fuck out of my room. But

I remembered her words about what had happened in Buffalo. That despite my outburst at graduation, she didn't think I was a raging psychopath. So I held in my anger and spoke as rationally as I could. "I can't even think, Kat. Let's talk in the morning."

"This deal may be gone by morning."

"I'll take my chances," I said. Then, groaning, I pulled the pillow over my head. And when I heard my door click shut, I was grateful that she was finally gone.

Is she literally insane? was the last thought that came into my mind before I drifted into nothingness.

The next morning I awoke thinking that I'd had a bad dream. Had Katrina really come into my room and woken me up in the middle of the night?

I stretched, then rolled over and looked at the bedside clock. Nine thirty-four! I'd slept in.

I threw off the covers and jumped out of bed. That's when I noticed the slip of paper on the floor:

I didn't wake you. Get rest and come downstairs when you're ready. Let's decide about Mexico. ☺ *Kat*

Exhaling a shuddery breath, I sat back on the bed. It wasn't a bad dream. Katrina had actually come into my room in the middle of the night to tell me that I needed to go to Mexico. Shit, *was* she insane?

And why the hell was she saying we should decide about Mexico? Did she not understand what the word "no" meant?

When I went downstairs forty-five minutes later, Katrina beamed at me as though she were the sweetest person in the world. I was tying my apron behind my back when she came over to me.

"Did you sleep well?" she asked.

"Yeah, sure," I responded, my tone clipped. "Which section do you want me working today?"

"Section one. Alexis is on the patio."

"Okay."

I made a move to head in that direction, but Katrina placed a hand on my arm. I faced her. "Hey, just wanted to let you know that Christian and I have made arrangements for Mexico. We leave on Monday."

"Monday?" I was surprised. "That's in four days."

"Yes, and I'm not going to have the shop open. All the more reason for you to go with us."

"Did you invite Alexis, too?" I asked. "Or just me?"

"Alexis is nice and all, but I wouldn't hang out with her."

"What's she going to be doing with the shop shut down?" Not that I thought she'd hang with me during Katrina and Christian's absence. Alexis and I got along at work, but the moment she clocked out she got on her boyfriend's Harley and took off.

"Alexis said she's going to head to Miami with her boyfriend. She's got family there."

I nodded. Maybe it was time for me to take a trip back to Erie? But as soon as the thought entered my mind I dismissed it. I'd barely arrived in Florida. Besides that, I wasn't certain that I wanted to see my sister. I was still annoyed with her for opening her big mouth. And home was a long drive away. It wasn't like I'd been gone for months.

"Maybe I'll go to Miami, too. I've always wanted to visit South Beach."

"Suit yourself," Katrina said. Then she turned and headed back behind the front counter.

Once again, Gordon wasn't here. Was he really a scumbag who'd been outed by Katrina? Or had she said something to scare him off?

I didn't entirely trust her anymore. More than once, she'd snapped at me when it was totally uncalled for. And the way she'd been in my room last night had creeped me out.

Why was she so insistent that I go to Mexico? And that bit about her wanting to set me up with the possible love of my life? Come on.

But as the morning went on, I started to wonder again if Katrina wanted me on the trip because she didn't want to be alone with Christian. I couldn't understand why she was bothering to go at all.

Clearly, their relationship was up-and-down. Maybe the stress of that rocky relationship was causing Katrina's mood swings. Maybe she figured if I was in Mexico with them things wouldn't be so unpredictable.

Which told me Katrina was wary of Christian. I didn't blame her. I was wary of him, too.

I was checking on the tables in section one when I felt my phone vibrate in my apron pocket. I quickly withdrew it, saw Wesley's smiling face.

Excitement tickled my stomach. Wesley was calling? That's right. I'd sent him a text a couple of nights ago. Maybe he was finally willing to get our relationship back on track.

I hurried to the back of the shop before swiping the TALK icon, then put the phone to my ear. "Hello?"

"What the fuck is wrong with you?"

I reeled backward, shocked by his words. "Excuse me?"

"Threatening me? Threatening Michelle. She wanted to call the police, by the way. I had to talk her out of doing that."

I slipped into the kitchen. "What on earth are you talking about?"

"Is that your game? Go off like a psycho lunatic, then play innocent?"

"Tell me what the hell you're talking about!"

Wesley scoffed. "I'm talking about those fucking pictures you sent to my Facebook page and messaged to Michelle. You may have set up a different account, but we know it was you."

I made a face, confused. "What?"

"Of all things, a German shepherd? When you know my dog was hit by a car last year."

"Wes—"

"Is this your idea of showing me that you've 'changed and deserve another chance'?" he asked, quoting the last text message I'd sent him.

"I didn't do what you think I did!"

"Sure, and you didn't call her a whore on my page, either, right?"

I said nothing. I couldn't deny that one.

"Every day, you keep showing me just how deranged you are. We're done, Jade. Never contact me or Michelle again."

"Wesley, why won't you listen to me? I didn't send any crazy pictures. I wouldn't—"

"Just leave us the fuck alone, Jade. You understand? And get some fucking help."

As the phone went dead, I held it in my hand, completely befuddled. What the hell was Wesley talking about? Pictures? I hadn't sent him any pictures.

I jumped when I heard the kitchen door open. Then I looked in that direction, saw Katrina eyeing me curiously. "Everything okay?" she asked.

A shuddery breath oozed out of me. "No, everything is not okay. I need . . ." I walked toward her. "Can I have a minute?" I asked.

"Sure," she said.

I scrambled into the staff bathroom at the back of the café. Then I opened up my Facebook page on my phone.

I tried to access Michelle's page, but I couldn't even see

it now, meaning she had gone beyond unfriending me and had blocked me. So I went to Wesley's page and scrolled down his wall.

And the image I saw there made me gasp. It was a graphic picture of a pig that had been gutted, its entrails in a pile beside its body. It had been sent from someone named JANE DOE.

Obviously a pseudonym.

The words read: *This is what happens to scumbag cheaters. Consider yourself warned.*

"What the heck?" I said aloud. Wesley thought I'd sent him this? Didn't he know me better than that?

I scrolled down farther. The next picture made tears come to my eyes. The decapitated head of a dog, a German Shepherd, made me sick to my stomach.

Look in the mirror, dog.

"My God," I gasped. This was horrific. Absolutely sickening.

I had a couple of messages, so I opened my in-box. I saw Wesley's name, first, and clicked to read his message. But I quickly learned that the message was actually from Michelle:

Bitch, this is Michelle. I've blocked your ass, so I'm using Wesley's account to send you this final warning.

Do you really think I'm stupid?

You message me pictures of gutted animals on Facebook from some fake account and think I won't realize who it is?

You threaten me again and I'm reporting your ass to the cops. And you wonder why Wesley chose me over you? Get some help, you fucking psycho!

Hot tears spilled onto my cheeks. Tears of frustration. My God, why would they think I would do something so heinous? I hadn't set up any fake account.

Michelle and Wesley, it wasn't me. Honestly. I don't know who did that, but it wasn't me. I swear.

I sent the message but didn't know if either of them would believe me. Wesley of all people should know I wouldn't send him a picture of a dead dog. I loved dogs. I loved all animals.

But that whole bit about *this is what happens to scumbag cheaters* . . . Anyone looking at the page would think that I had been the one to send it.

My head swam as a memory hit me. Katrina in my room in the middle of the night. The sound of fingers on a keyboard that had initially roused me from my sleep.

Good God, had *she* done this?

CHAPTER SIXTEEN

When I went back into the café, I debated confronting Katrina. Debated but dismissed the idea. How could I accuse her of something so . . . so crazy?

Instead, I set about taking care of my customers. But I was on edge now, suspicious of Katrina and the timing of her having been in my room last night. Had she gone into my computer and found the Facebook info for Wesley and Michelle?

It made sense.

But why would Katrina do something like that? That's what *didn't* make sense. Was I paranoid for even being suspicious of her?

All I knew was that I was pissed. Pissed that someone would threaten Michelle and Wesley and pretend to be me. I guess I was wearing my anger for all to see, because less than an hour after I came back into the café Katrina came up to me and said, "We need to talk. In the back. Now."

I followed her into the kitchen, and I could feel my anger growing as I did. It was the fact that she'd been in my room last night that didn't sit well with me. Had she accessed my Facebook account while I'd been sleeping?

Facing me, Katrina said, "What is going on with you?"

"Did you send my ex and my friend vile messages on Facebook?"

She looked at me as if I had grown a third eye. "What? I don't even know who they are."

"That doesn't answer the question."

"If I don't know who they are, how could I send them messages? And why on earth would I?"

"I don't know. Maybe you thought you were doing me a favor?" I suggested, grasping at straws.

"Do you need to take the rest of the day off? Because you're walking around the café looking pissed off and that's just not acceptable. No matter what's going on between you and your ex—"

"Someone created a fake account and sent Wesley and Michelle pictures of gutted animals with threatening messages. They think I did it."

"What?"

"Wesley called over an hour ago. He was livid. And Michelle sent me a really nasty message. She thinks I threatened her life and wanted to go to the police. Wesley convinced her not to."

"Well, if you didn't send them any crazy messages, you didn't send them. The police can't do anything about it."

I paused, drew in a deep breath. But I forged ahead, because I had to be sure. "Last night, when you were in my room . . . Were you only checking out Mexico deals on my computer?"

Katrina's expression darkened. "You know what, Jade? I let you come down here, I offered you a job, I allowed you to stay with me . . . despite knowing what I know about you. You lost it at your boyfriend's graduation; you tried to kill yourself. Now you're accusing me of sending nasty messages to your boyfriend? Do you even hear yourself?"

I opened my mouth to speak, then promptly shut it. *Did I seem like a lunatic?*

"If you're going to accuse me of shit, maybe you ought to just go home. I'm done taking abuse when I've been nothing but nice to you."

"I'm sorry," I said, and placed my hand on my forehead. "This is too much stress for one person. Wesley's mad at me; now you're mad at me. And honest to God, I don't know what's going on."

Unexpectedly, Katrina put her arms around me. "It's okay, Jade. But I am worried about you. All this stress . . . it can't be good."

Given what Marie had told her about my car accident, Katrina probably thought I was on the verge of a breakdown. "I'll be fine," I told her.

"Regardless, take the rest of the day off. Or, if you feel better by the evening, you can come down and work then."

I was going to argue, insist that I was fine to work. But I thought better of it. I needed time to decompress.

Upstairs, I made the mistake of going on to Facebook—only to find a flurry of nasty messages.

If my friends had thought I was crazy after grad, they were convinced of it now.

I always liked you, but you're fucked up! That was the first message I saw on my wall, and the rest of the nasty messages were in the same vein: *Psycho! Deranged bitch!*

But the worst one was from Gail, one of Michelle's friends. She wrote: *Your mother should have aborted you.*

I cried. For a solid ten minutes, I lay in bed and bawled. Everybody hated me.

And then a name sounded in my brain.

Brian.

He didn't hate me. Brian liked me.

Brian was a fresh start.

Sitting up, I wiped my tears. Then I found his number in my phone. For a solid minute, my thumbs hovered above my screen. I wasn't sure what to say.

I decided to keep it simple:

Hey.

About thirty seconds later, my phone trilled. My mood lifted as I saw his name flash on my screen.

Does this mean you're not mad at me?

I responded right away:

On the fence about that. ☺ Where are you?

I waited for a reply, my stomach sinking when there was none. *Come on, Brian. Don't you bail on me, too.*

About two minutes later, my phone rang. My heart did a crazed pitter-patter when I saw Brian's name and number displayed on my screen.

I quickly answered the call. "Hello?"

"Hey."

That deep, sexy voice was like a warm blanket on a cold day. It enveloped me, erasing the chill I'd been feeling.

"Are you still in Key West?" I asked.

"Actually, I left yesterday."

"Oh." Disappointment washed over me. I wanted to see him, badly.

"I'm not too far away, though. I'm in Miami. I was hoping to hear from you before I left."

"Are you coming back?"

"I'm not sure I can."

"How long will you be in Miami?"

"Why? What's up?"

I blew out a frazzled breath. "I'm just having a bad day."

"What happened?"

"I don't want to get into it."

"Hey," he said softly. "You're upset. Tell me what's going on."

So I did. I told him about Wesley and Michelle and what they thought I did.

"They're upset right now," Brian said, "but they'll realize the truth soon enough. And if they don't? Move on and forget them."

"You make it sound so easy."

"No, it's not easy. But don't beat yourself up over what they think."

I sighed softly. "Can I meet you in Miami? Katrina, the owner of the coffee shop, is heading to Mexico and I'll have a few days off."

"She's heading to Mexico? When?"

"In four days. On Monday. And I don't want to be here on my own."

"Aw, man. I have to head back to Ohio tomorrow."

His words deflated me. "You do?"

"I wish I didn't."

"God, I don't want to be here," I muttered, more to myself. "Katrina asked me to go to Mexico with her and her boyfriend, but that's crazy. I don't want to do that."

"What if I met you there?"

For a moment I was speechless. "What?"

"I have to head back to Akron, show my face at my job. But if I can swing it . . . sure, I'd meet you in Mexico. Which part?"

"Cancun." I said the word slowly, not sure I could believe what he was saying.

"Why don't you let me know the details. When, where. I'll see if I can make it."

My eyes misted, but this time because I was happy. Brian had come into my life and changed everything for the better.

"Okay," I told him. "I'll let you know."

After talking to Brian, I popped two painkillers to help alleviate the throbbing in my head. The conversation with him had brightened my mood, but I'd still had a stress headache.

Thankfully, I fell asleep. A solid ninety minutes of rest helped me to wake up feeling refreshed.

And with a whole new positive outlook on life.

Brian might join me in Mexico. I was over the moon.

I went back downstairs to work shortly after six that evening and immediately approached Katrina, who was behind the counter. "About Mexico," I began without preamble, "you guys leave on Monday?"

"Uh-huh."

I bit the inside of my cheek before continuing. "I've been reconsidering your invitation."

Her eyes lit up. "You changed your mind about coming with us?"

"Maybe you were right. I think I *could* use a vacation. A real one. And what am I going to do here by myself with the shop closed down and Alexis in Miami?"

Squealing, Katrina threw her arms around me. "Yes!"

As we broke apart, I said, "Seriously, though, you're not bothered about me being a third wheel?"

"I wouldn't have invited you if I didn't want you along."

"And Christian?"

"Is totally cool with it." Katrina looked at me expectantly. "You're going?"

"I got my passport last year," I replied. "I may as well use it."

"Yay!" Katrina threw her arms around me again. "Oh, I'm so happy. We're gonna have a blast!"

"Obviously I'm going to get a separate room." But I hoped I wouldn't be alone. I hoped Brian would be with me.

"Duh." Katrina giggled. "I've already spoken to a travel agent about the trip. I can give her a call and find out the price for you."

"Four days," I said, sighing softly.

Katrina draped her arm across my shoulder. "In four days, we'll all be in paradise, without a care in the world."

CHAPTER SEVENTEEN

SHAWDE

Shawde tossed her research binder onto the bed beside her, then rubbed her eyes with the heels of her hands. Her vision was blurring from going over the information she'd compiled on Katrina again and again—only to find nothing new.

Reaching her hand over her shoulder, Shawde tried to massage a knot in her spine below her neck. But she couldn't quite reach the spot. And then she sighed, wistful, missing Maurice. He used to give her the best massages.

Her eyes ventured to the empty side of the bed, where Maurice used to sleep when they were together. Now the binder lay near his pillow.

Why are you choosing the past over me? Maurice had asked her. Shawde had argued the point, telling him that it wasn't fair for him to make her give up her quest to see her brother's killer brought to justice. But as she looked at the binder on Maurice's side of the bed the reality of his words hit her full force. Instead of the man she loved being with her, she had that damned binder of information that hadn't helped her one iota.

"Did I make the right choice?" she asked aloud.

She was no closer to nailing Katrina. And Shawde's quest for justice had cost her Maurice. Had the price been too steep?

"I know you wouldn't want this for me, Shemar," Shawde said softly. "For me to be here alone and broken-hearted. But shouldn't Maurice love and support me one hundred percent?"

As pain filled her heart, Shawde's eyes ventured to her cell phone on her night table. Was he missing her right now, as she was missing him?

Maybe she should call him. Or at least send him a text to let him know that she was thinking of him.

Summoning courage, she reached for her phone. Then flinched when it started to ring in her hand. *Maurice?*

A quick glance at the screen told her that it wasn't Maurice. Someone with a 323 area code was calling, a number she did not recognize. Shawde swiped her screen to accept the call, wondering who was calling her after 11:00 p.m.

"Hello?"

"Shawde Williams?" a woman asked.

Shawde crossed her legs. "Yes?"

"I'm Monica Langdon. Sorry to call so late, but I'm on the West Coast and your messages sounded urgent."

"Monica, hi." This was why Shawde answered all calls, no matter the hour. Because it could be someone calling her about Katrina. "No worries regarding the time. I'm just glad you got back to me."

"I've been out of the country," Monica explained. "I was in Chile for the past few months working as a missionary."

"Wow. That's wonderful."

"Which is why I couldn't return your calls sooner."

"Of course."

"You wanted to talk to me about Katrina Hughes?" Monica said.

"Yes." Shawde's stomach tensed with nervous energy. "What do you remember about her?"

"I was the treasurer for the Alpha Sigma Pi sorority, so I worked with her a lot, as she was the sorority president."

"So you know her well."

"As much as anyone could get to know her," Monica said.

"What does that mean?"

"Just . . . she could be aloof. People tried to impress Katrina, get close to her, but she only let a few people into her inner circle. I tried to get close to her, and superficially we seemed to be, but it was like there was a glass wall between us."

So she wasn't particularly warm and fuzzy. "What else can you tell me about her?"

"I definitely remember that Katrina was power hungry. She took her role as sorority president way too seriously."

"What do you mean?"

"Everything had to be her way. If it wasn't, she'd dole out punishments for the girls. Stuff like that."

"These punishments . . . how bad did they get?"

"You mean did anyone get hurt?" Monica clarified.

"Yes." There was no point in sugarcoating the issue. Shawde needed proof, and she needed it now.

"Before I tell you anything else," Monica began cautiously, "exactly who are you and why do you want to know?"

"Katrina used to date my brother. Shemar Williams."

"Right. He died in a car crash."

Shawde swallowed. "Yes. He died. But I'm not entirely convinced it was an accident." She blew out a frazzled breath, then continued. "Look, I want to know if there was ever anything about Katrina that scared you. Or anyone else."

Monica didn't answer right away, and Shawde feared she was going to end the call. "She could be intense," Monica finally said. "There was always this sense of fakeness around her, like her smile wasn't real. If she liked you, she liked you. But if you were on her bad side . . ."

Like my brother. "What happened if you were on her bad side?"

"You'd get extra punishments, attitude."

"What do you know about her relationship with Shemar?"

"Not much. They seemed really close. But if I remember correctly, in the weeks before his death he wasn't coming around the sorority house as much. I figured they were having relationship issues. And . . ."

When Monica's voice trailed off, Shawde sat up straighter. "And what?"

"I don't know if this is true. . . ."

"If what is true?"

"It's just . . . I'd heard from someone that Katrina thought Shemar was seeing one of our sorority sisters. He wasn't. I was friends with the girl in question—"

"Who?" Shawde asked.

"A woman named Angelina Wright."

"Angelina!"

"What—you've heard something?" Monica asked.

"Actually, I wanted to ask you about her. What I heard was that she was attacked on campus. Shortly afterward, she left UB."

A beat. "She was. There was a rapist on campus—"

"And that's why she left?"

Monica paused. Then she sighed and said, "No. She let people believe that, but that's not why she left."

Shawde got to her feet, too tense to sit. "Why did she leave, Monica?"

"Angelina didn't trust too many people in our sorority, and she didn't even trust me with the truth until years later. She made me promise not to say anything."

An idea was formulating in Shawde's head. Had Katrina believed that Shemar was involved with Angelina? Was that why Katrina had murdered Shawde's brother? Mere jealousy?

"Katrina thought Shemar was cheating on her?" Shawde said, a question in her tone. "And you just told me that when you got onto Katrina's bad side you were treated badly."

"Angelina wasn't sleeping with Shemar," Monica said.

"Then why did Katrina believe that?"

"Angelina and Shemar got together to talk a few times. Katrina apparently saw them once, and assumed the worst. I heard her confront Angelina in the sorority house—who denied a relationship with Shemar—but Katrina became insufferable toward her."

"Something else was going on," Shawde surmised. The phone call from Shemar, his cryptic words about Katrina . . . If he'd simply been sleeping with someone else, he wouldn't have called Shawde and told her that he needed to discuss something important. "Do you know what it was?"

When Monica said nothing, Shawde continued. "My brother is dead, and I think Katrina may be behind it. Please—you have to tell me what was really going on."

"Angelina was afraid. That's why she left UB."

"Afraid for her life, you mean?"

"Yes."

"Afraid of Katrina?"

"Look, I really can't betray her confidence."

"Why, Monica?" Shawde pressed. "Shemar was killed, and Angelina was afraid for her life. What's the connection?"

"There was a lot going on that year. One of our sorority sisters had been murdered. Another, a girl named Phoebe, had been implicated. And on top of all that, there was the rapist on the loose."

"Phoebe . . . does she have something to do with this?"

"We had more drama that year than we could handle, and I think all of it influenced Angelina's decision to leave."

Monica was backtracking. Was she afraid, too? "If you're worried that I'm going to tell Katrina that I talked to you, rest assured I won't. Please, I need answers. You believe Katrina's dangerous; I know you do. I need to know why."

"I didn't, at first. I just figured that Katrina was frosty toward Angelina because of Shemar, and that Angelina left because of the rapist, the murder. With all that was going on, I didn't make the connection. Not until I talked to Phoebe once things began to return to normal. She said something, questioned the timing of Shemar's death. She wondered if it was really an accident. What she said to me, it was like she was hinting at something bigger. So I started to rethink things. Katrina's insistence that Angelina and Shemar were involved, the attack on Angelina, then Shemar's death . . . I started wondering if Katrina had committed a crime of passion."

Shawde wrote the name Phoebe on a notepad and circled it. She would try to talk to her. "So it *was* about jealousy? That's what you're saying?"

"That's what I speculated. But as time passed, I figured my imagination was simply running wild. And then, two years after Angelina had left and cut me and everyone at our sorority off, she contacted me out of the blue. I finally had a chance to ask her some questions. She filled in some blanks, but honestly she hasn't told me anything more than vague details."

"Give me something," Shawde said. "I need to know if I'm grasping at straws."

"All I'll tell you is that Angelina was going to report Katrina to the National Pan-Hellenic Council—the national sorority board—because of an issue. She didn't give me details—she felt it was better to keep me out of it."

"Even years later."

"Even years later," Monica echoed.

"But Shemar knew about it. That's why he and Angelina were talking."

"Yes. And right after Angelina threatened to go to the Pan-Hellenic Council, she was viciously attacked. Everyone suspected the Bike Path Rapist, but Angelina told me that she knew it wasn't him. There was no attempted rape, no sexual assault of any kind—which was atypical for the Bike Path Rapist."

"Why didn't she report Katrina to the police?"

"Because she didn't see her attacker. In fact, Katrina had been in the sorority house with a ton of alibis during the attack."

Shawde frowned. Then it came to her. *Of course.* "Katrina had someone else do her dirty work."

"Angelina suspected Katrina's best friend, Rowena, was involved. But Angelina couldn't prove anything. However, after Shemar died, she was sure that there had been a plan to kill her."

Shawde wrote down the name Rowena. Then she frowned. What were the missing pieces? "You don't know why she was going to report Katrina?"

"Even years later, she was afraid to tell me everything. I guess she saw in Katrina something the rest of us didn't. That she was truly dangerous. So dangerous that thousands of miles between them hasn't made Angelina feel safe."

"Wow. So she's afraid that Katrina will *still* hold a grudge at this point?"

"I don't know about now. I haven't talked to her in over two years."

"Damn it," Shawde muttered, deflated. "You're no longer in touch?"

"We haven't spoken, but I have a number for her. And we're friends on social media."

Hope filled Shawde's chest. "She's on social media? I couldn't find her anywhere."

"That's because she changed her name."

"She was so afraid of Katrina that she changed her name?" Shawde asked.

"No, she got married," Monica explained.

"Ah. Of course."

"But she keeps a low profile online—I mean very low. And she's not in touch with anyone from UB. Only me."

"I really need to talk to her."

Monica hesitated. "I can't give out her number."

"But you can contact her for me, ask her to give me a call."

Again Monica hesitated. "Sure. I can do that."

"I'd really appreciate it, Monica. Before Shemar left for home, he told me that he had something serious to tell me about Katrina. He wanted to talk to me in person. He never made it. He was killed in a car with no brake fluid—when he would have definitely checked his car out the day before his drive. He was that kind of guy. What you just told me about Angelina makes me even more convinced that I'm right."

"I'll get in touch with her and let her know that you'd like to talk to her. I'll give her your number. That's the best that I can do."

"Thank you," Shawde said. "My goal is to bring Katrina to justice. Perhaps what Angelina knows will help me do that."

"Perhaps."

Monica sounded wary, and Shawde understood. Clearly, Angelina had been terrified of Katrina. Perhaps she still was.

All the more reason to have the bitch put away once and for all.

Shawde ended the call, feeling truly hopeful about nailing Katrina for the first time in ages. She was so elated that she wanted to call Maurice and tell him about this promising new development.

But she didn't. Because she knew what he would say. If Shawde called him at any point before Katrina was behind bars, Maurice would be frustrated with her. Frustrated with her obsession.

No, she'd made her choice where Maurice was concerned and she knew where she stood.

She had chosen justice for Shemar.

But maybe once Katrina was finally apprehended, Shawde and Maurice could work things out.

And Shawde felt far closer to that goal today than she had ever before.

Excited to tell someone, Shawde called Gordon's number. For the second time today, his voice mail picked up. Where was he?

"Gordon, hi. It's Shawde again. I've got some news that I'm really excited about. And something else for you to look into. It's a bit late now. But call me in the morning. I can't wait to tell you what I've learned."

CHAPTER EIGHTEEN

On Monday, we left for Mexico. And even though I was happy about the idea of spending careless days on the beach and putting my stress behind me, my heart was heavy.

Brian hadn't confirmed one way or another if he would be joining me. I'd given him my flight and hotel details, and all he'd said was that he would try to make it.

I'd quickly agreed to go to Cancun with Katrina and Christian because I'd hoped Brian would join me there. Now I doubted that would happen.

My last two texts to him had gone unanswered, which made it pretty clear that he was avoiding me.

Avoiding me because he didn't want to have to tell me the truth.

Well, if he was playing me, so be it. I wasn't going to give him another thought.

We flew out of Key West at 2:00 p.m., with a short layover in Miami. And at four forty-five Monday evening, our plane touched down in Cancun.

I'd drifted off during the flight but awoke when the plane began to descend. I was in the window seat, and beside me Katrina and Christian were holding hands. And that glimpse of them, seemingly so happy together, made me feel a pang of sadness. I'd had Wesley in my life for so long, and now I knew there was no going back to him. It was an odd feeling to know that I was really alone.

But to numb those thoughts, I looked out the window and took in the view. It was spectacular. I could see white sand and the most stunning turquoise water. I had been impressed when I saw Key West from the sky when our plane took flight, but Cancun was even more beautiful.

"I'm thinking one day we can take a boat to Cozumel," Katrina said. When I glanced at her, she continued. "It's an island off of Cancun. I'd love to see it."

I shrugged. "Sure, if we can swing it."

She had the airline magazine from the seat back in her lap and was rifling through it. "There's also a snorkeling excursion where you get to visit Isla Mujeres. Island of women."

"Island of women," Christian chimed in. "That sounds good."

Katrina playfully whacked his arm. "I'll bet it does."

But he grinned at her, and she at him, and the kiss that followed didn't surprise me. I was no longer surprised by their public displays of affection.

I turned back to the view. The moment the plane touched down, people began to cheer.

And I found myself smiling. I'd left Wesley and all of my baggage back in the States. I was in Mexico, and I was going to make the most of it.

"Why are we renting a car instead of just taking a taxi to the resort?" I posed the question to Katrina, although Christian was the one who'd decided we should rent a car.

Our luggage in hand, Katrina and I were walking a few

feet behind Christian as he led the way to a rental car counter.

"He said he wants to be able to drive around and enjoy the real Mexico," Katrina explained.

"I'm sure the hotel will offer all kinds of excursions," I went on. "Renting a car . . . it might be a waste of money."

We were behind Christian now, and he turned to face me. "I always prefer to rent a car wherever I go. That way, I can just get up and go. Besides, there are excursions we can get to ourselves. Trust me, the hotel will charge you an arm and a leg. Having a car will be far more efficient."

I shrugged. Obviously, Christian had made up his mind. And what the heck? If he was going to be doing the driving, I guessed there was no reason to complain.

It took several minutes for Christian to do the required paperwork. Katrina and I sat on a nearby bench, mostly people watching while we waited. A man beckoned for us to go over to a counter where the sign read: EXPERIENCE MEXICO LIKE NEVER BEFORE! TOUR OUR LUXURY VILLAS.

Katrina waved a dismissive hand. Then she faced me. "Damn, I thought Key West was hot."

"You're the one who wanted to go to Mexico in the summer."

"You regretting that you came?" she asked.

I hesitated a moment. Then I said, "No." And that was the truth. It had been two years since I'd been on a plane, and it was nice to get away. Even if I'd only exchanged one perfectly fine tropical paradise for another.

Christian came over to us, a huge grin on his face. "Okay, ladies. Our chariot awaits."

"You're so goofy," Katrina said, getting to her feet.

As we stepped outside, a blast of hot air hit us. Wow. It was a *lot* hotter than Key West had been.

Then I thought of the most recent winter in Buffalo. A ton of snow and brutally cold temperatures had had me wishing I could hibernate until spring.

Naw, I wasn't going to complain. I could handle the heat.

We followed Christian to the rental car area, where he stopped at a white Chevrolet Malibu. He popped the trunk, then opened the driver's door.

"Start that air-conditioning," Katrina told him.

He did as instructed while Katrina and I worked on putting our luggage in the trunk. Christian joined us, lifting the larger suitcase.

We all piled into the car, me in the backseat. Christian handed Katrina a map. "Hold that, love."

"You know how to get to the hotel?" Katrina asked.

"Yeah. They showed me on the map how to get there. It's not too far. I'm sure I'll find it easily enough."

As Christian drove out of the airport, I looked around at the palm trees and the scenery. My anxiety began to ebb away. I was glad I'd agreed to come.

We were driving for about five minutes before I heard the whir of a siren. I craned my neck to look behind me. Sure enough, there was a cop car behind us, lights flashing, siren blaring.

"Why are we being pulled over?" I asked. "Were you going too fast?"

"No. I was driving under the limit." Christian pulled the car over onto the side of the road and stopped. He wound the window down as the police officer approached.

"Can I see your driver's license, please?" the officer asked. He spoke English perfectly, but with a thick Spanish accent. He looked into the car, seeing Christian and Katrina, then gazed into the backseat where I sat.

"Officer, what's this about?" Katrina asked.

"You were going too fast."

"But I wasn't, sir," Christian protested. "I was driving sixty kilometers an hour."

"But now it is a fifty zone. You were going too fast. Give me your license, please."

"I didn't see any sign indicating a lower speed limit," Christian said.

"You were not paying enough attention," the man said simply. "Please, I need your driver's license."

Sighing, Christian eased up his lower body from the seat so that he could reach into his jeans pocket. "If the speed is just going to change randomly, how is that fair to tourists?"

Saying nothing, the officer took the license, and I glanced over my shoulder again. I saw that there was another officer, one who was standing outside of the cruiser, and I wondered why he was just standing there. Perhaps to make sure none of us caused any problems?

The cop strode back to the other officer, and the two of them conferred for a few minutes. Minutes in which we talked among ourselves, wondering why Christian had been stopped.

"I wasn't speeding," Christian said. "If the limit had changed, why weren't there new signs?"

"It's bullshit," Katrina said. "What—is this what they do? Harass tourists?"

"Maybe he'll let us go with a warning," I commented.

When the officer came back to the car, he looked at each of us in turn before speaking. "Speeding is very dangerous. Many people are killed each year in Cancun because they drive carelessly. The fine for speeding is very high. It will require a court date, and until then, I will have to take your license."

"Take his license?" Katrina exclaimed.

"Señora, you need to be quiet, please. You are not helping the situation."

"It's a simple misunderstanding," Christian said. "If I'd seen another sign with a lower speed limit, I would have of course driven slower."

"That is no excuse, señor."

"Surely you can give him a warning," Katrina said.

"Señora, you are trying my patience. All of you, exit the car."

"No, wait." Christian held up a hand, then faced Katrina. "Kat, let me handle this." He turned back to the officer. "Please, is there anything I can do? As I said, I didn't realize the speed limit had changed. Obviously I agree that speeding is a very serious thing."

"What do you have in mind, señor?" the officer asked. "Because I'm sure it will be a very big inconvenience for to have to go to court. And of course, for me to take your license and this car until the matter is settled."

"Is that seriously how it's done here?" Christian asked.

"Many people come to Mexico, drive like maniacs. When they get a ticket, you know what they do? They go back home and never come back. So, señor, we have become wise. Keeping your license until the matter is settled is the way it's done."

"How much is the fine?" Christian asked.

"The fine, because you're a tourist, is five thousand dollars."

"What?" Katrina and Christian exclaimed at the same time.

"As I said, we take speeding very seriously in Mexico."

"This is insane," Katrina muttered.

"Señora." The officer leveled a hard stare in her direction. "Please do not try my patience."

"Hon," Christian said to her, "just chill."

I stayed silent in the backseat, watching with a knot in my stomach.

Christian finally said, "I'm sorry. I didn't realize I was

speeding. If you let me off with a warning, I promise I'll be more careful. It's my first time in Mexico, and I didn't realize."

I watched the cop as he pursed his lips, the seconds passing. He looked in the car at each of us again and then said, "Perhaps we can come to some arrangement."

"What kind of arrangement?" Christian asked.

"What do you have in mind?" the cop asked.

It was the second time he'd said that, and I quickly caught on. And so did Christian.

"Maybe I can give you a little bit of money. For the fine. Because I can't pay it all."

"How much money?" the cop asked.

"Jesus," Katrina muttered. "This is ridiculous."

The expression on the cop's face darkened. He looked into the car, facing Katrina with steely eyes. "Señora, you are being very disrespectful. Do you know that I can arrest you for interfering with an investigation?"

"No, no, please. That's not necessary." Christian raised a hand, showing his acquiescence. "I have some money." Christian opened his wallet. "Three hundred dollars. American. That's all I can pay."

The officer contemplated Christian's suggestion. Then he looked at Katrina. "What about her? How much does she have?"

This was a shakedown. I'd heard vaguely about corruption in the police force in Mexico. But I'd never dreamed we would experience it. And certainly not so soon after arriving here.

Christian faced Katrina saying, "Babe, how much you have?"

Katrina was angry, but she reached into her purse and opened her wallet. She passed Christian a hundred-dollar bill. "There," she said tersely. "That's all I have."

I knew what was coming before the officer looked my

way. I already had my purse on my lap. And when his eyes met mine, I withdrew my wallet and opened it. "I have . . ." I quickly tallied the cash in my wallet. "I have one hundred and thirty dollars," I said. I pulled out the bills and passed them forward.

Christian took the money from me and passed everything to the officer. Then he asked, "Is this okay? Will it be enough for the fine?"

The officer folded the money into his palm. "Thank you, señor." He pasted a smile on his face as he passed Christian his license. "Enjoy your vacation in Mexico."

Then he wandered off, heading back toward the cruiser.

"Prick!" Katrina yelled.

"Shhh!" Christian put a hand over her mouth to quiet her. "The last thing we need is for him to hear you carrying on." He quickly rolled up the window. "You think he won't come up with a reason to arrest you?"

Katrina's nostrils flared as she looked in the direction of the police car. "You're right," she said after a moment. "But that was bullshit."

"I agree," Christian said, "but there's nothing we could do." He faced me. "I'll give you the money back. I'm sure there's an ATM at the hotel."

"We should complain to someone," Katrina went on.

"Complain to whom?" Christian challenged. "If a cop can bloody well shake down tourists for cash on the side of the road, you think you can trust any of them?"

I didn't bother to say that I had been against renting a car, because it would have been rubbing salt in a wound. Had this been what my anxiety had been about before we'd left Key West? Some sort of premonition that we'd have a run-in with the law down here?

I didn't know, but I was glad that the situation hadn't been worse. "Nothing we can do about it now," I said. "Let's just head to the hotel."

Christian started the car. "From now on, I'll know to slow down, and everything should be fine." He was looking at Katrina, who was still sulking. "The money's not an issue, love. Let's not let this ruin our vacation."

A long beat passed; then Katrina leaned across the seat and gave Christian a kiss on the cheek. "You're right. What's done is done. Let's get to the resort. Because I need a margarita. Like immediately."

CHAPTER NINETEEN

Once we arrived at Serenity, our resort in Cancun, I began to feel a lot better. It was hard to feel anxious when you looked out at turquoise blue water as far as the eye could see and the stretch of pristine white sand. The place was stunning—and, as the name suggested, serene.

The run-in with the cop was all but forgotten as we stepped into the swanky lobby of the hotel. The floors were a polished white marble, and four decorative columns surrounded stylish sofas. Salsa music played over the speaker system.

"This place is spectacular," I said.

Katrina squealed, "It's fabulous! Can you believe we got it for a steal?"

"Ah, there's an ATM," Christian said. "Hold on, love."

I watched Christian head off to the far right, then noticed a group of women entering the lobby from the elevator area. They were wearing bikinis and sarongs and headed to the opposite side of the lobby, which was open to the outside. Sheer curtains billowed in the breeze. Beyond that, I could see a seating area and a tiki hut. And I could hear happy laughter.

It wasn't just finally being at the hotel that had me feeling better. I was also feeling optimistic about Katrina and Christian. The conflict with the cop could have been a stressor to send them into a war zone, but they'd weathered the storm and looked like a happy, amorous couple.

To look at them now, as we followed the bellman through the impressive lobby, no one would ever know that they had a sometimes volatile relationship.

It turned out that our rooms were side-by-side. The travel agent had arranged it. I didn't mind. But I did hope that the walls were thicker here than back at the shop in Key West.

"Which suitcases go in which room?" the bellman asked.

"We'll take care of it," Christian told him. Then Christian began to help the bellman take the suitcases off of the trolley and place them outside of our doors.

The task complete, Christian reached into the back pocket of his jeans for his wallet. He passed the bellman a twenty. I knew it was the smallest bill Christian had, but still, that was a significant tip.

"There you go, mate."

"Thank you, sir."

"De nada," Christian told him. Then Christian turned to me and passed me seven bills. "And here's your money."

"I'll give you back your ten when I can get some change."

"Don't worry about it," Christian said.

Katrina opened their hotel room door. But before she could step inside, Christian scooped her into his arms. She gasped, then let out a playful giggle.

"Oh no, you don't," Christian said. "I've got to carry you across the threshold."

When I saw Katrina kiss his lips, I took that as my cue to open my door and check out my own room. It was beautifully decorated, with bright colors that spoke of the tropics. But the king-sized bed was a glaring reminder that I was here alone.

No, I told myself. *Not alone. You're here with friends.* And maybe I would even end up meeting and hooking up with someone. Why not? I was officially single now. Ready to mingle and move on.

I went back into the hallway to get my suitcase and carry-on bag and saw Katrina and Christian there, too, also getting their remaining luggage.

"Isn't this place beautiful?" Katrina asked me as Christian took the two big suitcases and disappeared into their room.

"Gorgeous," I agreed. "I'm going to head down to the beach. Get a drink and lounge around."

Katrina looked over her shoulder into the room, exchanging a playful look with Christian. "We'll join you later."

"Sure," I said. But I wasn't counting on that. I could see in their eyes that the first order of business was to do some serious screwing before setting foot on the beach. Which was fine with me. I wanted the alone time. "I'll be downstairs whenever you want to find me."

I changed into my bathing suit, secured a red wrap around my waist, plopped the large straw hat I'd bought for this trip on my head, then slipped on my sunglasses. I put a towel and a novel in a beach bag and went downstairs.

As I walked along the pool's patio that led to the stretch of white, sandy beach, I saw eyes flitting toward me. Men were checking me out, which did help my bruised ego. But I kept my gaze straight. Yes, I was open to the idea of meeting someone, but I wasn't ready for that quite yet. I wanted a drink to loosen up and some quiet time to enjoy my stunning surroundings.

The pool area was packed, more than I'd expected at this time of year. There were lots of other college kids, also something I didn't expect. But with school having just finished, I guessed that they were here celebrating. Perhaps celebrating graduation or just enjoying a well-earned break after months of studying.

Ten minutes later, I had a piña colada in hand and a spot at the far end of the beach, away from the crowds, where I had been able to find an available lounge chair. It didn't bother me being so far away from everyone else. In fact, it was exactly what I wanted. It was quieter here.

I sat down and took in the view, determined to enjoy the peace and tranquility. I sipped my drink, then looked down the beach. And as I saw two people walking in the distance, I felt a jolt.

My eyes narrowed. Was that . . . *Brian*?

I pushed up my sunglasses and craned my neck to get the best view I could of the two men. Was the one on the right actually Brian?

Suddenly the men stopped. Then they turned and started off in the opposite direction. And as I watched them walk away, I noticed that my pulse was racing.

Certainly that *couldn't* be Brian.

No, that didn't make sense. We had talked about him coming here. Surely if he had come to Cancun, he would have told me. And we'd be hooking up right now.

But that body . . . This man bore a striking resemblance to the one I'd met in Key West.

Would he have actually come to Mexico and not told me?

As I watched the men become smaller and smaller in the distance, the answer was obvious. He wouldn't.

And yet my pulse was racing, my senses telling me that it was him.

CHAPTER TWENTY

"Are you sure you want me to come along?" I asked.

Hours later, I was back upstairs in the hotel. Katrina and Christian hadn't connected with me downstairs, so I'd knocked on their door to check on them. I half-expected no one to answer, but it took about four seconds for the door to swing open. Katrina, fully dressed, had greeted me with a smile.

Now I was sitting on a chair in their room and Katrina had just extended an invitation for me to go to a bar with her and Christian.

"Of course," Katrina responded.

"We don't want to leave you here all on your lonesome," Christian added.

"I get that. . . . But if you're more in a mood to be a couple than to have a third wheel tag along . . ." It was already weird enough that I was here with them in Mexico. Not that I wasn't enjoying the change of scenery and pace. Key West was beautiful, no doubt about it. But here I was definitely on vacation.

"Nonsense!" Katrina beamed. "We would love to have you come along."

I couldn't help thinking that the Mexico sunshine had certainly done a lot to improve her mood. Both she and Christian were still happy. No sign of any cracks in their relationship to be seen.

"All right," I agreed. "If you insist."

We had dinner at the hotel first. Since we had the all-inclusive package, there was no point in paying for dinner anywhere else. We sat outside, where the ocean breeze was lovely. The entire ambience was beautiful, but with me sitting across the table from Katrina and Christian I still felt like an intruder on their romantic time.

After dinner, we all got ready for a night on the town. I put on a white halter and a denim skirt, an outfit that highlighted my hourglass figure. I was fussing with my hair, making sure it was perfect, when there was a knock on my door.

I exited the bathroom and pulled open the hotel door. Katrina grinned at me. She was wearing a red tube dress that looked as though it had been painted on. Perhaps to make the dress appear a bit more modest, she wore a short denim jacket as well. My eyes ventured to her feet. The red strappy pumps had to be at least four inches high.

Then I looked at my own feet. I was wearing flat sandals, with a bit of bling on the straps. "Do you think I'm underdressed?"

"You look great!"

"But look at you."

She waved a dismissive hand. "You look hot."

"Love the shoes," I told her. "But I couldn't walk in those all night." I'd gone out in heels on numerous occasions and regretted it. Ultimately, I'd decided that I preferred comfort as opposed to feet that hurt for days.

"I'm from Atlanta. I'm used to it."

"I'd want to take those off after an hour."

Katrina shook her head. "That's a no-no. My mama

always said that a lady never takes her shoes off. Make sure you can wear them out, because it's not classy to take them off on a dance floor."

I shrugged. "I didn't realize there was shoe etiquette."

Christian appeared. "You ladies ready?"

I nodded.

"And to put everyone's mind at ease, we'll be taking a taxi," he announced. "I plan on drinking."

It was a catch-22. On one hand, taking a taxi was preferable. Not that I expected we'd have another run-in with the cops so soon, but taking a taxi would eliminate the possibility altogether. On the other hand, if Christian was drinking, he could be unpredictable.

We headed downstairs, where we caught a cab. At dinner, the waitress had suggested a local bar called Tequila Grill, saying that it had a more authentic Mexican flavor than the other establishments on the strip. It was a hip place that played a variety of music, so she thought we would enjoy it.

Authentic Mexican was what we wanted. That's why we'd come to Mexico, instead of hanging out in Key West.

"Tequila Grill," Christian told the taxi driver.

I was in the front with the driver, while Katrina and Christian were in the back. A couple of times, I peered over my shoulder at them and saw them sharing a kiss.

Thankfully, it didn't take long for us to arrive at Tequila Grill. I swear, if the drive had been any longer Katrina and Christian could have ended up naked in the back. I understood that they were into each other, but how could they not rein in their affection even in public?

Christian passed the driver some money. "Thank you, mate."

I exited the car first, my eyes taking in the exterior of the establishment. The nondescript large building was made interesting only by its sign. TEQUILA GRILL was lit up in yellow lights, with a bottle of tequila at the end of the words, also lit up, but in red.

No one checked our IDs as we entered. Stepping inside, I smiled as I glanced around. I liked the place. The decor was still touristy to me—palm trees inside the bar, strings of lights hanging from beams on the ceiling—but it was more rustic than polished, and I liked the decided Mexican flavor.

From the looks of it, the crowd here was a mix of tourists and locals. A group of Mexican men stood together in one corner and checked us out as we walked in. On the far side, I saw men in T-shirts, khaki shorts, and flip-flops—and knew they were American. College kids, I surmised.

"What are you having?" Christian asked me. "I'm buying."

"Get us a round of tequila shooters," Katrina said. "When in Mexico, and especially when in Tequila Grill, tequila needs to be the order of the day." She beamed at him.

"Right, love."

"See that table?" Katrina pointed. "We're going over there."

"Okay," Christian said. Then he gave her a kiss on the cheek before heading off in the direction of the bar.

Katrina began to walk, and I followed her. The good thing about having arrived here before nine was the fact that there were plenty of tables to choose from. I expected that later the place would be filled.

I thought Katrina might sit, but she shucked her denim jacket, put it on the table, then took me by the elbow and began to lead me. A lively Latin tune was playing, and she was gyrating her hips even as she was making her way to the dance floor. Then she turned and faced me, moving her body in a totally sexual way. I tried to match her movements, but I couldn't match her enthusiasm. But I supposed that if I had spent an afternoon getting laid, I would certainly be sexually liberated on the dance floor, too.

When the first man approached us no more than a minute later, I wasn't surprised. Katrina was sex on a stick, winding her body and smoothing her hands over her stomach and hips as if she were begging to feel a man's hands there instead.

I didn't hear what the guy said to her, but I saw her smile. Saw the man place his hands on Katrina's hips and try to dance with her. She extricated herself from him, then came behind me and started dancing, as if to say we were together.

The man watched, pulling his bottom lip between his teeth.

And that's when I felt the hand smooth over my hip. At first I thought it was Katrina, giving this guy a real show. Until I looked to my left and saw a man standing beside me.

"Hey, you want to dance?" he asked, his Mexican accent thick. He looked at me as though I were a tall glass of water on a hot day.

He was one of the short, local guys I had seen when we'd first come in. He came up to about my chin, but apparently that didn't discourage him.

"Um, no."

As if on cue, Katrina took me by the hand and twirled me around.

"I think you need a man," the man said to me when I was facing him again. He reached for my hand. "Dance with me."

"Actually," I began, pulling my hand from his, "I was just heading to the bar."

"Let's go together," he told me. "Whatever you want, I will get it for you." He spoke English well.

"No, that's okay." I started walking off of the dance floor.

"I insist."

"My boyfriend's waiting for me at the bar." I offered him an apologetic smile. "Sorry." Then, before he could say anything else, I hurried off to where I joined Christian at the bar and quickly slipped my arms around his waist in case the man was watching. I had to make it look good.

The bartender was just pouring the last of the three shooters when Christian turned, his eyes widening a little as he saw me. "Oh?" His voice held a note of question.

"Go along," I said. "I'm trying to escape someone."

"Ahhh, of course."

"What took so long, by the way? This place isn't packed."

"I think everyone in here wanted a drink at the same time as I did," Christian said.

I faced the bar and watched as the bartender put three lemons onto a small plate beside the shooter glasses. Christian put the money down onto the counter.

"Excuse me. What's going on here?"

At the sound of Katrina's voice, I turned and let my hand fall from Christian's waist. "Nothing. He was just my decoy so I could escape that other guy."

Katrina was grinning, her expression saying that she got it and that she was just messing with me. But she placed a hand on Christian's back, almost proprietarily.

"Here." Christian lifted two shooters and passed one to Katrina and one to me. Then he passed each of us a lemon as well before lifting the last shooter glass for himself.

"Here's the salt." He licked between his thumb and forefinger and sprinkled salt onto that area. He passed

Katrina the saltshaker and she did the same, and I was the last to complete the first phase of the tequila shot ritual.

Katrina took charge, counting to three, and we all threw our heads back and downed the shooters, then quickly grabbed the lemons and sucked on them immediately afterward to kill the bite of the strong liquor.

I dropped my shooter glass onto the counter with an audible slam, crying, "Ah!" And then, "I could use another!"

Katrina looked at Christian. "Order us another round, will you? We'll be right back." She took me by the arm and started to drag me off.

"Where are we going?" I asked. I didn't want to go back to the dance floor.

"The ladies' room."

The restroom was one of those dark, murky places. For the life of me, I didn't understand why club bathrooms were so often painted black and why the lighting was so poor. I could barely make out how good or bad I looked in the mirror.

"Here."

Turning away from the mirror, where I'd been trying to adjust the lock of curls hanging at the side of my face, I faced Katrina. She unfolded a Kleenex in the palm of her hand. There were little white pills in there, and she extended her palm for me to take one.

"What is this?"

"Ecstasy," she explained, as casually as if she had just said *aspirin*. "Take one."

"Oh, I don't know about that."

"Don't be a wimp. Take one."

"I don't do drugs." It was the one thing I'd refused to partake of in college. Sure, I'd drink. But after the one time I'd smoked pot with Wesley and suffered the most intense bout of paranoia afterward, I'd sworn off all drugs.

"It's just gonna make you feel good. And you could loosen up."

"Why?"

"You seem a bit uptight."

I frowned. "That's not true."

"You can't see it, but everyone else can. Even Christian said that you seem distant."

"How do I seem distant?"

"Come on. Try one. It's no big deal."

I reached for a pill, not wanting to appear uncool. But as my fingertips closed around it, I thought about what I had done for Wesley. How I had, without question, delivered that package of weed because he'd asked me to. I had risked my freedom for a man, and he'd gone ahead and dumped me anyway.

So this time, I knew that I didn't want to follow the crowd or be influenced by anyone to do something that I really didn't want to do. Even if I did appear uptight.

"Maybe later," I told her, a way to soften my rejection of her offering. Then I dropped the pill back into the Kleenex.

Katrina shrugged, nonchalant, as though it didn't bother her. And I hoped it didn't. I should be able to make my own decisions about this without feeling guilt.

I watched her dry swallow a pill before returning the Kleenex to her purse. Then she looked at herself in the mirror, smoothing the short strands of hair at the sides of her face.

"Ready?" I asked.

"Not quite," she said. "You go on without me."

I exited the bathroom. I kept my eyes fixed ahead of me, determined not to talk to any other guys right now. But despite the fact that I didn't want to talk to anyone, a man suddenly stepped into my path.

I glanced up. He was about six foot two, ruggedly

handsome, with dark skin and closely cropped hair. And he had a muscular frame, something that was shown off by the T-shirt he was wearing.

I liked what I saw. There was a little edge to him, a hint of bad boy in his eyes and in the smirk he subsequently laid on me.

My heart began to race. Then, feeling an odd sense of panic, I looked away and kept walking.

"Hello," he said, his voice like silk. He was walking beside me.

"Hello," I replied, not making eye contact with him.

"Where are you rushing to?" he asked.

"The bar," I said. The same line I had given the other man, but this time it was true.

"Why are you rushing like it's last call?" he asked with a hint of humor in his voice.

You seem a bit uptight. "I know. It's just . . . I'm in a relationship."

Damn, maybe I *was* uptight. This guy was easy on the eyes, and I was giving him the brush-off?

"Then where's your man?" came the question. "If you were my girl, I wouldn't leave your side."

That drew a small smile from me, and I faced him. "I appreci—"

He put his arm around my waist, truly startling me.

I looked him in the eye. "I just told you that I have a boyfriend."

"I might have something else you need," he said, confusing me. Then, in a lower voice, he continued. "I've got some *other* stuff. Stuff to make sure you have a good time tonight. A good price."

My eyes widened. Now I knew why I hadn't been drawn to this guy, no matter how cute. I'd sensed he wasn't worth my time.

I wriggled myself out of his arms. "I'm okay."

"You sure? You look like you could use something. . . ."

"Which is why I'm heading to the bar."

I walked faster, my stride strong. First Katrina, now this stranger. Did I have something written on my forehead saying that I wanted to get high?

As I hurried back to the bar, I found myself wishing that I had stayed back at the hotel. I wasn't ready for this, clearly. Wasn't ready to be out in a crowd of happy partiers looking to enhance their evening with drugs. I wanted to be in my hotel room, curled up in bed and watching a romantic comedy on television.

At the bar, I found Christian waiting with our second round of shooters. "Where's Katrina?" he asked me.

"I left her in the bathroom," I explained. "She'll be out in a minute."

He nodded. Then, "I really love her. I know it must seem like I don't sometimes. But I do."

The comment had come out of left field. "Why are you telling me that?"

"Because I know you're concerned. I know Kat pretty much had to twist your arm to get you to come here with us."

Was that why Christian thought that I was uptight— because I'd been unconvinced about going to Mexico with them? "We've all made mistakes," I said to him.

"We're passionate," he went on. "When we love, when we fight. We don't do anything halfway," he added with a chuckle.

"I get it. And it's kind of nice," I found myself saying. "Not when you fight, obviously. But at least when you two fight, it doesn't mean your relationship is over. Not like me and my ex."

I noticed that Christian was looking beyond me, a curious expression in his eyes. And then his face fell. Something was wrong.

I whirled around to see what had gotten his attention. To my surprise, Katrina was with the guy who had just offered me drugs. He was all over her—his hands exploring her back and her ass. He had done the same to me and I had pushed myself out of his arms. But Katrina was throwing her head back and laughing as he groped her. Enjoying the attention.

"Bloody hell!"

Christian charged through the crowd, and I stood back almost helplessly as I watched, fearing the worst. This wasn't going to be good. How could it?

I swallowed as Christian grabbed Katrina by the arm and jerked her away from the guy.

Her laughter died on her lips. Even from where I stood, I could see the fury in her eyes. Then she shoved Christian. And the next thing I saw was a flurry of hands flying everywhere. Christian shoving her back, Katrina slapping him. The guy who'd been pawing Katrina pushed Christian, who stumbled backward. But a moment later Christian stood tall and charged at the other guy—who was at least a couple of inches taller and far more muscular—jamming a shoulder into his stomach. Barely affected by Christian's efforts, the man laughed—then punched Christian in the face, sending him flying into a crowd of women. Gasps and screams erupted.

I raced over to them, jumping in front of Christian just as he righted himself and raised his fists. "Hey!" I yelled, placing a hand on Christian's chest and extending my other hand to keep Katrina and the drug dealer at bay. "Stop it, everyone!"

If Katrina's eyes could kill, Christian would be dead. "Don't you ever put your hands on me again!"

"What the hell are you doing with this guy?" Christian demanded.

"You want to take this outside, bro?" the other man yelled.

Releasing Christian, I moved forward and put my hand on the other man's chest. God only knew what he was capable of. "Please, we don't want any trouble." We were in Mexico, and the last thing we needed was to get into a confrontation with the wrong person. And God knew we didn't want another run-in with the police. "Please."

His eyes held mine for a long moment; then his lips curled in a smile. "Don't worry your pretty little self, sweetie. This dude ain't worth my time."

And with a shrug, he turned and wandered through the crowd. I released a breath I didn't even know I was holding.

"You're an asshole," Katrina said to Christian.

I gave Katrina a warning look, hoping that she would take the hint and let the conflict drop. "Katrina, forget it."

"At least I'm not a whore," Christian spat out.

I glanced around at the onlookers, and that's when I saw two bouncers heading in our direction. "Shit, we need to get out of here."

Panic filled Christian's eyes as he saw the bouncers, too. He reached for Katrina. "Let's go."

She jerked her arm free of his hand. "Like hell," Katrina retorted. "I'm not going anywhere with you."

"You're pissed at me when you're the one acting like a slag? That wanker was all over you, for Christ's sake. And I wasn't even twenty feet away!"

"I'm a grown woman," Katrina shot back. "I can do what I want."

"Katrina," I said in a warning tone. "You want the bouncers to call the cops? After what happened today?"

"Fuck you, Jade!" she snapped. "Stay out of it."

I reeled backward at her harsh words and tone.

"Is there a problem?" one of the two brawny bouncers asked as they reached us. This one was the taller of the two, about six foot one, and built like a linebacker.

"I'm perfectly fine," Katrina said. Then she walked off in the direction of the drug dealer, who was watching us from among the crowd. She wrapped her arms around the man's waist as though they were longtime lovers. She leveled a dirty look at Christian before she snaked her hand around the man's head and forced it down. The next instant she was planting her lips on his.

"Fucking bitch," Christian muttered.

"Christian," I said, reaching for him. But he shrugged away from my touch and stalked toward the club's exit.

So much for our first happy day of vacationing in Mexico. It had just gone to hell.

CHAPTER TWENTY-ONE

I watched Christian leave. Then I marched over to Katrina, confused and angry. Was it the Ecstasy that was making her act so completely irrationally?

The only thing I knew for sure was that I was pissed. I had come to Mexico—at her urging—for a peaceful vacation. Not drama and chaos.

"Katrina, what the fuck are you doing?"

Her eyes lit up, and a smile erupted on her face, as though she were seeing me for the first time. Yeah, the Ecstasy had clearly taken effect already. My gaze went to the guy, who also was also in happyland with Katrina.

Sternly I said, "Can you please get off my friend so I can talk to her for a moment?"

"Feisty. I like it." He stepped back, raising his hands in a sign of surrender. Then blew me a kiss.

Rolling my eyes, I grabbed Katrina by the upper arms and shook her. That's when I noticed the sort of bug-eyed look on her face.

Just how out of it did a person get on Ecstasy? I'd never taken it, so I had no clue what it did to a person. But it had done something. Because Katrina didn't look like herself.

"What are you doing?" I asked, hoping to talk some sense into her. "You just sent Christian away—for this guy. A stranger. Why did you start making out with him like that?"

Katrina leaned in close and whispered, "He wanted to give me something. And he had to use his mouth."

Was this how they exchanged the drugs? From each other's tongues? I felt sick.

"Christian left," I told her.

Katrina shrugged.

"Look, whatever game you're playing, you need to realize that it's dangerous. First of all, you already know Christian has a temper." I respected that he'd left before doing something worse, which I almost couldn't blame him for at this point. In fact, I was seeing Katrina in a new light. If this was how she acted with Christian, it wasn't hard for me to believe that she had pushed him to violence. "Second, you can't just let strange guys—"

"Relax; Christian will be back. You know it, and I know it. He always comes back."

As I stared at Katrina, my anger grew. She wasn't completely out of her mind. She was doing this on purpose. Pushing Christian as far as she could just to see how much he would put up with? What a bitch.

But it wasn't my life; it was hers. I couldn't control her, and I didn't want to.

In fact, maybe I didn't even want to work for her anymore. I didn't need to be caught up in her drama. As if I didn't have enough of my own.

She stepped away from me and looked around, as though searching for the pig she had just exchanged saliva with. I too looked for him. The guy had given me a bad vibe from the moment I'd met him, and I hoped that he was gone.

I saw him nowhere.

But as my eyes scanned the place, I saw someone else. And this time, I knew I wasn't imagining him.

Brian!

He *was* here. In Mexico.

And he was heading in my direction.

I was dumbfounded.

And pissed.

Brian really was here?

My stomach lurched with anxiety when his gaze connected with mine. No doubt about it, he was making his way toward me through the crowd. I could hardly believe my eyes.

"Jade," he said, and opened his arms, expecting me to hug him.

Was he for real? "You're here?" I asked. "And you didn't tell me you were coming?"

"I wanted to surprise you."

I gaped at him. "Surprise me? After you're the one who suggested meeting me here?" I paused. "I thought you weren't coming. I thought . . ."

"That I was leading you on?" he supplied.

I turned, giving him my back at the bar.

"What—you're that mad at me?" he asked.

"You're playing games with me. I don't like games."

"All right, I can see why you're unhappy. I didn't think. I just figured I'd show up, and—"

"How did you even know I was here?" I asked, gesturing to the bar. "I certainly didn't get to tell you that."

"Coincidence."

I narrowed my eyes. "Where are you even staying? You know what, forget it. I don't want to know."

Brian edged into the space beside me at the bar and gently placed a hand on the small of my back. And damn, was I insane? Because that simple touch flooded my body with heat.

"Don't touch me," I said, and eased away from him.

Despite my body's reaction, I didn't want to be a fool. His behavior wasn't adding up.

He raised his hands. "All right. I get it. I should have told you I was definitely coming. I'm sorry."

He was quick to own up to his flaws, which was a good quality. But I didn't want a guy who figured he could keep disappointing me and simply apologize to make everything better. "I thought I saw you on the beach today," I said. "With another guy. Near the Serenity Resort."

"I'm staying at a resort near that one," Brian said. "Yeah, I was out checking out the beach with my buddy, Keith. I told him I was coming to Mexico, and he decided to come with me."

"Did you see me? Did you see me and turn the other way?"

He shook his head. "No. If I saw you, I would have approached you. You're the reason I came here, Jade."

A few beats passed. I stared at him. Studied him, really. He said the right things, but something was off. "I don't get you," I said.

He put his hand on the small of my back again, and just like the first time, my body reacted. I felt the stirring of arousal in my gut.

"What if I said that something's going on that I can't tell you about? That I need you to take a leap of faith and trust me. Can you do that?"

His touch was distracting me. Maybe I didn't really care what his excuse was. I wasn't looking to make a love connection, but I could definitely see myself making a sexual one with him. Something about Brian made my whole body come alive.

"A fitness trainer with such secretive work?" I asked, my voice laced with sarcasm.

"I will admit that I'm not a fitness trainer."

"What do you really do?"

Brian grinned, the kind of grin that made me realize he had a few secrets. My brain told me that I should run, not walk, away from him.

"It's not something I want to get into right now."

"Is it legal?" I asked.

"Definitely legal."

"Then why can't you tell me about it?"

"This isn't the time," he said simply. And then his hand began to move up my back. When it got to my neck, he trilled my skin with his fingers.

"When is the time?" I managed to ask, surprised my voice even escaped my lips.

"After we get to know each other a bit better," he whispered into my ear.

My eyelids fluttered shut. Sex first, questions later? Was that what he was proposing?

Slowly, my eyes perused his body. How did he make a simple T-shirt look so good? His black shirt hugged his muscular chest and highlighted his biceps. His jeans were also black, and damn if his thighs didn't look incredible. He looked even better than the first time I'd met him.

"Where's that drink, bro?"

At the sound of the foreign voice, I glanced beyond Brian. There was a man standing began him, the same one who'd been walking on the beach with him. He was a little taller than Brian, with darker skin.

"Sorry, Keith," Brian said. He faced his friend quickly before meeting my eyes again. "I got distracted."

I swallowed. Why was I so fiercely attracted to this guy?

"This is Jade," Brian went on. "The woman I told you I was coming here to surprise."

Keith's eyes lit up, as if he was excited to finally meet me. "Ah, you're the famous Jade. Hello. I'm Keith."

"Hello," I said, and shook the hand he offered me.

"Adele," Brian said as a new song began to play. "This is a great song. Want to dance?"

"I don't know, Brian."

He took my hand in his. "Trust me," he whispered.

I swallowed. Then I said, "All right."

Brian led me to the dance floor, where we danced close to each other but not touching. His eyes were so striking, light brown in color, and as he regarded me I could feel the heat emanating from his gaze.

Leaning forward, he whispered, "You're beautiful."

Glancing away, I smiled bashfully. Two simple words had me feeling giddy inside. Suddenly I understood why Katrina was so giggly around Christian—when things were good between them. It was that attraction to a new person that had you euphoric, something I'd forgotten after dating Wesley for so long.

One dance turned into two, and when a slow song began to play, Brian didn't hesitate. He pulled me into his arms.

And Lord, the feel of his strong hands on my back and the way his hard chest pressed against my breasts sent my body into overdrive.

I wanted to get naked with him.

But wanting that and going for it were two different things.

An upbeat hip-hop tune began to play, and we pulled apart. I glanced beyond Brian then and saw Katrina about ten feet away. I'd pretty much forgotten about her and was surprised to see her chatting with Brian's friend, Keith.

"Looking for someone?" Brian asked me.

"I just realized that the friend I came here with is talking to your friend."

Brian glanced over his shoulder, then faced me again. "Talking. Is that what you call it?"

I jerked my head in Katrina's direction again. No longer just talking, she was acting like the high school slut, gyrating against Keith. As I watched in horror, Katrina ran her hand down his chest to his waistline, then kissed him on the cheek.

"Oh God," I uttered.

"Is she always like that?"

"I've never seen her act like this before." I cringed when I saw Keith remove Katrina's hand before it lowered to his groin. At least he wasn't one of those guys who would take advantage of an inebriated girl throwing herself at him. "Shit, she is totally out of control. Even your friend can't handle her."

"Keith is fine."

"I'm sorry about that," I said.

"Don't apologize," Brian said. "Your friend is grown. So is Keith."

"Katrina's not normally like this. I think she took some—" I stopped short, realizing that I'd been about to blurt out that Katrina had consumed drugs. Not a smart idea, even if Brian was a happy tourist who wouldn't care about illegal activity.

"Hmm?" Brian prompted.

"Um." I paused to think. "She took some pain medication with her alcohol," I lied. "She had a migraine before we left the hotel. She should know better, but . . ." My voice trailed off, and I shrugged.

"Enough about your friend," Brian said. "Can I finally get you that drink?"

"I guess I'll have a margarita," I told him.

He took my hand and we walked together through the crowd, past the happy guests who were pumping their bodies to the music. It felt nice, him holding my hand like that.

And it was nice to feel wanted.

He'd asked me to trust him. And that was what I was doing. Because the way he was making me feel, I just couldn't believe that he was lying to me.

CHAPTER TWENTY-TWO

A short while later, Brian and I were on the dance floor, working up a sweat, when Keith came over to us. I thought he was going to address Brian, but instead Keith spoke to me.

"I think your friend might need you," he said.

I narrowed my eyes. "What's the matter?"

"She went into the bathroom about fifteen minutes ago," Keith answered. "Said she wasn't feeling well, and she hasn't come out."

"Shit," I uttered. Then, "Excuse me for a minute?"

I took a step, but Brian put a hand on my arm, stopping me. I faced him. "What?"

"By the way, did you tell Katrina that we met before?"

I shook my head. "No."

"Then let's keep that between us."

I narrowed my eyes. "Why?"

"I have my reasons."

More secrecy. "I don't understand."

"I'll explain later, I promise. Just . . . don't tell her we met before. Trust me," he added.

"You're asking a lot." Perhaps too much. When Brian

said nothing, just gave me an imploring look, I said, "Fine. All right."

I made my way to the bathroom. Inside, two girls, both with dirty blond hair, stood in front of the sink, adding more mascara to eyes that definitely had enough. The two made me think of those girls from *Jersey Shore*— identical hot messes. But they smiled at me, and I returned the smile.

A quick glance beneath the doors told me that all three stalls were occupied. "Katrina?" I called out.

No answer.

When I called her name again and still got no answer, I waited. I figured she was in a stall, trying to compose herself. Or possibly puking.

One after the other, the stalls emptied. But Katrina hadn't been in any of them.

Frowning, I made my way back out to the club floor. And that's when I saw Katrina, standing against the wall at the back of the restaurant.

I started over to her. As she saw me, she eased off of the wall, and I noticed her sway. No surprise there.

"Katrina," I said as I reached her. "Why are you standing over here? Are you okay?"

"I don't feel so good."

"Maybe we ought to go."

She mumbled something unintelligible.

Shit, she was out of it. I took her by the elbow and started leading her back toward Brian and Keith. I wasn't impressed. I would have to get her back to the hotel, which undoubtedly would throw a kink in my plan to get naked with Brian.

"I don't want to leave," she said as I walked with her.

"You're not feeling well, and I'm sure Christian is looking for you."

"I'm fine." She slurred her words.

"Christian hasn't come back in since your fight. We need to find him."

"Christian's fine."

"Obviously, you're inebriated out of your mind, because I know you're not this callous."

She said nothing as I led her back over to Brian and Keith. Brian's warm smile immediately set me at ease. He was strong and gorgeous, and I got the sense from him that he was a take-charge kind of guy who would protect a woman.

Maybe he would be willing to help me get Katrina back to the hotel . . . then we could continue with our evening.

"Is she okay?" Brian whispered in my ear.

I shrugged. "She seems okay." Then I groaned. "I'm so embarrassed by her behavior tonight."

"You said she's not normally like this?"

"The truth is, I'm not totally sure what she's like." When Brian gave me a curious look, I explained, "I only met her recently. Like a couple of weeks ago."

"And you're already on vacation with her?" Brian asked.

"She's a friend of my sister's. My sister's the one who set it up for me to work at her café in Key West. They knew each other in college, and I'm guessing Katrina has really changed since then. My sister doesn't drink excessively, nor do drugs."

Brian's eyes widened. "Drugs?"

Shit! But if I tried to backtrack now, I knew I would look stupid. So I told him a half-truth. "Some guy offered her something earlier. I don't know what it was, but ever since then she has totally not been herself. I think I should get her back to the hotel."

"You want me to go with you?"

Brian didn't even hesitate when he asked the question, which made my heart fill with happiness. The situation with Katrina wasn't turning him off. I smiled, but when

I spoke I tried not to sound too excited. "Sure. If you want to."

"Picture time!" Katrina leaped in front of us, her smartphone already raised high.

"No pictures," Brian said.

"Come on," Katrina insisted.

Brian shook his head. "I'd rather not."

Katrina, giggling, snapped the picture anyway. The flash went off, blinding me.

"I just asked you not to take my picture," Brian said. "Can you please delete that?"

"What's the big deal?" Katrina asked.

"I don't like my picture ending up on social media," Brian responded.

"I promise not to post it on Facebook or Twitter," Katrina said, and made the sign of a cross over her chest. "Okay?"

"I'd prefer you delete it."

And with Brian's insistence I felt niggling doubt in my gut. Did he not want to appear on social media because he was afraid of *who* might see the picture? Like a girlfriend or a wife?

"Is it really that big of a deal?" I asked him.

"Keith, smile," Katrina said. When Keith posed, Katrina snapped his photo. Then she faced Brian. "Keith isn't making a fuss. Why are you?"

Brian snaked his arms around my waist and pulled me close. "Trust me," he said.

"That picture's just for you," I heard Keith say. "I don't want that posted online anywhere."

"What is it with you two?" Katrina narrowed her eyes with suspicion. "Are you two criminals or something?"

"We're just private people," Keith replied.

My stomach fluttered. *Were* they criminals? And why didn't he want me to tell Katrina that we'd met in Key

West? God only knew who they really were. I'd met Brian in Key West; then he'd mysteriously disappeared. At the time, I'd thought that it was another woman who'd sent him running, but what if it was a drug dealer? Someone Brian owed money to? We were in Mexico, after all. Maybe I was being judgmental, but how did I know that he wasn't involved in the drug trade?

"What are you thinking in that pretty head of yours?" Brian asked. "Because I see the wheels turning."

"I'm thinking that you have a lot of secrets," I answered, not meeting his eyes.

"Look at me," Brian said.

Slowly, I raised my gaze to his. Mixed with the desire I saw in his light brown eyes I also saw honesty. My gut told me I could believe him.

"I'm not lying to you about what matters. Now isn't the time to talk, but I will tell you everything." He stroked my cheek. "When the time's right."

Katrina, getting a second wind, wasn't ready to leave. So Brian got me another drink, and we continued dancing. I was feeling no pain, as they say, another margarita having given me a nice buzz and a feeling of being free.

I wanted sex. And I wanted it with Brian.

But Katrina's second wind didn't last more than twenty minutes. Looking ashen, she approached me and Brian on the dance floor and tugged on my arm. "I feel like shit."

"What's wrong?"

"I'm gonna puke."

"Damn it," I muttered. "You want me to go with you to the bathroom?"

"I just want to go," she whined.

"We'll go with you," Brian said. "Help you get Katrina back to your hotel."

"Oh, thanks." I tried to hide my smirk of satisfaction. I was sure he was offering more than that, but either for his sake, Katrina's, or mine, he was playing like he didn't have designs to get me into bed back at the hotel.

We all made our way out of the club. Once outside, Katrina asked, "Where's Christian?"

Honestly, I wanted to throttle her. Now that she was sobering up, she suddenly gave a damn about her boyfriend?

I only drank alcohol, and even the one time I got stoned I was aware of everything going on around me. I never got so shit faced that I didn't know what was happening, and it pissed me off that Katrina was so self-centered that she had caused a scene with Christian, disrespected him in grand style, then let him leave without a second thought until now.

"He's probably back at the hotel," I told her. *But if he knows what's good for him, he'll be on a plane back to England.*

"I was a total bitch, wasn't I?"

"Yeah, you were." No point sugarcoating the truth. Covering crap with honey didn't make it any more appealing."But I'm sure Christian will be back at the hotel, waiting for you."

As usual. It had to be the sex that kept him around, because what I was learning about Katrina was far from appealing. What guy in his right mind put up with being disrespected and humiliated if not for some amazing sex between the sheets?

Keith flagged down a taxi that was pulling up in front of the restaurant, and moments later he was opening the door for all of us. The night air was cool and sobering. But even so, I still knew I wanted to get laid. My perception of Brian hadn't changed with a clearer head.

I got into the back of the taxi beside Brian. He pulled me onto his lap, surprising me, and I made a little *oomph* sound. Then in came Katrina. Kevin took his seat beside the driver.

As the taxi started off, Brian reached up to curl a hand around my neck and urge my head down. My heart began to thud—hard. And then he began to kiss me, right there in the backseat of the taxi, with Katrina beside us.

My whole body tingled with desire. His tongue swept over mine, hot and urgent. I let go of any reservations and kissed him back with abandon, letting him know that I was his for the night.

CHAPTER TWENTY-THREE

I was sitting beside Brian when the taxi pulled up to the hotel—after I had been admonished by the driver for sitting on his lap—but we were snuggled close and holding hands. All of my reservations were gone. I was, as he'd asked me to, trusting him.

"Here we are," I said when the taxi came to a stop, my voice fluttery. "This is our hotel."

Katrina gripped my arm. "Jade, I feel awful."

I faced her. "We're at the hotel now. We're going to get you upstairs."

"No," she said, and I heard a hint of panic in her tone. "I don't want strangers going upstairs with us."

I quickly glanced at Brian, before facing Katrina again. She had both hands on her stomach and an expression of pain on her face. "It'll be okay," I told her.

"No, it's *not*," she told me, an edge to her voice. "I need you tonight, Jade. I feel like I'm going to die."

"It's okay," Brian said. "We can see each other later."

"But—"

He opened the door and got out of the taxi. As I got out

after him, he went around to the other side of the car to help Katrina out. She stumbled in her heels, and Brian caught her before she fell. She began to wail.

The bellman looked in our direction, and I inwardly groaned. I was so humiliated!

Brian walked Katrina over to me, and she quickly wrapped her arms around my shoulders, clearly needing me to even stand upright. She was whimpering.

"Brian—"

"Take care of your friend," he said to me. "She needs a lot of water. And get some crackers into her. Or French fries. Some sort of starch."

My stomach plummeted. He was leaving?

"But . . ." My voice trailed off. Suddenly I felt like a fool voicing what I wanted. Didn't he want the same thing?

"We'll connect later," he said.

"When?" I asked.

But I wasn't even sure if he heard me, because Katrina began to wail like some wounded animal. "Jade, please! I've got to get to the room."

As I secured an arm around Katrina's waist, I saw Brian head back into the taxi. He was leaving.

Katrina swayed, and I tightened my arm around her. Her wailing faded to a groan. "Why did I drink so much?"

I heard the taxi door shut. A quick look in that direction and I saw the taxi starting off. Brian waved.

Katrina's inebriated state had cost me a night with a guy I was really into.

And then it hit me, the mistake I'd made. I hadn't let him know that I had my *own* room. He no doubt assumed that I was sharing a room with Katrina . . . and who would want to get busy with a drunk in the next bed?

Was he going to call me later? Tomorrow, after Katrina slept off her hangover? And why did it feel like Brian was disappearing from my life once again?

Because he didn't even tell you the hotel where he's staying, was the thought that popped into my head. I felt like a puppet on a stick—a stick Brian had control of.

He'd left me in Key West, and he was leaving me again in Mexico. Rightly or wrongly, I was feeling rejected.

Maybe he just wasn't that into me.

My disappointment was palpable as I walked through the front doors of the hotel with Katrina. The staff at the front desk gave us concerned looks.

"It's okay," I told them.

"You're sure?" one of the men asked.

"Yep." I forced a smile. "I can get her to the room."

I helped Katrina to the elevators, consoling myself with the fact that Brian hadn't intentionally abandoned me. With the chaos of Katrina feeling ill, Brian had simply forgotten to tell me where he was staying. And obviously a decent guy wouldn't expect me to cast aside my friend in order to spend a few hours in bed with him.

Maybe he'd have his cell phone on so that I could reach him, despite the outrageous roaming fees. Or maybe he planned to connect with me tomorrow.

Had I even given him my last name? Would he be able to find me at the hotel?

Where there was a will, there was a way.

My heart filled with hope. He said he had come to Cancun because of me. Which meant he would find me, one way or another.

I believed that he would. Because surely what I'd felt with him wasn't one-sided.

"I think I'm okay to walk on my own," Katrina said, and eased away from me.

"You're sure?" I asked.

"Uh-huh."

As we continued to the elevators, I noticed that she was far steadier on her feet. Miraculously so.

She pressed the UP button. Then casually said, "I know you like Brian, but I don't trust him."

"What?"

"There's something shady about him and Keith. And what's with him being all over you and not wanting to take any pictures with you?"

I stared at Katrina, realization dawning. "Minutes ago, you looked like death warmed over."

"I had to get rid of them, Jade."

Anger began to brew inside of me. "That was all an act?"

The elevator arrived, and Katrina walked onto it. "You'll thank me later."

I wanted to punch her in the face. Instead, I stood outside of the elevator, glaring at her.

"Are you coming in?" she asked me.

"No." I turned.

"He's long gone, Jade!" Katrina called out to me.

That manipulative bitch! She was enjoying this.

Balling my hands into fists, I kept walking. Because I didn't want to say something I would regret.

I sat in the lobby, trying to cool off. But also hoping. Hoping that Brian would show up at the hotel in an effort to connect with me.

Of course, he didn't.

I went upstairs about an hour later and found a slip of paper stuck in my door. I pulled it out, opened it, and read:

Christian's not here. I'm worried.

"Now you're worried?" I asked sarcastically. Crumpling the note as I entered my room, I couldn't help hoping that Christian had come to his senses and left. Katrina had some serious issues.

But as much as I hoped that, I was certain that he would be back by the morning and he and Katrina would have incredible makeup sex.

Although after Katrina's behavior last night, if Christian had even a semblance of a brain he would be gone.

And never come back.

I was asleep in my hotel room when the sound of frantic knocking on my door jarred me awake. At first, I thought I was having a bad dream. Then, in my barely conscious state, I was seized with panic, fearing that someone was trying to break into the room.

But then I heard: "Jade! Open up!"

Katrina?

The pounding continued, and I scrambled out of the bed and opened the door.

"Jade, he's not back," Katrina said without preamble.

I had been jarred from sleep and wasn't entirely coherent. "What?"

"Christian. He's not back."

"What time is it?" I asked groggily.

"About quarter to six."

"Fuck, Katrina." My brain was slowly waking up, and I couldn't contain my anger. "Why would you come to my room at this time in the morning?"

She bit down on her bottom lip, and that's when I saw that her eyes were puffy and misted with tears. She'd been crying. Was she really this worried? Or was it simply the aftereffects of the alcohol that had her so emotional?

"I—I'm sorry," she said. "But I'm worried."

I felt bad for my harsh reaction. "It's early," I told her. "I'm sure he's fine." And then, "Maybe just making you sweat for what you did. Last night was pretty crazy."

Hugging her torso, Katrina nodded. "I was so stupid."

"That's a gentle way of putting it." Perhaps if it had

been later, and I hadn't been jarred from sleep, and *she hadn't* deliberately sabotaged my night with Brian, I could sugarcoat my feelings over Katrina's behavior. But she needed a reality check, big-time. "What were you doing, Kat? Playing some sort of bizarre mating game with Christian? To make him jealous and cause serious drama? Is the sex only good when you two are fighting?"

Her face crumbled. "Oh God. What if he's found someone else?"

Then he's not as dumb as I thought, was the thought that popped into my mind. But I said, "I'm sure he'll be back. That's what you told me at the club yesterday, remember? That Christian always comes back."

Katrina nodded, but her expression said she wasn't entirely convinced.

"Look, I've got to go back to bed. But call my room or come back if you hear anything. If he returns to the room and he's angry, feel free to come back here," I added, acting more gracious than I felt. But I had a few more days with her here in Mexico, and I didn't want there to be tension between us. "In fact, if you want to sleep in the extra bed, you're more than welcome."

Katrina shook her head. "No, that's okay. I'd better go back to my room. If Christian comes back and I'm not there, I don't want him to be angrier. I think our stupid fight has played itself out."

"I'm sure it has," I agreed.

Katrina turned to walk away but then suddenly faced me again. "I caught him sexting an ex."

"What?" I asked.

"That's why I was . . . trying to make him jealous last night. He'd been sexting an ex-girlfriend in England. Obviously, I was pissed. So I just wanted to make him jealous, too."

I looked at her—and didn't believe her.

I'd seen her and Christian together from the time we left Key West, and I hadn't detected a hint of conflict. They'd been amorous until the time we got to the restaurant.

If Katrina had caught Christian sexting, surely I would have seen some anger on her part before her antics at the club.

"I just wanted you to know," she said. "So you don't think I'm a total bitch."

I covered my mouth as I yawned. "It's fine," I said. Obviously, she was trying to make herself look better by coming up with a lie to explain her behavior. But I wasn't about to get into it with her. "Go back to bed. I'm sure that by the time you wake up, Christian will be back, and you guys will work things out."

CHAPTER TWENTY-FOUR

My eyes popped open when I heard the pounding on my door. For a moment I wondered if I'd been dreaming about what had happened earlier when Katrina had come to my door.

But as I lay still, listening, I thought I heard the sound of sobbing. Then the pounding started again.

Throwing the covers off, I looked at the digital clock. It was ten forty-three. Time to get a strong coffee if I was going to have to deal with more drama today.

With a sigh of exasperation, I went to the door. I could guess what was happening. Christian wasn't back. And Katrina was beside herself over that reality.

But the truth was, I wasn't surprised. I could only imagine that after last night Christian realized that he didn't want to end up in jail over a woman who was intentionally pressing his buttons.

I opened the door a crack, my lips parting to tell Katrina that she needed to calm down. But before I could speak, she did.

"He's dead!" she shrieked.

A moment passed. Then another. Time seemed to have

slowed down. I blinked, certain that I hadn't heard her say what I thought she'd said. "What did you say?"

Katrina pushed herself into the room, then spun around to face me. "He's dead, Jade! Someone killed him. Oh my God!"

A cold chill swept over me. I heard the words now, loud and clear, but there was a disconnect. I couldn't comprehend them. "Who?" I asked. "Who's dead?"

"Christian!"

I shook my head, not believing what she was saying. "Kat, if he isn't back yet, maybe he's not coming back. Your fight last night . . . it was major. I'm sorry, but I can understand if Christian has had enough."

"Listen to me, goddamn it! I just got off the phone with the police. They found Christian's ID. That led them to the hotel, and to me. His body was found. . . ." Her voice cracked. "He's dead, Jade. And it's all my fault!"

The police? She'd spoken to them? My chest constricted and my head swam. This wasn't Katrina just being paranoid, which had been my initial thought. I had assumed that in her quest for drama she had created some scenario where something bad had happened to Christian since last night, as opposed to the fact that he'd come to his senses and left her in Mexico.

"You talked to the police?"

"Yes!" She sounded hysterical.

"Kat, this doesn't make any sense." My mind refused to accept her words. Just yesterday, we'd arrived in Mexico. How could Christian be dead?

"I spoke to the police, Jade," she reiterated. "You think I'd come in here and make up a story like this?"

"No, of course not." I drew in a breath but found it hard to breathe. It was like a black cloud had suddenly enveloped the room. "They're absolutely sure?"

Katrina moved toward me now, wrapped her arms

around me, and started to sob against my shoulder. I felt odd, cold, consumed with disbelief.

"Oh God, Katrina." I gasped, the news finally seeming to hit me like a sledgehammer to the gut. "How?"

"He was found . . . he was found . . . behind . . . he was behind the club." Katrina struggled to get the words out. "His throat—his throat was slashed. Cut from ear to ear."

She croaked, then went to my bed and collapsed, her despair overwhelming her.

As I watched her curl into a fetal position, her words slammed into me with the force of a train. "You're saying someone slashed his throat?"

"They want me to go to the station, identify him. They . . . they took pictures."

I swallowed, the horrific image of Christian with his throat slashed making my knees buckle. But still, I didn't want to believe it. "If you haven't seen the body, it might not be him. You can't be sure. Maybe someone stole his ID and that's why the police think it's Christian."

"His picture is on his ID," Katrina continued. "They must . . . they have to . . ." Her voice trailed off, and she began to wail.

Katrina was right. Certainly the police would have matched the picture to the victim.

My stomach twisting painfully, tears began to sting my eyes. I hadn't known Christian all that long, and I didn't wish him dead.

"I don't even want to go to the police station," Katrina said. "After what happened when we were leaving the airport, how can we even trust them? They're totally corrupt."

"This isn't vulnerable tourists in a rental car. This is a murder. The murder of a foreigner." I paused. "We have to go the station, Katrina. We have to be sure."

A chill swept over me, and I shuddered. That guy in the bar! The one Katrina had been dancing with and kissing.

He'd gotten into that ugly fight with Christian. Had he gone outside to finish what he'd started—with no witnesses?

But to kill someone you didn't even know over something so ridiculous? A part of me couldn't believe—*wouldn't* believe—that this was true. "Kat, I know what you heard is terrifying, but let's try to stay positive. Until we get to the police station and know for sure. There could be some mistake."

Katrina sat up and brushed at her tears, looking as though she was lost in a world of grief. "Christian didn't want to come here. He said there were so many problems with drugs. Tourists getting killed."

I remembered something very different. Christian promoting the idea of a trip to Mexico. And to think that at the time I'd suspected he might want to do harm to Katrina . . .

"That's what you think?" I asked. "You think he got caught up in drugs? Because I only saw him drinking—"

"All I know is that he's dead!"

I flinched from the velocity of Katrina's voice, but the next moment she was weeping again.

I'd been trying to offer her a shred of hope to cling to, but I wasn't succeeding in making her feel better. Until we knew for sure, there was simply nothing I could to do alleviate her grief. Clearly, she wasn't the type to try to hold on to a smidgen of hope.

And maybe with good reason. Maybe I was the one who was being naïve in wanting to keep any shred of hope intact.

I sat on the bed beside her and gently touched her back. "Kat, I'm so sorry." It was all I could say. "I'm here for you, okay. I'll go to the police station with you. We'll deal with this together."

"Why would anyone do this?" she sobbed.

Again I thought about the man she had been dancing

with in the bar the night before. The man she had been leading on in her game of drama.

Had it been a game that had cost Christian his life?

The trip to the police station seemed endless. I had thought that the police would send an officer to pick us up, but instead we had to make our way there.

Katrina was a mess, crying nonstop in the cab, while I sat numbly. Somehow I kept myself composed. Because I didn't want to believe it until we knew for sure. When we got to the police station, we would have real proof. Until then, I clung to the hope that this was all a misunderstanding.

The taxi pulled up to the police station, which was a beige-colored one-level building. The words POLICE STATION were in huge letters and also in English. Below were the Spanish words ZONA HOTELERA.

I felt a little better. This was the police station for a highly populated tourist destination. It wasn't a decrepit building in the middle of nowhere.

Katrina was still too emotional to speak, so I took the lead. I went to the front desk, where a female officer sat. She looked up at me as I approached her.

"Hello," I said. "Um, my friend and I were told to come here. Her . . . her boyfriend went missing last night. The police think they may have found his body." I swallowed, unsure of my words. But never in my life had I ever expected to have a conversation even remotely like this, and I had no clue how to go about it.

"Your name?"

"I'm Jade Blackwin. And my friend is Katrina Hughes."

The woman gestured to the seating area. "Please, have a seat."

Taking Katrina by the arm, I led her to the far side of

the room, where we sat in well-worn cushioned chairs.
There was a blond woman in here, her eyes red rimmed.
Two Mexicans were handcuffed to their chairs and sitting
on the opposite side of the room. Two male tourists also
sat in the waiting area, both of them also handcuffed to
their chairs. One had a black eye.

"We've been here for hours," the man with the black eye
said. "Good luck getting any justice in this country. Can't
trust the Federales!"

I edged closer to Katrina, feeling very uneasy. We were
in a strange country and in a horrible situation. And de-
pending on what we learned, the situation would either get
better or get a hell of a lot worse.

I watched the female officer as she spoke to someone
on the phone. All I understood was, "Si, señor."

And then, despite the fact that we had arrived after
the other people in the waiting area, the female officer
called our names: "Katrina Hughes and Jade Blackwin!"

My heart began to thud as my unease intensified. Why
would we be called ahead of the others here . . . unless it
was bad news?

"Please come to this door."

By the time we got there, it was opening. A man appeared, about six feet tall. He offered his hand, and I
shook it.

"Hello. I am Second Sergeant Roberto Ramirez."

He offered his hand to Katrina, but she didn't take it.

"Come this way," the sergeant said.

We followed him through the door, into an area where
some police officers were at desks doing paperwork and
working on the computers.

The sergeant's office was to the right. He entered, and
we followed him. Then he gestured to the two chairs opposite his desk.

"Sit."

I sat, but Katrina didn't. "Please, I need to know," she said. "I can hardly breathe."

"Please, sit," Sergeant Ramirez reiterated. "We will discuss."

Moaning softly, Katrina sat beside me. Her butt was perched on the edge of the chair, and she was leaning toward the desk. She was literally on edge. As was I.

I knew that like me, she was hoping the sergeant would tell us news that would change everything for the better. That it wasn't Christian who had been found but another man.

Second Sergeant Ramirez sat and opened a folder on his desk. "You are the one I spoke to at the hotel?" he asked.

Katrina nodded. "Yes, that was me." She paused briefly. "My friend here . . . she said that maybe you're wrong. That it's another man you found. Not Christian."

The sergeant lifted a passport from the folder. Before he even opened it, I could see that it was a British passport. My stomach sank.

He opened it and turned it so that we could see the photo. "Christian Alexander Begley. Is this your friend?"

Katrina's hand went to her mouth. "Oh God."

"Yes." The word hardly escaped my throat. "That's him."

"Then I am very sorry, but yes, he is dead."

Katrina slumped forward and burst into tears, and I put a comforting hand on her back. But still, I wasn't convinced. "What if whoever you found had his ID and you only *think* it's him?" I asked. "Isn't it possible that he was robbed—"

"I saw his face," the sergeant insisted. "The man in the alley is the same one pictured in this passport."

"Katrina was told that you had pictures so we could identify him for ourselves."

The sergeant looked me in the eye, his expression grave. "Trust me, señora. You do not want to see the pictures."

The proverbial last straw vanished, leaving me with the cold, hard truth. Christian had been murdered. The fight oozing out of me, I whimpered.

"I understand this is difficult," the sergeant said. "But can you tell me what is your relationship with Christian?"

"I'm a friend," I explained. "But Katrina and Christian were dating."

"Are you British, or American?"

"American," I told him. "We both are." Katrina was too distraught to speak. Sergeant Ramirez realized this, too, and had directed the question to me.

"Did you meet in Mexico?"

"No. Christian and Katrina met in Florida. He's been staying with her there. We all decided to head to Mexico for a vacation."

"How can this be true?" Katrina suddenly asked, whipping her head up. "We were at the club; we were . . . he's not supposed to be dead!"

"I'm sorry for your loss," the man said in a tone that didn't sound the least bit sympathetic. Maybe he saw far too many murders to invest himself in the grief of one person. "But please, tell me. Why did you come to Mexico?"

Katrina frowned. She looked taken aback. "Why does anybody come to Mexico? We came for a vacation."

Sergeant Ramirez looked at her, holding her gaze a little too long. It made me feel uncomfortable.

Then he spoke. "People come to this country for all sorts of reasons. Many times, we have to clean up the mess left by American tourists who think that Mexico is about one thing. Drugs."

"Drugs?" I asked, my eyes bulging. "Are you—are you accusing us of coming here for drugs?"

I remembered the man's comment in the waiting area. *Good luck getting any justice in this country.*

"You said you were at a club last night," the sergeant began. "Did you meet with anybody about drugs?"

"How dare you?" Katrina asked. Her eyes were narrowed, her face full of anger. "I'm not here because of drugs. I'm here because someone killed my boyfriend."

"And we need to determine why. Why would somebody slit a man's throat at the back of a club? Because he was having a good time on the dance floor?"

The sergeant's question was sarcastic, making it clear that he didn't believe Christian's death had been a random attack on an innocent tourist.

And hearing the sergeant state how Christian had been killed was like hearing it for the first time. My stomach roiled. "His throat was really slit?" I asked.

"From ear to ear."

My head swam. I thought I might pass out.

"This is why it is important for me to know everything. Sometimes the cartels will cut off a person's head. Or they will shoot you. This murder doesn't quite have the mark of the cartels. But one never knows."

Katrina was no longer crying, but her breathing was haphazard. Was she about to have a panic attack?

"We were at the club," I said. "We were dancing. And then Christian—" I stopped, suddenly unsure if I should say that there'd been a fight between Katrina and Christian. But wasn't it important to tell the truth? Maybe the guy Christian had fought with was the perpetrator. The sergeant needed to know that.

I looked at Katrina, but her eyes were losing focus. *Come on, Katrina,* I silently urged. *I need your help here.*

"Please go on," Sergeant Ramirez said. "What were you going to say?"

I glanced at Katrina again. She was like a shell of her former self. Could she even hear what we were saying?

I took a deep breath, then told the truth. "Katrina and Christian had a fight. She was flirting with another guy, and maybe that guy is the one who—"

"Jade!" Katrina threw a lethal look in my direction.

I was surprised that she had even processed what I'd said. "Don't you think that guy might have something to do with this?" I asked her. "You were flirting with him; Christian got pissed and went over to confront you two. Who else would hurt him?" When Katrina said nothing, I turned back to Ramirez. "Christian and this guy fought over Katrina. Physically. He's got to be the killer."

Katrina wasn't convinced. "He was just some guy at the club. He wouldn't kill Christian over me."

"Some people are psychopaths, Kat. They seem normal, but they've got a dark side. Anything can set them off."

"Brian seemed pretty normal, too, didn't he?" Katrina muttered.

Sergeant Ramirez held up a hand. "Please. Let me be clear. Your boyfriend fought with a man you were dancing with?"

"He did," Katrina admitted.

"And you think he is the killer?" The sergeant's tone told me that he was unconvinced. "Because this man was flirting with you, he does this to your boyfriend?" With that, Ramirez produced a picture from the folder, held it up. And as my eyes landed on the graphic image, my stomach lurched violently. I had to hold my breath to keep the bile from rising.

Katrina's outburst was instantaneous. A sob clawed at my throat. It was a picture of Christian lying on his back, his throat sliced from ear to ear, his blood covering the concrete, a look of agony etched on his face forever.

I could no longer hold in my tears. They spilled onto my cheeks in a steady stream.

"I thought you weren't going to show us the pictures," I said. And now I could understand why he'd initially said that he wouldn't. What I saw was an image I would never be able to forget.

"I am through playing games," Sergeant Ramirez said. "Why would someone do this to a man because he was dancing with his girlfriend? There is something you are not telling me. You want me to find your boyfriend's killer, you need to start telling me the truth."

The image of Christian murdered flashed in my mind again, and unsteadily I got to my feet. "I need . . . I need a bathroom."

"Right across the hallway," Ramirez told me, pointing in that direction.

I raced out of my room and into the door with the sign BAÑOS. I barely made it to the toilet before I hurled.

And then I cried, letting it all out. Christian was dead. There was no more pretending.

He'd been slaughtered.

I turned on the faucet and scooped some water into my hands. The water was warm and tasted like crap, but I swallowed some anyway. I needed to get the taste of vomit out of my mouth.

As composed as I possibly could be under the circumstances, I made my way back to the sergeant's office. As I entered, Katrina was saying, "I swear. Nothing else is going on. My boyfriend and I had a fight. That's why I feel even worse about this. If we hadn't fought, if I hadn't been trying to make him jealous . . . don't you think I realize that maybe I could have prevented all of this from happening?"

As I sat, Katrina glanced at me. She offered me a weak smile.

"I'm going to need to speak to both of you separately," Sergeant Ramirez said.

"What?" Katrina exclaimed.

"Is there a reason you don't want to be questioned separately?" The question was almost an accusation.

"Of course not," I said. "We have nothing to hide."

Ramirez smiled, but it didn't reach his eyes. "Good. Who will talk to me first?"

Katrina scowled. "Fine. I'll stay."

"Very well." Then he looked at me. "Miss, please head back to the waiting area."

I did as instructed, hoping that Katrina would keep her cool. She was starting to get angry, and the angrier she got, the more likely the cop would suspect that we had something to hide.

In the reception area, the American tourists were still there. The one with the black eye looked at me and said, "Now the fun's about to start."

CHAPTER TWENTY-FIVE

If by *fun* he meant aggravation beyond anything I'd ever known, he was right. Not only was I questioned by the sergeant, I was also questioned independently by another officer. Now, after a good hour and a half of being at the police station, I was released from the second detective's office and heading back into the reception area.

Katrina looked up as I trudged over to her. I plopped down onto the chair beside her.

"What did he say?" she asked me.

"I was questioned by some detective named Acevedo. He just kept asking the same questions." I looked to where the two American tourists had been sitting. "Were they finally released?"

"I don't think so. A cop came out here and took them through that door on the left."

Damn. They were being locked up?

"I wish we'd never come here," Katrina complained. "I should have known better."

I gathered that she was referring to the police station. "I don't understand why they keep bringing us back in to question us. By now, they should be letting us go and working on finding the killer. We've already told them everything. And why are two different cops questioning us independently? Do they think we're *suspects*?"

Katrina said nothing. What was there to say? After all, she didn't have the answers any more than I did.

I was exhausted, so I knew it had to be even worse for her. I hadn't loved Christian. The shock and horror were setting in, and I could only imagine that she was barely keeping it together.

And were we even going to get out of here or end up in a jail cell? The very fact that the detective had mentioned drugs had me extremely worried. Did he think that we were holding something back? And was the fact that Katrina had offered me drugs of any significance? What about that guy she'd been flirting with? He'd offered me something.

Ramirez said that the cartels had a specific modus operandi, and while Christian hadn't been decapitated, his head had been severed. What if this killing wasn't about flirting and jealousy but the fact that that guy Katrina had met was a drug dealer?

I touched Katrina softly on the arm to get her attention. "Hey," I said in a soft voice. "What if this *is* about drugs? What you offered me in the bathroom, where did you get—"

"Shut up!" she hissed.

Her words felt like a slap. But I swallowed my hurt and proceeded in a calm voice. "Ramirez and Acevedo are smart. They know we're holding something back." I'd told them about Brian and Keith, how we'd hung out with them at the club and gotten a cab ride with them back to the hotel. "What if there were surveillance cameras in the bar, and they . . . they saw you getting . . . *stuff*? I mean, the guy you were dancing with specifically offered me—"

Katrina glared at me. "Do you see where we are? As it

is, who knows if we'll get out of here. You start talking about stuff that makes us sound suspicious and good luck getting any justice. We might just get thrown in jail. Like those other guys did."

For several seconds, I said nothing as I contemplated her words. Then I spoke, making sure to keep my voice low. "But what if that guy is a big-time drug dealer or something? That's what I'm saying. They keep questioning us, and maybe it's because they know that we're leaving something out. And that's probably making us look guilty. Maybe if we tell them—"

"I'm not about to get arrested in Mexico for a crime I didn't commit. If you want to be stupid and open your mouth, leave me out of it."

The back door suddenly opened, and the sergeant appeared. He pointed to Katrina and said, "Miss Hughes."

Slowly, she stood. As she made her way to the sergeant, she glanced over her shoulder at me. In her eyes, I saw a warning: *Shut the hell up.*

I'm not sure how much time passed before Katrina exited from the back offices. Maybe twenty-five minutes. Perhaps forty. I'd stopped checking. Every time I'd looked at the clock, mere minutes had passed, and checking the time was stressing me out.

Hearing the door open, I looked up. And there was Katrina. Sergeant Ramirez beckoned to me. "Miss Blackwin. Please come with me."

Katrina, arms folded over her chest and a look of exasperation on her face, passed me without saying a word.

I followed the sergeant into his office once more. Honestly, if this wasn't the last round of questioning I was going to tell Katrina that we should leave after this.

I exhaled audibly as I sat in the same chair I'd assumed before. I was tired of this now, ready for it to be over.

"Tell me about this man you were talking to," the sergeant said without preamble. "The one who fought with Christian."

My eyes widened in alarm. "Excuse me?"

"According to your friend, he spoke to you first."

I stared at the sergeant, barely breathing. Why would Katrina throw me under the bus like that? Was she trying to make it seem like I knew the guy or had nefarious dealings with him?

"Miss Blackwin?"

"Yes, I did speak to him, very briefly."

"Do you know this man?"

"No. Of course not. He was just some guy who approached me in a bar."

"Are you sure about that?"

"Of course I'm sure about that."

"Your friend seems to think that perhaps you knew him from before."

I narrowed my eyes in confusion. "What?" Was that what Katrina had said? Or was Ramirez lying? I had seen enough cop shows to know that police didn't always tell the truth. In their quest to get people to confess to crimes, they elaborated and downright lied.

That had to be what they were doing. She wouldn't say that. I knew she wouldn't.

"I don't know him," I stressed. "I'd never seen him before last night."

"What did you talk about? You and this mysterious stranger?"

I hesitated. "I—I . . ." My voice trailed off. "He asked me to dance, I think. I don't really remember. I declined and he went over to Katrina." I refrained from telling the full story, because I remembered the look Katrina had given me and wondered if she was right: The more we talked, the more we might implicate ourselves.

The sergeant eased back in his chair. "Interesting. Because Miss Hughes tells me that he offered you drugs."

My heart stopped in my chest. Literally, I felt as though I might drop dead. What the heck was Katrina doing?

The sergeant leaned forward and folded his hands on top of the desk. "See, this is exactly the kind of information I need to know. And when people aren't honest with me, I have to wonder what they are trying to hide."

Panic spread through my blood, leaving me cold. What could I say now? Now that I looked like I had been lying to cover up my own guilt. "Okay, you want the truth? I spent maybe three seconds with him. He asked if I wanted some stuff. I didn't know what he was referring to, but whatever it was, I told him I wasn't interested."

My pulse was pounding. What was Katrina's game? Did she figure it'd be either her or me and she was trying to protect herself?

"He knew I wasn't interested," I went on, "so he didn't bother wasting his time with me. He moved through the crowd, and the next thing I knew, he was flirting with Katrina. They ended up dancing. He had his hands all over her body. Christian saw them and got angry. He went over to confront them. That's when a fight broke out. Christian and this guy exchanged blows." I told it all. No point protecting Katrina now, not after she'd betrayed me!

Sergeant Ramirez continued to stare at me, and I could hardly breathe. "I'm telling you the truth," I said. I made the sign of a cross over my chest. "I swear, that's everything I know."

"Thank you for your honesty, Miss Blackwin."

I shifted uncomfortably in my seat. "I wasn't trying to deliberately mislead you. I just don't think Christian's killing is about drugs. If this guy did kill him, I think it's about ego and jealousy."

"Jealousy is a strong motive," the sergeant agreed. "People kill for love every day. What about your friend? Do you think Miss Hughes could have killed her boyfriend?"

My eyes bulged. "What?"

"You said she was dancing with another man. Flirting. I have to assume she didn't love Christian."

"Katrina was with me all night. Christian was angry after their fight. He left . . . and that was the last we saw him." I blew out a frazzled breath. "That is honestly everything we know. Why don't you go to the bar, see if there are surveillance cameras so you can get pictures of everyone? There's a killer out there."

"Tell me again what happened after the fight. You said you met someone else. A man named Brian."

We had been through this twice already. I was getting tired of it. "Yes, but he came into the bar after Christian left. He's not responsible."

"How do you know?"

"I—I—because I just do," I said, knowing that what I'd said wasn't anything close to concrete proof. But I certainly couldn't say that I was certain of Brian's innocence because he was a good kisser.

"May I see your phone, Miss Blackwin?"

"My phone?"

"You met some men, had some fun. You didn't exchange numbers?"

I pulled my phone from my purse. "As a matter of fact, we didn't. I don't know about the guy Katrina was flirting with, but Brian and Keith hung out with us for a bit, then went in the cab with us back to our hotel."

"And pictures?"

"I took no pictures of anyone. Using your phone in a foreign country can cost a fortune. I didn't even turn it on."

I was about to pass it to him, then thought better of it. What if he took my phone, never gave it back? "With all due respect, am I under arrest or something?"

"No. I am simply trying to find answers. And the more I ask questions, the more things you may remember. For example, your friend remembered that she had taken pictures of Brian and Keith."

"Yes," I said after a moment. "She did." Though why she thought that was of any consequence was beyond me. Though I did remember what she'd said back at the hotel, that she didn't trust Brian. I'd been too pissed with her to ask her why not.

"Perhaps you took pictures of other people in the bar?" the sergeant suggested.

"I took no pictures, I can assure you. I didn't even have my phone with me."

"You're sure?"

"One hundred percent."

The sergeant produced a piece of paper. "Thanks to your friend, I have pictures of Brian and Keith. But write down everything you remember about the other men you came into contact with. And anyone else you may think of. Height, weight, eye color, skin color. And yes, I have an officer checking with the bar to see if there are surveillance cameras."

"Everyone? Is there another way?" I asked. "Maybe you have a book of pictures with criminals you can show me?"

The sergeant laughed as though I had said the funniest thing in the world. "Do you know how long that would take? Please, write everything you know. Everything you remember about these people you came into contact with. Leave nothing out."

After I wrote descriptions of all of the men we'd come into contact with, Katrina and I were told that we were free to go. Once we reunited in the reception area, I learned that Katrina had had to do the same taxing exercise. It had been an exhausting and grueling few hours at the police station. The sergeant told us that an officer would give us a ride back to the hotel. Although I didn't know if I wanted to spend time with any more cops in this country, Katrina and I gratefully accepted.

Neither of us spoke during the ride back. Not only were we silent; Katrina barely looked my way. I wondered if she was mad at me.

Once in the hotel, I said to Katrina, "I forgot all about those pictures we took with Brian and Keith."

"So did I. But that sergeant kept grilling me, wanting to see my phone, if I'd taken pictures . . . and I was shocked to see them. You know I was drunk, and stoned. I barely remember anything that happened last night."

She hadn't been *that* out of her mind, because she'd known what she'd been doing when she made sure Brian didn't come into the hotel with me. But I focused on what mattered. "What about the other guy? The one who was fighting with Christian? Did you get pictures of him?"

"No."

I followed Katrina to the bank of elevators. "You don't think Brian and Keith had anything to do with this?"

"I have no clue what to think."

"Why were you so suspicious of Brian last night?"

"Just a feeling," she said. "That he was a liar. I wanted to protect you."

If she'd wanted to protect me, why had she told the sergeant that *I* had been talking to that guy in the bar first? Had she simply relayed the facts as she knew them, or had she been trying to cast suspicion onto me?

"Hey," I began softly. "That detective kind of implied that you thought I was being too chummy with the guy who had the fight with Christian." I exhaled a sort of snort, letting her know I thought the idea was ridiculous. "But obviously you don't feel that way."

I waited for her to tell me that she didn't. Instead, she walked toward the elevator and jabbed at the UP button.

I moved to stand beside her, placing a hand on her shoulder, urging her to turn. "Kat?"

"You never liked Christian," she said.

I gaped at her. She looked up toward the floor numbers, clearly trying to avoid me.

It took me several seconds to process her implication. "So—what? You think because I didn't like Christian that I arranged to have him *killed*?"

"I don't know what to think."

My eyes bulged. I almost couldn't suck in a breath. "You were the one ramming your tongue down that guy's throat. I barely said two words to him."

The elevator dinged, and two young, smiling couples exited. Then Katrina rushed on and I followed quickly behind her.

"Please tell me you don't think that I . . . what . . . met some random guy in a bar in Mexico and arranged to have him kill Christian?" I ended my words with a questioning tone, one that said a more ridiculous idea had never been thought of in the history of mankind.

Katrina didn't speak.

"Katrina?" My voice held a desperate note. "Why on earth would you—"

"The detective kept asking me questions, analyzing every little thing that happened. Twisting my every action. Second-guessing everything." She exhaled sharply. "Of course I don't think that you had anything do to with this."

"I thought we'd have each other's backs, Kat. For you to say that to the detective could easily make me look guilty. But when he suggested that maybe you didn't love Christian, I told him that he was wrong."

"So he thinks *I* killed him?" Katrina asked, a panicked expression coming onto her face.

"He's grasping at straws. Like you said, he has to analyze everything. But I made sure to tell him that you were with me the entire night. That you couldn't have killed Christian."

The elevator dinged and stopped on our floor, and we exited. Katrina walked on ahead of me down the hall.

"Kat," I said when she got to her door. "Please tell me you told the sergeant that I was with you, too. That you didn't give him a reason to think I may have had something to do with Christian's death."

"It's been a long, awful day and I'm tired," she said. "I just want to go to bed."

"You realize you're not making me feel better."

"We're both home-free, Jade. That's what matters."

"Home-free?" I frowned.

"You know what I mean. We're not stuck in a Mexican jail. Isn't that the point here?"

"I thought the point was to find Christian's killer."

"Are you gonna twist my words, too? Of course that's the point." She groaned, frustrated. "Look, Jade. I need to get some sleep."

"Sure," I said, not wanting to push her.

But as she opened her door and slipped into the room without looking back at me, I was left feeling confused and uneasy.

CHAPTER TWENTY-SIX

I couldn't sleep. Instead, I checked out flight options and how much it would cost me to leave Mexico early.

The vacation had turned into a nightmare. The officer hadn't said anything about us having to stay in the country, but with Katrina casting suspicion on me—as unlikely as it may have seemed—I wasn't sure that I wanted to stick around. If I was back on U.S. soil, I would feel that much safer.

Talking to Katrina hadn't alleviated my anxiety. Instead, I had been left feeling worse. Because I didn't know if she actually believed I may have had something to do with what happened to Christian and if she had convinced the detective of the same.

I also wasn't impressed with her two-faced behavior. She'd told me to keep my mouth shut, then had blabbed about the guy offering me drugs in a way that made me look like a liar.

Maybe I was being too hard on her. Her boyfriend had just been brutally murdered, and I knew she couldn't be thinking entirely straight. Still, I would only feel safe once I got back home.

I wondered who would deal with Christian's body. He must have a family. Did Katrina know how to contact them? Someone would have to make arrangements for him to be returned to England, to be buried.

Not your problem, a voice in my head said. *Right now, like Katrina, you need to worry about yourself.*

The question as to who would take care of the arrangements for Christian's body was answered the next day when I heard raised voices through the hotel wall.

Quickly throwing on some clothes, I exited my room and went to Katrina's door. When I put my ear against it, the voices became louder, but I could only make out snippets.

". . . told you. I don't know what happened."

"He came here with you."

". . . just stop!"

I knocked on the door.

". . . no clue what you want from me."

I pounded this time. Several seconds later the door flew open. Katrina faced me, her nostrils flaring with anger. At first I thought she was upset with me, until she said, "You deal with her. I'm outta here."

Katrina charged past me, and I looked into the room, where I saw a white heavyset woman with short brown hair that looked like it hadn't been combed. She looked at me, held my gaze. Her eyes were moist and red, and she held a crumpled Kleenex up to her nose.

I glanced in Katrina's direction, but she had already disappeared down the hallway. Then I looked at the woman again.

"Who are you?" she asked.

It was then that I heard her British accent. Guarded, I stepped into the room. "I'm Jade. Katrina's friend."

"You came here with her and Christian, then?"

I closed the door behind me. "Y-yes. Sorry, you are?"

"Christian's sister. Melody. I got on the first plane here when I got the call."

I walked farther into the room and stood opposite her.

"I'm so sorry," I told her.

"What happened?" she demanded.

I told her what I could. That'd we'd been out for a night of fun. I wasn't completely honest, however. I didn't want to say that Christian had left the bar angry. So I told her that Christian had stepped outside and that we never saw him again.

"Why?" Melody asked. "Why would Christian go outside and leave you two in the bar? He didn't smoke."

"I . . ." Should I tell her that Katrina and Christian had had a spat? Or would that make her feel worse about the situation?

"How on earth did this happen?" Melody went on, her throat raw. "You go on a vacation to Mexico—though God knows why when you were already in Florida—and my brother ends up dead? And no one can give me any bloody answers?"

She began to sob into her already-overused Kleenex. The woman was completely grief-stricken, and I felt her pain but had no answers for her.

"I wish I had answers," I said softly. "Katrina and Christian wanted to go to Mexico. I suppose for a change of pace. Or just to travel. We were in the bar, and Christian . . . he said he needed air," I lied. To tell Melody the truth would certainly add to her rage and grief, and I wanted to spare Katrina that. Not to mention myself.

"He went out for air and ended up murdered?" Melody sounded suspicious.

I shrugged. "I really don't know what else to say," I told her. "It's as shocking to me as it is to you. After spending much of yesterday at the police station, I still don't believe it's real."

Melody stared at me, her anguished gaze assessing me. "And none of this has to do with the fact that Christian and Katrina fought all the time?"

My eyes widened. Had she heard about the fight at the bar?

"Excuse me?"

"Oh, you don't have to pretend. My brother's dead and gone. No need to pretend he and Katrina had some kind of special relationship. I came here to hear from her what happened, and all she did was get defensive and leave. Christian told us that they had a rocky relationship, that he worried he'd made a mistake. He would call us and tell us about their fights. I told him to be wary of her. That with our family money, he needed to be careful of her intentions."

"You thought she was using him?"

"Of course she was using him." The woman looked angry. "The moment I heard about Katrina, I was worried. Everything was moving so fast with her and Christian. Why? I never believed that Katrina loved him for him. To me she sounded like a classic gold digger. A dirty, gold-digging whore who sank her teeth into my brother and didn't let go until he was dead!"

The words were harsh, but Alexis had also implied that Katrina's attraction to Christian was at least in part fueled by his bank account. Still, I hadn't seen signs of Katrina using him for his money. No lavish spending sprees, for example. And Katrina certainly worked hard in the café. She seemed determined to make her own money and take care of herself.

Perhaps Christian had paid for the trip to Mexico, but that wasn't a big deal. That hardly made Katrina a gold digger.

Not to mention the bigger flaw with Melody's theory. If Katrina was a gold digger, Christian would be better off alive so that she could marry him.

"I know you're upset. Lord knows I can't imagine what you're feeling right now. But I'm not sure if you're implying that Katrina killed him—"

"Of course she killed him!"

I flinched at the words. Then continued. "If you're right about Katrina wanting Christian for his money, then she couldn't have killed him. Why kill him and cut off any access to his money? In fact, if she really wanted his money, wouldn't it make more sense to marry him?"

Melody's eyes narrowed as she stared at me. She regarded me as if I had sprouted a second head.

And then she said, "You don't know?"

"Know what?"

"You said you were friends. How could you not know?"

"Know what?" I repeated.

"They were married. Last week."

Suddenly the room became very still. Then my stomach bottomed out.

"W-what did you say?"

"I thought it odd, you going on their honeymoon with them."

"Honeymoon?"

"Why on earth do you think they came here? Christian told me that they got married and they were going to Mexico for their honeymoon. I still never understood. They could just as easily have stayed in Florida. Now I know. Katrina wanted him here so she could get rid of him!"

The room was spinning. I was so unsteady on my feet that I had to walk over to the nearby table and grip the back of the chair.

"I knew it was trouble," Melody was saying now. "I told Christian not to marry her, but he didn't listen. But I tell you this: It'll be a cold day in hell before she gets her dirty hands on his money."

"No," I rasped. "No . . . it can't be . . . it isn't . . . true."

As I took in a few deep breaths to calm myself, I felt Melody's hand on my back. "It's clear to me that you didn't know. And for that, I'm glad. I worried that the two of you had planned this. Concocted some way to kill him."

I whirled my head around to face her. "I would never." My breaths were ragged, my heart beating wildly. "And Katrina . . . I don't think she had anything to do with it. They were . . . they'd had a fight. You were right about that. She and Christian fought a lot. And they did at the bar that night. Katrina was flirting with another guy, and Christian got pissed. Then he left. And that was the last we saw him."

"Oh, I'm sure Katrina hired someone. Probably paid a local a few dollars. Or offered a sexual favor. I saw this happening the moment Christian told me he was marrying her. Do you really think his murder here was a coincidence?"

A lump had lodged in my throat and I swallowed, but it wouldn't go away. "Married?" I asked. "Are you sure? I mean, I've been in Florida with them. If they got married last week, I would know."

"I'm certain. Before Christian and Katrina left for Mexico, he married her. Against my protests, he married her, and Mexico was their honeymoon. I can't tell you how upset I was when he refused to even get a pre-nup." Melody paused, a look of anger cutting through the anguish on her face. "Katrina didn't tell you about their marriage. Doesn't that make you wonder why? And doesn't that make you wonder what she has to hide?"

A short while later, Melody left to go to the police station and I went back to my room, where I sank onto the bed and buried my face in my hands.

I was numb. Confused.

And not altogether sure that I believed Melody's bomb-shell. If Katrina and Christian had gotten married last week, how could I *not* know about it? I'd been there, day in and day out with them at the café. When would they have had the time? And even if they had snuck off to tie the knot, wouldn't Katrina have told me?

Katrina didn't tell you about their marriage. Doesn't that make you wonder why? And doesn't that make you wonder what she has to hide?

I shook my head as I remembered Melody's question. No, it didn't make sense. Melody was wrong. Plain and simple.

Then, out of nowhere, something popped into my mind. A snippet of that argument they'd had when things had gotten ugly after Christian had been drinking and I'd intervened to stop it.

What about today? You're supposed to be my wife.

I felt a jolt, as surely as if I had touched a live hydro wire. My chest constricted. *Oh God . . .*

Closing my eyes tightly, I wracked my brain, trying to remember what Katrina had said in response to Christian's comment. She had immediately scoffed, saying something to the effect that Christian was drunk and out of his mind and that she wasn't his wife.

But hadn't that also been the day that they'd disappeared for a good part of the afternoon?

Slowly, I lowered my hands from my face. They'd gone off and come back even more romantic than ever.

My God, was it true? Had they gotten married that day? And if so, why had Katrina lied about it?

I went to Katrina's door, hoping that she had returned. I needed to talk to her. But she didn't answer. So I returned to my room and tore a piece of paper off of the notepad, wrote a message asking her to come to my room when she got back, and then slipped it under her door.

In the hour that it took Katrina to knock on my door, I had gone over the facts as I knew them countless times. And I finally decided to dismiss what Melody had said. More than likely, she had her facts wrong. Christian and Katrina had talked about marriage; Katrina told me that he'd proposed to her. But if she had married him and Mexico was their honeymoon, too many things didn't add up. For one thing, why was I here with them? That was just crazy. And two, why would a newlywed be all over another man in a bar?

When I heard the knock, I jumped up from the bed and ran to answer the door. I looked through the peephole first and saw Katrina, looking distraught.

I opened the door. Then hugged her. "Hey. I was worried."

"I needed some space. I couldn't handle Melody's accusations."

"She's upset. And that's understandable. Her brother was just killed. She's looking for someone to blame."

"I guess so. But still, she's got to understand how devastating this is for me. I loved Christian."

Emotion caused Katrina's face to collapse. The stress had aged her practically ten years overnight.

I led her into the room, where she sank onto the armchair and pulled her knees to her chest. Then I waited for her to regain her composure, because I needed to address what Melody had said.

"Look," I began gently. "Melody said something. I'm sure she's mistaken, but I figured I would mention it. Because I bet she's going to bring this up with the police, and you need to be ready." I took a breath. "For some reason, she's under the impression that you and Christian got married?"

My voice ended on a questioning note, and I waited.

Waited for Katrina's eyes to grow wide, for her to ask how on earth Melody would have gotten a ridiculous notion like that.

Instead, something unreadable passed in Katrina's eyes. Then she rose from the armchair and walked past me to the window that overlooked the vast blue ocean.

A few beats passed, beats in which my stomach began to twist painfully. "Kat? You didn't—"

She faced me, and the look in her eyes conveyed the truth.

But still I went on, not wanting to believe what now seemed irrefutable. "Tell me it's not true. You wouldn't have married Christian without telling me?"

Katrina expelled a loud breath. "We thought it best to keep it secret for the time being."

And with her words, I felt the sensation of falling, as surely as if someone had pushed me through my hotel room window and I was now sailing through the air from the sixth floor.

"You—you *married* him?"

"And that's exactly why I didn't tell you. Because I knew you would think I was crazy."

My feeling of disorientation passed, leaving anger in its wake. In fact, I could hear my pulse thundering in my ears.

I was enraged. I felt betrayed. And stupid. "When? And my God, why? The way both of you were always fighting?"

"It was a small ceremony last week. And I didn't tell you because I knew how it would look—we'd been fighting all the time, and you would have tried to talk me out of it. But I loved him, and I wanted it to work between us. I figured that once we got married, everything would work itself out."

I scoffed. I'd never heard something so ridiculous in my entire life.

"So this is really your honeymoon? You made up all

that bullshit about going to Mexico for a few days in the sun?"

"If I wasn't telling you that we got married, I certainly couldn't tell you that this was our honeymoon."

"And why am *I* here?" I'd never felt good about going on this trip with them to begin with, and now I felt even worse.

"I've already gone through the inquisition with Melody. Can you please give me a break? My husband was just murdered."

My husband . . . This was absurd. I narrowed my eyes as I regarded Katrina, wondering if Melody was right. Had Katrina married Christian for his money? Was that why she hadn't told me about it? And was Christian dead now because she stood to inherit a fortune?

Katrina saw the look in my eyes, and it was clear she read what I was thinking when she said, "Melody has her suspicions, but she couldn't be more wrong. In fact, after we got back from Mexico, Christian and I were going to go to a lawyer. I was going to sign an agreement saying I didn't want his money."

"Oh my God. *After* the wedding?" I guffawed. "Do you know how that sounds?"

"I do. Which is why I need to head back to Florida. Once Melody starts weaving her sordid tale, I might be detained here. And I don't plan to live out my days in a Mexican jail."

My head was spinning. My whole world was spinning. I didn't know what to believe anymore. If Katrina loved Christian and was on her honeymoon, why the hell had she been all over those guys in the bar? Unless she didn't really care about Christian but had married him for what he could do for her.

Even Ramirez's question didn't seem so far-fetched

anymore: *Do you think Miss Hughes could have killed her boyfriend?*

"I spent the last hour looking into flights," Katrina said, jarring me from my thoughts. "I'm leaving later today."

I gaped at her. "And what about me?"

"Why do you think I'm telling you?" she asked, an edge to her tone. Then she sighed softly. "Look, Christian's dead, but his sister's here now and she can deal with getting his body."

"You're his *wife*." I couldn't keep the biting tone from my voice. "Aren't you the one who's supposed to make the arrangements?"

"And piss off his family? We've been married less than a week. It's only fitting that his sister deals with the body, takes him back to England."

"So that's just it? Christian is dead, and you go back to the States as though nothing happened?"

"I loved Christian, but he's gone. So there's no point in me staying here. Yes, I'm heading back to the States. Are you coming or not?"

So cavalier . . . so nonchalant. Or was I judging her?

"I'm coming. Obviously."

"Good. There's a flight in four hours. If you're coming with me, you better get ready."

CHAPTER TWENTY-SEVEN

SHAWDE

Shawde paused the television and picked up her phone. Her adrenaline was pumping after seeing this news report, and she *needed* to talk to Gordon.

Instead of ringing as the phone had the last time she'd called him, it went directly to voice mail. "The mailbox of the cellular subscriber you are trying to reach is full."

Shawde swiped her screen to end the call, frowning. She had a niggling feeling in her gut. Where the hell was Gordon?

He hadn't gotten back to her after she'd left him the message about the promising phone call she'd had with Monica and now his phone was going straight to voice mail?

Unless . . .

Unless he'd learned of Katrina's plans and was in Mexico.

Of course! That would explain why she hadn't been able to reach him. He'd learned that Katrina was heading to Cancun, and he'd quickly gone there as well to continue to keep an eye on her. He just hadn't been able to contact

Shawde yet. Not with all the hell that was breaking loose in Mexico.

Shawde turned her attention back to the television. Using the remote control, she rewound the news story and watched it again, a sense of hope filling her despite the story's gruesome nature.

A British tourist had been killed in Cancun. His throat had been slashed from ear to ear. The man's sister had appeared on television, talking about the killing, letting the world know that she and her family were completely devastated by what had happened.

It was a devastation that Shawde understood. She'd seen her only brother laid to rest five and a half years before.

Although how could his soul be in peace when his killer was still on the loose?

"I am hopeful that the police will soon have the killer arrested," the distraught sister said. "This crime will not go unpunished."

The spark of hope from this tragic story had come for Shawde when she'd heard the name of one of the women who had gone to Mexico with the murder victim.

Katrina Hughes.

"I believe that my brother's new wife, Katrina Hughes, holds the key to this murder. They were honeymooning in Mexico at the time. If she has nothing to hide, where is she now?"

Katrina Hughes. Shawde's lips had parted in shock when she'd first heard the story, and her pulse had picked up speed. Now, as she watched it again, her feeling of elation was so intense she literally thought she could float.

Looking heavenward, she said, "Thank you, God."

For five and a half years, Shawde had prayed for justice. For five and a half years, she had feared that Katrina had gotten away with cold-blooded murder. Shawde had tried overturning every stone from the past for a real lead that would nail that bitch once and for all, all the while praying that Katrina would make a mistake.

And she just had.

Shawde was damn sure going to capitalize on it.

Judging by the tone of the woman on the television, she had her own suspicions about Katrina. But she was doing a good job of reining in her emotions and not coming right out and accusing Katrina of cold-blooded murder. She had far more restraint than Shawde did.

Of course, it had only been thirty-six hours since her brother had been killed. Not five and a half years.

My brother's new wife . . . When the hell had that happened? It must have been a secret wedding, because Gordon hadn't known about it. But if Katrina had married this Christian Begley guy, it had been for one reason. For the financial gain that would come from his death.

There wasn't a doubt in Shawde's mind. Katrina had killed her own parents for the same reason.

But why had Jade Blackwin been on the trip? Gordon had mentioned that she'd been working for Katrina. Jade's older sister, Marie, had gone to school with Katrina. Had Jade been involved in the murder plot?

"Of course not," Shawde said, and couldn't help chuckling as the answer came to her. "She's Katrina's alibi. Or her scapegoat."

Katrina never did anything without thinking it through. And for her to bring a third person on a honeymoon with her meant she'd planned to use Jade in some way.

Shawde watched the news story for a third time, then jumped up from the sofa. Nervous energy flowed through her, and she simply couldn't sit still. She was anxious, excited, and wanted to do a happy dance. Instead, she forced in slow breaths to calm the adrenaline flowing through her veins.

Then she looked heavenward again. "Katrina made a

mistake, Shemar," Shawde said softly. "She's finally made a mistake, and now she's going to pay."

Instinctively Shawde raised her phone and started to punch in Maurice's number. Then she stopped short.

No, not yet.

She was far closer to her dream of seeing Katrina punished once and for all, but Shawde couldn't contact Maurice until the task was done. Only then would there be any hope of them reconciling.

Right now, it was time for Shawde to head to Key West. She wanted to be there when Katrina's life imploded.

CHAPTER TWENTY-EIGHT

I started packing the moment Katrina left my room.

I was no fool. If Katrina was getting out of Mexico, I wasn't about to stick around. This was a completely different country, with a whole other justice system. We'd learned that firsthand when that cop had extorted cash from us on the side of the road.

This wasn't a country where my rights would necessarily be respected. Rumors of police corruption ran deep. I remembered seeing a documentary about a man who'd been thrown into jail here without a trial as a drug charge was sorted out. It took a few years of the U.S. government and his supporters raising a stink before he was finally released for lack of evidence.

That wouldn't be me.

At least I knew that I was innocent. *I* had nothing to hide.

I wasn't altogether certain that I could say the same thing about Katrina.

I knew that I needed to call my sister before heading to the airport. I'd turned on the television, and of course the story had made the news. Complete with my name and all.

Melody had already been interviewed and was publicly questioning Katrina's involvement. She must have left the hotel and gone straight to a press conference with the media.

Which was another reason that it made sense to get the heck out of Mexico. With news outlets coming here to report on the latest grisly tourist death, I didn't want to get caught up in the spotlight.

I punched in Marie's number and was glad when she answered after the second ring. "Jade?"

"Yes, it's me."

"Thank *God*! What's going on?"

"I take it you heard the news."

"Of course. It's all over the major news networks. Why the hell are you even in Mexico?"

"Kat wanted me to come along." I exhaled harshly. "Look, I can't get into this now. I just wanted you to know that I'm on my way back to the States. We're leaving the hotel right now."

"Thank God. Are you okay?"

There was a knock at my door. I heard Katrina call, "Jade, are you ready?"

"Kat's at my door right now. We have to leave. But yes, I'm okay. As okay as I can be, under the circumstances."

"Good. Call me the moment you're back on U.S. soil."

"I will," I told her. Then I hurried to the door and opened it.

"Are you ready?"

"Yeah. I just called my sister to let her know what was going on. Let me just get my luggage."

A minute later I had my small suitcase, purse, and carry-on bag and was joining Katrina in the hallway. Together, we made our way downstairs.

As we made our way through the lobby, my eyes registered what was outside. The small crowd, the cameras.

"Oh my God," I uttered, my feet halting. "Shit!"

"Damn, what do we do?" Katrina asked.

Looking at her, I saw her chest rise and fall with a heavy breath. "What *can* we do? There's only one way to the taxi stand. Let's check out first."

There was a handful of people in the lobby, and they were watching the media with curiosity. Once Katrina and I checked out and returned the room keys, she announced, "Wait here. I have a plan."

She went over to the concierge, leaving me with the luggage. She spoke to the man there, then came back over to me.

"He's going to make sure a taxi's ready for us before we go outside."

The minutes that passed seemed much longer, and then the concierge came back into the hotel and beckoned to us.

"Ready?" Katrina asked me.

"As ready as I'll ever be."

We had no choice but to exit the hotel doors and face the media scrum. They rushed toward us, like a wall closing in. Which meant they knew what we looked like. Video cameras went onto shoulders. Microphones and portable recorders were thrown into our faces.

"Girls, what happened? Who do you think murdered Christian Begley?"

"Did you have anything to do with the murder?"

"Is Christian's sister right about this being a cold-blooded murder plot?"

So many questions at once, and it was hard to concentrate. Katrina was pushing her way through the crowd, trying to follow the concierge, who was leading us to the taxi. He splayed his arms wide in an effort to try to shield us from the reporters, but it was no use. Their bodies crushed against ours as we tried our best to hurry to the car.

"Katrina, Christian's sister Melody says that you married her brother weeks after his vacation in the U.S. and that your interest in him was financial. Is there any truth to her claims?"

Katrina stopped then, faced the cameras as the concierge opened the back door of the taxi. "Yes, I did marry Christian. Because I loved him. I had no interest in his money. As for what happened, I have no clue. I only know that I came here to celebrate our new marriage and now he's dead."

A microphone appeared in front of my face. "Was this some sort of twisted love triangle?"

For a moment I was like a deer caught in headlights. Frozen and unable to speak. But as the question registered—the preposterousness of it—I found my voice. "Of course not. Look, I don't know what happened to Christian, but please, focus the attention where you should. Make sure the police fully investigate this case. There were people in the bar that night who might have answers. Put pressure on the police to do their jobs."

There were more questions, but both Katrina and I ignored them as we stuffed our belongings and our bodies into the back of the taxi. Katrina passed the concierge a ten; then he closed the door.

"Airport, please," Katrina instructed the driver.

"Are you two famous or something?" the driver asked, gesturing to all of the reporters surrounding his car.

"Just drive," Katrina said. "Please."

The taxi driver began to move, and slowly but surely he passed the reporters without killing anyone.

Only then did I draw in a relieved breath.

Then I reached for Katrina's hand and gripped it, happy to be on our way home.

I couldn't remember ever being more relieved than when our plane began to taxi down the runway. A part of me feared that as we tried to leave Mexico we would be told that we were on a no-fly list. That we were being detained for further questioning.

But we boarded the plane and then the plane took flight. And both Katrina and I relaxed.

If anyone recognized us from the news broadcasts, they didn't show it. Though I'd made sure to tie my hair back and I never took my sunglasses off during the flight.

Katrina and I hardly spoke. What was the point in engaging in small talk? With the gravity of what happened, I appreciated the time to be alone with my thoughts.

I was still afraid while on the plane, fearing that once we landed in the States there might be hurdles. Perhaps more reporters. Or I wouldn't have been surprised to find FBI agents coming onto the plane before anyone disembarked.

But it turned out that my imagination was running rampant. We got to the Key West airport, and there were no air marshals, no FBI, no police whatsoever. Nor was there a line of reporters waiting to barrage us with more questions about what had happened in Mexico.

By the time the taxi pulled up in front of the café, I was ready to sleep for a few days. Katrina must have felt the same way, because once we made our way inside she said, "I hope you're not offended. But I need to go to bed. I just want to sleep."

"God, me too," I said.

Katrina pushed open the door from the kitchen and peered into the café at large. "I can't believe it," she said, her voice cracking. "Christian's never coming back here."

I went up to her and put my arm around her waist. "It still feels like a dream."

"If only we hadn't gone to Mexico. We could have stayed here, still had a good time."

She sobbed softly, and I stayed with her until she'd cried her fill.

"I don't think I'll open tomorrow. It's going to be too hard."

"Don't even think about the café for now. You've been through a harrowing ordeal. Of course you can't open yet."

She nodded as she wiped her tears. "Thanks for understanding."

Then we went upstairs and to our respective rooms. As promised, I called Marie, let her know that I was back and safe.

"Are you going to come home?" she asked me.

"I don't think I can leave Katrina. She's a mess. And she's got no one. Her parents died, and now Christian's dead."

"Right. That makes sense." Marie sighed softly. "I'm just . . . I'm worried, but I was more worried when you were in a strange country. I feel better that you're back in the U.S. What happened? Shit, Jade, they said that that guy's neck was slit. And his sister is making it seem as though Katrina might have killed him?"

I told my sister everything I knew. About the guy in the bar, Katrina's flirting, the shocking truth that she had married Christian but also the fact that she'd been in the bar with me all night and *couldn't* have killed Christian.

"Of course she didn't kill him," Marie agreed. "How many tourists are murdered in Mexico? It wouldn't be on my top list of places to visit. I don't even know why you guys went there."

I didn't have an answer for that, so I said nothing.

"This is the kind of story you hear about happening to other people," Marie went on. "You don't expect *other people* to be your sister and your friend."

"Tell me about it. Honestly, I'm still processing that this even happened." I sucked in a breath, blew it out slowly.

"Marie, I wanted to let you know that I got back safely. But I'm really, really tired. Can we talk tomorrow?"

"Yeah, of course. If anything changes, call me."

"Anything like what?"

"Well, if you get word that they've caught the killer."

"Right. You might know that before I do. I'm heading straight to bed."

"I love you," Marie said. "Talk to you tomorrow."

It was rare that Marie and I said we loved each other and it felt awkward, but I returned the sentiment. "I love you, too, Sis."

Once I ended the call with my sister I tried to sleep, but it turned out that I was too wired. I lay in bed for a good hour, unable to sleep, when I decided that it was pointless to try to drift off. So I got up and opened up my laptop and watched a bit of CNN.

The news was the same as it had been before. There was nothing new.

Then I checked my Facebook account.

I was surprised to see that I had a dozen messages in my in-box. I clicked on it and scanned the list, saw that I had messages from friends I hadn't heard from since grad. It soon became clear to me that they'd seen the news. All of them wanted to know what was going on.

I scoffed. They didn't care about me. They simply wanted to be able to get the gossip firsthand.

To my surprise, there was a message from Wesley. After he'd practically told me to screw off and die, I was shocked to hear from him. But this was a big story.

Jade, what the hell happened in Mexico? Why were you even there? Call me, okay?

"Yeah, right," I muttered, then deleted the message. I'd debated at least letting him know I was okay but decided against it. I just wanted to be done with him once and for all.

I supposed I would ultimately reply to him later or send him a text to let him know that I was okay and he didn't have to worry about me. But first, I wanted to get through the messages in my in-box.

My interest was piqued by the photo of a woman I'd never seen before. She was pretty, with dark skin, a stunning smile, and a full head of curly, natural hair. Her name was Shawde Williams, which I didn't recognize.

I could only see the first line of her message without clicking it open totally:

You don't know me, but it's very important . . .

I clicked on the message, fully opening it:

You don't know me, but it's very important that you contact me as soon as possible. It's about your trip to Mexico and what happened there. Call me, or send me your number and I'll call you. Trust me, it's of vital importance that you get in touch with me.

The woman had ended her message to me with her phone number.

I frowned, wondering who she was and why she wanted to reach me. Probably some psychic who'd seen the story about Christian's murder on the news and wanted to "reach out" to me to give me advice . . . for a fee.

Likely, Katrina had also gotten such a message.

I deleted it.

Finally I fell asleep and slept for hours, awaking the next morning surprised to see that it was after eleven. Though

I shouldn't have been surprised that I'd slept a solid twelve hours. The whole ordeal of Christian's murder, the questioning by the police, and then the trip home had drained me.

I climbed out of bed and went to check on Katrina. The place was quiet, so I assumed that she was still sleeping. Lord knew, after what happened she might not want to get out of bed for a long time.

I knocked on her door softly. "Katrina?"

I waited, knocked again, and when I got no response I turned the knob. Her bed was empty and unmade.

Folding my arms over my chest, I made a face. Had she opened up shop?

I went downstairs to check it out but found the place dark and empty. I frowned. Where was she?

There was no point in staying downstairs, so I went back up to my room. I checked my phone for a message from her, found nothing.

But I did have a few messages from Wesley. I still didn't feel like replying to him yet. Maybe I was trying to make him suffer. I didn't know.

I noticed that I had a new Facebook notification. There was another message from that same woman, Shawde Williams:

Please, it's absolutely urgent that you contact me. I'll call you if you want. Just give me your number. My brother went to school with Katrina.

As I read her last sentence, my eyes bulged. Was this a ruse?

I clicked on the woman's profile and could see an enlarged version of her profile picture. She didn't look like a deranged person. She was attractive, smartly dressed. The

profile said her hometown was Albany, New York. Her relationship status reflected *IT'S COMPLICATED*. Her
profession, *MEDICAL*.

Well, she hadn't called herself a psychic . . . and with
her claim that her brother had gone to school with Katrina
I was intrigued. I didn't think she would simply make that
fact up. Better that she pretend she was the one who'd gone
to school with Katrina if she was hoping to get me to contact her.

But still, who knew? Some people liked to insinuate
themselves into other people's drama.

For the next several minutes, I debated what to do. My
gut told me she wasn't lying, but I didn't want to contact a
person with ulterior motives.

And then something else occurred to me. Months ago,
after I'd delivered that package of weed for Wesley, he'd
had a dispute with his dealer. Wesley had worried that the
dealer might try to contact me or his other friends to get
the money he believed he was owed. To be on the safe side,
Wesley had warned me to be suspicious of random people
trying to contact me. Just in case. I'd all but forgotten about
that.

Was it possible that someone had created a fake account, complete with a fake picture, as a way to get me to
contact them? But why? All for a bit of weed money I had
nothing to do with?

I jotted down the woman's number. I would block my
number and call her. That way, I could find out what the
deal was. And if she didn't appear to be who she claimed,
I could hang up and she would never have my information.
Then I would block her on Facebook.

A minute later I blocked my number, then punched in
the digits to Shawde's number. It rang three times before
she picked up.

"Hello?"

I hesitated.

"Hello?" the woman repeated.

"Hi," I said. Tentative. "You contacted me on Facebook."

"Jade?"

"Yes."

"Thank you," she said, and sounded relieved. "Thank you for getting back to me."

"What's this about?"

A beat. "It's about Katrina. What happened in Mexico."

"With all due respect, how can you possibly know anything about it?"

"I'd like to get together with you. See you face-to-face and explain everything."

I didn't respond. First of all, God only knew where this woman was. If she was in Albany, I certainly wouldn't be going there, and I didn't imagine she'd come down here. And second, I didn't have enough information to feel that meeting her would be wise.

"I know this sounds crazy," she went on, "but with what's going on . . . you're in danger."

"Because of Katrina?" I asked doubtfully. "Or is this really about Wesley?" There, I'd said it. If this was a ruse by some small-time weed dealer, I was certain that I would have thrown the person off of their game.

"Wesley?" The woman sounded genuinely confused. "Is he involved with Katrina?"

"No." There went that theory.

"Look, will you meet me? I'm in Key West."

My jaw dropped. "You—you're here?"

"I came as soon as I could. Like I told you, this is serious. And I'd rather not talk about it on the phone."

I was unsure. And yet curious. "And if I say no?"

I heard the woman sigh. "I'll be disappointed. But I'll also tell you to watch your back where Katrina's concerned."

"If you saw the news, then you know that her boyfriend was murdered in Mexico. I'm not sure what kind of beef you have with her, but I was with her at the time and I know she didn't kill the guy. Or maybe you just want to involve yourself in this story for some reason." Lord knew there were far too many crazy people in the world.

Shawde chuckled, but the sound held no mirth. "She's got you believing her, too. She's good at that."

I bit my inner cheek. This was insane. Some crazy guy had just murdered Katrina's boyfriend, and the woman on the line was acting as though Katrina was a villain.

The same as Melody believed.

"Maybe you saw Christian's sister on the news and some *spirit* has compelled you to come here and save me. I'm sorry you wasted your time, because there's nothing you can tell me—"

"Five and a half years ago, at the University at Buffalo, Katrina dated my brother. And he ended up dead." Shawde paused for a few seconds, letting her words sink in. "Now will you meet me?"

CHAPTER TWENTY-NINE

I agreed to meet Shawde at one that afternoon at The Inn at Key West, where she was staying. We would go to one of the restaurants on-site to have our talk.

And he ended up dead. Her words had played over in my mind all morning, and now as I neared the hotel I had a sickening sensation in my gut that I couldn't shake. Another dead boyfriend? Like in Mexico when I'd learned that Katrina had married Christian, my world had shifted on its axis, leaving me strangely disoriented.

I called my sister as I started to walk toward the hotel but got her voice mail. Hanging up, I found Brian's number and called him. I needed to talk to someone about this.

Brian's phone didn't ring at all, just went immediately to voice mail. An automated voice announced, "Please leave a message after the tone."

I frowned, then tried again. Once again his phone didn't ring. I got the same automated message.

Before Mexico, the fact that Brian didn't have a personal voice mail greeting hadn't fazed me. But now I remembered Katrina's comment about Brian and Keith being shady. How she'd wondered if they were involved in criminal activity. Was she right? Was that why Brian didn't announce who he was in a message on his cell phone?

And why did he have a Key West number when he didn't even live here? He had probably picked up a burner phone just to be able to correspond with me.

He'd told me to trust him, but what was with all the suspicious behavior? It was probably best that I forget him once and for all.

Of course, he'd probably heard the news about what had happened by now and likely wasn't going to contact me again anyway.

Pushing Brian from my thoughts, I continued to the hotel to meet Shawde. We'd agreed to meet in the lobby, and Shawde had told me that she would be wearing a pink dress to help me identify her more easily. Although having seen her picture online, I knew I would recognize her.

My first thought upon entering the hotel was that it was absolutely lovely. The lobby was like a grand entrance to a mansion, with a double staircase that led to the second level.

And as I looked up to that level, that's where I spotted the woman who had to be Shawde. She saw me the moment I saw her, because she instantly got up from the armchair where she'd been sitting and started down the right side of the staircase. She was wearing a long pink sundress as she said she'd be wearing, but what I recognized was the full head of curly hair, styled in an Afro.

I walked toward the steps and reached them as she finished descending. "Jade?" she asked me.

I extended my hand. "Hi."

She took my hand and shook it. "Thank you so much for agreeing to meet me."

She didn't look like a crazy person. In fact, she had an air of sophistication about her. And there was something else that struck me. Behind the beautiful face there was a hint of sadness in her eyes.

"Hammock's Café is serving lunch and has a lot of variety." She gestured to her far right. "It's that way, so it's close. Unless you want to head out somewhere else."

"No, Hammock's Café sounds fine." I wasn't really hungry. My stomach had been in knots since I'd spoken to her. Everything that had happened over the last few days, capped with her bombshell about her brother, had my head spinning.

"I'll buy." For the first time, she smiled, and my sense was that she was a warm and caring person.

But I didn't return her smile, because I didn't want to be a fool. And until I knew what she really wanted, I couldn't relax.

She led the way to the restaurant, which was outside. A cheerful hostess asked us if we were a party of two. Shawde took the lead, telling her yes and asking if we could have a table in a corner.

Less than a minute later we were seated on the far right, beside a wall of lush palms. I could see the blue water of the pool a short distance away and hear the laughter of people frolicking in it.

Just being here made me think of the fact that I hadn't even explored the beauty of Key West yet. Now, with Christian's murder, I wondered if I ever would.

Shawde lifted one of the two menus that the hostess had placed on the table and passed it to me. "Anything you want. It's my treat."

I took the menu but said, "I'm not too hungry. I think I'll just have coffee."

"Are you sure?"

I was in no mood to be breaking bread with a stranger, especially not under the circumstances. "Yes, I'm sure. But thanks anyway."

A few seconds later a waitress appeared, all smiles. "Good afternoon. Welcome to Hammock's Café. Can I get you a cocktail while you look over the menu? We make amazing frozen margaritas."

"Actually, I'd love a cappuccino," I told her. "Do you have any flavored shots?"

"We do."

"Vanilla?"

"Sugar-free or regular?"

"Regular, thanks."

The waitress turned her attention to Shawde. "I'll have a coffee," Shawde said before the waitress could speak. "Black. Plus an order of your Island Chips and Queso."

"Great." The waitress took our menus and walked away.

I studied Shawde as she placed her purse strap over the side of her chair. She was older than I was, probably by ten years.

She faced me, smiling again. "I'm sure you're wondering if I'm crazy."

"The thought has crossed my mind. I mean, you don't know me, yet you come all the way to Key West to see me? Are you actually living in Albany?"

"Yes."

When she gave me a quizzical look, I said, "I checked out your Facebook profile."

"Of course. I'm glad you did. I'm a pediatric nurse. Have been for ten years."

I was certain that at least some people with psychiatric problems had been able to hold down steady jobs. But I didn't say that.

"And," she went on, "so you know, I didn't come just to see you."

I narrowed my eyes. "Vacation?"

"No. I wish." She paused, then leaned forward, resting

her elbows on the table. "I had a friend down here. You talked to him several times at the café. A guy named—"

"—Gordon," I finished for her, a prickling sensation spreading across my nape. A sixth sense. "What about him?"

"I haven't been able to reach him for over a week."

"He hasn't been in touch at all?"

"Nothing. Which isn't like him."

"He used to come into the coffee shop every day and work on his novel. We talked quite a few times. Then suddenly he stopped coming in."

"When was that?"

"Gosh, at least a week ago."

"And did he contact you after that? Text, call?"

"No, we never exchanged numbers. We talked about getting together to see Hemingway Home once, since we were both into writing, but after that I never saw him again." I paused, thinking. "No, wait. I saw him the morning after that. He was outside of the café. Katrina was talking to him. He turned and left. That was the last time I saw him."

"Katrina was talking to him?"

My stomach sank. *Oh God. Was that of any significance?* "She thought Gordon was playing me. I think that's why she talked to him. She probably told him to stay away."

"Maybe Katrina was on to him," Shawde said, more to herself. "Damn it. This isn't like him. He was supposed to stay in touch daily."

"Wait," I said, trying to figure out what was going on. "What exactly are you saying? Was Gordon down here to spy on Katrina? Spy on me?" Even as I asked the question, it sounded ridiculous.

"This isn't about you," she said. "Like I said before, this is about Katrina Hughes."

Gordon had asked a lot of questions, especially about

my connection to Katrina and sorority life. "Is he really a writer?"

"No."

"Oh my God." I felt betrayed. "So he lied to get close to me. He asked me all those questions. I thought he was interested in me."

"He had to find out who you were, what you knew."

This woman had had someone investigating Katrina? Investigating me? Maybe she *was* crazy. Or seriously misguided.

Suddenly I was unsure that I should even be here. My loyalties lay with Katrina, who'd been good to me—even if she wasn't the nicest person in the world. Not this stranger.

"You're making Katrina out to be a villain, but the truth is, I have no clue who *you* are. What your agenda is."

The smiling waitress returned at that moment. "One vanilla cappuccino, and a black coffee. Is there anything else I can get you right now?"

"Nope," I said.

Once the waitress was a good distance away from the table, Shawde asked, "How long have you known Katrina?"

"Not all that long," I said. "A couple of weeks. But my sister has known her for years. And why are you asking *me* these questions, instead of telling me what you know? You said your brother died?"

"Bear with me. Just as you want to be careful, so do I. So your sister is the connection to Katrina." She made a face. "Either your sister didn't really know her, or . . ."

Her voice trailed off, and I leaned closer to her, eager to hear what she had to say. "Or what?" I prompted.

"Or she was a part of it. I have long suspected that Katrina has had help doing what she does. Heck, *someone* has to know."

"My sister was a part of what?"

Shawde said nothing, just looked deep in thought.

"Are you deliberately being cryptic?" I asked.

Shawde studied me for several seconds before answering. "It's just . . . and please don't be offended . . . but I need to make sure you're not one of the people in Katrina's circle who know what's she's really doing. I mean, you went to Mexico with her on her *honeymoon*."

My anger flared. "If you're trying to imply that Katrina is involved in some sort of sordid activity and that I know about it—condone it—you're wrong. Is that why you had me meet you? So you could accuse me—"

"No," Shawde interjected, and held up a hand. "I'm just . . . my brain is spinning with a million thoughts, but no, I suppose that doesn't make sense. And Gordon found no reason—"

"Why are you here?" I interjected. "Why am I here?"

"Because I agree with Christian's sister. I don't think her brother being murdered was a tragic case of wrong place, wrong time. Another family has lost someone they love—all because Christian had the misfortune of getting involved with Katrina."

I glared at her. "That's a pretty cruel thing to say." This woman had had me meet her, but she hadn't said anything that proved Katrina was a killer. "You weren't in Mexico. You have no clue what happened. But I was, and I can tell you that it's not fair to blame Katrina because some insane guy killed her boyfriend. All you need to do is read the news to know that there are serious issues in Mexico. Tons of tourists have been killed there. We shouldn't have even gone to Cancun."

"*Exactly.* So why did you? Wasn't it just a couple of weeks ago when a couple was murdered in Cancun? Why would anybody say, *Hey, let's go to Mexico,* when they were already in a tropical place?" She gestured around.

It was a fair question and one I didn't have an answer to. So I stuck to what I knew. "As I said, you weren't there. Neither was Melody. I was, and I can tell you that speculation isn't proof. You think I haven't questioned what happened? But the bottom line is, Katrina was in the club with me the entire time. And she got way too drunk to kill anyone."

Shawde shook her head, giving me a look of disappointment. "I don't know how she does it. She has everyone in her life under her spell."

"Excuse me?" I had to draw in a deep breath to keep my anger under control.

"One boyfriend dying under questionable circumstances, that's bad enough. But two?"

My jaw went slack. "Your brother died under questionable circumstances?"

But was I really surprised? It was clear that this woman had come here because she thought Katrina was responsible for her brother's death. But on some level, I'd tried to avoid the obvious. I hadn't even come out and asked her about her brother.

Because you're afraid to hear . . .

Shawde didn't answer. She was busy fiddling with her phone. And when she turned it to face me, I saw a man who looked a lot like her. He was gorgeous and had a smile that radiated warmth through the phone's screen.

"This is Shemar. My brother." And there was that sadness in her eyes again, more pronounced now. "Five and a half years ago, after dating Katrina, he died in a car crash. The police ruled it an accident, but I know it wasn't that. It was murder."

CHAPTER THIRTY

"Murder?" I repeated the word, speaking louder than I'd planned. I quickly glanced around, checking to see if anyone was within earshot and had heard me.

No one was close enough, which was a relief. Still, I lowered my voice before continuing. "Why do you think your brother was murdered?"

"I don't think it. I *know* he was murdered," Shawde stressed. "And that bitch thinks she's gotten away with it."

As I stared at Shawde, at her eyes that had filled with tears, I felt a pang of empathy for her. I knew what it was like to lose someone. To lose someone you loved dearly. And I imagined if that loss was sudden it was even harder to cope with.

"Don't look at me like that," Shawde said, brushing away her tears. "I'm not crazy. The police said there was no proof, but that's because Katrina knew what she was doing."

I noticed then the pale skin on Shawde's wedding finger where a ring had been. Had she recently ended a marriage? Another loss could be causing the pain over her brother's death to be even worse.

"I don't think you're crazy," I began gently. "It's obvious you loved your brother, and a sudden loss like that—"

"I assure you, if I believed it was simply a tragic accident, I could move on. You have no clue what this quest for justice has cost me."

Maybe part of that cost had been losing her marriage. "I'm sorry," I said. "I'm sorry about your brother."

"But you don't believe me. I ask you this: How would a person who knew his way around cars leave for a long trip with broken brakes? My brother was great about checking his car from top to bottom the day before a long trip. He always did that. We had a cousin who died in a car wreck. He *knew* the dangers on the road. And he was heading to Albany the day he . . . he died." She paused, swallowed. "He would have checked his car. There isn't a doubt in my mind."

I held Shawde's gaze, contemplating what to say. I had no doubt that she believed what she was saying. Believed it with every fiber of her being. But believing it didn't make it true. "Did the police investigate your claims?" I finally asked.

She scoffed. "Not hard enough. They said the car was so damaged after the crash that they couldn't find any evidence of sabotage. But the witnesses all said that Shemar didn't stop. Traffic was slowing down, and he kept barreling ahead, finally swerving to avoid the traffic in his path. His car collided head-on with a truck and burst into flames." Stopping, Shawde grabbed one of the napkins from the table and dabbed at her tears.

"Oh my God," I uttered. "That's awful." No wonder she was devastated.

"It's just so hard," Shawde went on. "Five and a half years and you'd think I wouldn't break down like this."

"Losing someone you love is devastating," I said. "I recently lost my father. And . . . well, I had to miss a semester of school because of it. It's not easy."

"My brother had dirt on Katrina," Shawde went on, sounding stronger now. "He had dirt on her, and he was going to expose her."

My back went straight. "What kind of dirt?"

"He didn't say. He was vague when he spoke about it, asking me advice about what he should do. But I think she hurt someone. And he knew, and he was wrestling with his conscience as to whether or not he should turn her in. He was heading home to Albany for a few days to get some rest and relaxation and decide his next course of action. It was also then that he was going to tell me exactly what was going on."

"And you have no clue what he was going to tell you?"

Shawde shook her head.

A few beats passed. "You're not even sure what was going on with your brother and Katrina. And you assume that she tampered with his car to kill him?"

"It's the only thing that makes sense. I've talked to some people from UB, and I'm even more convinced. Katrina and my brother weren't just having a relationship spat. When I talked to him, he sounded . . . conflicted. Scared, even. Something big was going on. That's why he was heading home. To talk to me and my family about it. And I know my brother. He would never get into a car with faulty brakes."

I felt for her. I did. Losing someone—and so suddenly and horrifically—was no doubt crushing. It left a person needing to place blame, to find a reason for the inexplicable.

Melody was obviously doing the same thing.

"You don't believe me," Shawde said, "but before you dismiss me, there's more you need to hear."

I met her gaze. "Go on."

"I think Katrina is also behind the deaths of her parents."

The proclamation left me speechless for several seconds.

And not because I believed it to be some sort of bomb-shell. But because it was the kind of statement that pushed Shawde's theory into the realm of the unbelievable. She was blinded by grief, finding sinister motives in tragic accidents.

"I'm sorry," I said, shaking my head with disbelief. "Her parents? Now that's just crazy."

"It is. That's exactly what I'm saying. Katrina is crazy."

I refrained from making the obvious correction . . . that Katrina wasn't the one who was crazy. Instead, I pushed my chair back and stood. "I think I've heard enough."

"Sit," Shawde commanded.

Perhaps it was the unexpectedly stern tone in her voice, but I found myself obeying her. I sat back down, saying, "Look, I don't understand why you're telling me any of this. You think Katrina killed your brother, her parents, Christian. . . . Even if she did, what am I supposed to do about it?"

"For five years I've been waiting for Katrina to slip up, make another mistake so that I can get justice for my brother. I think she just did."

I stared at Shawde, not sure what to say. I wasn't entirely convinced. But I could tell that she was entirely convinced that she was right.

"How?" I asked, sounding exasperated. "I already told you, I was with her. She was with me at the club. She didn't kill Christian." And I seriously doubted that she had killed Shawde's brother. Especially if the police didn't even buy the story.

"If she didn't hold the knife herself, then she got someone else to slit that poor man's neck."

It was the same thing Melody had said, and my body flinched at the allegation. But that's all it was. An allegation. And yet I could suddenly see the possibility of it. Why would Katrina ram her tongue down a stranger's throat?

Unless . . .

No, I told myself. *It isn't possible.* "I wasn't lying when I told you that I was with Katrina in the bar. The guy she was with—her boyfriend—they'd had a fight and he left. Katrina and I were in the bar for the rest of the evening until we went back to the hotel. I know that because I watched a lot of her bad behavior. Lots of flirting and drinking, and some other inappropriate stuff that doesn't matter. The point is, at the time that Christian was being killed, she was with me. We left and went back to the hotel together. She couldn't have killed him."

"I heard the guy was her husband, not her boyfriend. That she married him last week."

I swallowed. "Yes. That's something I found out later. After his death. His sister told me."

"So when you went to Mexico with them, you thought that Christian was her boyfriend?"

"Yes."

"So Katrina obviously lied about that."

"She said that she didn't want to tell me. She thought it would look bad. Because they had a rocky relationship. She figured I would judge her for marrying him. They hadn't known each other all that long."

Shawde scoffed. "Right. More likely, she wanted you along for their honeymoon . . . so you could be her alibi. Nobody brings a third person with them on their honeymoon. Nobody."

I swallowed. I thought of Melody's adamant stance that Katrina had killed Christian and Sergeant Ramirez's own questions. *Oh God . . . could Katrina really have planned something like this?*

I shook my head. No, the idea was ludicrous. Wasn't it?

"Katrina told me her parents died in a carbon-monoxide accident in their home," I said, hoping that if I debunked the allegation that Katrina had killed her parents Shawde would realize that the story she was spinning was coming from a place of grief.

"Right after Katrina was in town. Did she tell you that part—or conveniently leave it out? She left town the morning her parents died. One minute she's there; the next they're leaving a car on in the garage? You know she inherited a fortune after they died?"

"They wouldn't be the first people to leave their car running in the garage." Though my voice quavered. I hadn't known all of the details, and I had to admit that Katrina having been there didn't bode well.

"Katrina's a very clever killer."

"So you say. How can you know any of this?"

"Because I've been waiting for her to slip up for five and a half years. I've paid attention to everything she does."

Silence fell between us. After a long moment, Shawde said, "I can see you're finally getting it. You're finally seeing the big picture."

"I'm seeing the picture you're painting, but who's to say you're right? You're spinning events and facts to make it look like Katrina's a killer. But if you're right, how could every cop be so blind?"

"People get away with murder, Jade. It happens."

I exhaled sharply. "Even if you want me to help you, I wouldn't have the first clue how."

"Gordon told me that he'd seen you go upstairs at the shop. You're living with Katrina, right?"

I gave Shawde a look of dismay. I still couldn't believe she'd had someone watching us. "How long has Gordon been spying on us?"

"For a while. After I learned she opened up shop here, I knew it would only be a matter of time before something tragic happened. She's a psychopath." Shawde paused. "You *are* living with her?"

I nodded. "Yes."

"Then you're in the best position to find evidence about what she's done."

"Evidence?" I shot back, incredulous. "How?"

"I've studied serial killers over the past five years. I think . . . I think it's likely that Katrina has kept trinkets from her victims."

"Oh my God," I uttered. "Do you hear yourself?"

"Or maybe a journal. With every kill she gets away with, she feels more and more invincible."

I stared at Shawde, wondering for a moment if I was having some weird out-of-body experience. Surely this wasn't really happening.

"You may not be crazy, but you're deluded by grief."

"Grief?" Shawde countered, and I could detect anger in her tone. "You think my fight for justice is about grief? My God, do you know what it's cost me?" Her jaw flinched. "More than you can imagine. And I assure you that I have not put my personal relationships on the back burner for five years simply because I'm sad over losing my brother."

Things were becoming clearer now. She'd probably lost her husband—or perhaps fiancé—over her quest. "What you want, I can't be a part of it. You want me to spy on Katrina?" I shook my head. "Your brother died, and I'm sorry for that, but I'm not convinced it was murder. And neither are the cops." I pushed my chair back.

"Please," Shawde said, "don't leave."

I stepped away from the table. "Whatever your issues are, you're on your own. I don't want to be involved."

"Jade."

"Don't contact me again," I added over my shoulder.

"Ask yourself, where's Gordon?" Shawde said, and I halted. "Suddenly he's nowhere to be found. I thought he was in Mexico following you guys, but I still haven't heard from him. And by your own admission, the last time you saw him he was talking to Katrina."

The implication was clear. That Gordon had met with foul play at Katrina's hands.

"Watch your back, Jade. Katrina's dangerous."

I resumed walking, hurrying out of the restaurant, hoping that I would never hear from Shawde again.

CHAPTER THIRTY-ONE

My pulse didn't stop racing after I left Shawde, not even during my long walk back to the shop.

The story Shawde spun was incredible. She made Katrina sound like a cold-blooded serial killer. One who had killed her college boyfriend and now Christian. Heck, Shawde alleged that Katrina had even murdered her parents.

That was where Shawde lost me, for good. Even if I'd been able to suspend my disbelief and see Katrina as some sort of black widow, I couldn't believe that a person would kill her parents. Not without being seriously evil.

I hadn't seen that kind of evil in the weeks I'd spent with Katrina. And even if that wasn't long enough to truly know someone, my sister had known Katrina for years. I might not always get along with Marie, but there was no way she'd ever send me down here to be with someone who had a dangerous side.

But Katrina was in your room. Was she the one who sent those nasty messages to Wesley and Michelle?

I halted on the sidewalk, my stomach knotting as I remembered the feeling of fear when Katrina had woken me in the middle of the night. She'd been desperate to convince me to go to Mexico with her and Christian.

Had I been a critical part of her plan?

Stumbling over to a nearby light pole, I placed a hand on it to steady myself. Then I drew in a few deep breaths and tried to regain my composure. How could I believe that I'd been living with a killer? Coincidence wasn't proof.

The police hadn't found any evidence to connect Katrina to Shemar's accident, and Katrina had been in the bar with me when Christian had been murdered. And as for her parents, when Katrina had told me about their deaths I'd felt her grief. She hadn't been faking it.

I knew firsthand how awful it was to lose not one parent, but two. No one would kill their parents. At least not loving, caring parents. And that was how Katrina had described hers.

"Miss, are you okay?"

I looked over my shoulder, saw a tall woman regarding me with concern. Easing off of the light pole, I forced a smile. "I'm fine. Just hot."

The woman nodded and continued on her way. Then I did the same. Despite the heat of the day, I shuddered as I neared the café. Christian's murder and now Shawde's allegations . . . All of it was surreal. I felt as though I'd been thrown into an alternate universe, one where nothing made sense.

The only thing I was certain of as I went to the café's back door was that grief could cripple a person. And Shawde was clearly crippled. She'd been devastated by her brother's death and hadn't been able to move on for years. It wasn't surprising that she'd conjured a story where Katrina was the villain. It was a place for Shawde to focus her attention and energy because she simply hadn't been able to make sense of the loss of her brother.

I opened the door and entered, finding the lights off and

the place quiet. I had contemplated telling Katrina about my meeting with Shawde as I'd walked home but decided against it. Katrina was dealing with enough. She didn't need to hear that someone from her past was accusing her of murder.

Upstairs, it was also dark and quiet. Katrina still wasn't home?

And then I heard a sound. Was that . . . *laughter*?

I moved forward slowly, putting each foot in front of the other as quietly as possible. Yes, Katrina was here. In her bedroom.

Another sound. Words I couldn't make out, followed by more laughter.

I made a face. Not that she had to be curled up in bed crying, but the laughter struck me as odd. After everything that had happened, I wasn't sure I'd be able to smile for weeks.

I crept closer.

". . . well, what can you do?"

Was she talking about Christian's death?

". . . police in Mexico, do they ever solve any crimes?"

She didn't sound frustrated or even worried. But perhaps . . . sarcastic?

I was at her door now and took a step closer. The floorboards creaked beneath my feet, and I cringed just as Katrina whipped her head in my direction. The smile that was on her face instantly went flat, and she looked at me with an accusing, angry glare.

"Um, hi." I raised a hand in a wave and smiled, hoping that she would think I had just gotten home and was checking on her. Rather than the truth that I was eavesdropping.

Into the phone, she said, "I'll have to call you back. Touch base with me about what we said."

"You're home," I said uneasily.

Katrina tossed her cell phone onto the bed, then got to her feet. "How long have you been standing there?"

I didn't answer right away. I didn't want to seem on edge. So I drew in a slow breath and replied, "I just got back. I heard your voice so I figured I'd say hi."

"Where were you?"

"I got up, you weren't here. So I decided to walk around Key West. Explore. You know, do something relaxing to ease my mind after all the stress we've been through." My voice ended on an uneasy note, but I hoped she wouldn't suspect that I was lying.

"I see."

"And where were you?" I asked. "You left early."

"I—" She stopped abruptly, and then her face seemed to crumble. And whether it was the conversation I'd had with Shawde or my own intuition, I suddenly thought that the action looked insincere.

"I was missing Christian," Katrina went on. "So I wanted to go to the last place we were together that meant something. I went to the beach where he proposed. I stayed there for hours."

"That must have been hard," I said.

"Actually, I felt a sense of peace there." A little smile came on her lips, and again I was suspicious. Perhaps because I had experienced my own recent loss, I was skeptical about a memory of something so wonderful bringing her joy at this point. My sense where Shawde was concerned was that every happy memory also brought with it pain. And that was what I was experiencing now, even a year after losing my father.

But people grieved differently. I found the memories—the happy ones especially—the hardest to bear. Those memories remind you of everything you've lost—at least in the beginning. Maybe it was exactly the opposite for Katrina.

Would I even be second-guessing her if I hadn't met with Shawde earlier today?

"You're stronger than I am," I said. "Doing something like that, for me it would be hard. The happy places . . . I could hardly stand to go there right after my dad passed."

"Everyone grieves differently," Katrina said, a tad defensive.

"No, I know that."

"Going to that spot on the beach was good for me. I know Christian was there with me. I felt him. And I know that he would want me to be remember him fondly."

I nodded. Her explanation was reasonable. I shouldn't be suspicious of her simply because of what Shawde had said.

And yet Shawde's parting words, her warning for me to watch my back, suddenly struck more effectively than they had when she'd uttered them.

I was glad I'd made the decision not to bring up Shawde with Katrina. What if Shawde was right about her? Letting her know that someone else was accusing her of murder might actually put me in harm's way.

Not that I believed Shawde, but I had an unsettling feeling. Likely because of the stress of the last few days. But I suddenly knew that I couldn't be too careful. I would have to watch Katrina and see whether or not I believed she was being honest. And perhaps I needed to talk to my sister, find out what she really knew about Katrina's character.

"Any idea what you're going to do?" I asked. "Are you going to reopen the café anytime soon?"

"I know you came down here to earn money for the summer—"

"That's really the last thing you should be worrying about. This was an awful tragedy. And who knows what might happen. We left Mexico, but do you think they might want to question us again?"

"We're back in the States now. We're out of their reach. They can't obligate us to do anything."

Shawde's words sounded in my head. *So you could be her alibi. Nobody brings a third person with them on their honeymoon. Nobody.*

I pressed my fingers to my temple and massaged. My head was throbbing.

"Are you okay?" Katrina asked.

"Not really." I shrugged. "How can either one of us be okay right now?"

Katrina got up and hugged me. "We'll be okay," she said softly. "We'll get through this."

Watch your back, Jade. . . .

I needed to talk to my sister. See what else she could tell me about Katrina. I didn't want to believe Shawde's story, but what struck me about her was just how adamant she'd been.

"I'm going to take a shower," I said as I pulled out of Katrina's embrace.

"Sure. See you in a bit."

As I showered, I wasn't thinking about cleaning my body as much as I was recalling everything Shawde had said to me. Although I had earlier dismissed her words, now I wasn't so sure. Could it possibly be true? Was I living here with a psychopath?

When I exited the shower, I saw that Katrina's bedroom door was closed. I assumed she was in there, and I went into my bedroom and closed the door. With her door closed and mine, I figured the risk of her overhearing me was minimal.

I called my sister and she picked up on the second ring. "Hey, Jade. How are you?"

"I'm not sure."

"What do you mean?"

I hesitated. Then I asked, "How well do you know Katrina?"

"I know her pretty well. We went to UB for four years together."

"But are you best friends? Close friends?"

"Well, we weren't really *that* close. We saw each other in the sorority house all the time, of course." She paused. "Why?"

"I'm just wondering why you sent me all the way down here." Shawde's story was getting to me, even her claim that some people had to have known what Katrina was up to and turned a blind eye. Certainly my sister wouldn't be complicit in any crime . . . would she? "Why did you have me come to Florida to work for her?"

"Because you needed a job. You needed an escape. It was perfect timing."

"But if you weren't that close with her—"

"I still knew her. I've stayed in touch with her on Facebook." Marie paused a beat. "Why are you asking me this?"

"Just wondering. Wondering how well you know Katrina."

"There must be something else. Obviously, you're not just calling me because you're curious. Did something happen?"

"You mean other than the murder?"

My tone was snarky, but Marie didn't offer a retort. Instead, she waited a few beats and said, "I'm not really sure what's going on here, Sis."

"Someone called me," I said, sounding harried. "Actually, she did more than call me. She came all the way down here to see me. So I need to know. Is there something about Katrina that you never told me? Something I should have known before I ever got here?"

"Like what?"

"Is there anything about Katrina—anything at all—that would make you not trust her?"

"If I didn't trust her I wouldn't have sent you down there."

My sister's words put my mind at ease. I knew she wouldn't have sent me down here to be with a deranged person. But still, Shawde's story haunted me. The reality that I couldn't simply dismiss her as crazy led me to wonder if there was a grain of truth to her claims.

I told Marie everything that this woman had told me. About Shemar, Katrina's parents, and now of course Christian.

"She contacted me, too," Marie said. "I got a message on Facebook from someone asking me to call her, but I didn't."

"She said she'd spoken to some people who went to school with Katrina."

"Williams. I didn't even make the connection with the names. Of course, it's been years since I was in college." Marie paused. "I remember when Shemar died. It was a tragic car wreck. Why would his sister think it was more than that?"

"She seems pretty confident it was murder. But I know family often have a hard time accepting the truth."

"There was something," my sister said suddenly, her voice sounding distant, as if she was recalling a memory.

My back stiffened. "Something like what?"

"There was a girl. Another soror. She left, went back home. She'd been attacked, something like that. I remember there being some talk about Katrina somehow being involved. Maybe the girl was scared? I can't even remember the details."

"Think," I pressed, my pulse quickening. "This could be important."

"I don't really remember. I just remember there being some sort of rumors about Katrina and that this girl had been scared." My sister paused, and I waited. "At the time, a girl in our sorority had been murdered."

"Someone was murdered!" *Another murder that involved Katrina?*

"You may remember the story. There'd been a rapist on the loose. The Bike Path Rapist. Some people had been attacked at UB. Then this girl from our sorority house had been murdered, and people were even more scared. We were all on edge. So when Angelina—yeah, I think that was her name—when she left to go back home, a lot of us felt that it had to do with the murder of our soror. That anything to do with Katrina intimidating her had just been speculation. Katrina was a bit of a hardnose. She was sorority president, and she was very by the book. So she did rub some of the girls the wrong way. Some girls talked about wanting to drop out of the sorority because of her."

"So your soror was murdered? Did they ever find her killer?"

"Yeah. It was crazy. Another soror killed her and then tried to kill someone else. It had to do with a boyfriend, and this girl being jealous. Totally insane, obviously."

"So it had nothing to do with Katrina?"

"Nothing at all."

I frowned. "And that's all you remember about Katrina?" I asked. "Nothing else?"

"No. Not that I remember. But you know, her best friend was Rowena. I can get in touch with her and ask her if she remembers anything else."

"Oh, would you?" Someone else who'd been close to Katrina, that could be good. "She might remember the details you don't, and that would be great."

"Why? Are you worried? You believe this woman?

Because I have to say, the idea of Katrina being some sort of crazed murderer . . ." My sister's voice trailed off, and she chuckled.

Her chuckle put me at ease. If she thought the idea was ludicrous, clearly I had no reason to worry. It was highly likely that Shemar's death had been what it appeared to be. A tragic accident.

"I'm not worried, but I would love to have as much information as possible. If I know for sure what happened, then I can deal with it. That's all I want to know. If everything was kosher, then I don't have to cause myself any added stress by letting Shawde's words haunt me at night."

"I'll give Rowena a call. See what she remembers."

"Great. And call me back as soon as you know something."

CHAPTER THIRTY-TWO

SHAWDE

The hours that passed seemed endless as Shawde waited for *something*. She wanted the phone to ring, to finally hear from Gordon. There were so many damn hotels in Key West and she had been painstakingly going through the list of all of them, but it was taking hours. And so far, she'd had no luck locating Gordon.

The problem was, Gordon could have already checked out—especially if he'd gone to Mexico to continue his surveillance of Katrina there.

With all her heart, Shawde wanted to believe that. But she had a bad feeling in her gut, one she couldn't shake: Something had happened to Gordon.

"I can't take this anymore," Shawde uttered, and bounded up from the bed. She went over to the suitcase on the floor and fished out her swimsuit. She wasn't down here for a leisurely vacation, but several laps in the pool would help ease her tension, just as it had when she'd used to swim in college.

She was stripping out of her dress when her cell phone rang. Quickly tossing her dress onto the floor, Shawde sprinted over to the night table and scooped up her iPhone. PRIVATE NAME was flashing on her screen.

"Gordon," she rasped, and quickly answered the call. "Hello?"

A beat passed. Shawde almost thought no one was going to speak until she heard: "Is this Shawde Williams?"

"Yes," Shawde said in reply to the woman's query. "Yes, it is."

Another beat. Then, "Monica said you wanted to talk to me. I'm Angelina."

Shawde's heart nearly stopped. She'd hoped for this call, prayed for it, but never expected it to transpire. "Angelina." Shawde sank onto the bed. "I'm so glad you called."

"You're really Shemar's sister?"

"Yes. He was my baby brother."

"God." Angelina made a sort of strangled sound. "I still think about him. Every day."

"Thank you," Shawde said. "That means a lot."

"I'm so sorry. I'm so sorry he's gone."

"It's not your fault."

"But it is," Angelina insisted. "If I hadn't talked to him, I know he would still be alive."

"You think Katrina killed him?"

"I *know* she did," Angelina said. "And after seeing on the news what happened in Mexico, I can't stay silent. Not anymore. She will keep killing until someone stops her."

Tears sprang to Shawde's eyes. Finally someone was validating her long-held belief that Katrina was a murderer. The heavy burden of everyone's doubts over Shawde's sanity lifted from her shoulders, giving her much-needed release.

"I know you were attacked," Shawde said. "And that you believe Katrina was behind it. Possibly she was working with Rowena, who I've heard was her best friend."

"Yes. And I spoke to Shemar after it happened. He was livid. He wanted to confront her. I told him not to, but I'm sure he did. And I think that's what got him killed."

"But something else was going on, wasn't it?" Shawde asked. "There's a reason you and my brother were talking *before* your attack? Monica mentioned you were going to report Katrina to the sorority board. What was that about?"

Shawde heard Angelina's deep intake of breath. "Actually, I wanted to go to the police about my suspicion."

"What suspicion?"

"There was another murder. Another girl, not a part of our sorority, named Carmen Young. Of course, when she was killed, we thought it was the Bike Path Rapist. Until I learned something from my then boyfriend, a guy named Ned. A friend of his knew Carmen, knew that she had tried to pledge our sorority, and was denied. She lodged a complaint against Katrina with our governing body, the National Pan-Hellenic Council, and had a whole list of grievances. I heard there was an investigation. Then the complainant died, and the matter was dropped.

"I don't know why, but I went to Rowena about it. She was the vice president, and I figured she needed to know. Katrina had a tendency to be rough on some of the girls, and I figured Rowena would support me, help me go to the Pan-Hellenic Council so we could get facts about the grievance to possibly bring to the police. If Katrina had nothing to hide, what would it hurt for them to ask her some questions? I expected Rowena to agree with me, but she instead became livid. She said I couldn't go around making wild accusations without any proof. I was stupid, because I told her that if she wasn't interested in pursuing the matter, I would do it on my own. It wasn't that I *believed* Katrina was a killer, but I wanted to rule it out, ya know? I didn't realize then that Rowena was in bed with Katrina, figuratively speaking. Next thing I know, I'm being attacked. It wasn't a man. As I fought with my attacker, I realized it was a woman. And that's when I grasped the seriousness of the situation. Rowena had tried to kill me to silence me for good."

"So Rowena and Katrina are in this together," Shawde said. "It makes sense. Katrina had to have help to do what she did. But how does my brother fit into this picture?"

"Ned. Ned knew that Shemar was dating Katrina, so he talked to him, expressing some of his concerns when I was initially unsure about what to do. Shemar was shocked and horrified to learn about Carmen Young, and found her death suspicious, as I did. He sought me out to talk about the situation and what we ought to do. There really wasn't enough proof to go to the police with our suspicion. That's when I told him I would handle it by talking to Rowena. I'd always known Katrina was a narcissist, but thought that Rowena was fair. I mean, what were the chances that they'd both be psychopaths?"

"So Shemar was dating Katrina, yet he believed his girlfriend was guilty of murder?"

"I'm not sure if he initially believed it, or just wanted to hear more, sort of hash things out with me. I do know he was surprised that Katrina had never told him about Carmen. If she had nothing to hide, why wouldn't she ever mention the issue to her boyfriend?"

"So he was starting to be suspicious of her."

"And once I was attacked, I think he was convinced. But the situation was big, and there was no real proof. I talked to him before I left, told him that Katrina was dangerous. I told him he had to let the matter drop, that Katrina would slip up on her own one day. But Shemar, he didn't—"

"Want to see her go unpunished," Shawde supplied, a smile touching her lips. That was her brother. He'd always had a keen sense of right and wrong. If he'd believed

Katrina guilty of assault, he would have wanted to see her brought to justice.

Shawde had that in common with her brother.

"He told me he was going to get proof. And that if he couldn't get proof regarding the murder, he was determined to get justice for me. I begged him to let it go, but I doubt he did. All I can assume is that he confronted Katrina at some point, or she found out what he was up to."

"And that's why she killed him. Maybe with Rowena's help."

"That's my feeling, that they're a team. Katrina wanted me dead, all because I was going to report her to the National Pan-Hellenic Council. Rowena tried to make it happen. But she failed, which was a huge loose end for them."

"Because with you around, they could possibly be arrested for assault. You were a live witness. So you knew you had to get away."

"I knew I wasn't safe. I believed in my heart that either Katrina or Rowena—or both—killed Carmen so that her complaint would be quashed."

"And once my brother tried to take her down . . . she had to get rid of him, too."

"Exactly."

"Finally," Shawde said, and stifled a cry. "You've given me the missing pieces. Shemar never got to tell me why he wanted to talk to me urgently about Katrina. He was on his way home to talk to me when he was killed."

"I tried to get him to forget about it," Angelina said. "I was safely out of Katrina's reach. And I wasn't telling anyone else at UB about what had happened. I'd learned my lesson. I was going to keep my mouth shut. I just . . . I just wish that Shemar had listened to me."

Though Shawde's heart was heavy, it felt fractionally lighter after she heard Angelina's story. A sense of pride filled her. She was proud that Shemar had taken a stand for what was right, even if it had gotten him killed.

"My brother took a stand," Shawde said. "Which validates exactly what I'm doing. I've dedicated my life to getting justice for Shemar. Thank you for sharing your story."

"I'm glad we got to talk. I always liked Shemar, and I've always felt a measure of guilt over—"

"Please, don't feel guilty. It's not your fault."

"Still, I know that if not for him wanting to defend me . . ." Angelina's voice broke. "I owe him, Shawde. And I want you to know that I'm no longer afraid to speak out. If you need me to tell my story to help nail Katrina, I'll do it."

"I appreciate that more than you know," Shawde said. "But now that Katrina's killed another boyfriend in Mexico, I think she's finally made the mistake that's going to take her down. She just hoisted her own noose over a tree branch, Angelina. And she's about to hang herself. I'm sure of it."

CHAPTER THIRTY-THREE

My sister called me later, and I answered the phone before it could ring a second time. "What did you find out?" I asked without preamble.

"Well, I sent a message to Katrina's closest friend on Facebook, asking her to call me because I needed to talk to her. She just got back to me. And she said that any idea about Katrina being some sort of crazed killer is insane. Which is what I think."

"What about the incident with the girl?"

"I brought that up, and she said the same thing that most of us had thought at the time. That because of the rapist on campus, and the murder of our soror, Angelina was naturally terrified after her own brush with the rapist. That's why she left school."

I bit my inner cheek. For some reason, the answer didn't satisfy me. "Though I suppose if Rowena and Katrina were best friends, how much of what she says can you actually trust?"

"Are you looking for something where there is nothing? Are you trying to play Nancy Drew? Katrina is not this person that Shemar's sister made her out to be."

"I'm just saying, Shawde said she had friends who would lie for her."

"And you don't know Shawde from Adam. I went to school with Katrina. I know her."

"All right. I just wanted to hear whether or not there was any merit to Katrina being . . . I don't know . . . a bit shady? But I guess if the friend thinks there was none, and the fact that the police never investigated anything . . . my mind should be at ease."

"Exactly. I wouldn't take anything this woman told you seriously."

Why would your sister send you down there? Shawde's question came into my mind. But I shook it away, because as many problems as my sister and I had had over the years, I didn't believe that she would willingly put me in harm's way.

"All right. Thanks."

"Good night. And just try to relax. You've had a stressful few days, and this person coming to see you obviously hasn't made things any easier. If you want to come back home, please do. Perhaps we'll both feel better that way anyway."

"I'll think about it."

I ended the call, and for some reason I turned my attention to the door. Had I heard a sound?

My eyes went downward, and I don't know if I was imagining it, but I thought I saw a shadow pass by. And if I hadn't been imagining it, had Katrina just been listening to what I'd been saying through my door?

And if so, how much had she heard?

I frowned, but I didn't get up and go to the door. I didn't feel like talking to her, and I could only hope that she hadn't heard what I'd been saying.

She likely wouldn't have been able to make sense of my part of the conversation anyway.

Besides, was it wrong for me to want to know the truth? If she had nothing to hide, then I had nothing to fear.

Despite what my sister had told me, I still had questions. So, minutes later, I was on my laptop and looking up the University at Buffalo. In particular, I was searching for stories about the Bike Path Rapist and the sorority girl who'd been killed.

I learned that three girls in the same sorority as the victim had first been suspected of the student's murder, but ultimately someone else had been charged. Like Marie had said, another sorority sister who had apparently been jealous had been charged with the crime.

Then I found myself looking up Shemar Williams and the car accident. The article about it wasn't very long. And it was the same thing that I'd heard from the sister. Out of control car collided with a truck. Shemar appeared to be driving as though he didn't want to stop. Speculation of suicide.

There was a knock at my door. I nearly jumped out of my skin.

Slamming the laptop shut, I said, "Come in."

"Just wondering if you're okay. You haven't come out all evening."

"I'm not really that hungry, and I just feel like chilling. It keeps hitting me, you know? One minute we were having a good time in Mexico, the next . . ." I shook my head. "It's just tough."

"If you watch a movie or something . . ."

"Thanks. But I think I'm gonna just go to bed tonight."

"I was actually thinking that I should open up the café tomorrow. Instead of spending all of my days just thinking about Christian, I should probably do something more productive with my time. And of course, the bills are still gonna come in."

"That's an idea," I said, perking up.

"So you won't mind?"

"No. In fact, I agree. It will give us something to do. Did you talk to Alexis?"

"I called her. She said she can come in."

"Good. I think opening the shop is a great idea."

The next morning, Katrina and I got up bright and early and went downstairs to begin the task of getting the café up and running. There was some comfort in the familiar routine that I had only just become accustomed to. Of course, Christian being missing from the trio was hard, but by the time we started brewing coffee and letting customers in I felt better.

And Katrina seemed to feel better, too, because she was talking and smiling with customers. We were busy. Many wanted to know about Mexico, because of course they'd seen the story on the news. Katrina respectfully told them that she didn't want to talk about it, and I said the same.

The only person I did talk about it with was Alexis, and I didn't bother to fill her in on the mysterious visit from Shawde. Instead, I just repeated what I'd told the police and my sister. That Katrina and I had been out, that Christian left the bar and the next thing we heard he'd been killed.

"I heard she married him," Alexis said to me, whispering in a conspiratorial tone.

"Apparently she did."

"I don't get why she would have you go on their honeymoon." Alexis made a face. "I mean, unless the three of you had something going on . . ."

"No! Definitely not!" Was that what people thought? Well, I supposed that was better than the alternative. That I had somehow been involved in the murder.

"I've thought about the same thing," I began, "and my honest opinion is that because they fought so much, she just wanted someone else there to help make sure they stayed sane around each other. I don't know if that makes sense, but maybe she thought that with me there, they'd be less likely to fight?" But as I said the words, they sounded stupid. Like a lame excuse.

And it was the one thing I really didn't understand, the one thing that gnawed at me. Why had I been on their honeymoon with them?

Alexis shrugged. "The whole thing is way too strange for me. Then again, I've always found Katrina a little bit weird."

Alexis wandered off, and I headed to the front of the restaurant to wipe down a table that had recently been vacated. As I cleaned the table, I looked outside.

And saw Shawde.

She was standing across the street, looking at the coffee shop.

Seeing her, I remembered her parting question to me. Where was Gordon? He was the one loose end that didn't make sense. If her claims about Katrina were true and she'd gotten wind that Gordon was investigating her . . .

I shook my head. I was letting my imagination run wild. Perhaps it was the writer in me, trying to see some validity to Shawde's outrageous claims.

My eyes widened when I saw Shawde look both ways for traffic, then step into the street. Good God, she was coming over here. I quickly craned my neck around, searching for Katrina. I hadn't seen her in a while.

The door chimes sang as Shawde entered the shop. She started toward me, purpose in her steps.

"You need to leave," I said in a hushed voice when she reached me. "You want Katrina to see—"

"Katrina left a while ago. I saw her head down the street."

She'd left? "It doesn't matter," I said. "You shouldn't be here."

"I learned some stuff. We need to have another talk. First of all, I found the hotel where Gordon was staying. They said he never checked out. But no one's seen him since last week."

I swallowed. "So?"

Shawde narrowed her eyes. "So? I sent him down here to investigate Katrina, and now he's gone. Just vanished."

"I told you to stay away from me."

"There's more."

Hearing footfalls behind me, I quickly whispered, "You have to go!" Then in a louder voice I said, "I'm not sure where you got the idea that the owner was offering franchises." I glanced over my shoulder, and there was Alexis, carrying a tray of drinks. I forced a smile.

Shawde glanced at Alexis before meeting my gaze again. "I guess I wasted my time, then."

"Looks like you did," I agreed, giving her a pointed look.

Shawde flashed a tight smile, then turned and was off, whisking out of the café without a look backward.

A slow breath escaped my lungs.

"Franchises? Where'd she get that idea?"

"Who knows?"

Alexis walked off with her tray, and I turned—I supposed to see if Katrina truly wasn't in the building. I saw Irene, an occasional worker who had come in to work today, putting coffee beans into the grinder.

Katrina wasn't here. When the hell had she left? And where had she gone?

CHAPTER THIRTY-FOUR

It was about three hours later, nearly 5:00 p.m., when Katrina came through the front door. I looked in her direction, my gaze questioning.

As she reached me, I asked, "Where'd you disappear to?"

She took me by the arm and led me to the kitchen area. Once inside, she closed the door before speaking. "I went to the local TV station."

I made a face. "What? Why?"

"Have you seen the news today?"

I shook my head. "No. I didn't want to watch."

"Yeah, well, Christian's sister keeps talking about how she's convinced that I'm responsible for her brother's death. And fine, she thinks I'm a killer. But it is totally clear to me that the Mexican police aren't interested in justice. I gave that sergeant pictures of Brian and Keith, and you know what—there's been *nothing* about them on the news. What does that tell you?"

I hesitated. "They're not looking for them?"

"Obviously not. And God only knows how long it will be before they're deciding to pin this on me because there are no other suspects. So I went to the media. I gave them the pictures of Brian and Keith and told them that the Mexican police aren't really interested in justice. I mean, don't you think it's weird that I gave Ramirez the pictures and they're not mentioned in the media even once? Instead, it's all about me, how I'm some lying gold digger. Obviously, they don't want to solve this crime. And now the reporters are starting to nose around here."

I wondered how Brian would react to being thrown into the media spotlight as a possible murder suspect. Honestly, I didn't think he or Keith had anything to do with it. After all, Brian and I had met in Key West before I ever knew I'd be going to Mexico on vacation. Clearly he didn't target us in Cancun. In fact, he'd gone to Cancun to meet me there.

"Maybe the cops *are* looking into other suspects," I said. "I'm sure they don't tell the media everything they're doing."

"Maybe not, but I needed to deflect attention from me."

"Why didn't you have me come along?"

"Because it was a spur-of-the-moment decision. After that reporter came in here pretending to be a tourist and ordered coffee. I was so ticked, I left and headed right to the news station."

"You don't really think that Brian and Keith had anything to do with it?"

"I had a bad feeling about them. Remember what I said about Brian when we got to the hotel? Think about it. I believe they targeted us. They killed Christian, then took us back to our hotel . . . I honestly believe that they were going to try to come upstairs with us if I didn't put a stop to it—probably to kill us, too."

"What?" I gaped at her. "Since when was that your theory?"

"How do we know they didn't slaughter Christian and weren't having a secret kick about it behind our backs? That's why I made sure to take their pictures."

I made a face. "But you didn't know Christian was dead at that time."

Katrina's eyes widened ever so slightly, and her lips parted. But it took another moment for her to speak. "But I knew something was off about those two. That's what I'm saying. What's so hard in that to understand?"

"Nothing," I said. "I just didn't know you felt that way." I frowned. "Why didn't you take a picture of the guy who actually fought with Christian?"

"What are you trying to say?"

"I'm not *saying* anything. I'm asking a question. Something compelled you to take pictures of Brian and Keith, who'd been nice to us, yet—"

"Jesus, Jade. I had an instinct, okay? Call it a premonition. I don't know. What I don't need is to be grilled by the one person who knows I had nothing to do with this."

"I'm only try—"

Sharply turning, Katrina walked away from me. More confused than ever, I stared at her retreating back. What the hell was with her attitude? Did she seriously expect me *not* to ask questions?

She marched behind the counter and started dumping coffee grinds. What she'd said, it didn't make sense. She'd taken those pictures of Brian and Keith because she'd somehow *known* we might need the evidence? How would she have had the presence of mind to do that when she'd been as drunk as she was?

And then it hit me. Unless she'd been *pretending* to be drunk . . .

She met my gaze from across the café, her irritation evident.

I turned away, my breathing growing shallow. *Had* she been pretending? That would explain why she was annoyed with me for asking logical questions.

But why would she need to fake being inebriated?

Unless she'd had an agenda.

An agenda to kill her husband and set someone else up for the crime?

I looked at her again, at the bright smile she wore while serving a customer a slice of cake.

And a chill ran down my spine.

CHAPTER THIRTY-FIVE

I had an unsettled night, my mind replaying everything about my time in Mexico with Katrina. As much as I wanted to believe that she wasn't a killer, there were questionable things I couldn't ignore. Like why she had insisted that I go on the trip with her and Christian when it was actually their honeymoon. And that angry call from Wesley, in response to nasty messages I hadn't actually sent. Katrina had denied any involvement, but now I wasn't so sure. The timing of those messages when she'd been in my room that night was suspicious. Had she sent those messages, knowing Wesley would be livid with me, hoping I would then decide I needed a getaway? It was Brian telling me he might go that had encouraged me to say yes to the trip, but Katrina could never have known that would happen.

And now there was the fact that she'd deliberately taken those pictures of Brian and Keith, which struck me as far too calculated.

Pandemonium struck the next day. Reporters appeared en masse and were camped outside of the café. Early in the day, Katrina went out and warned them not to step foot inside. That if they did she would be calling the police.

If it were up to me, I would have shut down the shop and stayed out of sight. But Katrina kept the doors open and welcomed the regulars and new patrons alike. In a twisted way, she seemed to be enjoying the attention.

The television was set to a twenty-four-hour news station, and every time Katrina's interview aired she made sure to point it out—especially drawing her attention to the photos of Brian and Keith and sharing her theory about them.

I hated that I was in the pictures with Brian and Keith, as I didn't want any added notoriety. Unfortunately, it was too late for that.

Around three o'clock, Katrina came up to me and said, "I'm going outside. I want to thank the media." She took me by the arm. "Come with me."

She dragged me to the front door, but that's where I pulled my arm from her grip. "I don't want to go outside," I told her.

"Suit yourself."

Katrina opened the door, and the reporters came to life. They moved forward with their portable recorders, started their video cameras, and snapped photos of Katrina.

I watched as Katrina raised her hand before speaking. "I want to thank you for keeping a respectable distance so that my customers have still been able to enjoy my café," she began. "I also want to say that I've been watching the news reports and I'm really grateful that you all have run the photos of Brian and Keith. Obviously, the Mexican police aren't interested in justice. I believe that these two men hold the key to finding out what happened to my husband.

"They befriended me and my friend that night," Katrina went on. "And when I look back, I find their actions highly suspicious. I think we may have been targeted, and right now I'm grateful that I too wasn't a victim."

Hearing Katrina spout this theory again made me want to scream. Of all the people to suspect, she was focusing on Brian and Keith. Not the creep who'd actually fought with Christian. Did she actually believe what she was saying, or had she come up with this story as a way to deflect any and all attention off of herself?

Alexis sidled up beside me. "Can you believe how packed the place is today? Negative attention makes you more famous than positive attention. It's crazy."

"Tell me about it." Maybe that's why Katrina seemed to be in a chipper mood. More business meant more money.

"At least I'm making great tips," Alexis said.

The café was busy until after 9:30 p.m., which I was grateful for. It kept my mind occupied and gave me something to do other than stay in my room upstairs and mope.

We had more garbage bags than usual piled outside the back door because of the extra business, so at ten thirty I began the routine of taking the garbage out to the Dumpster behind the café. The sooner the cleanup was done, the sooner we'd be able to get to bed and get rest for tomorrow, which I imagined would be as busy as today.

I heaved the third bag into the Dumpster, then turned to head back toward the café door. That's when I felt the hand clamp down on my mouth.

Panic washed over like a giant cold wave. I was too startled to even try screaming initially, but as my assailant began to drag me down the alley I started to fight. I began to flail and kick.

Suddenly I was being pushed against a brick wall. And then my attacker came into view.

My heart damn near exploded as terror swept through me.

It was Brian!

My eyes bulged. First confusion hit me. Then realization. Katrina's allegations . . . they didn't seem so far-fetched anymore. I'd assumed that Brian hadn't targeted us because I'd met him *before* Mexico. But what if he had targeted us after all? Right here in Key West? Then he'd gone to Mexico as part of some nefarious plan?

All that secrecy. All that talk about trusting him. I'd been a fool.

Oh my God . . .

I did my best to scream, but Brian's hand was like an iron clamp.

"Shhh," he implored me.

My breathing was ragged, my heart rate out of control. And tears were forming in my eyes.

"I'm going to let go of your mouth," Brian said, "and I don't want you to scream. Nod if you understand."

I did nothing. I was paralyzed with fear.

"I need you to calm down," Brian said. "I'm going to take my hands off of your mouth, and you need to relax."

There was something wrong with me. Because as terrified as I suddenly was of him, there was a small part of me that was happy to see him again. A part of me that didn't want to believe that he could ever be the type of person responsible for what Katrina was alleging.

"Do you understand me?" he asked, an edge to his voice.

I nodded.

He released his hand from my mouth tentatively, as though waiting to see if I would obey him. I debated screaming bloody murder, then thought better of it. I was alone with him, and surely he could hurt me before anyone could come to my aid. The fact that he was here had me terrified, and Katrina's claims no longer seemed outrageous. Had he targeted Christian, perhaps for money? And if he had so easily killed Christian behind that bar, what would he do to me?

"I'm not going to hurt you."

Yeah, right! a voice in my brain screamed. *That's why you're attacking me in an alley?*

"Why are you and your friend calling me a murderer?"

My chest rose and fell with erratic breaths. I was too afraid to say anything.

"You're afraid of me," Brian said, sounding mystified. "Jade, I didn't kill anyone."

"Then why are you attacking me in a dark alley?" I whimpered. "The same way Christian was killed."

"Attacking you?" He genuinely looked perplexed. "You think I'm attacking you?"

I said nothing.

"Have I hurt you?"

He hadn't, but that didn't mean that he wouldn't. I had no clue who he really was, nor what he was capable of.

"Think about it," Brian went on. "If I wanted you dead, I would have snapped your neck the moment I grabbed you."

His words made me shiver. "Or slit my throat."

Brian lowered his hands from my body, and in his eyes I saw disappointment. "You really think I'd do that to you?"

I swallowed. He'd released me, and yet I wasn't trying to get away.

"I . . ." My voice trailed off. The truth was, I could imagine him doing other things to me . . . murder not being one of them. "Then why are you here?"

"I'm here because I'm a cop. And you and your friend have all but blown my cover."

CHAPTER THIRTY-SIX

My mouth fell open. My first instinct was disbelief. But the hard set of Brian's eyes and the determination on his face made me rethink my position.

"If you're a cop, why don't you seem like one?" That was the only thing that I could think to ask, and I knew it sounded lame.

"I shouldn't be here. I shouldn't even be telling you this. But Keith and I are DEA. Undercover. That's why we were in that bar. Because a drug dealer we've been trying to get close to was there. And it just so happens he was talking to your friend, Katrina. Which of course made us curious."

"What?" I wouldn't have been more surprised if he'd said that they thought Katrina was involved in child pornography.

"We haven't been able to prove a connection, or if their interaction was a coincidence."

"It had to be coincidental," I said.

"Are you sure about that?"

I opened my mouth to say that yes, I was sure. And then I remembered the pills Katrina had offered me in the bathroom. The truth was, I didn't really know her all that well.

My brain was scrambling, trying to make sense of what he'd said. "Wait a minute. When you met me in Key West . . . was that a coincidence? Or did it have to do with Katrina?"

Brian didn't respond.

Horror filling me, my eyes grew wide. "Oh my God. That . . . that wasn't random. What—you've been investigating Katrina? Of course. That's why you didn't want me to tell her that I'd met you in Key West."

"Look, this stays between us. She's been on our radar, yes."

"So you weren't really in town for a wedding," I said. And then I remembered how Brian had disappeared from the bar just before Katrina and Christian had joined me. "Of course not. And that's why you left me that night. Because Katrina came into the bar."

"I had to give you a bullshit story because I couldn't tell you the truth."

I drew in a deep breath and let it out slowly. "Did you approach me in that bar because you think I'm some kind of drug dealer?"

"Drug dealers don't wear signs around their necks," he responded. "We follow every lead. We look at the friends of known dealers, their associates."

"Now I'm the associate of a drug dealer?"

"Listen to me. I'm not saying any of that. I targeted you, yes. But—"

"You *targeted* me? Oh God."

"Jade." He placed a finger under my chin and forced my gaze up to meet his. "With you living with Katrina, I had to talk to you. That's my job. I quickly deduced that you were not into the drug game."

I jerked my head away from his touch. "You expect me

to feel happy about the fact that you lied to me? Targeted me as part of your investigation?"

"Jade. Look at me, Jade." When I looked into Brian's eyes, he went on. "Our connection . . . that wasn't fake. Why do you think I came to see you at the café, gave you my number—"

"A burner cell, right?" I interjected.

"Yes," he said after a beat. "A burner cell. Jade, I wasn't even supposed to be talking to you on a personal level. But . . . I like you. And I wasn't ready to walk away from you. So I bent the rules."

"You weren't supposed to talk to me because I'm the associate of a drug dealer."

He didn't respond, which was all the answer I needed.

"So, what?" I began. "You think that I went to Mexico with Katrina to buy drugs?"

"That's not what I think. When I encouraged you to go to Mexico, it was because I knew I would be there." He exhaled sharply. "Probably not the smartest thing, but I wanted to see you. I had no clue all hell would break loose."

I tried to digest everything he was telling me. "So you think that Katrina is buying and selling drugs." Could this situation get any crazier?

"Katrina was associating with a known drug dealer in that bar in Mexico. Luis Romero. And it wasn't the first time."

My eyes grew even wider. "What?"

"This investigation started long before you arrived in Florida. We discovered Katrina's connection to Luis Romero about four months ago."

"By *we* do you mean you and Keith?"

"Yes. Look, I shouldn't be telling you any of this. For three years, Keith and I have been trying to get close to a drug lord in Mexico. Luis Romero was the next step in working our way up the ladder. But Katrina showed up in the bar that night, and with her husband's death and those damn pictures she took of us all over the media . . . Let's just say that the fact that Keith and I haven't been arrested after your allegations is gonna raise some eyebrows. Three years of hard work to get close to a drug lord, possibly gone downhill."

"Because of me?" The words were like a slap. "Me and Katrina? That *is* what you're saying?" And that hurt me. Actually, everything he'd said thus far had hurt me. Because when he'd met me he had clearly been playing a role. He claimed that our connection was real, but how did I know he wasn't lying to me right now?

"I'm explaining the situation," Brian said. "I'm not blaming you."

Now I understood why he and Keith hadn't wanted any photos to be taken. Because of their undercover status. Why Brian had been so damn secretive. Still, the story was incredible. "Why should I even believe you?"

"You want to see my badge?" He glanced around the alley, then reached into his pocket and withdrew a badge.

I said what I've heard many people say in the movies when my eyes landed on it. "How do I know that's real? You could have bought that at a novelty store for all I know."

"Take a look at the other side."

On the other side, opposite the badge, was a card that had his photo as well as an official-looking seal from the U.S. government. I had to concede it looked legitimate.

"Now do you believe me?"

"Yes," I said tersely. "But I don't understand why you're here."

"To ask you and Katrina to stop talking to the press about me and Keith. I didn't kill anybody. I certainly didn't slit a person's throat. And neither did Keith. But in light of the accusation, our cover could be blown because we've been thrown into the media spotlight. As it is, Keith and I are gonna have to lie low for a while, make it look like we were locked up. Or on the run from the authorities. But if you and Katrina continue to point the finger in our direction, suggesting that the police aren't doing anything to find us, then it's gonna be obvious that we were never picked up for questioning. And the people we're dealing with in Mexico are going to become mighty suspicious."

I swallowed, a small part of me feeling a little upset by what he'd told me. How stupid was I? To be disappointed over the fact that he wasn't saying he was here because he needed to see me. Rather, he was here to make sure I kept my mouth shut.

"Couldn't you have just called or texted to tell me this directly? Why grab me in an alley?"

"Yeah, that would go over well. Like you'd have believed a word I said." He gave me a pointed look, daring me to deny his words.

I couldn't.

"Fine," I said. "You came all this way to tell me to keep my mouth shut. I get it." I was disappointed, irrationally so. "Can I go now?"

"You know that's not the only reason."

He eased closer to me. I stared at him, and he at me. The sound of my raspy breathing filled the air.

"No, I don't."

"I had to see you, Jade."

"But I'm the associate of a drug dealer," I quipped.

"I don't care about Katrina."

"Sure you don't. You only used me as part of your investigation," I scoffed, then made a move to step past him.

He blocked me with his arm, forcing me to stay against the wall. "I understand you're mad, and that you probably don't trust me."

"You think—"

His lips came down on mine. At first, I was too stunned to move. Too stunned to react. But as his lips urged mine open with delicate skill I sighed in surrender and gripped his shoulders. I wanted to believe him. Wanted to believe that the connection I'd felt with him that first night was real.

Heat engulfed me. Suddenly the only thing that mattered was here and now.

Him.

His hands framed my face as his body pressed against mine, trapping me against the wall. I opened my lips wider, and his hot tongue swept over mine. I gripped his back, digging my fingernails into his shirt and loving the feel of his strong muscles.

Brian lowered one hand and cupped my breast. I gasped.

"Jade?"

At the sound of Katrina's voice, Brian tore his lips from mine, leaving me disoriented. As though I had awoken suddenly and didn't know what was going on.

"Jade, are you out here?"

"Shit," I whispered.

Brian placed a card in my hand. "Call me at this number," he whispered hotly into my ear. "I got rid of the burner phone."

And then he took off down the alley.

Shakily I stepped out from behind the Dumpster. "Hey. I'm right here."

Katrina stared at me oddly. "What are you doing?"

"I was bringing out the garbage and I just . . . I felt faint. I had to rest against the wall."

"Of course you feel faint. The smell out here will kill anybody. Come back inside."

I shoved the card into the pocket on my apron and followed Katrina back into the café.

* * *

Later, in my room, I held Brian's card in my hand. It was his official business card, with his DEA credentials and contact information. But on the back, he'd scrawled a phone number along with a room number.

I twirled the card around with my fingers, flipping it from the side with his credentials to the side where he'd scrawled that number.

In the wake of learning the truth about him, I felt both hurt and confused. He'd approached me under false pretenses. How could I trust anything he said to me now?

And yet that kiss . . . nothing about it felt fake.

Finally, around two in the morning, unable to sleep but certain that Katrina was, I called the number.

"Sunnyside Hotel, how may I help you?"

"Room three-twenty-one," I said.

The phone began to ring again, and two rings later it was answered. "Hello?" came Brian's groggy voice.

"It's Jade," I said softly.

"Oh. Hi."

"Sorry I woke you."

"No, it's okay. I figured you weren't going to call."

I hadn't been able to stop thinking about him. It was inevitable that I would call him. "I need to know what's going on."

"I'm not going to talk on the phone," Brian said. "Why don't you come to my hotel? It's a couple of blocks from the café."

My pulse throbbed. Go to his hotel . . . I wasn't naïve. I knew we would end up doing more than talking. Did I want that?

"Okay," I said, surprising myself. Though was I really surprised?

"How long will it take you to get here?"

"I'll leave in a few minutes."

We ended the call, and I slipped into my favorite pair of jeans and a formfitting pink T-shirt. The outfit was simple, but I loved the way it highlighted my figure. Then I applied lip gloss and fixed my hair until I thought I looked cute enough. There was no point pretending that I didn't want the night with Brian that we hadn't gotten in Mexico.

Satisfied with my appearance, I sneaked out of the apartment as quietly as I could.

Outside, I began to jog. I was aware of how crazy it was for me to be heading to the hotel room of a guy I didn't really know in the middle of the night. But I didn't stop.

As I neared the hotel, I could see someone standing by the window in the lobby. I halted. It was Brian.

And damn if he didn't look gorgeous. He was wearing gray sweatpants and a T-shirt—nothing fancy—but he made the clothes look like they were worth a million bucks. I began to walk slowly, allowing myself to check out his athletic body, those chiseled arms.

And that face . . . My pulse tripped. He was sexy as hell.

As I neared the hotel's doors, I saw his lips spread in a smile. And I remembered the first moment I'd seen him here in Key West. It was that smile that had drawn me in.

He began to open the door as I reached it. "Hey," he said softly.

"Hi."

Brian led the way to the elevators, and I folded my arms over my chest as I ambled behind him. I was suddenly conflicted, wondering if I should be here. If I could trust my judgment.

We went up in the elevator and got off on the third floor, and I followed him to the right. Moments later he was opening the door to his room and gesturing for me to go in.

I hesitated. Was I being smart right now or incredibly stupid?

"All right," Brian said, and stepped into the room ahead of me. "If you want to stand in the hallway and talk to me, we can do that. But I'd prefer if you come in here."

A beat passed. Then, my arms still crossed over my body, I entered the room. I knew I was sending the message that I wasn't completely comfortable, which was the truth.

But also true was the fact that I wasn't afraid of him. Even before knowing he was a cop, I had instinctively trusted him. It was his motives I was wary of.

I stepped into the room and closed the door, then leaned my back against it. "Is your name really Brian?" I asked. "It says that on your business card, but maybe that's part of your cover."

"Brian is my real name," he said. "And it's what I use in my work. It's just easier to use my real first name. But the criminals in Mexico don't know my true identity."

"Do you really think Katrina is some kind of drug dealer?"

"Will you please come over here?" Brian eased onto the bed. "Take a seat." He gestured to the armchair in the corner of the room.

I took a deep breath, then did as instructed. Once I was in the chair, I repeated, "You really think Katrina is some kind of drug dealer?"

"I can't really comment on an ongoing investigation. But . . . there's evidence, yes."

"Oh my God," I uttered. Then I went on. "Do you think this Luis Romero guy killed Christian?"

"It's a theory. He's killed before, for the cartels. Would he kill a tourist?" Brian shrugged. "Perhaps if he had the right incentive."

I buried my face in my palms briefly, then faced Brian again. "I'm so confused."

"About what?" he asked simply.

"I haven't wanted to believe anything bad about Katrina, but suddenly I find myself asking all kinds of questions. There are things now that I find suspicious. And what you're saying about her? I can't help wondering if she *did* kill Christian. Or paid this Luis guy to do it."

"I think you need to be wary of her," Brian said.

"Maybe I should go home."

A beat passed. I thought I saw disappointment flicker in Brian's eyes. "You want to leave already?"

"I'm not talking about right now. I mean leave Katrina's. Go back and live with my sister."

"Where's home?"

"Erie, Pennsylvania."

He nodded his understanding. "Maybe you should. The one thing I know from doing undercover work is that a lot of people aren't always what they seem. They're good at living lives where they appear to be decent people, but they've got an ugly side. A dangerous side."

I shuddered. Was Katrina dangerous? Was she a psychopath, as Shawde believed?

"Come here." Brian patted the spot beside him on the bed.

My breath caught in my throat.

"By now you should know that I'm not going to hurt you," he went on.

"Is this all part of an act?" I blurted. "An attempt to get information about Katrina by getting close to me?"

Brian regarded me with skepticism. "I know there's nothing you can tell me about Katrina that I don't already know."

He was right about that. I barely knew Katrina, and I wasn't involved in any illegal activity with her. And if he believed that I was, certainly he wouldn't have me in his hotel room. . . .

"Surely you don't think I invited you to my hotel room in the middle of the night because of Katrina," he said, echoing my thoughts. His lips curled in a smile, the same charming smile that had instantly had me smitten.

I swallowed.

"I get that you're confused. About everything. But what I said to you earlier, I meant it." He held my gaze. "What happened between us wasn't an act. . . ."

My heart thudded against my rib cage. I believed him.

"Come here," he said again, his voice soft, a gentle invitation. I knew that if I wanted to get up and leave he wouldn't stop me.

And maybe I should do exactly that. Get up, head to the door. Why should I make this easy for him?

I got to my feet. Took a couple of steps to my left, as if I were heading to the door. But then I abruptly turned. Took slow steps toward him.

As I reached him, his hands went up, cupped my hips. I glanced down at him, saw that damn smile. And all I could think was that I wanted to kiss him until the world around us faded away.

He urged me down, and I straddled his legs as I sat on his lap. Without missing a beat, my lips went down, too, finding his.

The kiss was like a minivolcano, erupting with heat. What was it about this guy that made all rational thought fly out the window?

His fingers found my face as his tongue flicked over mine. And he began to touch me, tantalizing strokes with his fingertips that added to the sensation of his kiss. I could feel his arousal against my center. Large and hard.

I moaned and deepened the kiss, then reached for the hem of my shirt and started to pull it off.

As soon as it was discarded, his palms were on my back, warm and enticing and holding my body against his as he eased backward on the bed. His lips found mine again, and his tongue delved into my mouth with broad strokes, his fingers trailing up my spine.

A sigh escaped me as he unclasped my bra. Then, in a flash, he spun us over, deftly switching positions. Now I was the one on my back and he was on top of me, his strong legs between my thighs.

I looked into his eyes, darkened and filled with desire for me, and hot lust shot through my veins. And then he was touching me, the tips of his fingers grazing my cheek, then moving down to my neck, and over to one shoulder. Brian slipped his fingers beneath my bra strap and eased it off of my shoulder and down my arm. I heard his sharp intake of breath as his eyes drank in the sight of my naked breasts.

"You're beautiful," he rasped, the words making me heady. Adjusting his body, he pulled the other strap down my other arm, then tossed my bra onto the floor. I curled my leg around his thigh, urging him closer.

He grinned down at me. "Looks like you're starting to trust me."

I chuckled softly. Then, quickly becoming serious, I lifted my head and nuzzled my nose against his cheek. "I wouldn't be here if I didn't," I whispered.

A groan rumbling in his chest, Brian angled his head, his lips finding mine. As he kissed me softly, one of his hands covered my breast. And then he deepened the kiss, his tongue sweeping into my mouth, hot and delicious.

Brian tweaked my nipple, coaxing it into a hardened peak. I gripped his shoulders and moaned into his mouth.

"Yes, baby," he said. "I'm going to do everything you like, for as long as you like."

And then he brought his mouth down onto my nipple. And as his lips tugged and his tongue tantalized, every thought of anything but him faded away.

CHAPTER THIRTY-SEVEN

Where was Christian? I weaved my way through the crowd in Tequila Grill, craning my neck left and right trying to find him.

Katrina saw me and beamed. I made my way over to her.

Where's Christian? I asked.

She didn't answer me. Instead, she raised her arms over her head and began to move her body to the funky beat playing in the bar. That's when I saw the blood on her hands.

Katrina! You're bleeding!

Look at the bird, she said.

As she said that, I looked up. Saw a bird sitting on a string of lights and chirping.

The next instant my brain registered that the sound I'd actually heard was my cell phone going off, indicating that I'd received a text message.

My eyes flew open. And that's when I realized that something was wrong. That I wasn't where I was supposed to be.

I looked to my left. Saw Brian's naked torso beside me. And it all came rushing back.

Going to his hotel room last night.

Making love to him for hours.

A smile broke out on my face.

He was on his stomach, his face turned away from me. The fact that he hadn't stirred told me he was sleeping.

I snuggled close to his body. The past several days had brought highs and lows, unexpected turns. The last place I'd expected to be right now was in bed with Brian. But he'd shown up yesterday, and here we were. My world had changed for the better.

My cell phone chirped again, and I glanced at the clock. It was minutes after eight. Who was contacting me at this hour?

I stretched my naked body over Brian's, reaching for the phone that was on his night table. He stirred.

"Sorry," I mumbled.

I grabbed my phone and settled back in the bed. Then I checked my texts. There were two from my sister. The most recent text appeared first:

Have you still been talking to Shawde? I thought I told you to stay away from her.

I frowned, then read the previous message:

Hey, what's going on? I'm watching the news right now. Shemar's sister is on.

I sat up and reached for the remote control. I turned the television on. The volume blared, and I quickly turned the sound down.

Too late. I'd awoken Brian. He rolled over onto his back, his narrowed eyes meeting mine.

"Sorry," I murmured. "I didn't mean to wake you."

"What's going on?"

I started flipping through the channels. "I got a text from my sister. Remember the woman I told you who came to me about her brother?" I'd filled Brian in on the whole story when we'd taken a break from making love. "She's apparently on the news."

I kept flipping until I found CNN. If my sister had seen the news, it had to be on a national news network.

"Come here."

Brian extended his arm, and I lay beside him, resting my head on his shoulder, my eyes still on the television set. "I should be getting back soon," I said. "Katrina will wonder where I was."

His fingers stroked my back. "What if I'm not ready to let you go yet?"

I angled my head to look at him, skeptical. "Seriously?"

His other hand went to my face, and I felt a rush of desire. Damn, I was becoming aroused again. "What, you think I came down here to see you for one night and that's it?"

The edges of my lips fought to curl in a smile, but I kept it under control. "Maybe."

"Oh, really?" His hand tightened on my back, and then he deftly adjusted our bodies so that I was now on my back and he was resting on top of me. "You need me to prove that last night wasn't about a one-night stand?"

He buried his lips in my neck, and I giggled at first . . . until his mouth began to move more slowly, with flicks of his tongue teasing my skin.

"Mmmm," I moaned, wrapping my hands around his neck.

". . . fishermen were surprised when they caught something unexpected in their fishing net."

"That's right, Taylor. Authorities here in Key West say that two fishermen were stunned to find the body of an unidentified man in their net last night. Shawde Williams, visiting Key West from upstate New York, is certain she knows the identity of the man."

"That's the story," I said, and quickly began to maneuver my body from beneath Brian's. He eased off of me and groaned in protest. I reached for the remote control and turned up the volume.. "The guy, the one I told you came down here to investigate Katrina. That must be him they found!"

Shawde was now on the screen, standing in front of the marina, the blue waters of the ocean behind her. "I'm certain that the man is Gordon Deaver. He went missing just over a week ago. He was in Florida, working for me. You know the story about the man recently murdered in Mexico? That victim was involved with the same woman my brother was involved with six years ago. My brother also died under suspicious circumstances. Now Gordon is dead, too."

The reporter, a man, looked visibly shocked. "You're saying you know this man and you believe that he was murdered?"

"Katrina Hughes killed my brother. I'm sure of it. Now her husband ends up dead during a trip to Mexico? And the man I sent down here to investigate her also ends up dead in the Atlantic? This is not coincidence. She needs to be arrested *now*—so that no one else dies."

"Those are incredible allegations."

"Katrina Hughes is a dangerous woman."

"Oh my God," I said. "Shawde came to see me at the café, told me that she'd found the hotel where Gordon was staying. He never checked out. I didn't . . . I didn't want to believe anything bad had happened to him."

". . . body is currently at the medical examiner's office," the reporter was saying when I turned my attention back to him. "Given the state of the body, it may be a while before an identification can be made and a cause of death determined."

"If Gordon's dead, too . . . how many coincidences can there be?"

"Hey," Brian said gently, sitting beside me and placing a hand on my back.

"One more death. Someone else connected to Katrina." I looked over my shoulder at him. "I can't keep denying the obvious."

"She may not be arrested for any crime yet," Brian began, "but that doesn't mean she's innocent. I don't want you going back there."

I swallowed. Maybe he was right. Maybe it was time I cut my losses, headed back home.

"We can stay here for a while," he went on.

"At this hotel?"

"Why not?"

Being holed up here with Brian, in our own little world, certainly held appeal.

He curled his arm around my waist and pulled me close. "If she *has* killed all of these people—she's clearly unstable. It's not smart to go back there."

"All of my stuff is there," I said.

One of Brian's hands crept up to my breast. "Well, there's no reason you have to go *right now*. . . ."

"I'm supposed to work," I said, then lolled my head backward as sensations of pleasure spread through me.

My cell phone rang, jarring me out of the moment.

Brian tweaked my nipple. "Let it ring."

"It's probably my sister calling to see if I saw the news report," I told him. "I should answer it."

With a groan of frustration, I pulled away from him and found my phone on the bed. Indeed, Marie's picture was displayed on my screen.

I swiped the TALK button. "Hey, Marie."

"Jade Blackwin?"

I frowned. That wasn't Marie's voice. "Yes?"

"I'm calling from Millcreek Community Hospital in Erie, Pennsylvania."

I blinked, my brain not quite making sense of what I'd heard. "What?"

"You're listed as your sister's emergency contact."

"Yes, I am." A chill ran down my spine. I was starting to understand. If someone from the hospital was calling me, that meant my sister couldn't. "What—what happened?"

"I'd say it's important for you to get here as soon as you can."

Panic gripped me with icy tentacles. "Oh God." I forced in a breath. "Is she—is she dead?"

Beside me, I felt Brian's hands on my shoulders.

"She's been in a car crash, and she's in critical condition. Can you come to the hospital?"

"No." I jumped to my feet. "I mean, yes. Of course. I'm on my way right now." I paused, trying to focus my frazzled thoughts. "Wait—but I'm in Florida. I—I'm not sure when I can get a flight."

"Just get here as soon as you can."

I held the phone in my hand, devastation filling my belly with the weight of a heavy boulder.

"Jade, what's happening?" Brian asked.

"It's my sister. She's—she's been in a car accident. I have to get to Erie as soon as possible."

"Shit," Brian said. "How bad is it?"

"The woman didn't say." My eyes scanned the discarded clothes on the floor for my underwear. "But it's critical."

"What can I do?" Brian asked me.

I got off the bed and scooped up my bra. And that's when it hit me. Shawde's words.

Five and a half years ago, after dating Katrina, he died in a car crash. The police ruled it an accident, but I know it wasn't that. It was murder.

My knees buckled, and I dropped onto the floor.

Brian bounded out of the bed and rushed over to me. "Jade!"

He held me in his arms, and I buried my face in his shoulder and began to cry.

"Shhh."

"This is what happened to Shawde's brother. He—he was in a car wreck. And I—I didn't believe her."

"Hey." Brian brushed my hair off of my face. "Don't you go thinking the worst. Your sister's alive, and I'm sure she's gonna be fine. Besides, Katrina's here, in Florida."

"I have to get to her. You don't understand. Shawde said that she believed someone close to Katrina had helped her commit her crimes. My sister contacted Katrina's best friend, talked to her about Shawde's suspicions. What if this friend was Katrina's partner in crime?"

"Let's not assume the worst, okay? Concentrate on the fact that your sister is going to be fine. That's what's important right now."

But would she?

Marie had talked to Rowena, Katrina's best friend. Now Marie had been in a car crash, just like Shemar had.

And I couldn't help thinking that my desire to learn the truth had almost gotten my sister killed.

CHAPTER THIRTY-EIGHT

Ten minutes later, Brian was driving down the street toward A Book and a Cup when I saw the crowd. Reporters. Even more than the day before.

"Damn," I said. "The reporters are back."

Though I shouldn't have been surprised. With Shawde's allegation in the news this morning, it made sense that the members of the media were at the coffee shop bright and early waiting for the first sighting of Katrina.

Brian started to pull up to a spot several feet away from the front of the shop, but I said, "Keep going. Turn left into the alleyway. I use the entrance at the back to get upstairs."

As he drove by the front of the coffee shop, I could see no action inside. The lights were off, and the CLOSED sign still hung in the door.

"Looks like Katrina didn't open up shop. I bet she's seen Shawde on the news."

"Are you worried?" Brian asked. "Because I can go up there with you."

I faced him as he turned into the alleyway. "No. She has no clue I spoke with Shawde. Besides, if she sees me with you . . . she's already proving to be far crazier than I ever imagined. I don't want to freak her out."

"I can take care of myself." He pulled past the Dumpster behind the café, where he had appeared the night before.

"I'm sure you can. But I don't want to have to spend any time explaining anything to Katrina. I have to get home as soon as possible." Somehow, I was remaining calm. I had to—because the moment I feared the worst I would fall apart.

"All right," Brian said. "Go in and get your stuff. I'll wait down here for you."

"You're going to wait for me?"

"Yeah. I'll take you to the airport."

"You don't have to do that," I told him.

"I want to."

"I might be a while," I told him. "I'm gonna look up flight options, see if I can book something while I'm here."

"I'll wait. I've got nothing better to do."

Under normal circumstances, I would have made some type of offhanded remark. But with the gravity of the situation—both my sister and the truth that was becoming clear about Katrina—my heart was too heavy for any lighthearted ribbing.

"It's gonna be okay," he said as if reading my mind, then gave my hand a supportive squeeze. "Go get your stuff."

I reached for the door handle and started out of the car. But suddenly Brian circled his hand around my wrist, stopping me from leaving.

"What?" I asked.

"You don't have my number," he said. "My cell number."

"Oh. Right."

"Call me," he said. "Then you'll have the number, and

I'll have yours. In case she gives you any problems and you need me to come up."

Despite the pain in my heart, I offered him a soft smile. I was glad to have him with me. I didn't quite feel so overwhelmed and alone.

He recited his cell number, and I called it. When his phone rang, Brian swiped the touch screen to reject the call.

"All right," I said. "You've got my number."

Then I exited the car and walked past the Dumpster to the entrance at the back of the building. I unlocked the door and went upstairs. All I needed was my ID so that I could catch a flight. I wasn't going to worry about clothes or anything else.

I took the stairs two at a time, then unlocked the apartment door. As I swung it open, I saw Katrina standing near the front window. The blinds were mostly closed, and she was using a hand to open one slat a little wider so that she could look outside.

"Hi," I said, stepping tentatively into the apartment. I raised a hand in greeting when she turned to face me.

"You're here." Katrina sounded surprised. "I thought you weren't coming back."

"Because of the media downstairs?"

She let the blind drop and moved away from the window. "It seemed weird to me. The media suddenly here in full force, and you gone before the sun even came up."

I swallowed. And then something occurred to me. She might assume that my being gone and the media being here were connected. Certainly she had seen the news by now. Did she suspect I'd been in contact with Shawde?

"No. I—I just—I was feeling antsy so I decided to go out last night. I met someone," I added with a sheepish grin.

"How did you get past the media just now?" Katrina asked. "I didn't even see you walking out there."

"Oh. I saw them from way down the block. So I cut through the back alley."

I continued walking, heading toward my bedroom door. That's when I noticed that it was ajar. Hadn't I closed my door when I left last night?

"Did you go in my room?" I asked.

"I was checking to see if you were in there."

"Oh."

I walked into my room, quickly scanning it to see if anything was out of place. Everything looked the way I had left it.

And then I noticed my open laptop on the desk. Hadn't that been closed when I left?

That itself wasn't a glaring red flag, but the fact that my screen was on definitely was.

"So, you met someone?" Katrina asked. She was in the doorway of my room. "What's he like?" She raised an eyebrow. "Or was it a she?"

"A she?" I forced a laugh. But I was worried. What had Katrina been looking for on my computer? Facing her, I said, "You were on my computer?"

She didn't answer, and I took a step closer to my laptop. The contents on the screen came into view. It was the story about Shemar's accident.

I squeezed my eyes shut. *Shit!*

"If you had questions about my college boyfriend, you could have just asked."

My pulse began to race. Damn it, what was she thinking? That I was looking into her past, that I believed she was a killer?

"I'll ask again. Was the person you met last night a man or a woman?"

Slowly, I faced her again. "A man."

"Right."

She didn't believe me. And it didn't take me long to connect the dots. It was a pretty good guess that she thought I'd met with Shawde.

Her next words confirmed that fact. "Let me guess. Shawde Williams spun a story about how I killed her brother. Of course, the police didn't believe her. But now Christian's dead, and I'm guessing she thinks that's proof that I'm some sort of crazed killer."

I walked toward the drawer that held my pouch with my ID. "What's your story?" I found myself asking. "That you're the unluckiest person on the planet?"

Katrina laughed—but there was an ominous tone beneath it that gave me a chill. "What are you trying to say?"

I didn't answer, just grabbed my pouch. Then I closed my laptop, unplugged it, and stuffed the items into a tote bag.

I started out of the bedroom, but Katrina blocked my path. "Where are you going?"

I didn't have time to get into this with her. I was finally seeing her without blinders on—the way Shawde and Melody saw her. "My sister was in a car accident," I said, trying to keep my voice even. "I have to head back to Erie."

"Oh. How unfortunate."

She sounded sarcastic, like she was taunting me, and in that moment I was certain that someway, somehow, Katrina was behind what had happened to Marie.

"Yeah, it is," I said, my tone a little clipped. But she was pissing me off. "I have no clue *how* the accident happened," I went on, stressing the word. "But obviously, I want to be there for her."

"Of course." Katrina's tone was overly sweet. "Please, send her my love."

I had to bite my tongue to keep from saying anything.

And as I stared at Katrina, I saw something in the depths of her eyes I had never seen before.

Evil.

There was no other way to express it. Her gaze caused goose bumps to pop out on my skin.

How had I not seen her sinister side sooner? Because she was a chameleon. A psychopath. She knew exactly how to play whatever role she wanted to.

"Rowena!" Katrina called.

My eyes widened in confusion. *Rowena?*

And then I saw the door across the living room slowly open. Another woman appeared. An attractive black woman with caramel-colored skin. She was about my height or a little taller. Maybe five foot six.

And it was like time stood still. I was frozen to the spot, an unfamiliar sense within me on high alert. *Why is Rowena here?*

"What's the matter, Jade?" Katrina asked. Again her voice was taunting.

My eyes flitted from Rowena, who was slowly walking toward us, back to Katrina. "What is this?" I asked.

"Oh, you don't know Rowena? You seem to know everything else about me. Jade, this is Rowena. My best friend from UB. Rowena, remember Marie Blackwin? This is her sister."

"Jade Blackwin," Rowena said, and her smile didn't reach her eyes. "So nice to finally meet you."

CHAPTER THIRTY-NINE

"Wow, you really look like your sister," Rowena went on.

I said nothing. I couldn't speak. The unfamiliar sense intensified. And I understood now what it was. A feeling of foreboding. It swept over me like a giant wave engulfing me, suffocating me. Why was Rowena here? And what was she holding behind her back?

"Did you think you and Shawde could plot against me and I wouldn't find out?" Katrina asked.

"What—you think *I* had something to do with her being on the news?"

"And the Academy Award goes to . . ." Katrina glanced over her shoulder at Rowena. "She's good, isn't she? *What— you think* I *had something to do with this*?" she mocked. Then she turned back to me, leveling a stony glare on me. "Do you think I'm stupid? I saw what you were reading on your laptop."

Did she *know* that I'd met with Shawde? Was that possible? "When I talked to my sister about Mexico, she mentioned that you'd had a boyfriend who died in college. That's why I looked it up. I was just curious."

"Right. Of course you were curious. And you had no

clue that Shawde was here in Key West. Honestly, you disappear last night and you expect me to believe that you hooked up with some random guy when you've been sniveling over Wesley since you got here?"

"It's the truth," I said. I looked at Rowena, standing behind Katrina on her left, and wondered if I was going to be able to make it out of this room.

"And that's why you're grabbing your stuff and trying to leave?" Katrina asked. "Because you *don't* think I'm a killer?"

"I just told you that my sister's been in an accident. It's pretty serious. That's why I have to leave right away."

"Rowena, do you have the needle?"

The hand of fear twisted my insides—hard. "N-needle?"

"You can't leave, Jade." Katrina spoke matter-of-factly. As if she'd just told me something innocuous, like, *I need to get more vanilla bean.*

"What the fuck?" I blurted out. My heart began to thump, wild and frenzied.

"I let you come down here," Katrina said. "I gave you a place to stay. And you betray my trust by conspiring with Shawde?"

Was she honestly making herself out to be some sort of victim? "As if you did me any favors. Because of you, people probably think I was in on a plot to kill Christian."

"Everything's on the line for me," Katrina went on, not acknowledging what I'd said. "I'm not about to let you fuck things up for me. Just like I couldn't let Gordon fuck things up for me."

My body trembled. She *had* killed Gordon. "You murdered Gordon, too? Oh my God."

"Me?" Katrina asked, feigning innocence. "You think I was able to beat him and dump him in the water?" She smiled, but it didn't reach her eyes. "Everything can be attained . . . for a price."

"Like Christian," I said. "You paid someone to kill him, too?"

Katrina turned to Rowena. "Get on with it, Ro."

Rowena began to lift her hand, then halted it, as though unsure.

"What are you doing, Ro?" Katrina demanded.

"Kat, look how many people are outside! Maybe this isn't smart."

"It *has* to be done," Katrina said. "You know what's at stake. Do you *want* me to die? You want that drug lord coming after me?"

"Of course not," Rowena said.

"Good. Then we have to do this. Jade's the only one who can open her big mouth. With her gone, I can get the money Christian left me in his will. Then the problem will go away."

Barely breathing, I tried to make sense of what I'd heard. "Drug lord?" I asked. "Will? You *did* marry Christian for his money! Because what—you were into drugs and you owe some drug lord money?" I shouted the last words.

"Are you hoping someone down there will hear you?" Katrina asked, smirking at me.

I swallowed. That had been exactly what I was hoping. "You used Christian, had him killed so brutally! How could you?"

"I did like Christian," Katrina said, and I actually saw a hint of remorse in her eyes. "But what was I supposed to do, just let myself get killed? I found a way out, and I took it."

"My God," I uttered. "You're so fucking callous."

Katrina's eyes flashed fire. "Ro, let's finish this."

"Here." Rowena extended her hand to Katrina, offering her the needle.

"Oh no." Katrina shook her head. "You have to get your hands dirty, too."

"My hands *are* dirty," Rowena said. "I took care of her sister."

My sister . . . a strangled cry escaped my throat. Rowena had been behind the accident? Seeing her here, I'd hoped that my theory was impossible. But she must have tried to kill Marie, then caught a flight to get her to Key West as soon as possible.

I reached for my phone in the tote bag. Quickly I pressed the button to wake it from sleep mode, then swiped my finger across the screen.

Before I could try to get to my call log to redial the last number, the phone was slapped from my fingers. It went flying and landed on the hard floor with a violent crash.

"No!" I raged. I refused to play haplessly into their murderous plan. Rushing forward, I jammed my shoulder into Katrina's chest. I must have caught her off guard, because she stumbled backward. I rushed past her, but Rowena was still in my way.

Instinctively I shifted the tote bag around my shoulder so that I could grip the laptop as a weapon. As Rowena moved toward me, I raised it and aimed for her head.

She yelped as the laptop connected with her arm when she deflected the blow. My heart soared, knowing I'd hurt her, even if not permanently. I started to sprint toward the door.

Someone grabbed my hair and pulled. I screamed, then reached for the hands to pry them from my head. Whoever had me pulled harder, and I tried to twist myself to get out of the vice-like grip. God, the pain that ripped at my scalp. But I didn't give up.

I began to kick a foot backward as hard as I could. When I heard the shriek, I knew I had connected with a kneecap, and I was relieved to feel the hands loosen in my hair. As quickly as I could I righted myself and continued for the door, not looking back.

I think I registered the crack and the sound of glass shattering before I even felt the blow. But then came the sharp pain, piercing through my skull and causing my knees to buckle. Next came the wave of dizziness, and my legs completely gave way, and I dropped to the floor.

"You bitch!" Katrina snapped.

I mustered the strength to look over my shoulder. Behind me, Katrina held the handle of a broken coffee mug. Damn, I was seeing double of her.

She glared at me, and a quiet, horrifying rage emanated from her dark eyes.

"W-why are you d-doing this?" I could hardly breathe, much less speak. The room was spinning.

She kicked me in the stomach, hard, and I cried out in pain. Tears filled my eyes. "Katrina, stop!"

"I let you live with me; I gave you a job."

On my butt, I tried to shuffle away from her. Rowena was right behind her now. Me against the two of them. I glanced around, trying to see if there was anything I could use as a weapon. "Please, I have to get to my sister."

Katrina advanced, a smug smile dancing at the corner of her lips. "Your sister . . . yeah, I think it might be too late for her."

"That's where you're wrong," I said, matching Katrina's smugness. "You failed. You wanted her dead, but she survived. She's in the hospital, not the morgue."

"Hospital?" Katrina laughed uncontrollably for several seconds, then faced Rowena. "Shit, we haven't told her yet."

My stomach sank. "Told me what?"

Rowena lifted a cell phone from the back pocket of her jeans. "You mean the call you got from the hospital this morning? Ooops, that was me."

I stared, blinking rapidly, not understanding.

"That's your sister's phone, idiot," Katrina said. "Did you even think about the timing? One minute she's texting you about Shawde being on the news; the next you're getting a call that she's in the hospital?"

As Rowena stuffed the phone back into her pocket, hot tears spilled onto my cheeks. I finally understood. I hadn't done the math, hadn't realized that the time line didn't add up. I'd been too frantic after getting that call from the hospital to be thinking straight.

"Jade Blackwin?" Rowena said, feigning the higher-pitched voice I'd heard on the other end of my phone at the hotel. "I'm calling from Millcreek Community Hospital."

Then she and Katrina laughed.

"No." My shoulders collapsed as the heavy truth settled over me. "God no."

"We needed to get you back here," Katrina went on. "Because we knew that you'd need to get your stuff to head to Erie."

"What did you do to my sister?" I asked.

"I wish I could tell you she didn't suffer," Katrina said, "but Rowena tells me she put up a fight."

Rowena nodded. "Sometimes these things get messy."

Hot tears filled my eyes. I'd lost everything now. My mother, my father, and now my sister.

In that moment, I could have been devastated. But instead, there was a shift in me. Learning the truth about my sister caused rage to build inside of me.

I wanted to kill Katrina.

Hot breaths shot through my nose. "You evil pieces of shit!"

The fight back in me, I jumped to my feet and advanced, ready to gouge out Katrina's eyes.

But she struck before I could, punching me in the face. Again my vision blurred.

"Nice try," she said as I stumbled backward.

"A for effort," Rowena chimed in.

They were so . . . nonchalant. So completely cold in their wickedness.

A primal cry escaping me, I lunged forward and clawed at Katrina's face. If nothing else, my DNA would be under her fingernails. She would not get away with my murder.

"Bitch!" she cried, and grabbed my hair again. She wrenched my neck to the left, then slapped my face.

I tasted my blood on my lips. I was in pain, I was terrified, but I forced a smile. "You won't get away with this. Not this time."

"I've had enough of this," Katrina announced. "Where's the fucking needle?"

Rowena moved a few feet away and bent to lift it off the floor.

"Good," Katrina said. "Let's get this over with."

I struggled, but Katrina yanked on my hair, causing new tears to fill my eyes. Then, with my head already lowered, she cracked the side of my skull against her knee.

Seeing stars and wailing from the pain, I stumbled. And all I could think as I fell was that I'd been stupid to refuse Brian's suggestion that he come upstairs with me. With him here, surely they wouldn't be able to get away with their murderous plan.

And I thought of something else. Instead of running for the door, I should have tried to get to the front window. With all the reporters downstairs, if I had banged on it I could have gotten the attention of someone below.

Damn it!

I'd lost, and I knew it now. And with that devastating realization, I began to cry. Loud, anguished sobs. I cried for my sister, who had been killed because I'd gotten her involved in this. And I cried for myself, because I knew there was nothing I could do.

"Awww," Katrina said, sarcasm dripping from her voice as she looked from me to Rowena. "I almost feel bad for her."

"Please," I begged. It was all I had left. "I won't say anything. I'll forget this ever happened. Please don't kill me. . . ."

"Enough fun and games." Katrina's expression hardened. "Rowena, do it now."

Rowena started toward me. I drew in a breath, trying to calm my shaking body. Then, resigned to my fate, I closed my eyes. I didn't want to see this.

One second turned to two, then to three, then to four. . . .
Come on already! Do it!

The sound of a bang, followed by a grunt, forced me to open my eyes. At first, I didn't register what I was seeing. Katrina's back against the wall, Rowena's fist curled against her friend's chest. Katrina's eyes bulging, confusion in their depths as she stared at her friend.

I watched, stunned. What was happening?

Katrina wheezed out a breath, then raised a hand to reach for Rowena's fist. And that was when I started to understand. Katrina's fingers flailed over Rowena's clenched ones, but she was too weak to remove her friend's hand. With another gasp, Katrina's palms went to the wall, searching—unsuccessfully—for purchase.

Only then did Rowena unclench her fist and take a step backward. At which point I saw the end of the syringe protruding from between Katrina's breasts.
What?

"Bitch." The word was barely more than a whisper. Katrina's breathing had become dangerously shallow. She was losing strength.

But suddenly she flung a hand forward, reaching for Rowena. Rowena jumped backward, out of her reach.

Katrina's head angled in my direction, and it seemed

to me that she was struggling to keep it upright. Her eyes met mine. Held. I stared back, mystified by this bizarre chain of events.

And then, in an instant, something changed. Katrina's eyes became vacant, and her knees collapsed. Her body began to slide down the wall.

I watched in horror, my chest rising and falling with each furious breath, my brain scrambling to make sense of what was going on. What was Rowena doing? Killing Katrina so there would be no witnesses? Was she the mastermind behind everything?

"What did you do?" I demanded.

Katrina's body finally hit the floor, her knees oddly positioned up to her face, as if she had merely sat down. But her limbs very clearly went limp, her head lolling forward, landing on her knees.

Was she . . . *dead*?

My eyes bounced from Katrina to Rowena. "You killed her!"

"Enough," Rowena said. She was looking at Katrina. "No more."

Then Rowena faced me. I should have tried to run, but I was mortified. Paralyzed. She took a step toward me, and that was when I snapped into action, scrambling backward on the tile floor.

One of my hands landed on a shoe, and instinctively I snatched it up. God, a shoe? What good would that do me?

But it had a high, thin heel, so I held Katrina's pump up with the heel extended. I only had to fight Rowena now. And damn it, I was going to do my best to get out of here alive.

Rowena raised both of her hands in a sign of surrender. "I'm not going to hurt you," she said softly.

I narrowed my eyes, unconvinced.

"Your sister . . . she's okay."

I began to shake my head, jerky movements. I didn't understand what she was saying.

She reached into her back pocket, and I tensed, fearing the worst. Did she have a gun?

She produced Marie's phone again. "This is your sister's phone."

She tossed it to me, and reflexively I caught it with my left hand. Then I examined the familiar blinged-out case and felt my stomach tighten. If I'd thought she was bluffing earlier, I now knew without a doubt that she had been with Marie.

And Katrina had boasted that Marie was dead.

"I didn't kill your sister," Rowena said. "But I *was* at her place yesterday evening. I had to take the phone so that Katrina would believe I'd done what she wanted. Yes, I used it to lure you back here. But . . . I was never going to kill you."

My head was pounding, my body still gripped with fear. "I don't understand."

"Marie's not hurt. I lied to Katrina. That's what I'm telling you."

Was this a trick? An attempt to make me trust her so I would let my guard down?

Rowena took another step toward me, and I jumped to my feet, raising the shoe high.

"Stop!" she yelled. "I'm not going to hurt you." She gave me an imploring look. Then her face collapsed and she started to cry. "I never wanted any of this . . . Shemar . . . killing him . . . every day I've been haunted by what I did. And Katrina, she always held it over my head. Threatened that if she went to jail, I would, too. Once your sister called me and asked questions, Katrina knew you were starting to figure things out. She wanted me to kill your sister, to kill you." Angrily she brushed away her tears. "I couldn't do it. I can't. I'm tired of living this lie. I have a family. A little boy, a husband. And I just can't do this anymore."

"Where's my sister?"

"She's at her house. She's unhurt."

I stared at her, knowing that I must look completely baffled. "She's not in the hospital?"

"No. I didn't hurt her. But I drugged her, tied her up. I couldn't have her calling the police before I dealt with Katrina. As long as Katrina was alive, I could never turn on her. If I did, she would hurt me. Or worse, she would hurt my husband. Or my son."

I shook my head again. Something wasn't adding up. "You had a syringe. You were giving it to Katrina to kill me. If she'd taken it and used it, I would be dead. So what you're saying doesn't make sense."

Rowena laughed, but the sound held no mirth. "You don't know Katrina. You think there was a way she was going to kill you herself? No, she wanted more ammunition to use against me. I offered her the needle, but I *knew* she would never take it. That she would insist *I* be the one to kill you."

My brain felt as though a hurricane were raging inside of it, but Rowena's words were finally registering. And they were making sense. In a crazy, twisted way, they were making sense.

"I had to make sure she was gone," Rowena said. "This was the only way."

Slowly, my shoulders began to relax. I was finally believing her.

Rowena looked to her right, at Katrina's unmoving body, and I followed her gaze. Katrina's eyes were open, her lips still parted, a look of surprise etched on her face. But she undoubtedly wasn't moving.

"She's dead?" I asked.

"Yes. What I gave her, it was guaranteed to kill."

I shuddered. It had been a dose meant for me.

"And now," Rowena went on, "I'm going to turn myself in. It's the only way. The only way to be free of the nightmare that has haunted me for years."

My lips trembled, and then the tears came. I let out all of my emotions in big, heaving sobs.

The door flung open. As Rowena's eyes widened, I spun around, once again tense.

But it was Brian.

"Brian!" Dropping the shoe, I ran toward him and threw myself into his arms.

He held me. "What happened?"

I looked up at him, saw his gaze jump from Rowena to Katrina's body, then back to Rowena.

"Katrina . . . she attacked me. I thought they were going to kill me, but her friend . . . she saved me."

Releasing me and urging my body behind his, Brian started toward Rowena. "Let me see your hands," he said. He was in cop mode, authoritative.

Rowena raised her hands. "I'm sorry," she said. "I couldn't let her do it again."

"You did this?" he asked, glancing at Katrina's body.

Rowena nodded. "The killing had to stop."

"Jade, call nine-one-one," Brian instructed me.

"Yes, please call the police," Rowena said. "I'm ready to turn myself in."

I was holding Marie's phone, so I used it to place the call. As I punched in 911, I heard Brian say, "Do you have a weapon?"

"No, I'm not armed."

"I think you better tell me what happened."

In my ear, the phone rang once before it was answered. "Nine-one-one operator, what's your emergency?"

"I'm in the apartment above the A Book and a Cup

coffee shop. And—and someone's dead. I need the police. Right away."

"Someone's dead?" the woman on the other end of the line asked. "What happened?"

"Tell her you're with a DEA agent," Brian was saying.

"I'm with a DEA agent right now, and the situation's under control. But someone was killed here. We need the police. And we need them as soon as possible."

CHAPTER FORTY

True to her word, Rowena willingly surrendered herself to the authorities. When the cops arrived, she stood from the sofa and immediately identified herself as the person who needed to be arrested.

Before they'd arrived, she had confessed all of her sins to Brian, which started with the murder of a girl named Carmen Young while in college. Carmen, denied admittance into the Alpha Sigma Pi sorority, had lodged a complaint against Katrina with the national board, alleging discrimination. According to Rowena, when she had agreed to go with Katrina to confront Carmen, murder hadn't been the plan. Katrina had simply wanted to scare Carmen into retracting her complaint. But when she threatened to go to the police and file a harassment complaint as well, Katrina snapped. She murdered Carmen and was able to make it look like the campus rapist and killer had been the culprit.

So when Angelina, one of their sorority sisters, had gotten wind of the idea that Carmen might have met with foul play at Katrina's hands, it made sense to kill her in the dark as she'd walked the campus trails, to make it look like the Bike Path Rapist had struck yet again. Rowena had attacked Angelina on Katrina's orders, meaning to kill her while Katrina was in the sorority house with a ton of alibis. Rowena, however, hadn't been able to beat Angelina to death. But at least the attack had succeeded in scaring Angelina into silence. Unfortunately, Shemar Williams, Katrina's college boyfriend, had figured things out. Which—in Katrina's mind—meant he had to be stopped. Because Rowena feared going to jail as an accessory after the fact in Carmen's murder, she did what she had to do to protect herself and helped tamper with the brakes on Shemar's car. Apparently, she had also gone to Atlanta with Katrina when Katrina's parents had died. While Katrina had been out publicly at a nearby fast food restaurant creating an alibi, Rowena had turned on the car in the Hugheses garage and left it running—ultimately causing the carbon-monoxide poisoning that took the lives of Katrina's parents.

My next call after 911 had been to contact the authorities in Erie, let them know that my sister was in her house and tied up. They promised to head there and deal with the situation.

While I believed Rowena, I wouldn't feel entirely at ease until I heard my sister's voice. Knew without a doubt that she was okay.

Now the apartment was filled with emergency personnel. Two EMTs had just finished checking Katrina's body for vital signs and were now loading her onto a stretcher. A formality, I guessed. Two uniformed cops were here, and one was reading Rowena her rights. There were also two detectives. Brian was standing with his arm wrapped around my waist as he, I, and the detectives watched the EMTs take Katrina's body out of the apartment.

One of the detectives, a man named Thrush, turned to me once Katrina's body was gone. "Are you ready to answer some questions?"

I glanced at Brian, and he nodded. It wasn't so much a

go-ahead from him as it was a way of letting me know that I had his support.

I led the way into my bedroom, and Detective Thrush, a tall, wiry man in his late fifties, closed the door behind us. Sauntering over to the window, I peered outside. I could see the side of the coffee shop above the alley, and a portion of the street. Camera crews were still out there. I could only imagine that after the arrival of the ambulance and the police the reporters were in a frenzy to know what was going on.

"What went on here today, Jade?" the detective asked me.

He'd already been briefed on the immediate situation—Katrina wanting to kill me and Rowena intervening. "Gosh, where do I start?"

"Start at the beginning."

So I sat on the window's ledge and told him everything, starting with the trip to Mexico and Christian's murder. I told Detective Thrush about Gordon, how he had apparently been down here trying to investigate Katrina on Shawde's behalf. The whole story, wild and crazy, spilled out of me.

"You're going to have to come to the station," the detective said to me. "Give a detailed statement."

I nodded. Of course, it had to be done. "It's just . . . my sister. The police from Erie haven't called yet. Should I be worried?"

"I don't know what to say," the detective said, opting for honesty. "All depends on whether Rowena was telling the truth."

"Is it possible you can give them a call?" I asked. "Talk to some—"

My voice broke off at the sound of a knock at the door. Detective Thrush went to answer it.

"Sorry to interrupt," I heard Brian say before he came into view, "but there's a call for Jade."

I sprang from my spot at the window and was at the door in under a second. Brian was holding Marie's phone. I'd given the authorities in Erie Marie's number to contact me at, since my phone had been destroyed when Katrina had knocked it out of my hand.

My eyes locked on Brian's as I reached for the phone, searching for the answer I so craved. After a beat, the edges of his lips curled in a grin. "It's your sister."

"Oh, thank God." Overwhelmed with emotion, I put the phone to my ear. "Marie?"

"Jade! You're okay?"

"Yes." A smile came over my face as happy tears filled my eyes. I moved to sit on the bed, and Detective Thrush exited the room, giving me privacy. "I am now."

"Rowena came here yesterday, acting all concerned about you being with Katrina. We had tea. And that's the last thing I remember before waking up and finding myself tied to a chair. I was terrified. I thought . . ." Marie's voice cracked. "I thought at any minute she was going to come back and kill me. And I had no clue what was happening to you."

"Oh, Marie." I'd been through my own harrowing ordeal, but my heart still broke for her. "So much has gone down, and I hardly know where to start. Rowena went to see you because Katrina wanted you dead. Wanted me dead. We were asking too many questions. But Rowena said that she was never going to hurt you. Getting you out of the way—temporarily—was part of her plan. She needed you out of the way so that she could kill Katrina."

"What?"

For the second time, I relayed the story of everything that had happened today. I ended with, "Rowena knew that with Katrina alive, she and her family would never be safe. She wanted to end this once and for all."

"Holy shit." Marie sighed audibly. "Oh, Jade. I'm so sorry. If I'd had any clue what Katrina was really like—"

"You wouldn't have sent me down here," I finished for her. "I know."

When she spoke again, I could hear the tears in her voice. "I just can't believe we lost Dad and I almost lost you, too."

It was exactly the fear I'd had about her. "For a few minutes, I thought I *had* lost you. Katrina said you were dead . . . and I . . ." My voice trailed off as I relived that awful moment. I couldn't hold back the tears.

"It's over, sweetie. And we're both okay."

"Yeah," I said softly.

"When are you coming home?"

I wiped away my tears before answering, "As soon as I can get out of here."

"I feel so bad for Shawde. It's one thing to lose a family member, but knowing her brother was murdered . . ."

"Oh shit," I uttered, wandering to the window. "Shawde. I have to call her, let her know what's going on. Marie, I'll talk to you later, okay? I want to call Shawde; then I'll have to go to the police station to give a formal statement." I glanced outside. "And I'm sure I'll have to speak to the media as well."

"I suppose you will. This story is going to be even bigger now. If you don't give them a statement, they'll hound you."

"No doubt."

"Call me when you're on your way home," Marie said.

"Will do."

As I ended the call with my sister, I remembered that Shawde's number was on my busted phone. Damn, how was I going to reach her?

But then I remembered that Shawde's number was also on my laptop. Which was in the living-room area.

Detective Thrush made eye contact with me when I exited the bedroom. "My sister's fine," I told him, beaming.

"That's great."

"Do you mind if I make another call?" I asked.

"Go ahead."

I meandered past the living room to the foyer, where I found the bag with my laptop. I'd used it as a weapon, and prayed that it would turn on.

It did. Quickly I opened my Facebook account and then opened the string of messages from Shawde. Seeing her number, I began to punch it into my sister's iPhone.

Shawde answered after the third ring. "Hello?" she asked, sounding tentative.

"Hey, it's Jade."

"Oh. Hi." She paused. "You heard? About Gordon?"

"I heard that a man's body was discovered in the water."

"It's Gordon. I know it is. I've been able to reach his father, and he's on his way down here."

"Well, that's good. Someone who can positively identify him."

"Yeah," Shawde said, and I could hear guilt in her tone.

"I have some news, too," I said, and I hoped that learning the whole ugly ordeal was over would give her some closure.

"What?"

"Katrina's dead."

A few beats passed. "Are you sure?"

"I am. She's definitely dead."

I heard a whimper and what sounded like a sob. "Thank God."

I told Shawde everything that had transpired. "I think she saw her world unraveling. I mean, she had Rowena go after my sister; then the plan was for both of them to kill me." I shuddered, the reality of what I'd gone through and how close I'd come to being murdered hitting me anew. "Her house of cards was finally falling apart."

"I can't believe it," Shawde said. "After all these years of wanting justice for my brother . . . suddenly, she's just gone."

"She won't hurt anyone ever again," I assured Shawde. "That is justice."

"Oh, I agree. It's the best justice. The only justice good enough for someone like her. Allowing her to live in prison would be unconscionable. She needed to be gone, and now she is. And I know this may seem shallow or just plain mean, but I'm glad she knew she was going to die."

I totally understood the sentiment. To think that Katrina had inflicted horror and pain on so many and had been gleeful about it . . . she'd gotten what she'd deserved.

"I hope this news helps you give some closure," I said. "Rowena admitted that they tampered with your brother's car the night before he was heading for Albany. That's irrefutable proof. Your efforts, they weren't in vain."

Shawde started to cry. "Finally. I've gotten justice for my brother. Shemar can now rest in peace."

And I hoped she could find peace now as well. She'd lost more than her brother because of what Katrina had done.

"I want to see Rowena," Shawde said. "Ask her about that night."

I wasn't sure that was the best idea, but Shawde had already invested so much in getting answers that I supposed she needed to hear every detail. "Well, she's cooperating. I'm sure she'll talk to you."

Shawde sighed, and it was filled with anguish. "I feel awful. I wish I hadn't gotten Gordon involved. But I had to know."

"I'm sorry. That everything had to come to this."

"I always knew that with Katrina going unpunished,

other people would die. I feel good knowing that she'll never hurt anyone else. Oh, and I have to let Angelina know. There was a girl who left UB because—"

"Because she was assaulted," I finished. "Yeah, Rowena told me. She confessed everything."

"Angelina's lived the past five and half years in fear because of Katrina," Shawde said. "She'll be relieved to know that Katrina is dead."

"I'm sure she will."

"I'm really glad your sister's okay," Shawde said after a moment, her voice soft now, wistful.

"Thank you." A tear slipped from the corner of my eye, and I wiped it away. My heart ached for her. I'd been lucky. Rowena had had a change of heart, and for that reason Marie had been spared. But Shawde had lost her brother, and there was nothing that could change that.

"Hold on a second, Jade," Shawde said. "Someone's calling on the other line."

"Oh. I should probably just let you go." I paused when I heard no response. "Shawde?"

She'd already put me on hold, so I did the polite thing and waited for her to come back on the line.

"Jade?" she said after less than a minute, her voice ripe with emotion.

"Everything okay?" I asked, concerned.

"That's my ex-fiancé. He said he saw the news and . . ." Her voice trailed off. "He knows I'm not crazy now. He still loves me."

The ring mark on her finger. She'd lost a fiancé because of Katrina, but it sounded as though they were going to work things out.

"I have to go," Shawde said.

"Of course. I'm sure you and your ex have a lot to talk about."

"Yeah, we do." I heard Shawde's shuddery exhalation

of breath. Then there was a smile in her voice when she said, "I know Shemar's looking out for me. Finally, I think everything's going to be okay."

"I think so, too," I told her, and my eyes misted. Shawde had put her life on hold in order to get justice for her brother, and now she could finally move on.

She'd lost so much. But at least now she hadn't lost everything.

"Please stay in touch," she said.

"Of course," I told her. "Now go work things out with your man."

CHAPTER FORTY-ONE

The rest of the day was surreal. I had to go to the police station to give my official statement and answer even more questions. It had been a harrowing and exhausting four hours, but Brian had waited there for me. The media, learning of Katrina's murder and Rowena's confession, had set up camp outside the police station, waiting to hear the salacious details from someone who had managed to escape the murderous plans of a deranged psychopath.

"I don't feel like going out the front door," I'd said to Brian. All I wanted was to rest and to escape the craziness.

"You don't have to. But even if you go back to Erie, you can probably bet that the media will show up there. You survived—they want to hear from you. My advice—give a statement. Answer their questions and put the matter to rest."

"Will you come out with me?" I asked.

"Not a good idea. Given what I do."

Undercover DEA. Of course, he wouldn't want to be seen on camera.

But another officer was by my side as I held an informal press conference. I answered questions honestly but without giving too many details. The officer also stepped in to answer certain questions with the standard, "We can't comment on an ongoing investigation."

When it was done, I slipped out the back of the station with Brian. Together, we walked to his hotel. I didn't want to go back to the apartment. Tomorrow, I would. But for tonight, I needed some distance from the place.

Brian and I made love again, and later we were lying together beneath the sheets when his cell phone rang. He turned and reached for it on the night table.

"Brian Hunter," he answered. For a while he listened. Then he said, "Really?" Pause. "Okay." Pause. "Yes, definitely. Thanks for letting me know." Ending the call, he edged closer to me.

"Work?" I asked.

"Yep. The autopsy on Christian Begley came back."

"There was an autopsy? Wasn't his cause of death obvious?"

"Yes, but an autopsy is still standard. Turns out he had barbiturates in his system. A pretty large dose."

"What?" I was astounded.

"My guess? He didn't ingest them knowingly."

"No," I said softly. "I doubt it."

"Which makes it far more likely that there was a plan to kill him. Weaken him with the barbiturates, then when the attack came he wouldn't be able to fight back."

My brain scrambled to make sense of this news. Had Katrina drugged him, then caused a fight because she knew he would leave the bar in anger? I'd replayed that night in my mind with deeper scrutiny, and the truth was, I hadn't been with Katrina every second. She'd gone to the bathroom without me. She'd hung out with random guys. And I'd spent a good chunk of time with Brian. Had she used an opportunity when we weren't together to slip out of the bar and attack the man she had clearly married for his money?

Or had she hired Luis Romero to kill him?

With Katrina gone, I supposed I would never know the truth. Unless Rowena was privy to the details and shared them with the authorities.

At least Katrina would never profit from Christian's death. For his family, that would be some small comfort.

"You sure you don't want to watch the news?" Brian asked me. "I thought you would have wanted to see your press conference."

"No," I said without hesitation. "I'm done. Today I was nearly killed, thought my sister was dead, witnessed Katrina murdered . . ." I exhaled sharply. "Emotionally, I'm done."

In fact, I was glad that my cell phone had been destroyed, because I didn't want any calls or texts from people. I had no interest in answering any more questions about what I'd been through.

"Yeah, I get that." Brian urged me closer and kissed my cheek. "Hey, you said you wanted to write a book. Maybe you could write this story? I bet it would be a bestseller."

I snuggled against him. "Maybe. After some time has passed."

It was an idea that had flitted through my mind earlier. That one day I might write about what had happened to me. Put the crazy story into a novel or a memoir.

Maybe.

But right now, I didn't want to think about the future or the past. I wanted to concentrate on Brian, make the most of our time together. By tomorrow or the next day, I would be starting my drive back to Erie. And I had no clue what the future held for me and this amazing man I'd been so fortunate to meet.

He must have sensed my thoughts, because he said, "So. You head back to Erie in a couple of days."

I made a little whimpering sound. "On one hand, I can't wait to get out of here, see my sister again." I paused. "But then . . ."

He eased his head back so that he could look at me. "But then, what?"

"You," I said, admitting what was on my mind. "I'm enjoying . . . this."

"Yeah, me too."

I pouted. "But you're going back to California, and probably Mexico, and I'll be going back to Erie. . . ."

A few beats passed. "Does that mean we'll never see each other again?"

I turned onto my side to better look at him, hope flittering in my heart. "You'd want to see me again?"

"I came to Key West to see you, didn't I?" Suddenly he scrunched his forehead. "Wait—is this when you drop the bomb that you were using me for my body?"

I laughed. Then playfully swatted his chest. "Of course not. Though what an incredible body." I sighed softly, becoming serious again. "Our lives, Brian . . . we live in two different states. Two completely different worlds . . ."

"Which will make it challenging," he said, "but not impossible."

The corners of my mouth fought to smile. "You're serious."

"I want to see you again, Jade." He held my gaze with steady, intent eyes. "Look, I understand the deal. Neither of us can really make any promises at this point. But I'd like . . . I'd like to keep the options open where we're concerned."

My smile couldn't be contained any longer, and I beamed like a teenager who'd just learned that the guy she liked, liked her back. I stretched a leg over Brian's body, running my foot along the back of his calf. "Would you, now?"

"Of course." He raised an eyebrow. "You wouldn't?"

"Oh, I do," I said, sliding my body onto his.

"You're killing me. Here I am, trying to have a serious conversation, and you're making it all about the sex." He faked a pout.

"Are you complaining?"

He circled my waist with his arms, holding me against him. Beneath me, his member grew hard. "Hell, no," he whispered.

"I absolutely want to see you again," I said softly. "What you said about our connection being real, I feel the same way. Whatever this is between us, it feels good. Really good. I want more of this, Brian. Of us."

Brian stroked my face. "Then where there's a will, there's a way."

"Is there a will to do me again?" I whispered hotly.

He grinned. "Most definitely."

"Then kiss me, baby."

Brian curled his hand around my head and drew my face down to his. And when his lips captured mine, the sweetest heat flooded my body. Each stroke of his hands on my skin and each tangle of his tongue with mine helped push the ugly ordeal I'd endured into the far recesses of my mind.

At least in this moment, the past no longer mattered.

The future lay ahead of me. And I just knew that it would be a bright one.

KAYLA PERRIN is the *Essence* bestselling author of more than twenty-five novels, including *The Delta Sisters*, *We'll Never Tell*, and *What's Done in Darkness*. She was featured in the documentary *Who's Afraid of Happy Endings?* She lives in Toronto, Canada.